SUSANNA MOODIE
ROUGHING IT IN THE BUSH

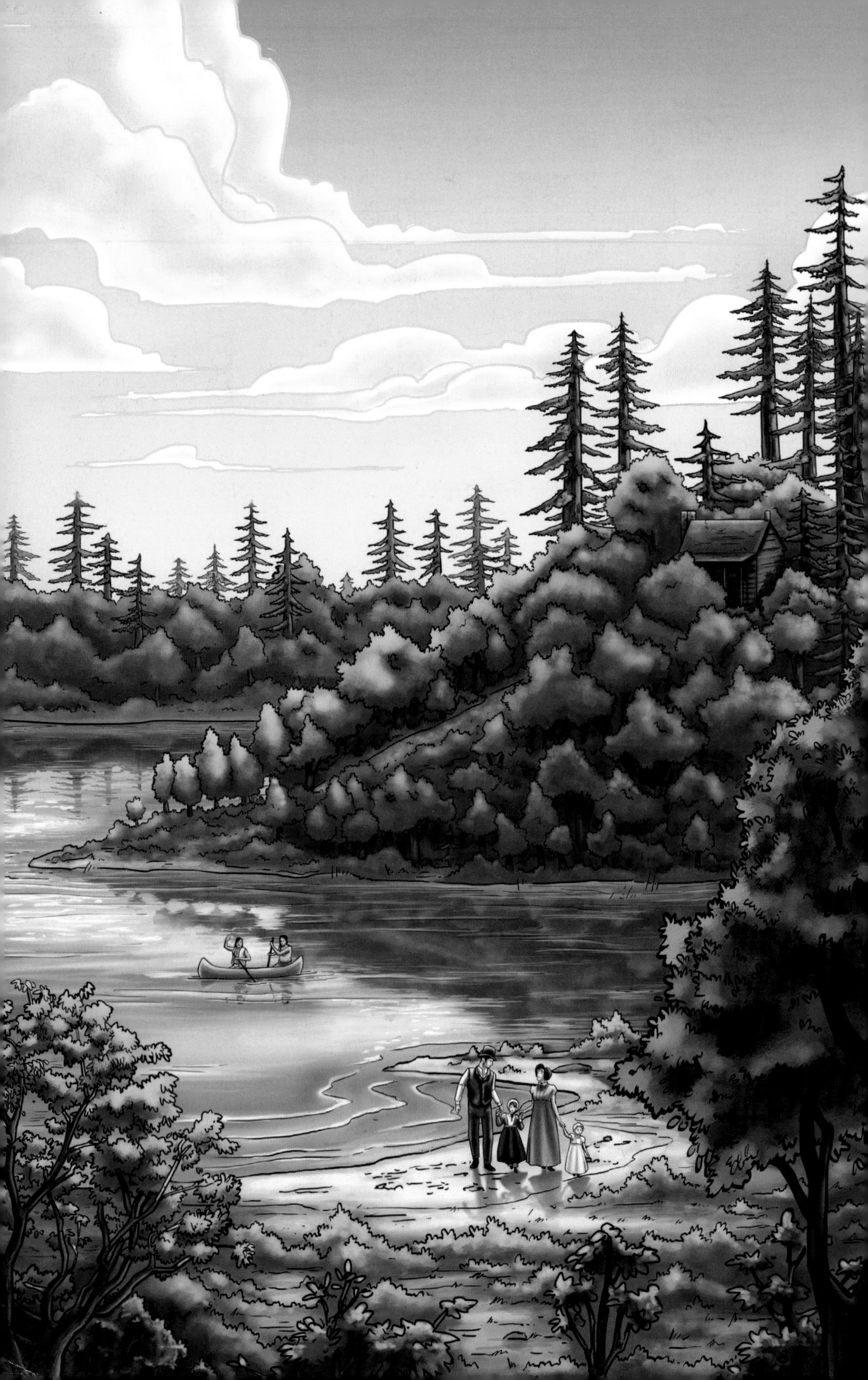

BY CAROL SHIELDS AND PATRICK CROWE

SUSANNA MOODIE
ROUGHING IT IN THE BUSH

GRAPHIC NOVEL ADAPTATION BY WILLOW DAWSON

ILLUSTRATED BY SELENA GOULDING

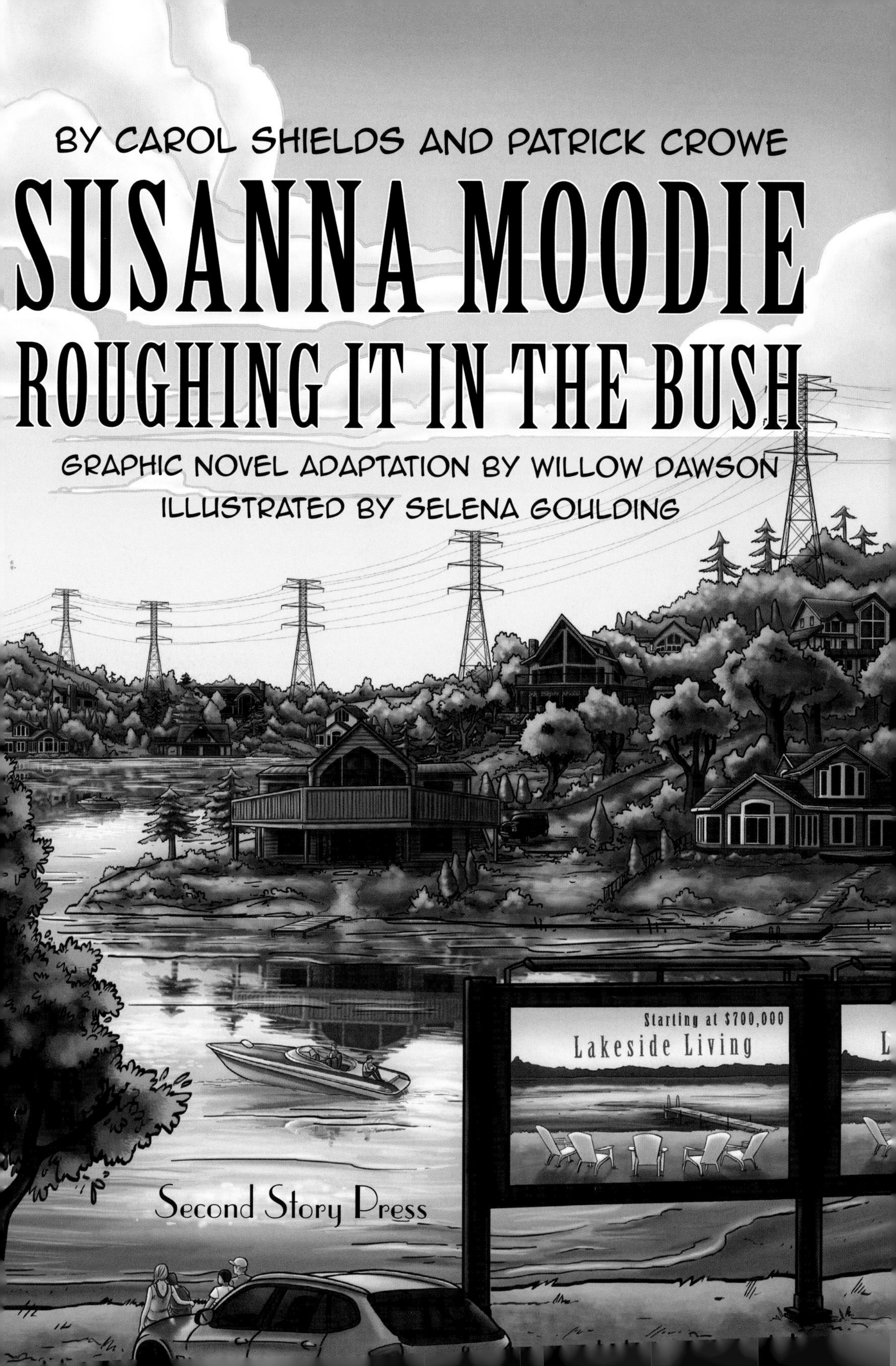
Starting at $700,000
Lakeside Living

Second Story Press

Library and Archives Canada Cataloguing in Publication

Shields, Carol, 1935-2003, author
Susanna Moodie : roughing it in the bush / by Carol Shields and Patrick Crowe ;
graphic novel adaptation by Willow Dawson, 2014 ; illustrations by Selena Goulding.

Issued in print and electronic formats.
ISBN 978-1-77260-003-2 (paperback).—ISBN 978-1-77260-004-9 (epub)

1. Moodie, Susanna, 1803-1885--Comic books, strips, etc. 2. Frontier and pioneer life—
Canada—Comic books, strips, etc. 3. Frontier and pioneer life—Ontario—Comic books,
strips, etc. 4. Women authors, Canadian (English)--19th century—Biography—
Comic books, strips, etc. 5. Graphic novels. I. Crowe, Patrick, 1967-, author
II. Dawson, Willow III. Goulding, Selena, illustrator IV. Title.

FC3067.2.S55 2016   971.3'02092   C2015-908394-X

C2015-908395-8

Printed and bound in Canada

Susanna Moodie: Roughing It in the Bush is also available in an interactive version
for iPad and Android Tablets, published by Xenophile Media on: iTunes and Google Play.
www.susannamoodie.com

A Note on Language
Upper Canada in the 1830s vibrated with a volatile mixture of many cultures, religious beliefs,
and political views. Common prejudices in the nineteenth century resulting from antagonisms
between Protestants and Catholics, or racism perpetrated by white Europeans against Blacks and
Aboriginals, were reflected in the everyday language people used to describe themselves and each
other. Today it is unacceptable to use words such as *Indian, squaw, darkie, Negro, Yankee,* or *Papist.*
Use of such language in this book should be viewed in the context of its time in history.
The authors and publisher of this book do not condone the use of disrespectful language.

Susanna Moodie: Roughing It in the Bush is a graphic novel
inspired by the life, correspondence, and published writing of Susanna Moodie.

*Second Story Press gratefully acknowledges the support of the Ontario Arts Council
and the Canada Council for the Arts for our publishing program. We acknowledge the
financial support of the Government of Canada through the Canada Book Fund.*

ONTARIO ARTS COUNCIL
CONSEIL DES ARTS DE L'ONTARIO
an Ontario government agency
un organisme du gouvernement de l'Ontario

Canada Council   Conseil des Arts
for the Arts   du Canada

Funded by the Government of Canada
Financé par le gouvernement du Canada

Canadä

Published by
SECOND STORY PRESS
20 Maud Street, Suite 401
Toronto, ON M5V 2M5
www.secondstorypress.ca

CONTENTS

INTRODUCTION

BY MARGARET ATWOOD

I am not only pleased, but astonished to have been asked to welcome this graphic novel version into the world. If you'd told me forty-five years ago – when I published my poem sequence, *The Journals of Susanna Moodie* – that such a thing would happen, I would have thought you were fantasizing. And if you'd told Mrs. Moodie herself, she'd have thought you were talking gibberish.

Yet here we are in the second decade of the twenty-first century, and here is Susanna Moodie, in full-colour comic-book form, living over the tribulations and triumphs of her life as an ill-prepared British emigrant to Upper Canada at the outset of the Victorian age. However did it come to this?

I myself first discovered Susanna Moodie on my parents' bookshelf in 1948, when I was eight. As my father was a forest entomologist and an accomplished woodsman himself, he had a large collection of books about forest life – Stuart Edward White, Earnest Thompson Seton, W.H. Blake, Ellsworth Jaeger – and a copy of Susanna Moodie's *Roughing It in the Bush* was among them.

My parents' edition had Arts and Crafts lettering on the front cover, and the two Os in *Moodie* were identical to the two Os in my own last name; also they looked like eyes. Lured by these typographical eyes, I made my way inside the book. It had tipped-in pictures in the watercolour style of Jeffries, and featured a gripping illustration of the Moodie log house burning down in the middle of winter. As I had lived in wooden houses in the forest myself and was aware of the dangers of fires, both forest and chimney, I was impressed. But the prose style of the book was too grown-up for me, so I soon abandoned it.

Had there been a Classic Comic available, however, I would have read that. The late 1940s was the golden age of the comic book. Comics were then a focus of parental worries, since children then consumed comic books in large numbers, and not all of these comics were savoury. Crime and horror, not to mention weepy romances, were especially deplored, though there was more wholesome fare to be had among the Donald Ducks, Mickey Mice, Little Lulus, and Archies of the comics world. Classic Comics were not lamented by parents and teachers: they were grudgingly accepted, since they might lead the youthful reader to the novels on which they were based.

Thus it was that I first encountered *Lorna Doone, Ivanhoe,* and other verbiage-crammed 19th century tomes. Classic Comics relayed the stories in condensed pictorial form, more or less like the Bayeux Tapestry version of William the Conqueror's invasion of England in 1066. In the deep background of this graphic rendition of Susanna Moodie, therefore, lies a group of French tapestry-sewing nuns.

In Grade Six, when I was ten, I encountered Susanna Moodie again. My school reader contained the burning house episode, and this time I not only looked at the picture – a different picture – but I read the text. There was poor Mrs. Moodie, standing in the snow with a few salvaged possessions and a gaggle of young children and a hysterical maidservant. It was a terrible moment, one of the worst in her life, but she got through it. As I was later to find when I read the whole book, she always did get through it, whatever it was.

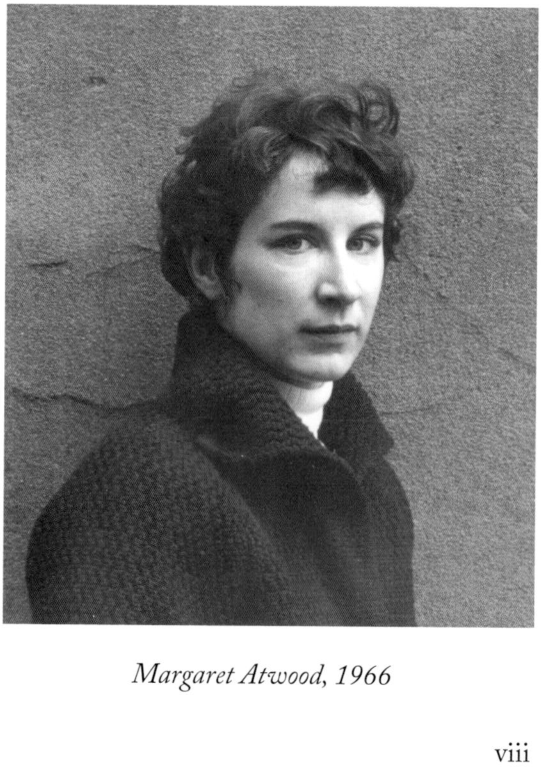

photograph courtesy of Charles Pachter

Margaret Atwood, 1966

Skip twelve years. All of a sudden I was in graduate school at Harvard, studying not only Victorian literature, but American Literature and Civilization. No comparable courses in Canadian Literature and Civilization existed then

in Canada, and I took to pondering why. Perhaps that was the cause of a dream I had. I dreamt I'd written an opera about Susanna Moodie – unlikely, as I was musically illiterate. But the dream was vivid enough to lead me to the Canadiana section of Widener Library, where I mainlined Susanna Moodie's two books, the second being *Life in the Clearings*.

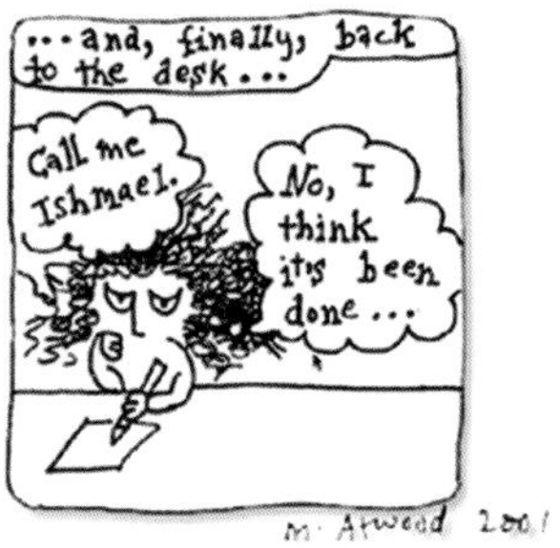
...and, finally, back to the desk...
Call me Ishmael.
No, I think it's been done...
M. Atwood 2001

From that sprang many things. First, my poem sequence, which later appeared in the gorgeously illustrated version by artist Charles Pachter. Second, a television play called *Grace Marks,* in the early 70s – based on a murder case described by Mrs. Moodie – which itself led to my 1996 novel, *Alias Grace.*

But meanwhile, Susanna Moodie herself was multiplying like mad on the page, a development that might have had something to do with the ferment of the early years of second-wave feminism: any woman who had ever done anything that involved breaking the mould – any mould – was suddenly not a weird eccentric, but a potential role model.

Moodie was the subject of Carol Shields' 1976 thesis, and appears also in Shields' novel, *Small Ceremonies*; she's there in Margaret Laurence's 1974 novel, *The Diviners*, though it's her sister, Catharine Parr Traill, who takes pride of place. She makes an undignified appearance as a snooty aristocrat in Rick Salutin's mid-70s play, *1837: The Farmers' Revolt,* which was unabashedly proletarian in its sympathies. Then Moodie popped up in some films – the first being Marie Waisberg's 1972 interpretation of my poems, the later ones being documentaries – and ultimately in a script by Carol Shields and Patrick Crowe, now adapted as one of the first interactive graphic novels for reading on tablets and in print.

Each incarnation of Moodie has been different: the Shields-Crowe graphic Moodie gives us her place of origin, a stately English home, which helps us understand the huge gap between Moodie's background and the circumstances she struggled with, often ineffectively, in the bush. It emphasizes, as well, her active involvement in the anti-slavery movement – making even more distressing her witnessing of a lynching on the very Canadian ground that prided itself on being a refuge for fleeing slaves. And it gives us the aftermath, her poignant late-age visit to the scene of her youthful struggles, now overgrown and abandoned.

Moodie's feelings about Canada were always mixed. On the one hand, striking beauty; on the other, intense physical suffering. She had many experiences she would never have had otherwise; she also had a good many experiences she could well have done without. This graphic version does justice to the many facets of her tale. It will introduce a new generation of readers to a figure who remains both iconic and – despite all the attention lavished upon her over the past forty-five years – mysterious. She may not be finished with us yet. What new Susanna Moodie may yet appear in the years to come?

-MARGARET ATWOOD
TORONTO, 2015

PROLOGUE

I SKETCH FROM NATURE AND THE PICTURE'S TRUE
WHATEVER THE SUBJECT, WHETHER GRAVE OR GAY
PAINFUL EXPERIENCE IN A DISTANT LAND
MADE IT MINE OWN.
      -SUSANNA MOODIE, *ROUGHING IT IN THE BUSH*

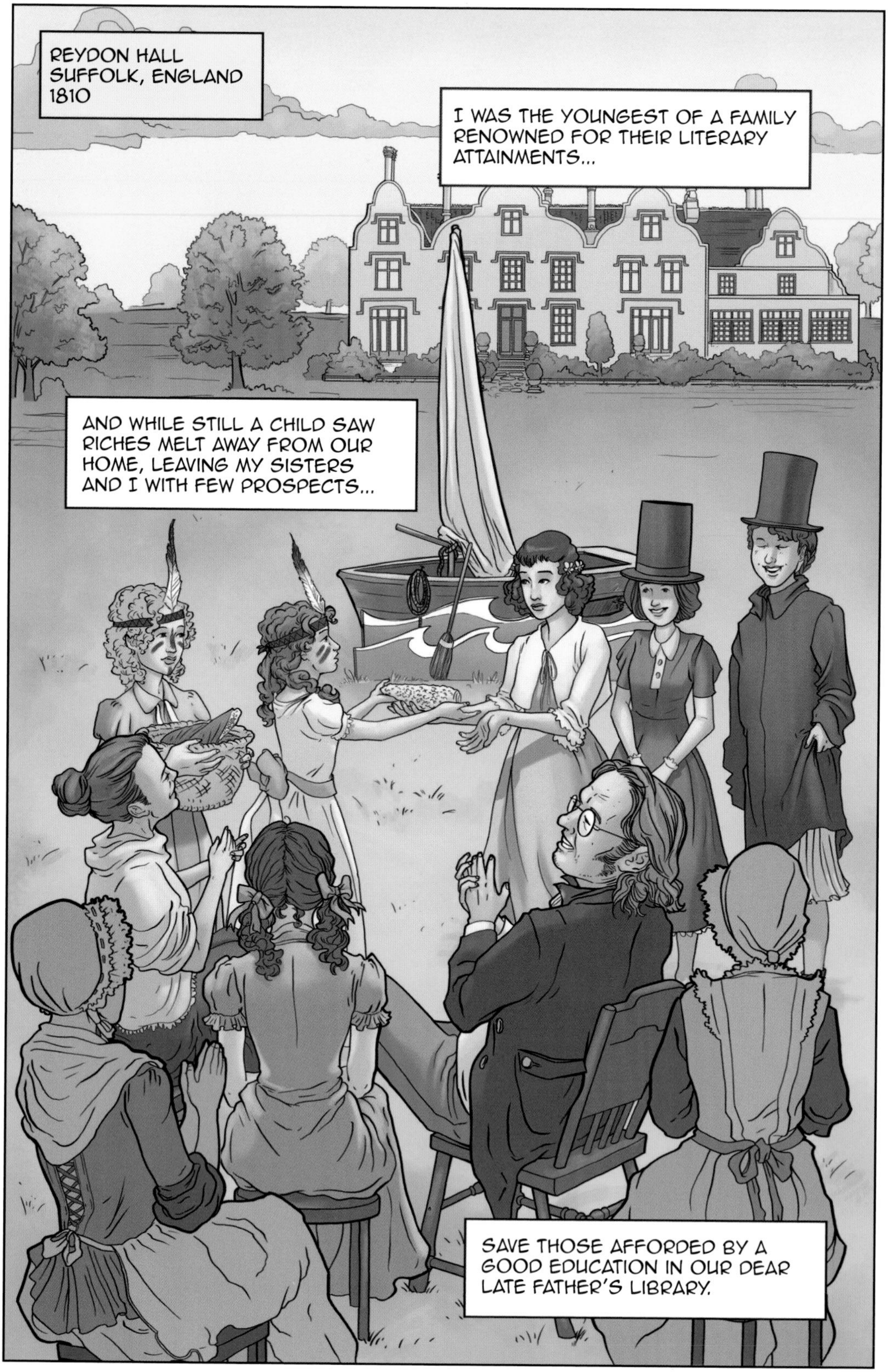
REYDON HALL
SUFFOLK, ENGLAND
1810
I WAS THE YOUNGEST OF A FAMILY RENOWNED FOR THEIR LITERARY ATTAINMENTS...
AND WHILE STILL A CHILD SAW RICHES MELT AWAY FROM OUR HOME, LEAVING MY SISTERS AND I WITH FEW PROSPECTS...
SAVE THOSE AFFORDED BY A GOOD EDUCATION IN OUR DEAR LATE FATHER'S LIBRARY.

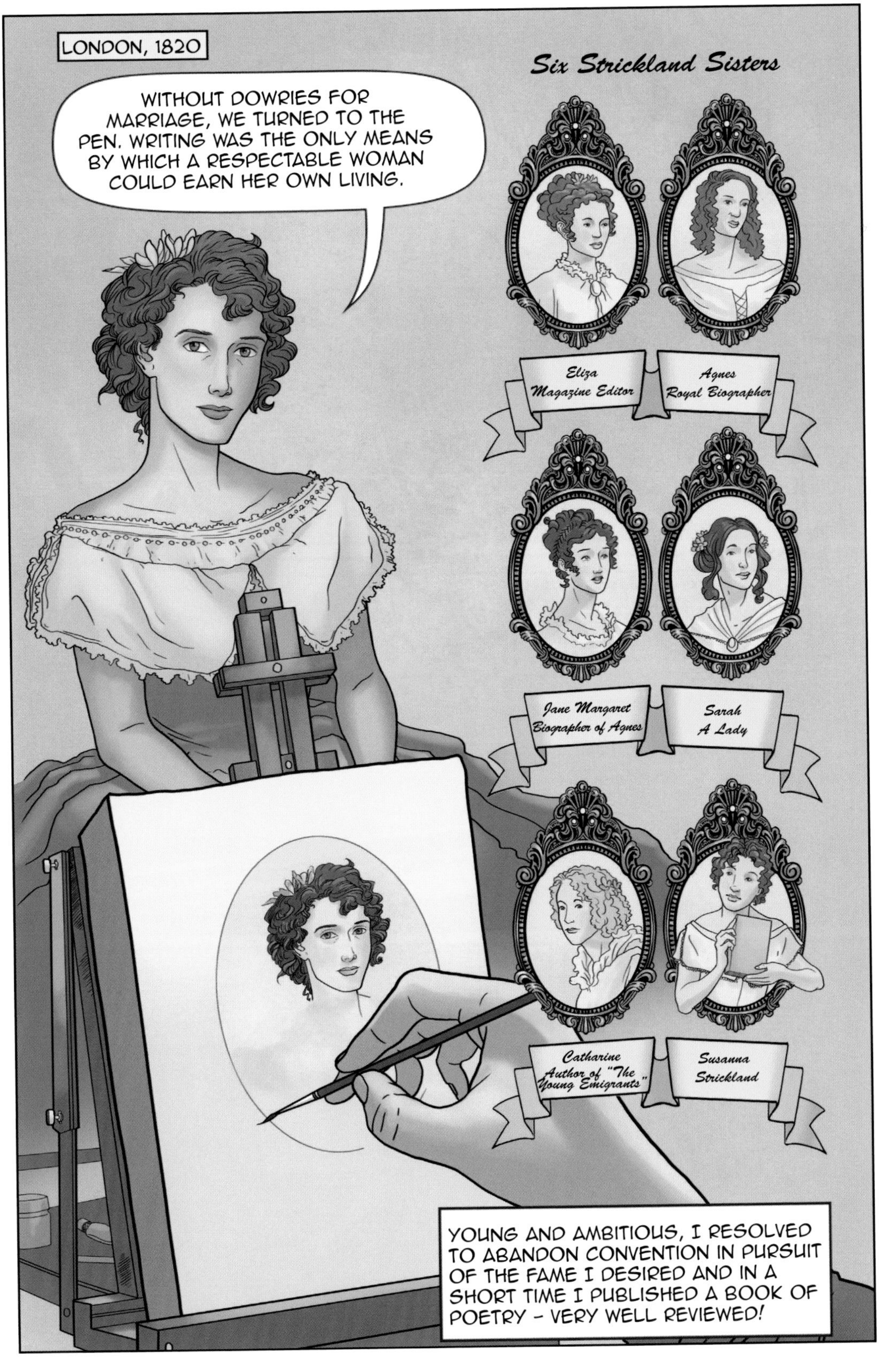
LONDON, 1820
WITHOUT DOWRIES FOR MARRIAGE, WE TURNED TO THE PEN. WRITING WAS THE ONLY MEANS BY WHICH A RESPECTABLE WOMAN COULD EARN HER OWN LIVING.
Six Strickland Sisters
Eliza Magazine Editor
Agnes Royal Biographer
Jane Margaret Biographer of Agnes
Sarah A Lady
Catharine Author of "The Young Emigrants"
Susanna Strickland
YOUNG AND AMBITIOUS, I RESOLVED TO ABANDON CONVENTION IN PURSUIT OF THE FAME I DESIRED AND IN A SHORT TIME I PUBLISHED A BOOK OF POETRY – VERY WELL REVIEWED!

CHAPTER 1

MATRIMONIAL SPECULATIONS

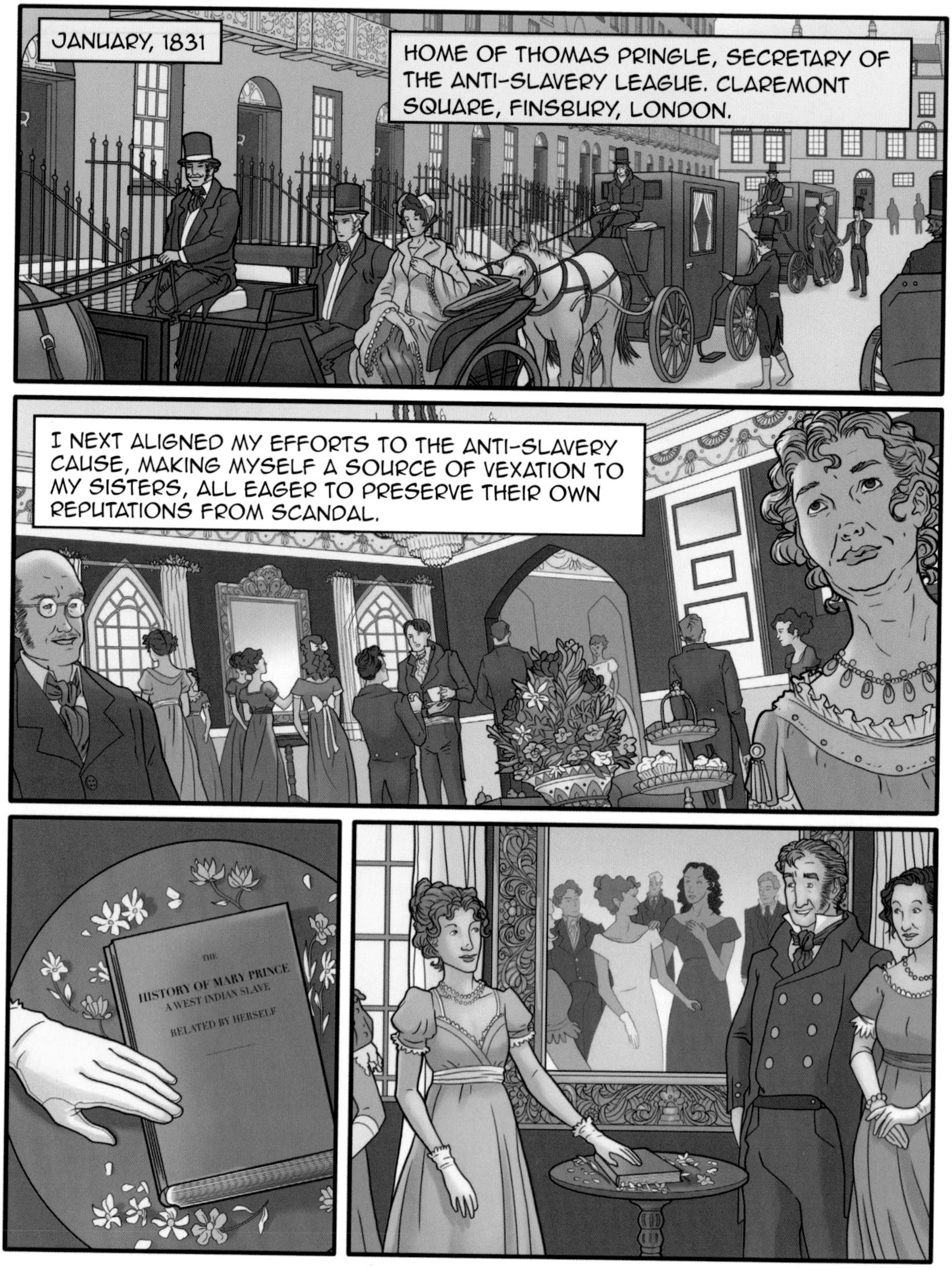
JANUARY, 1831
HOME OF THOMAS PRINGLE, SECRETARY OF THE ANTI-SLAVERY LEAGUE. CLAREMONT SQUARE, FINSBURY, LONDON.
I NEXT ALIGNED MY EFFORTS TO THE ANTI-SLAVERY CAUSE, MAKING MYSELF A SOURCE OF VEXATION TO MY SISTERS, ALL EAGER TO PRESERVE THEIR OWN REPUTATIONS FROM SCANDAL.
THE
HISTORY OF MARY PRINCE
A WEST INDIAN SLAVE
BELATED BY HERSELF

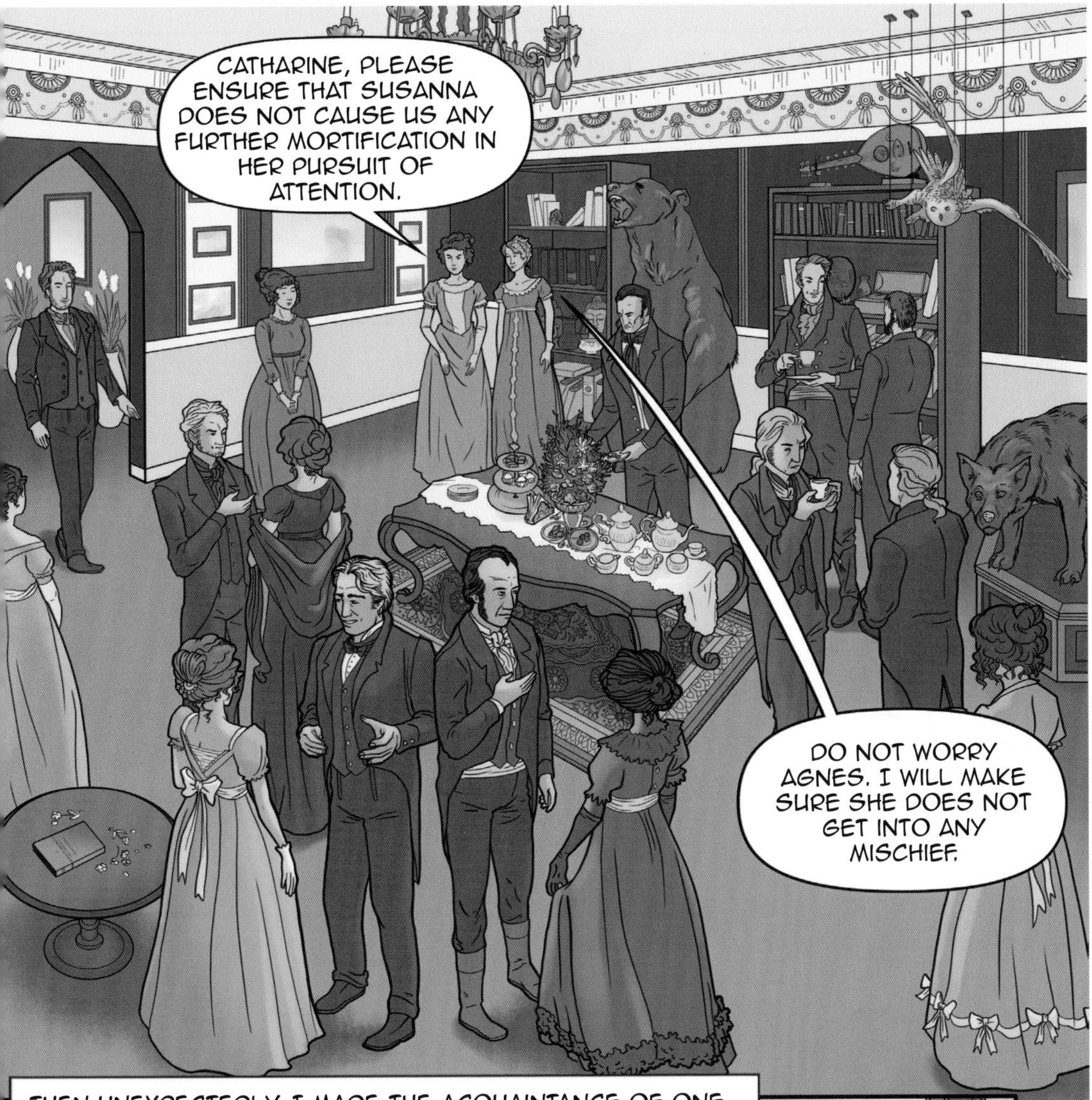
CATHARINE, PLEASE ENSURE THAT SUSANNA DOES NOT CAUSE US ANY FURTHER MORTIFICATION IN HER PURSUIT OF ATTENTION.
DO NOT WORRY AGNES. I WILL MAKE SURE SHE DOES NOT GET INTO ANY MISCHIEF.

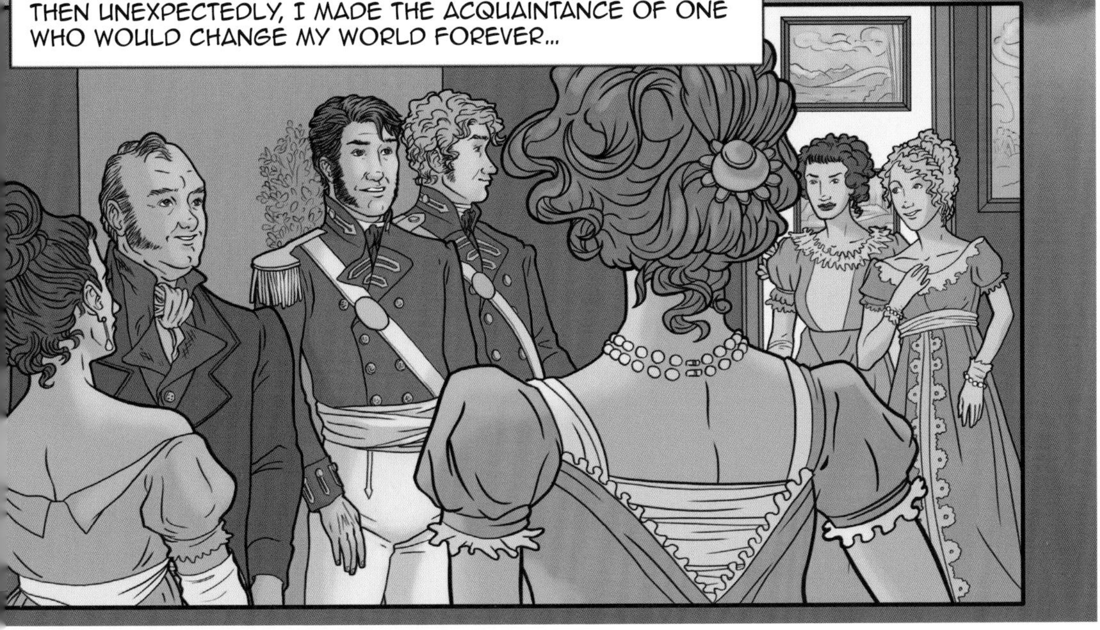
THEN UNEXPECTEDLY, I MADE THE ACQUAINTANCE OF ONE WHO WOULD CHANGE MY WORLD FOREVER...

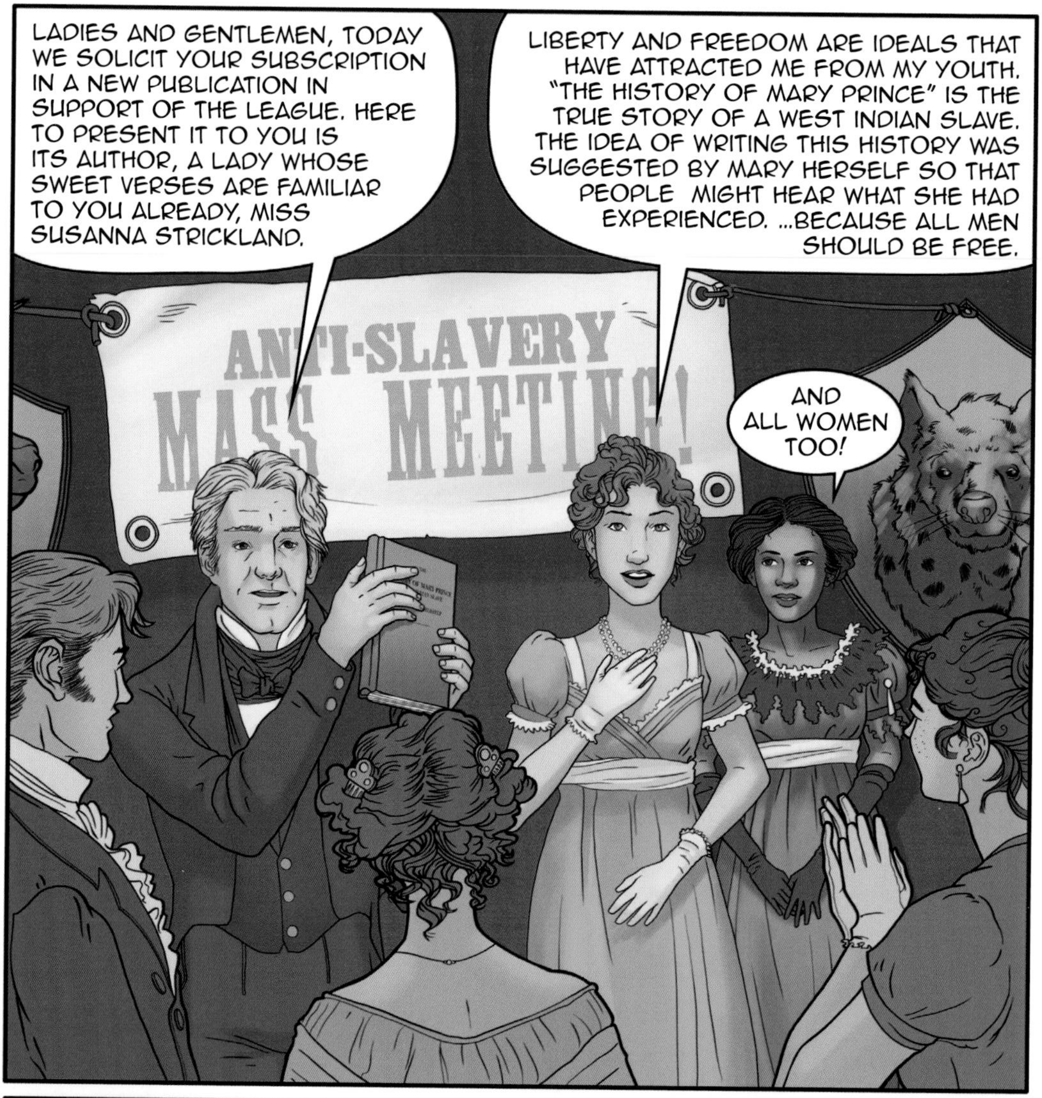
LADIES AND GENTLEMEN, TODAY WE SOLICIT YOUR SUBSCRIPTION IN A NEW PUBLICATION IN SUPPORT OF THE LEAGUE. HERE TO PRESENT IT TO YOU IS ITS AUTHOR, A LADY WHOSE SWEET VERSES ARE FAMILIAR TO YOU ALREADY, MISS SUSANNA STRICKLAND.
LIBERTY AND FREEDOM ARE IDEALS THAT HAVE ATTRACTED ME FROM MY YOUTH. "THE HISTORY OF MARY PRINCE" IS THE TRUE STORY OF A WEST INDIAN SLAVE. THE IDEA OF WRITING THIS HISTORY WAS SUGGESTED BY MARY HERSELF SO THAT PEOPLE MIGHT HEAR WHAT SHE HAD EXPERIENCED. ...BECAUSE ALL MEN SHOULD BE FREE.
ANTI-SLAVERY MASS MEETING!
AND ALL WOMEN TOO!

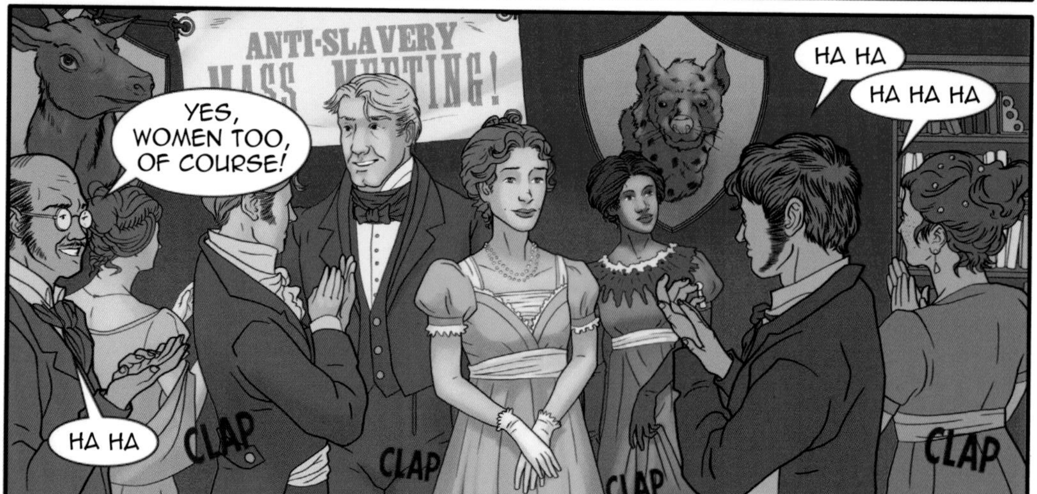
ANTI-SLAVERY
YES, WOMEN TOO, OF COURSE!
HA HA
HA HA HA HA
HA HA
CLAP
CLAP
CLAP
CLAP

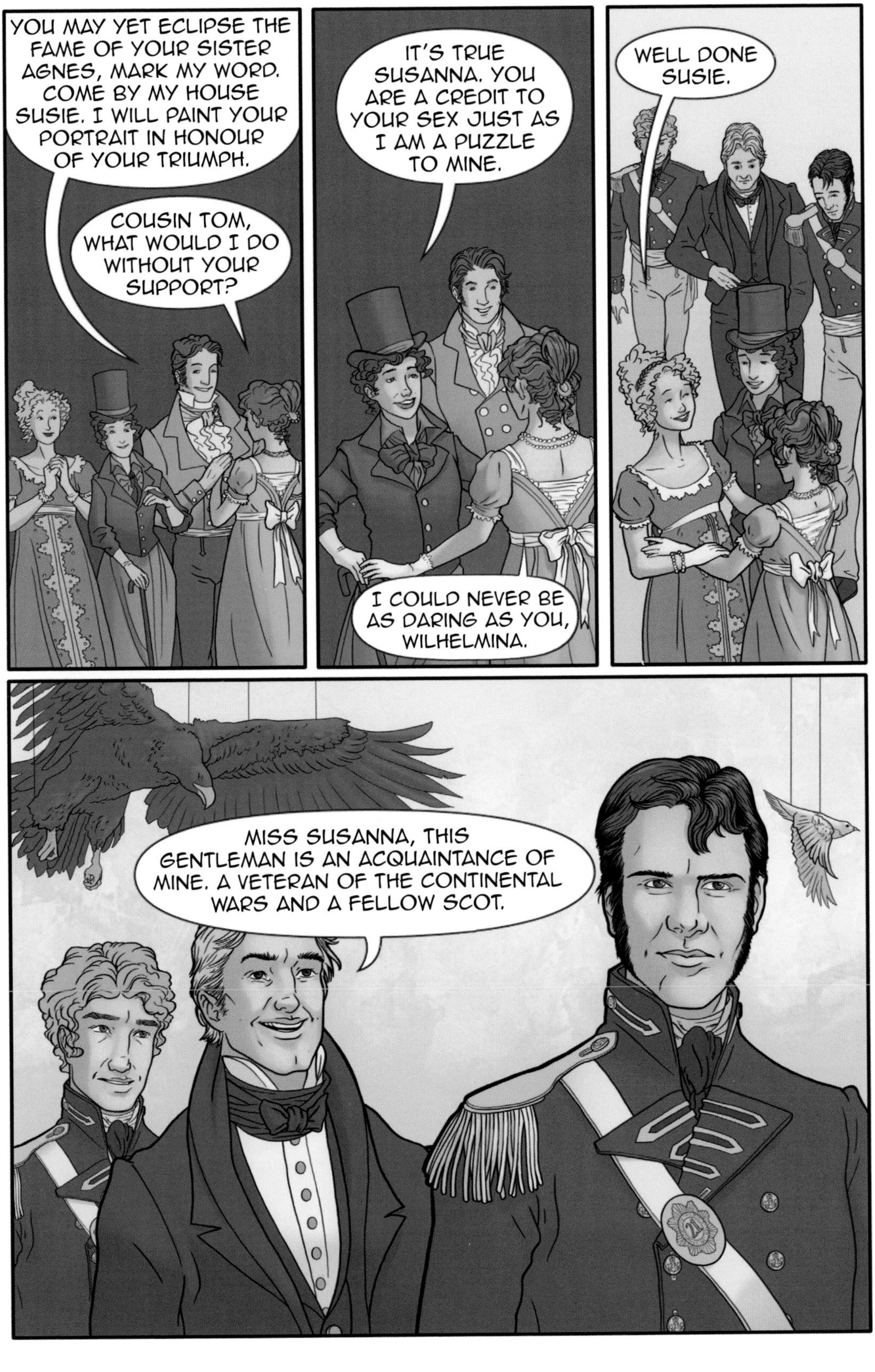

YOU MAY YET ECLIPSE THE FAME OF YOUR SISTER AGNES, MARK MY WORD. COME BY MY HOUSE SUSIE. I WILL PAINT YOUR PORTRAIT IN HONOUR OF YOUR TRIUMPH.
COUSIN TOM, WHAT WOULD I DO WITHOUT YOUR SUPPORT?
IT'S TRUE SUSANNA. YOU ARE A CREDIT TO YOUR SEX JUST AS I AM A PUZZLE TO MINE.
I COULD NEVER BE AS DARING AS YOU, WILHELMINA.
WELL DONE SUSIE.
MISS SUSANNA, THIS GENTLEMAN IS AN ACQUAINTANCE OF MINE. A VETERAN OF THE CONTINENTAL WARS AND A FELLOW SCOT.

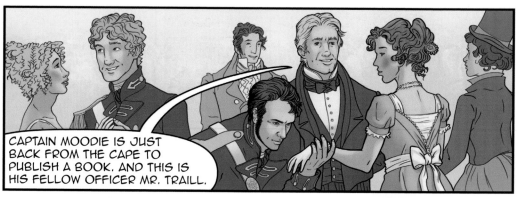

CAPTAIN MOODIE IS JUST BACK FROM THE CAPE TO PUBLISH A BOOK. AND THIS IS HIS FELLOW OFFICER MR. TRAILL.

SO, HAVING LIVED IN AFRICA, YOU MUST AGREE THAT THE FREEDOM OF THE NEGROES IS THE MOST CRITICAL ISSUE OF OUR AGE?

INDEED, HAVING FOUGHT FOR FREEDOM MANY TIMES I FEEL THAT I MUST BE ITS AGENT.

VERY COMMENDABLE. THOUGH AS A SETTLER IN THE CAPE, I IMAGINE THAT YOU WERE FORCED TO KEEP SLAVES YOURSELF?

HE OFFERED NO RESPONSE TO MY QUERY. VEXING.

I HAVE READ YOUR BOOK OF POETRY, *ENTHUSIASM*...

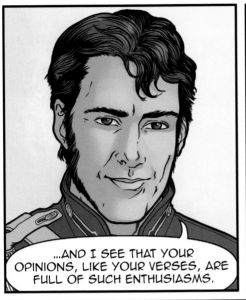

...AND I SEE THAT YOUR OPINIONS, LIKE YOUR VERSES, ARE FULL OF SUCH ENTHUSIASMS.

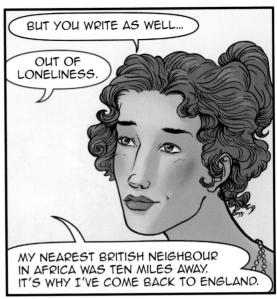

BUT YOU WRITE AS WELL...

OUT OF LONELINESS.

MY NEAREST BRITISH NEIGHBOUR IN AFRICA WAS TEN MILES AWAY. IT'S WHY I'VE COME BACK TO ENGLAND.

WILL YOU WALK OUT SOME DAY WITH ME? WITH A LONELY EMIGRANT?

BUT SIR, I DO NOT POSSESS YOUR APPETITE FOR ADVENTURE IN DISTANT LANDS.

WELL WE NEEDN'T GO AS FAR AS AFRICA.

SO HAMPSTEAD HEATH IT IS!

ALTHOUGH THE YOUNGEST, I WOULD BE THE FIRST IN OUR FAMILY TO MARRY.

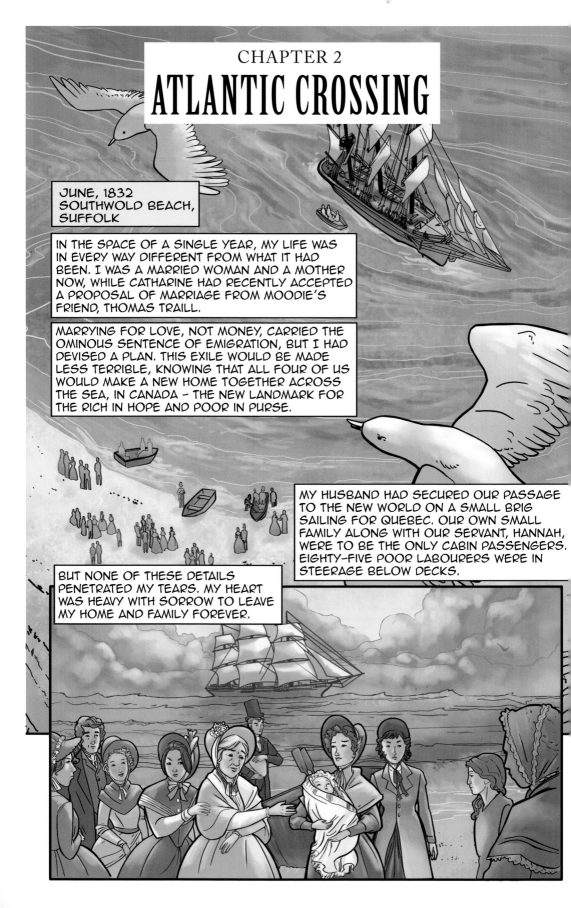

CHAPTER 2
ATLANTIC CROSSING

JUNE, 1832
SOUTHWOLD BEACH,
SUFFOLK

IN THE SPACE OF A SINGLE YEAR, MY LIFE WAS IN EVERY WAY DIFFERENT FROM WHAT IT HAD BEEN. I WAS A MARRIED WOMAN AND A MOTHER NOW, WHILE CATHARINE HAD RECENTLY ACCEPTED A PROPOSAL OF MARRIAGE FROM MOODIE'S FRIEND, THOMAS TRAILL.

MARRYING FOR LOVE, NOT MONEY, CARRIED THE OMINOUS SENTENCE OF EMIGRATION, BUT I HAD DEVISED A PLAN. THIS EXILE WOULD BE MADE LESS TERRIBLE, KNOWING THAT ALL FOUR OF US WOULD MAKE A NEW HOME TOGETHER ACROSS THE SEA, IN CANADA – THE NEW LANDMARK FOR THE RICH IN HOPE AND POOR IN PURSE.

MY HUSBAND HAD SECURED OUR PASSAGE TO THE NEW WORLD ON A SMALL BRIG SAILING FOR QUEBEC. OUR OWN SMALL FAMILY ALONG WITH OUR SERVANT, HANNAH, WERE TO BE THE ONLY CABIN PASSENGERS. EIGHTY-FIVE POOR LABOURERS WERE IN STEERAGE BELOW DECKS.

BUT NONE OF THESE DETAILS PENETRATED MY TEARS. MY HEART WAS HEAVY WITH SORROW TO LEAVE MY HOME AND FAMILY FOREVER.

HERE SUSANNA. I WANT YOU TO WEAR THIS ALWAYS...

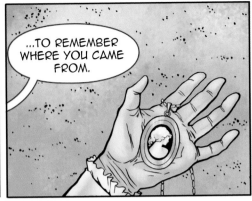

...TO REMEMBER WHERE YOU CAME FROM.

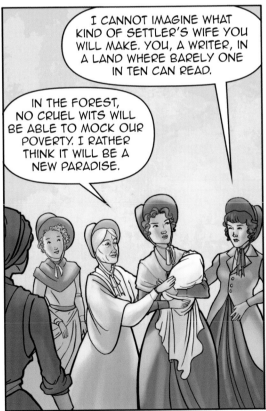

GOD BLESS YOU MY CHILD.

I CANNOT IMAGINE WHAT KIND OF SETTLER'S WIFE YOU WILL MAKE. YOU, A WRITER, IN A LAND WHERE BARELY ONE IN TEN CAN READ.

IN THE FOREST, NO CRUEL WITS WILL BE ABLE TO MOCK OUR POVERTY. I RATHER THINK IT WILL BE A NEW PARADISE.

YOU ARE DANGEROUSLY ROMANTIC – AND THAT YOU WOULD NOW INVOLVE SENSIBLE CATHARINE IN YOUR FOLLY...

SUSANNA, WE CANNOT DELAY ANY FURTHER.

THE SHIP WON'T WAIT.

I THINK I AM THE REALIST THIS TIME, AGNES.

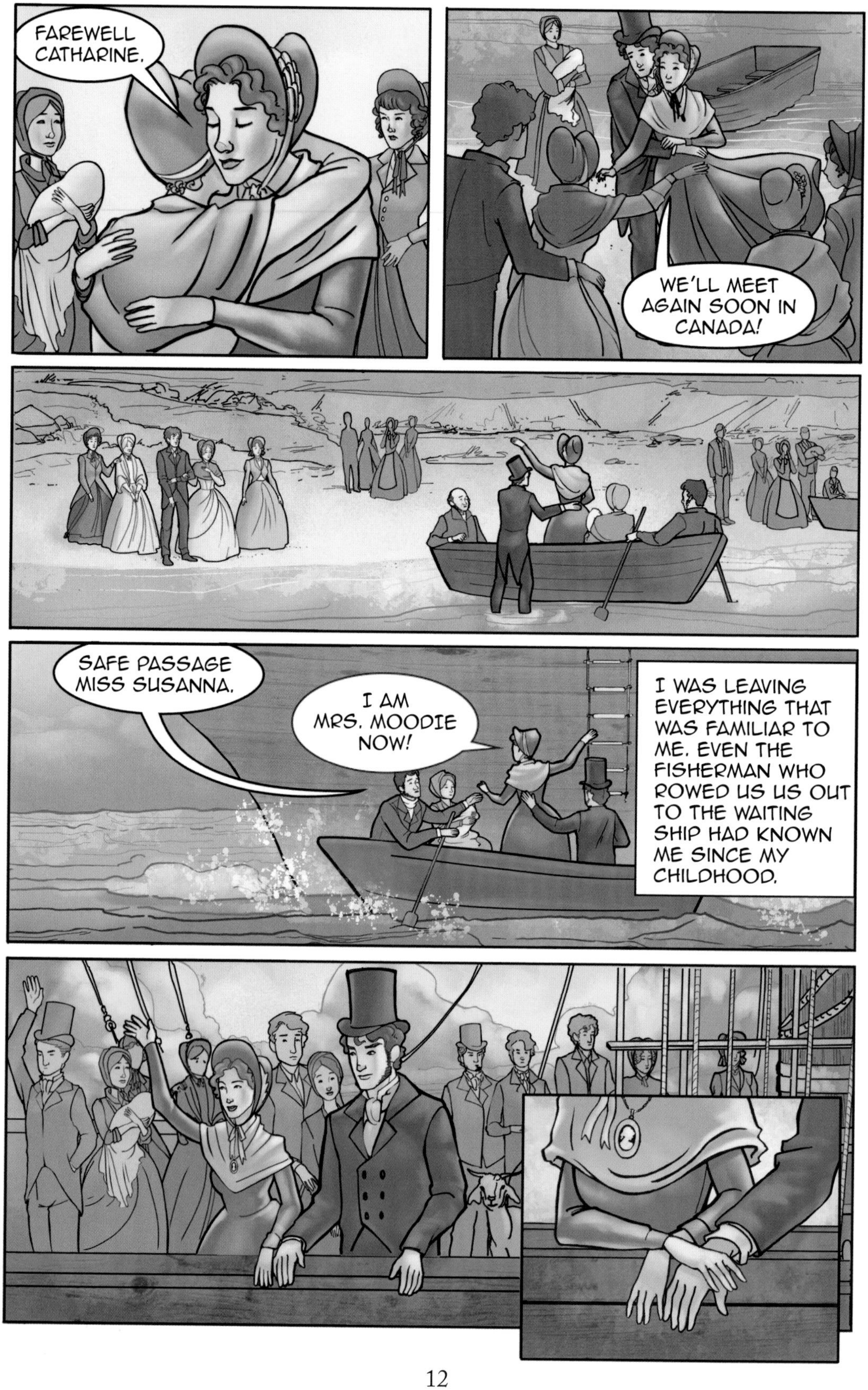
FAREWELL CATHARINE.
WE'LL MEET AGAIN SOON IN CANADA!
SAFE PASSAGE MISS SUSANNA.
I AM MRS. MOODIE NOW!
I WAS LEAVING EVERYTHING THAT WAS FAMILIAR TO ME. EVEN THE FISHERMAN WHO ROWED US US OUT TO THE WAITING SHIP HAD KNOWN ME SINCE MY CHILDHOOD.

FOR AS LONG AS I COULD REMEMBER, I HAD ALWAYS WANTED TO BE A WRITER AND MY HEART WAS FULL OF THE DREAMS OF YOUTH.

BUT SUDDENLY I HAD SET ASIDE MY AMBITIONS AND FOUND MYSELF HURTLING TOWARDS SOME STRANGE DESTINY.

WE HAD NO CHOICE. WE WERE OBLIGED TO EMIGRATE.

AS A RETIRED ARMY OFFICER ON HALF-PAY, MR. MOODIE'S MEANS WERE TOO SMALL TO SUPPORT A FAMILY IN ENGLAND.

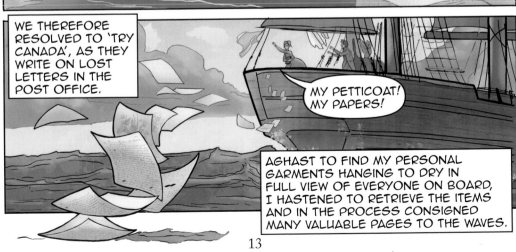

WE THEREFORE RESOLVED TO 'TRY CANADA', AS THEY WRITE ON LOST LETTERS IN THE POST OFFICE.

MY PETTICOAT! MY PAPERS!

AGHAST TO FIND MY PERSONAL GARMENTS HANGING TO DRY IN FULL VIEW OF EVERYONE ON BOARD, I HASTENED TO RETRIEVE THE ITEMS AND IN THE PROCESS CONSIGNED MANY VALUABLE PAGES TO THE WAVES.

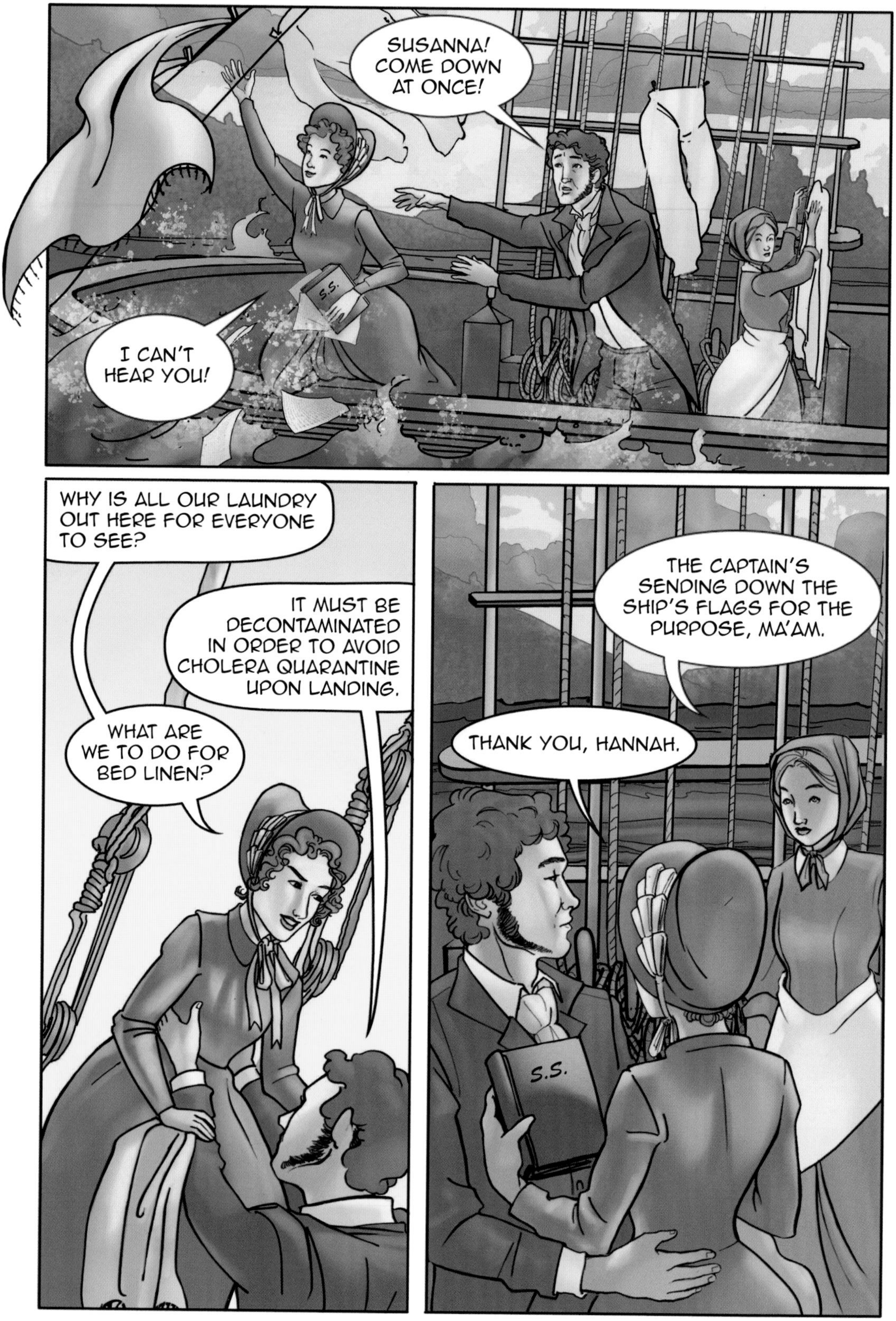
SUSANNA! COME DOWN AT ONCE!
I CAN'T HEAR YOU!
S.S.
WHY IS ALL OUR LAUNDRY OUT HERE FOR EVERYONE TO SEE?
IT MUST BE DECONTAMINATED IN ORDER TO AVOID CHOLERA QUARANTINE UPON LANDING.
WHAT ARE WE TO DO FOR BED LINEN?
THE CAPTAIN'S SENDING DOWN THE SHIP'S FLAGS FOR THE PURPOSE, MA'AM.
THANK YOU, HANNAH.
S.S.

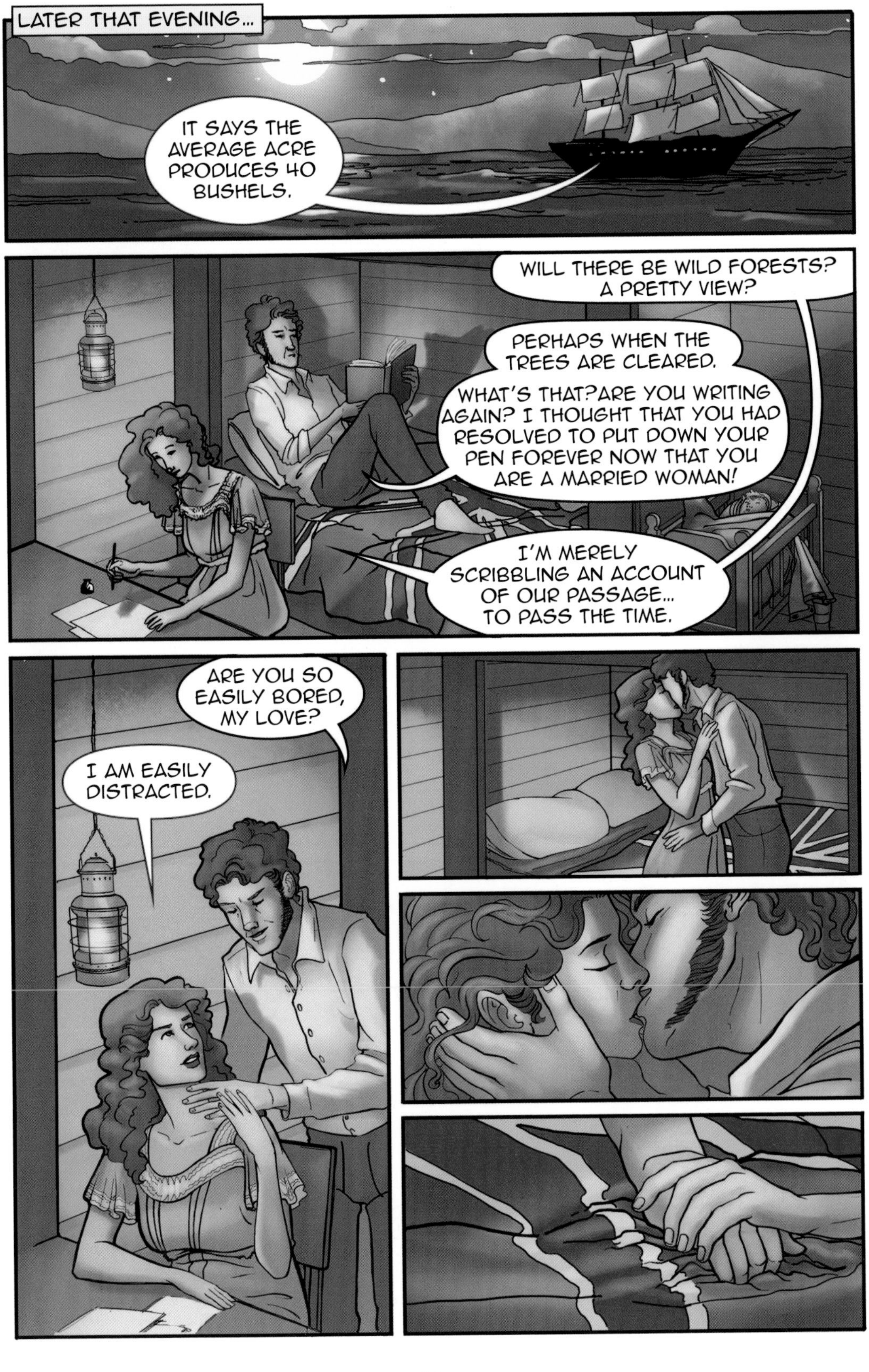
LATER THAT EVENING...
IT SAYS THE AVERAGE ACRE PRODUCES 40 BUSHELS.
WILL THERE BE WILD FORESTS? A PRETTY VIEW?
PERHAPS WHEN THE TREES ARE CLEARED.
WHAT'S THAT?ARE YOU WRITING AGAIN? I THOUGHT THAT YOU HAD RESOLVED TO PUT DOWN YOUR PEN FOREVER NOW THAT YOU ARE A MARRIED WOMAN!
I'M MERELY SCRIBBLING AN ACCOUNT OF OUR PASSAGE... TO PASS THE TIME.
ARE YOU SO EASILY BORED, MY LOVE?
I AM EASILY DISTRACTED.

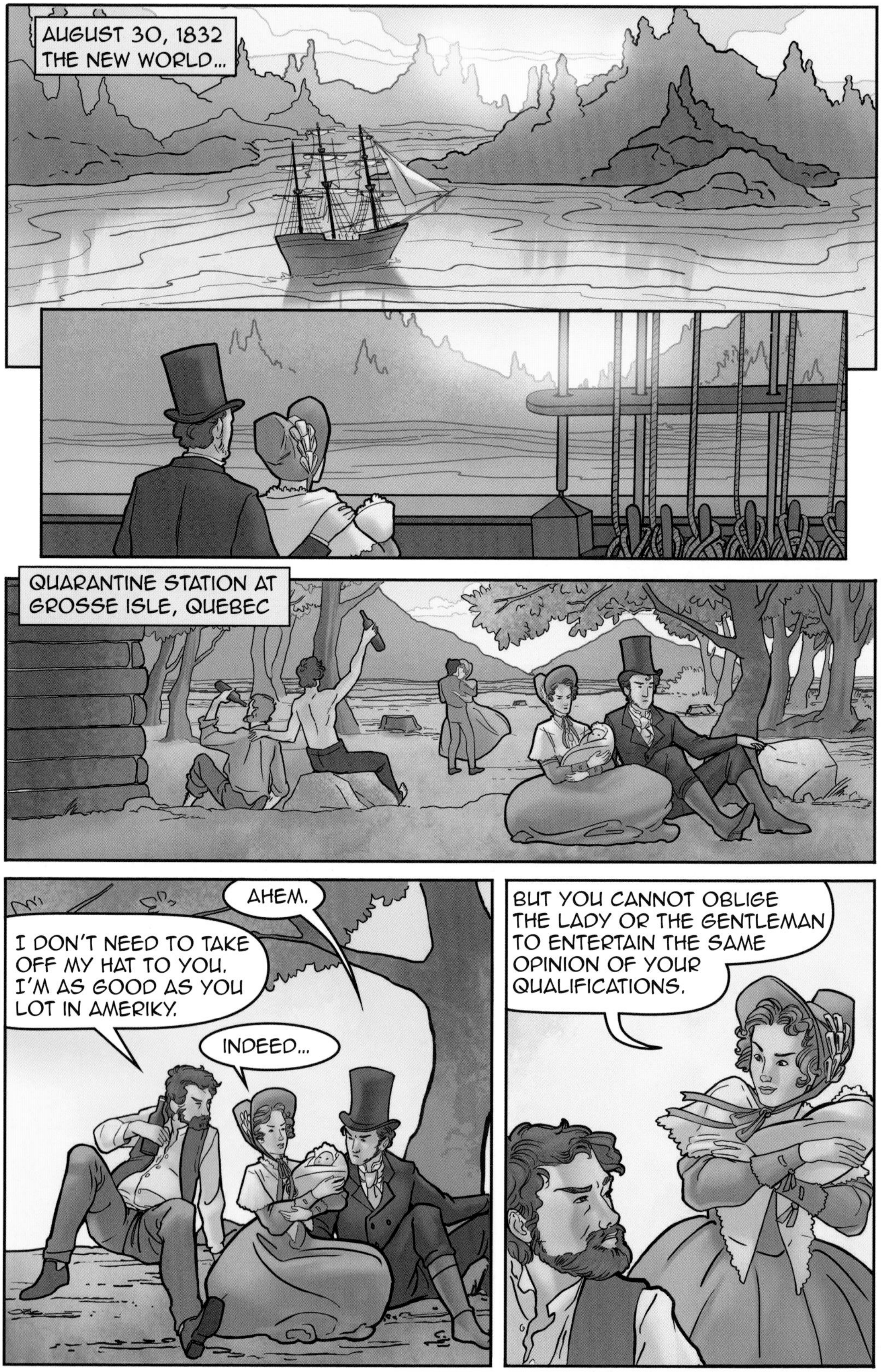
AUGUST 30, 1832
THE NEW WORLD...
QUARANTINE STATION AT GROSSE ISLE, QUEBEC
AHEM.
I DON'T NEED TO TAKE OFF MY HAT TO YOU. I'M AS GOOD AS YOU LOT IN AMERIKY.
INDEED...
BUT YOU CANNOT OBLIGE THE LADY OR THE GENTLEMAN TO ENTERTAIN THE SAME OPINION OF YOUR QUALIFICATIONS.

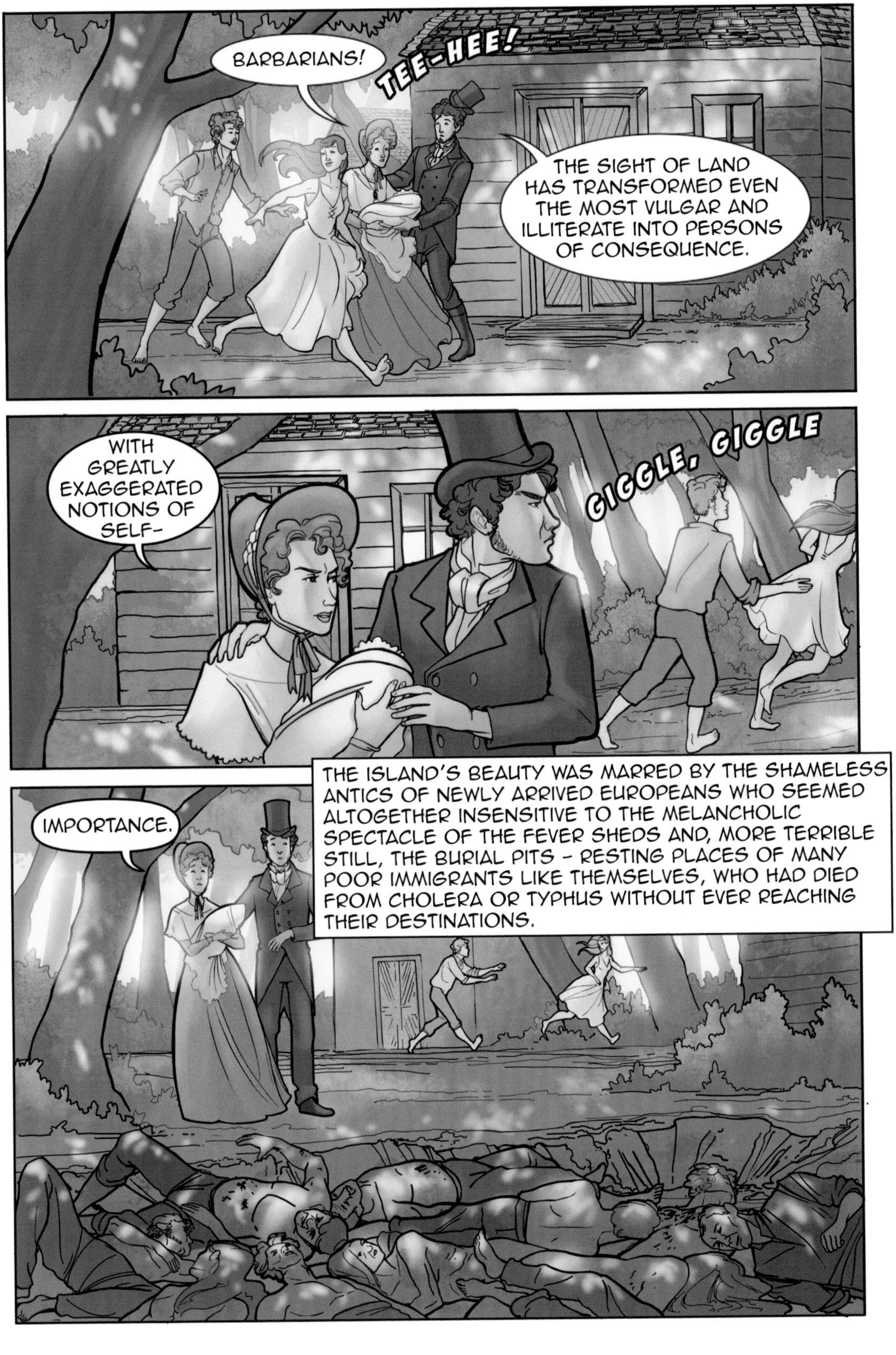

BARBARIANS!
TEE-HEE!
THE SIGHT OF LAND HAS TRANSFORMED EVEN THE MOST VULGAR AND ILLITERATE INTO PERSONS OF CONSEQUENCE.
WITH GREATLY EXAGGERATED NOTIONS OF SELF-
GIGGLE, GIGGLE
IMPORTANCE.
THE ISLAND'S BEAUTY WAS MARRED BY THE SHAMELESS ANTICS OF NEWLY ARRIVED EUROPEANS WHO SEEMED ALTOGETHER INSENSITIVE TO THE MELANCHOLIC SPECTACLE OF THE FEVER SHEDS AND, MORE TERRIBLE STILL, THE BURIAL PITS - RESTING PLACES OF MANY POOR IMMIGRANTS LIKE THEMSELVES, WHO HAD DIED FROM CHOLERA OR TYPHUS WITHOUT EVER REACHING THEIR DESTINATIONS.

CHAPTER 3
THE BUSH

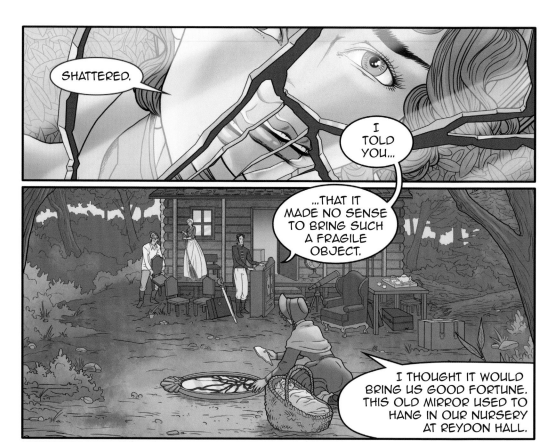

SHATTERED.

I TOLD YOU...

...THAT IT MADE NO SENSE TO BRING SUCH A FRAGILE OBJECT.

I THOUGHT IT WOULD BRING US GOOD FORTUNE. THIS OLD MIRROR USED TO HANG IN OUR NURSERY AT REYDON HALL.

SURELY THIS IS NOT A HOUSE BUT A CATTLE SHED OR PIGSTY.

IT'S ONLY A SHELTER FOR THE WINTER. WE'LL BUILD A PROPER HOUSE IN THE NEW YEAR.

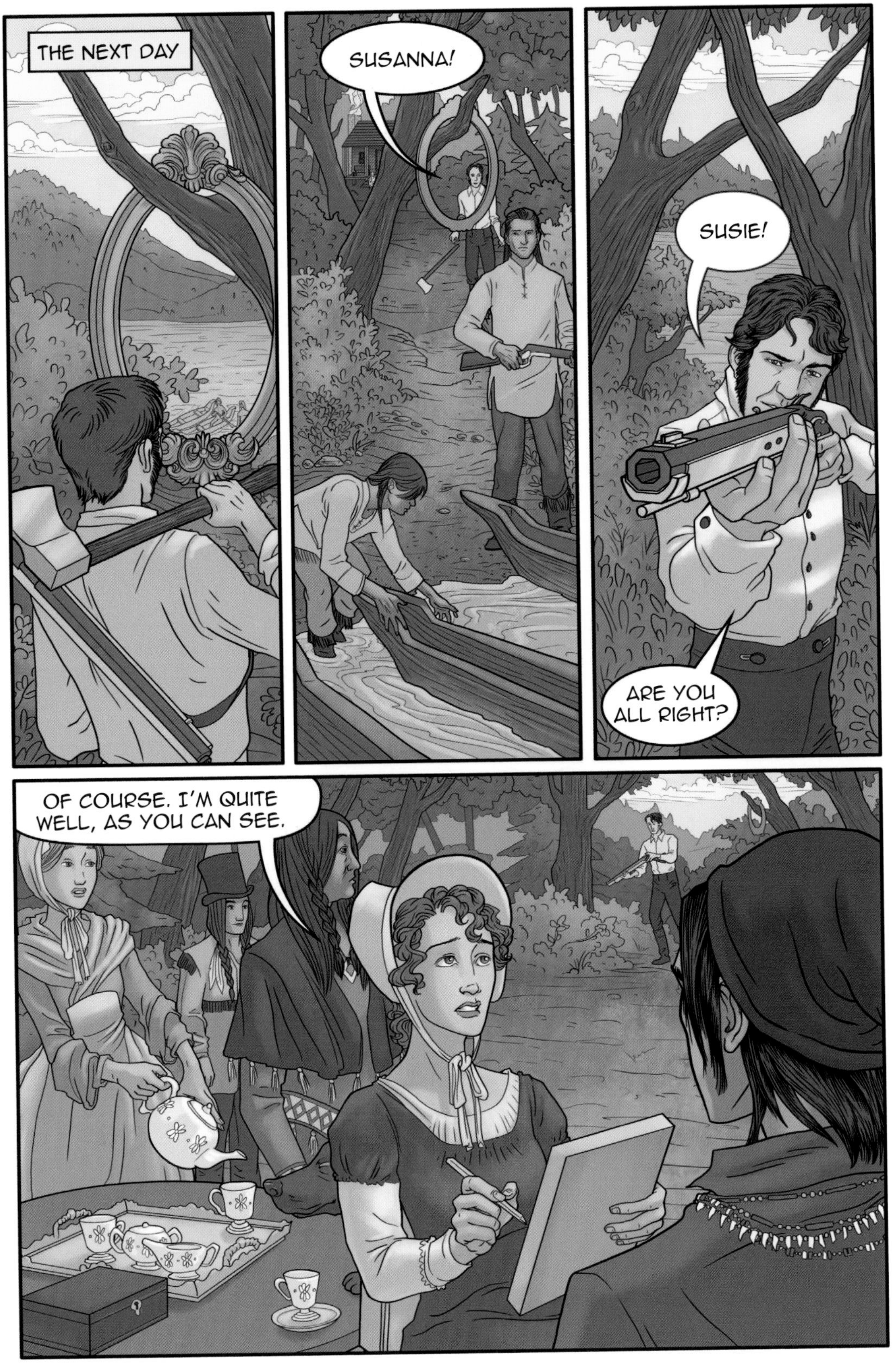
THE NEXT DAY
SUSANNA!
SUSIE!
ARE YOU ALL RIGHT?
OF COURSE. I'M QUITE WELL, AS YOU CAN SEE.

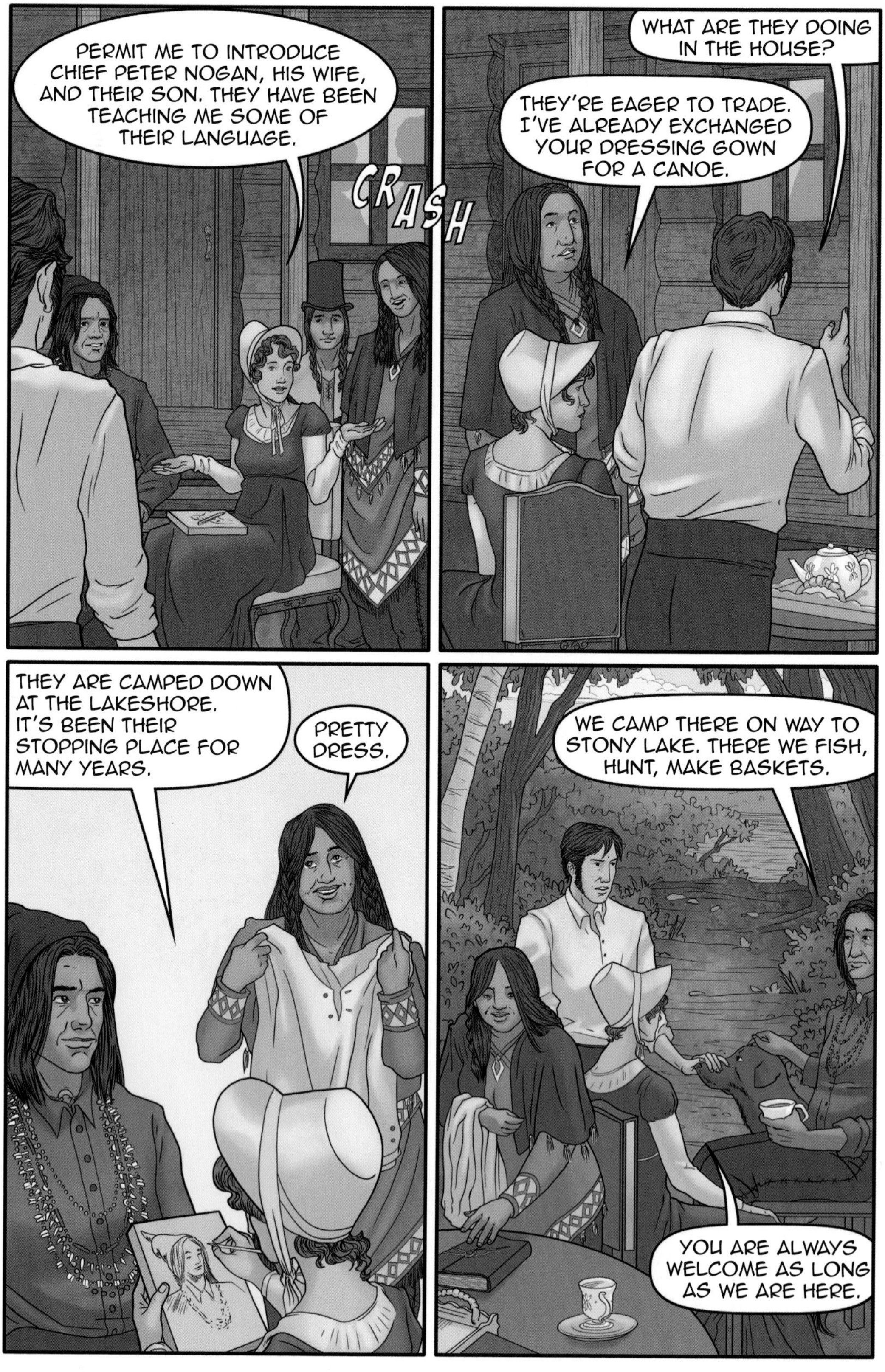
PERMIT ME TO INTRODUCE CHIEF PETER NOGAN, HIS WIFE, AND THEIR SON. THEY HAVE BEEN TEACHING ME SOME OF THEIR LANGUAGE.
CRASH
WHAT ARE THEY DOING IN THE HOUSE?
THEY'RE EAGER TO TRADE. I'VE ALREADY EXCHANGED YOUR DRESSING GOWN FOR A CANOE.
THEY ARE CAMPED DOWN AT THE LAKESHORE. IT'S BEEN THEIR STOPPING PLACE FOR MANY YEARS.
PRETTY DRESS.
WE CAMP THERE ON WAY TO STONY LAKE. THERE WE FISH, HUNT, MAKE BASKETS.
YOU ARE ALWAYS WELCOME AS LONG AS WE ARE HERE.

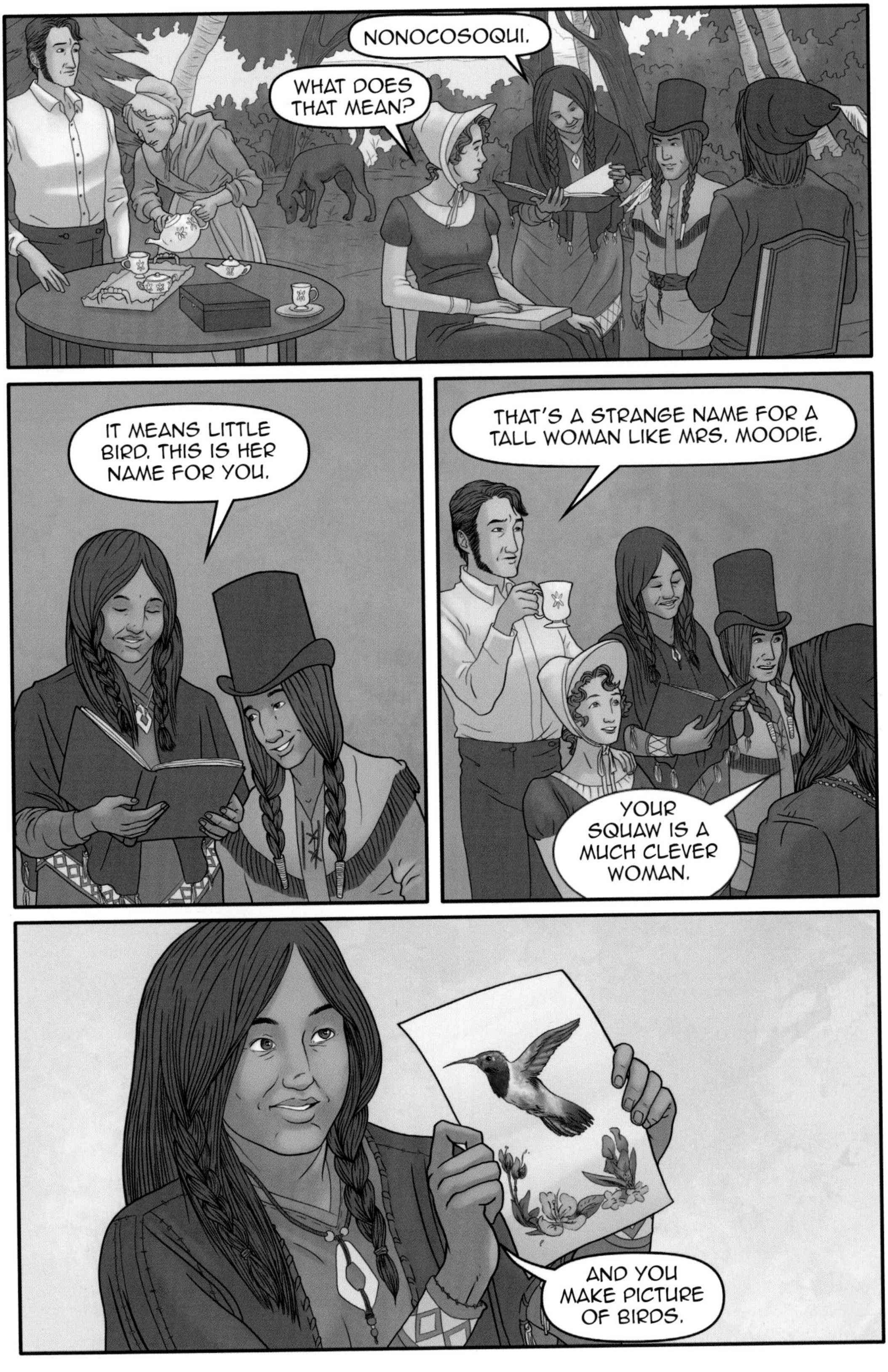
NONOCOSOQUI.
WHAT DOES THAT MEAN?
IT MEANS LITTLE BIRD. THIS IS HER NAME FOR YOU.
THAT'S A STRANGE NAME FOR A TALL WOMAN LIKE MRS. MOODIE.
YOUR SQUAW IS A MUCH CLEVER WOMAN.
AND YOU MAKE PICTURE OF BIRDS.

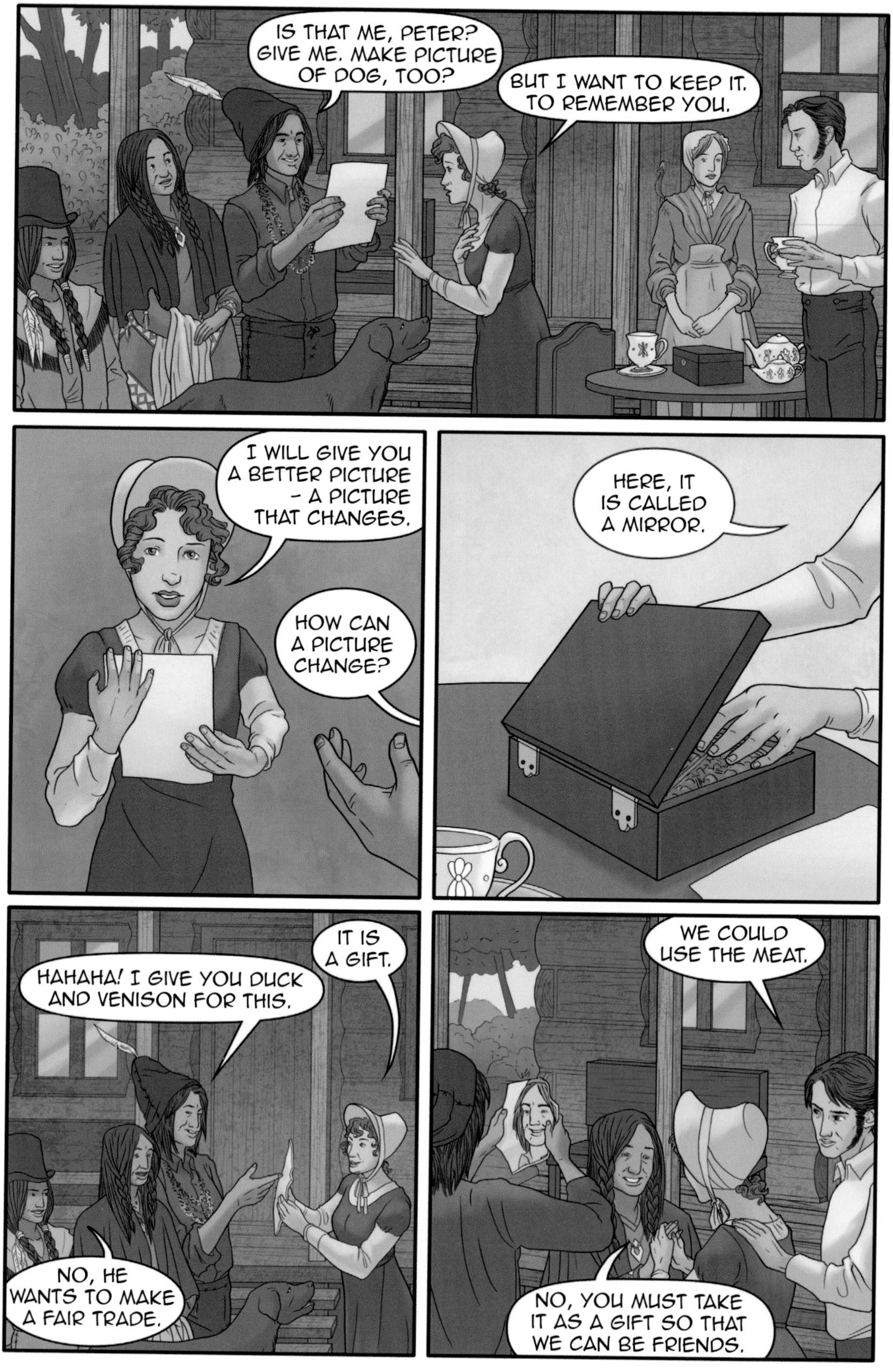

IS THAT ME, PETER? GIVE ME. MAKE PICTURE OF DOG, TOO?
BUT I WANT TO KEEP IT. TO REMEMBER YOU.
I WILL GIVE YOU A BETTER PICTURE - A PICTURE THAT CHANGES.
HOW CAN A PICTURE CHANGE?
HERE, IT IS CALLED A MIRROR.
HAHAHA! I GIVE YOU DUCK AND VENISON FOR THIS.
IT IS A GIFT.
NO, HE WANTS TO MAKE A FAIR TRADE.
WE COULD USE THE MEAT.
NO, YOU MUST TAKE IT AS A GIFT SO THAT WE CAN BE FRIENDS.

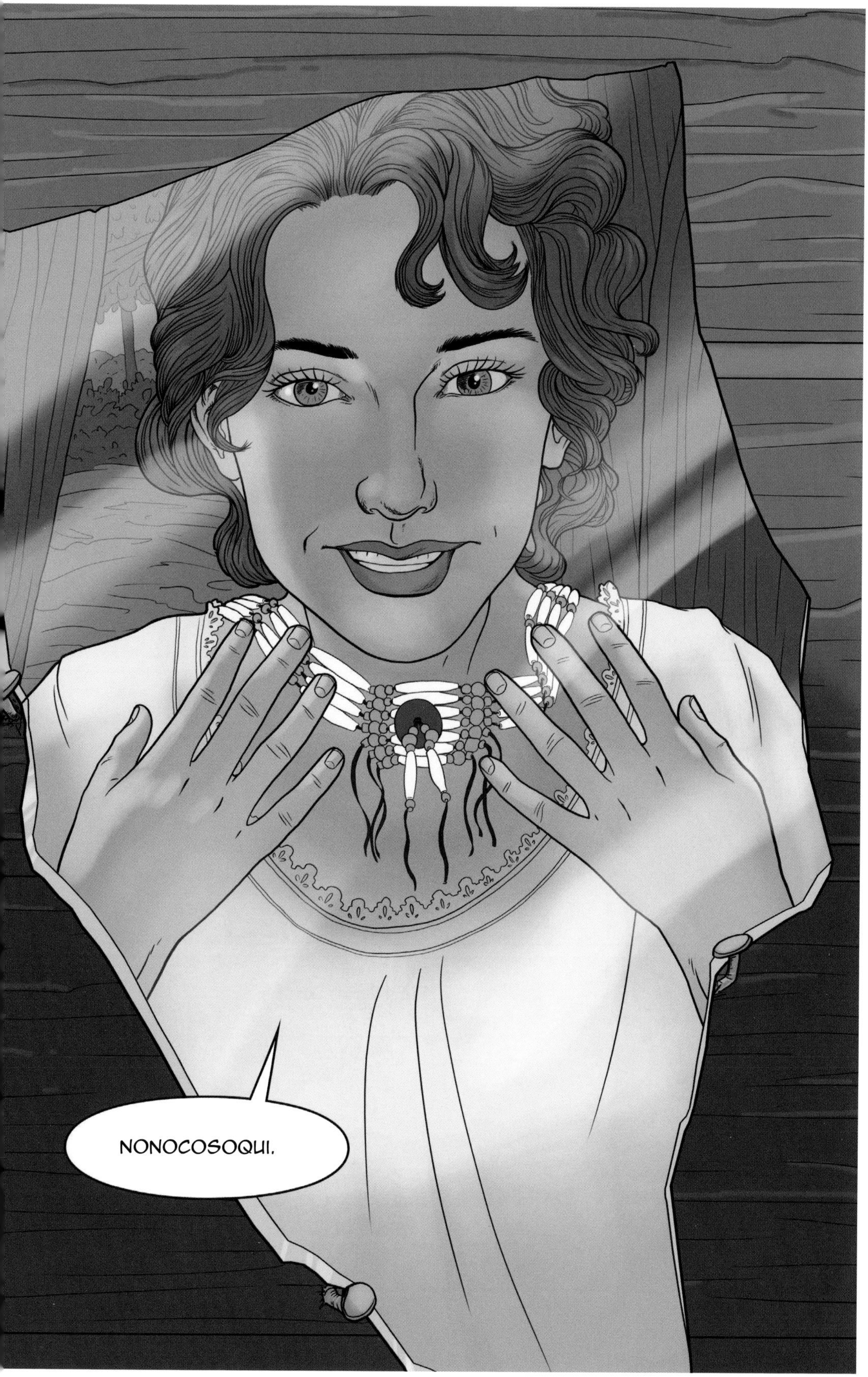
NONOCOSOQUI.

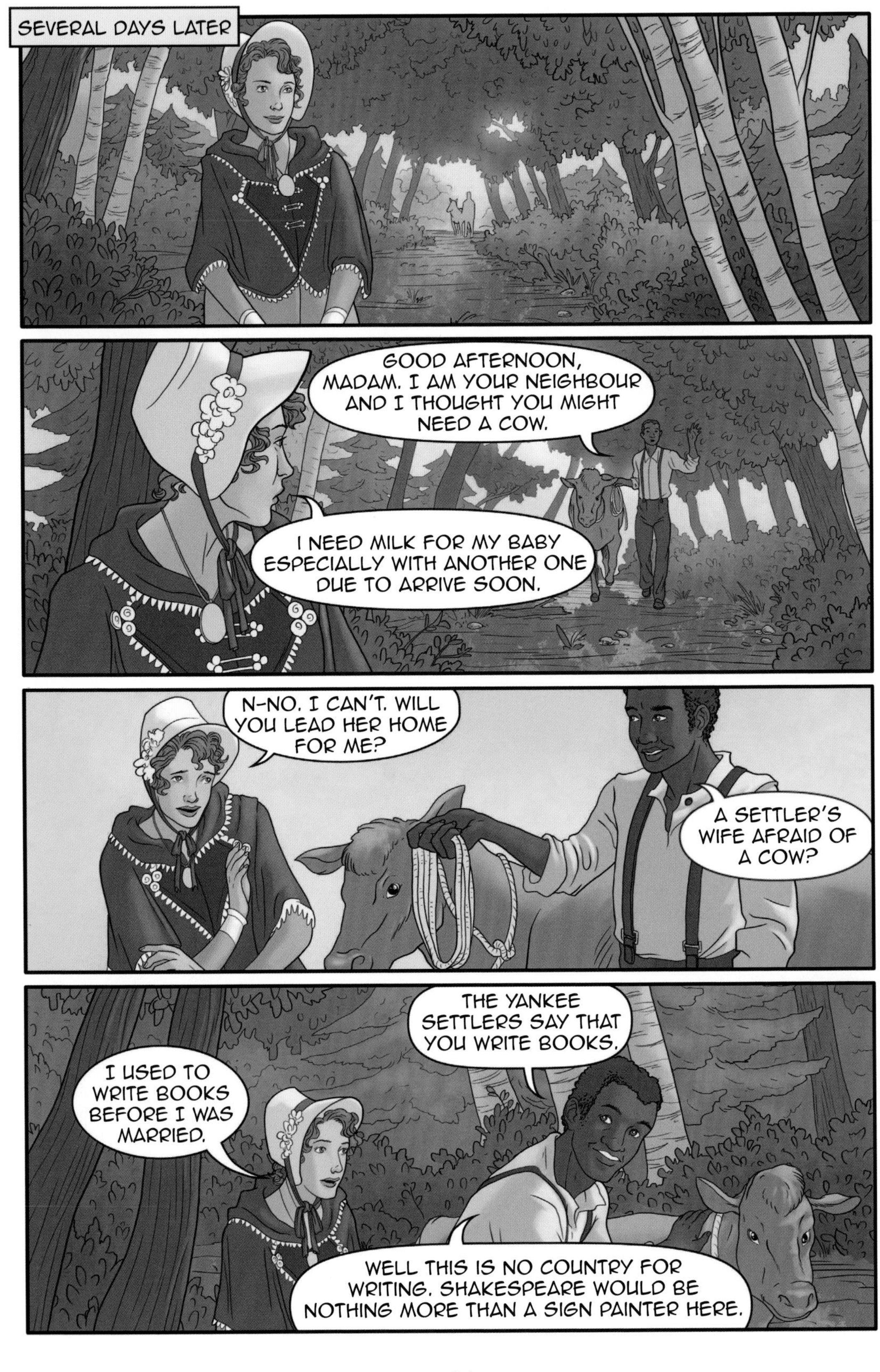
SEVERAL DAYS LATER
GOOD AFTERNOON, MADAM. I AM YOUR NEIGHBOUR AND I THOUGHT YOU MIGHT NEED A COW.
I NEED MILK FOR MY BABY ESPECIALLY WITH ANOTHER ONE DUE TO ARRIVE SOON.
N-NO. I CAN'T. WILL YOU LEAD HER HOME FOR ME?
A SETTLER'S WIFE AFRAID OF A COW?
THE YANKEE SETTLERS SAY THAT YOU WRITE BOOKS.
I USED TO WRITE BOOKS BEFORE I WAS MARRIED.
WELL THIS IS NO COUNTRY FOR WRITING. SHAKESPEARE WOULD BE NOTHING MORE THAN A SIGN PAINTER HERE.

AND HOW IS IT THAT YOU ARE ACQUAINTED WITH THIS GENTLEMAN?

I ONCE MANAGED A VIRGINIA PLANTATION AND MY MASTER GRANTED ME THE USE OF HIS LIBRARY.

THEN WHAT BROUGHT YOU TO THIS BEGGARLY WOODEN COUNTRY?

I WANTED TO BE FREE.

MOLLINEUX IS MY NAME.

I AM MRS. MOODIE.

AND WHAT DO YOU WRITE?

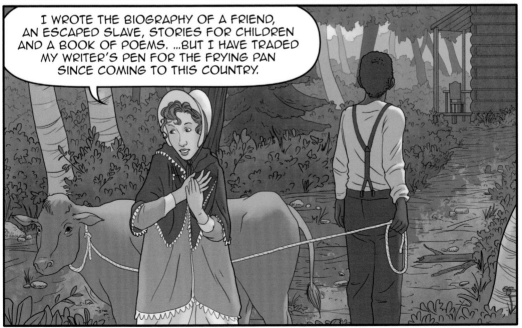

I WROTE THE BIOGRAPHY OF A FRIEND, AN ESCAPED SLAVE, STORIES FOR CHILDREN AND A BOOK OF POEMS. ...BUT I HAVE TRADED MY WRITER'S PEN FOR THE FRYING PAN SINCE COMING TO THIS COUNTRY.

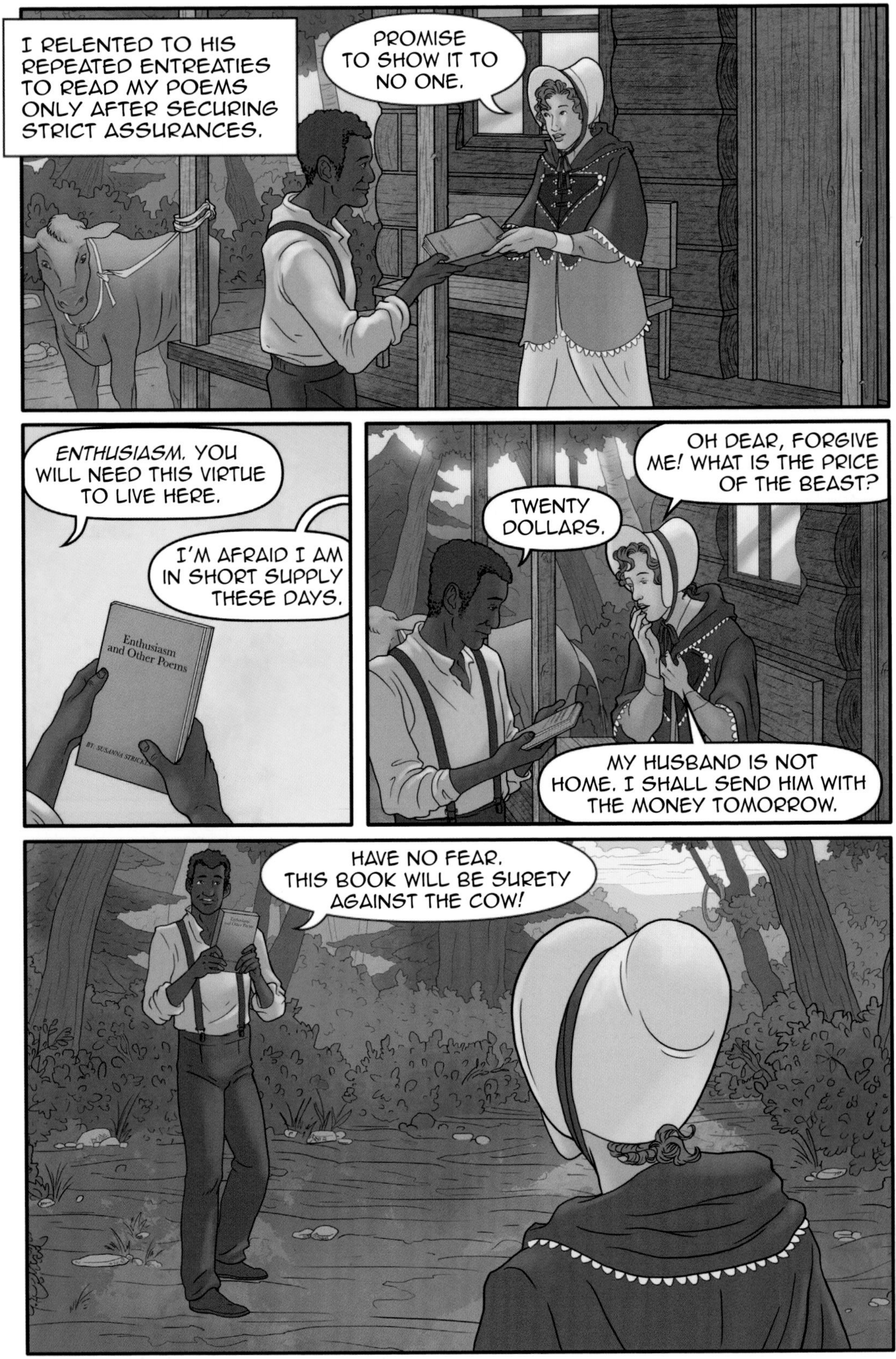
I RELENTED TO HIS REPEATED ENTREATIES TO READ MY POEMS ONLY AFTER SECURING STRICT ASSURANCES.
PROMISE TO SHOW IT TO NO ONE.
ENTHUSIASM. YOU WILL NEED THIS VIRTUE TO LIVE HERE.
I'M AFRAID I AM IN SHORT SUPPLY THESE DAYS.
Enthusiasm and Other Poems
OH DEAR, FORGIVE ME! WHAT IS THE PRICE OF THE BEAST?
TWENTY DOLLARS.
MY HUSBAND IS NOT HOME. I SHALL SEND HIM WITH THE MONEY TOMORROW.
HAVE NO FEAR. THIS BOOK WILL BE SURETY AGAINST THE COW!

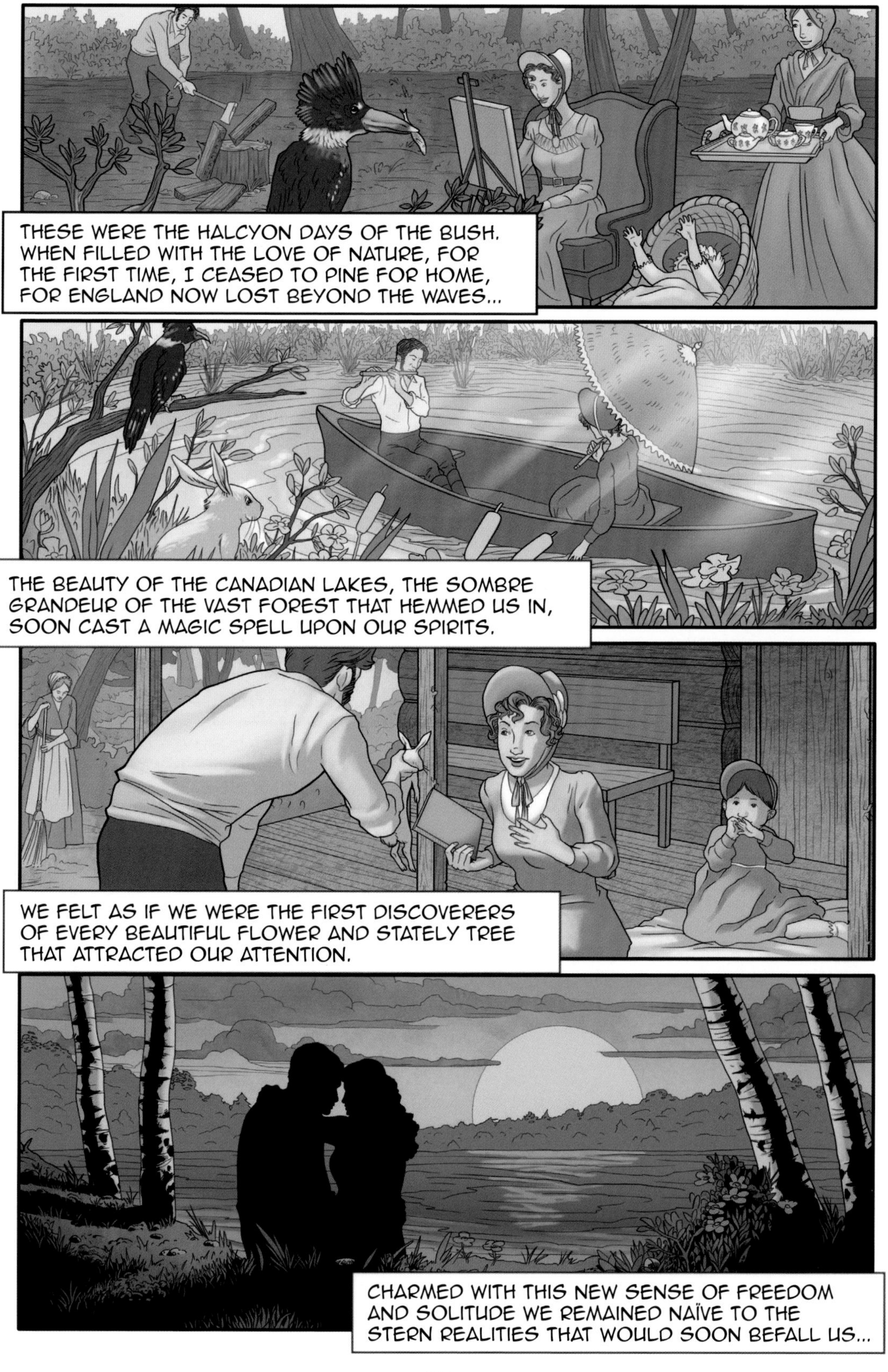
THESE WERE THE HALCYON DAYS OF THE BUSH. WHEN FILLED WITH THE LOVE OF NATURE, FOR THE FIRST TIME, I CEASED TO PINE FOR HOME, FOR ENGLAND NOW LOST BEYOND THE WAVES...
THE BEAUTY OF THE CANADIAN LAKES, THE SOMBRE GRANDEUR OF THE VAST FOREST THAT HEMMED US IN, SOON CAST A MAGIC SPELL UPON OUR SPIRITS.
WE FELT AS IF WE WERE THE FIRST DISCOVERERS OF EVERY BEAUTIFUL FLOWER AND STATELY TREE THAT ATTRACTED OUR ATTENTION.
CHARMED WITH THIS NEW SENSE OF FREEDOM AND SOLITUDE WE REMAINED NAÏVE TO THE STERN REALITIES THAT WOULD SOON BEFALL US...

CHAPTER 4

OUR LOGGING BEE

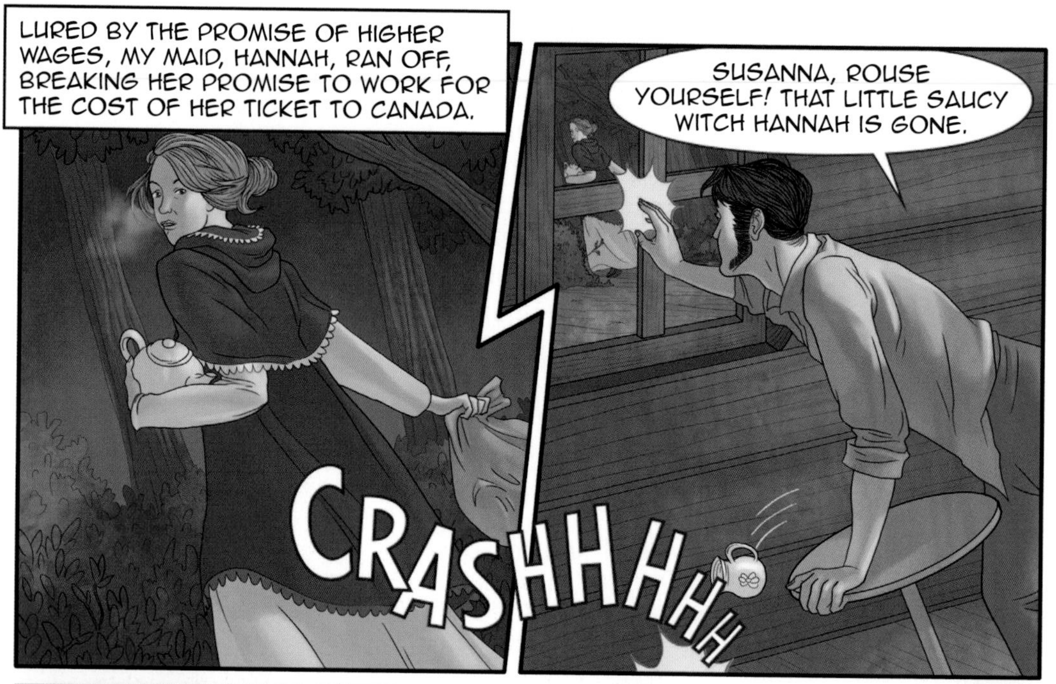
LURED BY THE PROMISE OF HIGHER WAGES, MY MAID, HANNAH, RAN OFF, BREAKING HER PROMISE TO WORK FOR THE COST OF HER TICKET TO CANADA.
SUSANNA, ROUSE YOURSELF! THAT LITTLE SAUCY WITCH HANNAH IS GONE.
CRASHHHHH

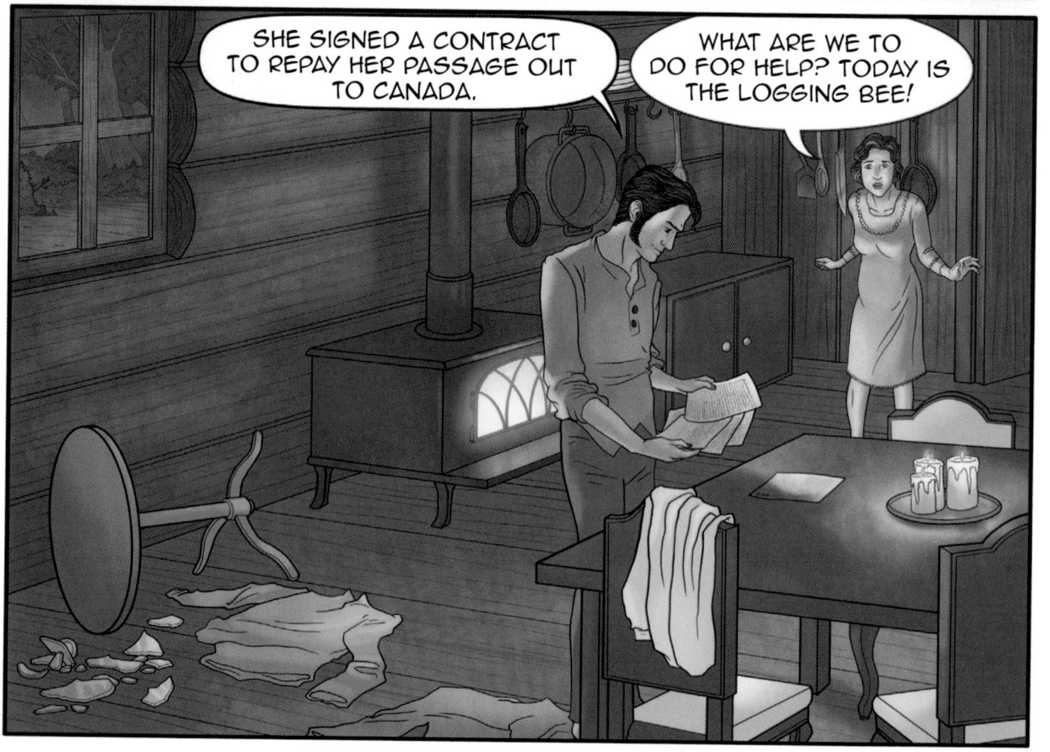
SHE SIGNED A CONTRACT TO REPAY HER PASSAGE OUT TO CANADA.
WHAT ARE WE TO DO FOR HELP? TODAY IS THE LOGGING BEE!

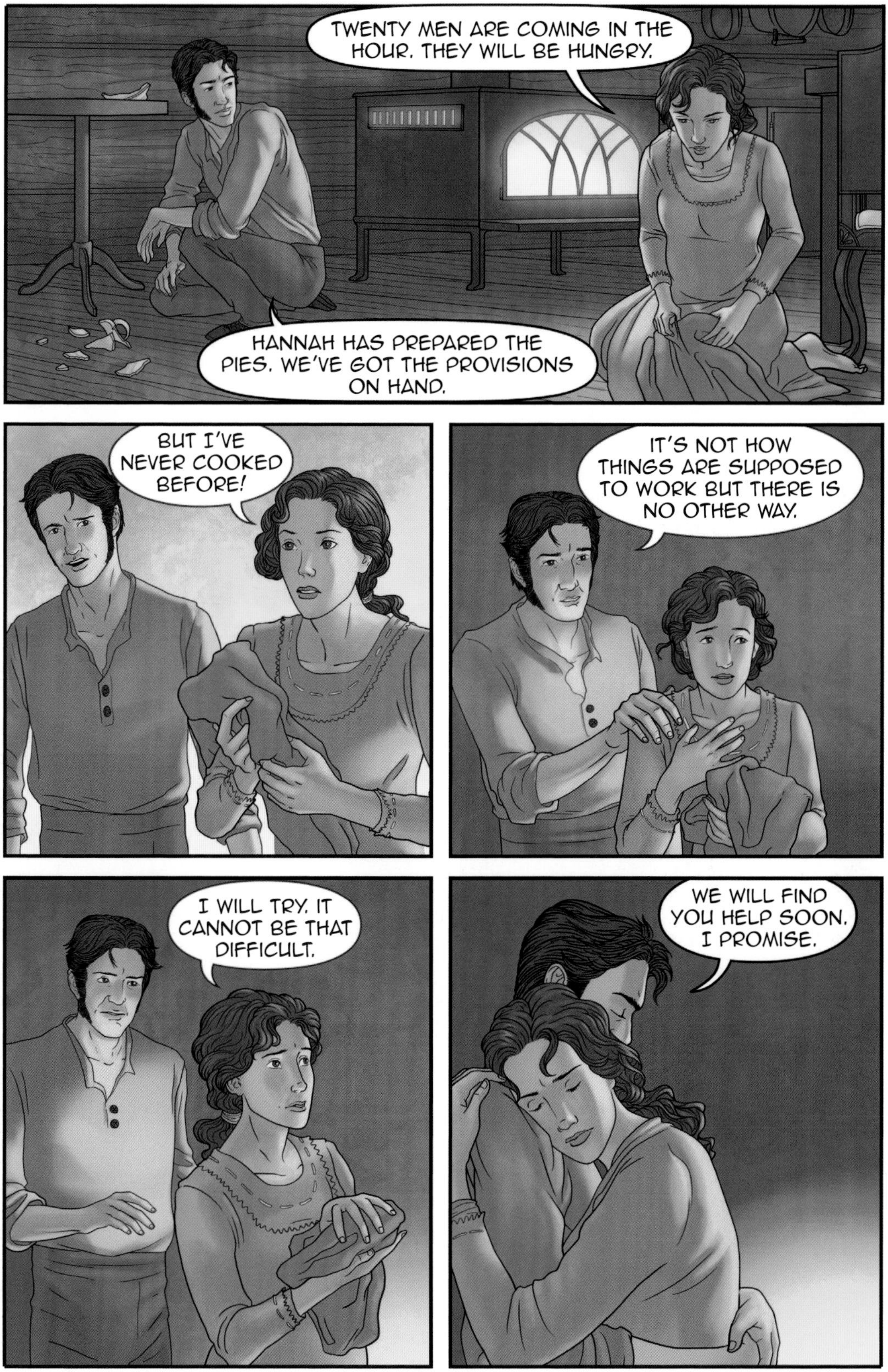
TWENTY MEN ARE COMING IN THE HOUR. THEY WILL BE HUNGRY.
HANNAH HAS PREPARED THE PIES. WE'VE GOT THE PROVISIONS ON HAND.
BUT I'VE NEVER COOKED BEFORE!
IT'S NOT HOW THINGS ARE SUPPOSED TO WORK BUT THERE IS NO OTHER WAY.
I WILL TRY. IT CANNOT BE THAT DIFFICULT.
WE WILL FIND YOU HELP SOON. I PROMISE.

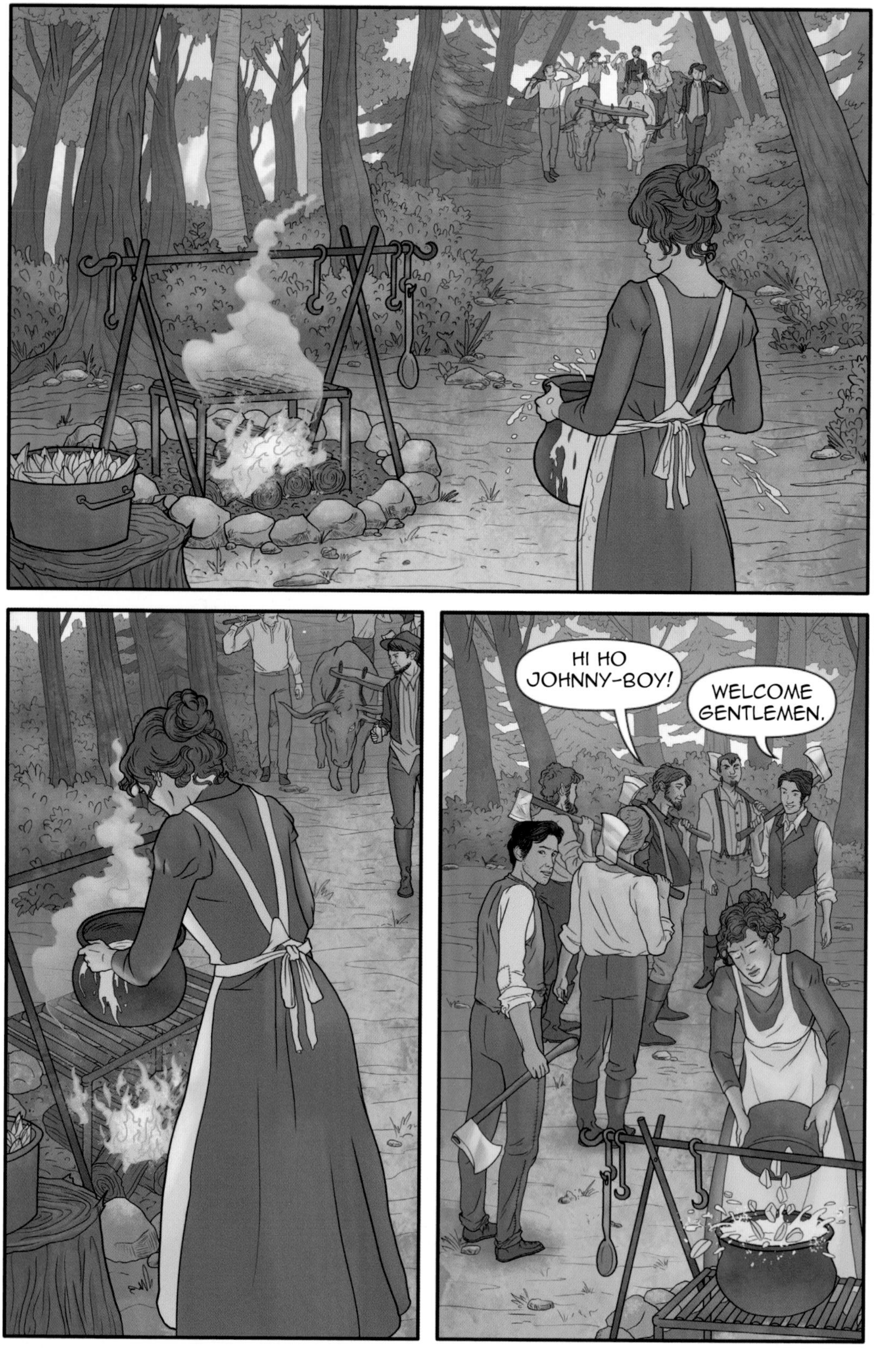
HI HO JOHNNY-BOY!
WELCOME GENTLEMEN.

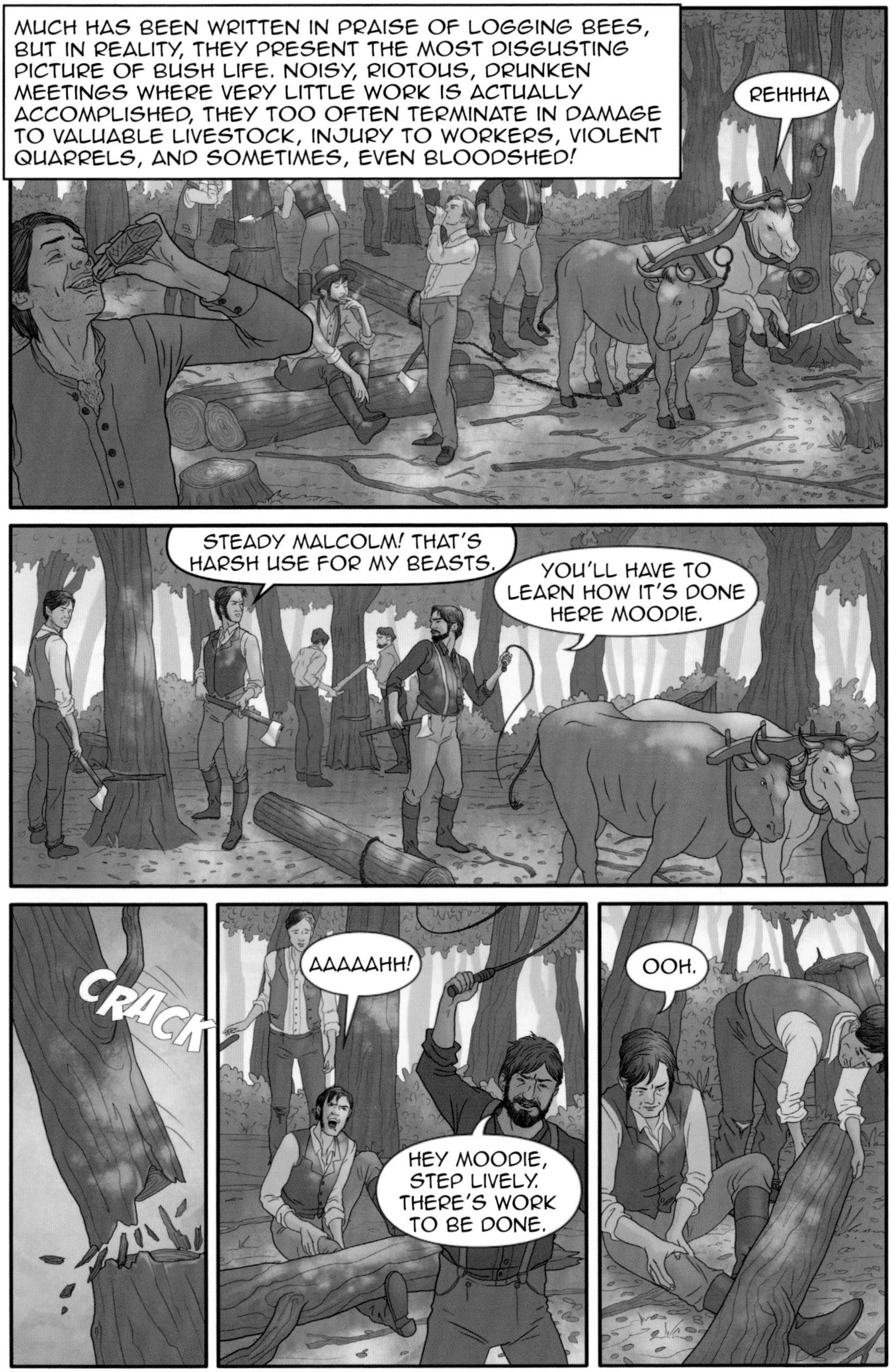
MUCH HAS BEEN WRITTEN IN PRAISE OF LOGGING BEES, BUT IN REALITY, THEY PRESENT THE MOST DISGUSTING PICTURE OF BUSH LIFE. NOISY, RIOTOUS, DRUNKEN MEETINGS WHERE VERY LITTLE WORK IS ACTUALLY ACCOMPLISHED, THEY TOO OFTEN TERMINATE IN DAMAGE TO VALUABLE LIVESTOCK, INJURY TO WORKERS, VIOLENT QUARRELS, AND SOMETIMES, EVEN BLOODSHED!
REHHHA
STEADY MALCOLM! THAT'S HARSH USE FOR MY BEASTS.
YOU'LL HAVE TO LEARN HOW IT'S DONE HERE MOODIE.
CRACK
AAAAAHH!
HEY MOODIE, STEP LIVELY. THERE'S WORK TO BE DONE.
OOH.

HA HAR HA

NEITHER MY HUSBAND NOR I WERE ACCUSTOMED TO TOILING LIKE LABOURERS AND WERE CONSTANTLY EXHIBITING OUR IGNORANCE. JOHN'S LEG TOOK MONTHS TO RECOVER, WHICH COST HIM DEARLY IN LOST WORK, WHILE MY OWN CLUMSY ATTEMPTS AT COOKERY COULD IN NO WAY BE CALLED SUCCESSFUL.

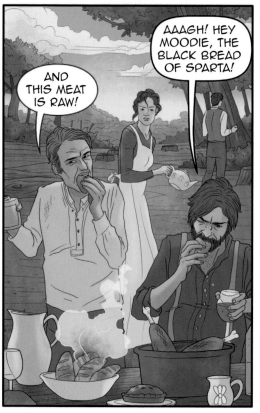

AAAGH! HEY MOODIE, THE BLACK BREAD OF SPARTA!

AND THIS MEAT IS RAW!

I CARE NOT AS LONG AS THERE'S GROG. HERE WOMAN, MY CUP HAS SPRUNG A LEAK.

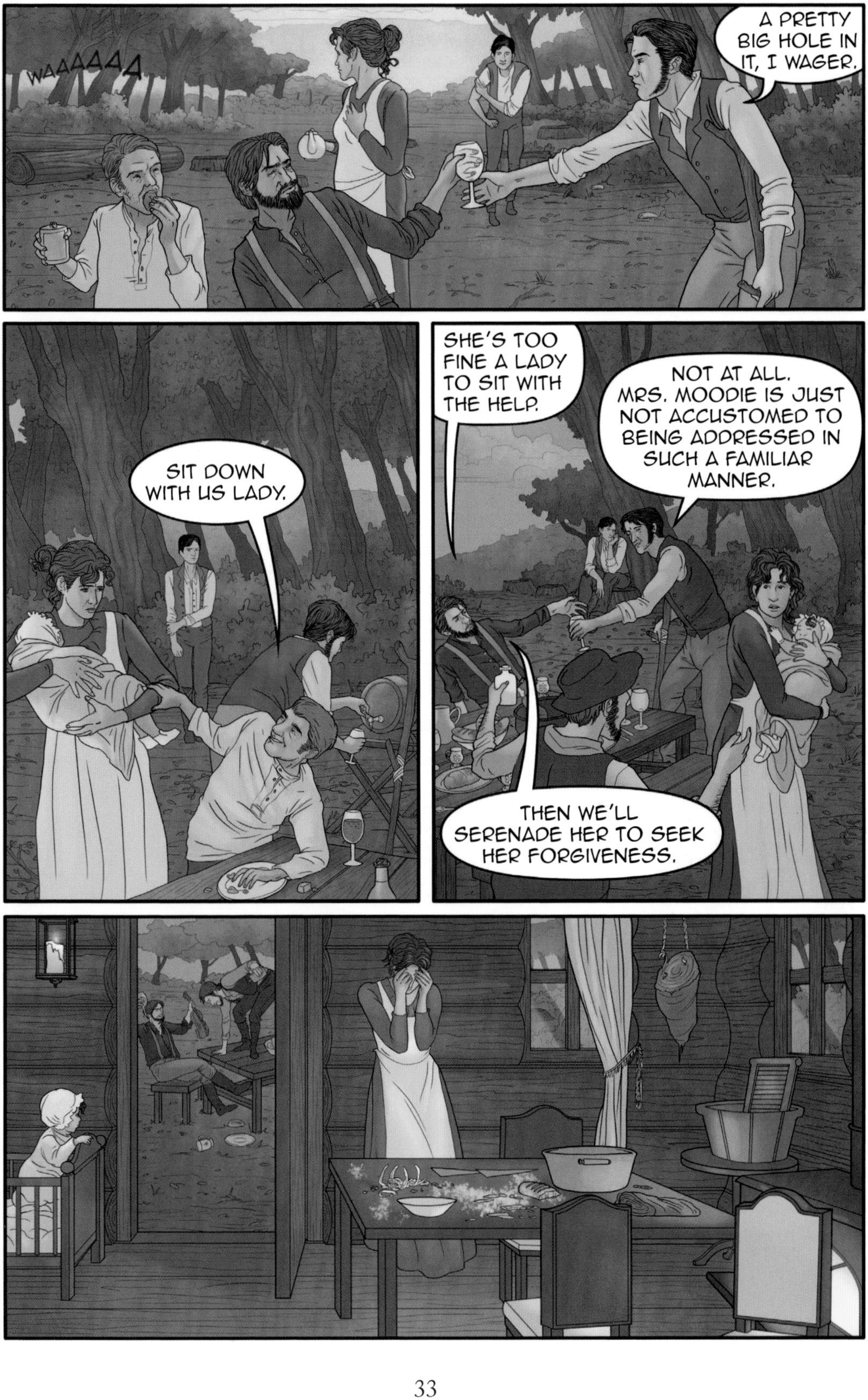
WAAAAAA
A PRETTY BIG HOLE IN IT, I WAGER.
SIT DOWN WITH US LADY.
SHE'S TOO FINE A LADY TO SIT WITH THE HELP.
NOT AT ALL. MRS. MOODIE IS JUST NOT ACCUSTOMED TO BEING ADDRESSED IN SUCH A FAMILIAR MANNER.
THEN WE'LL SERENADE HER TO SEEK HER FORGIVENESS.

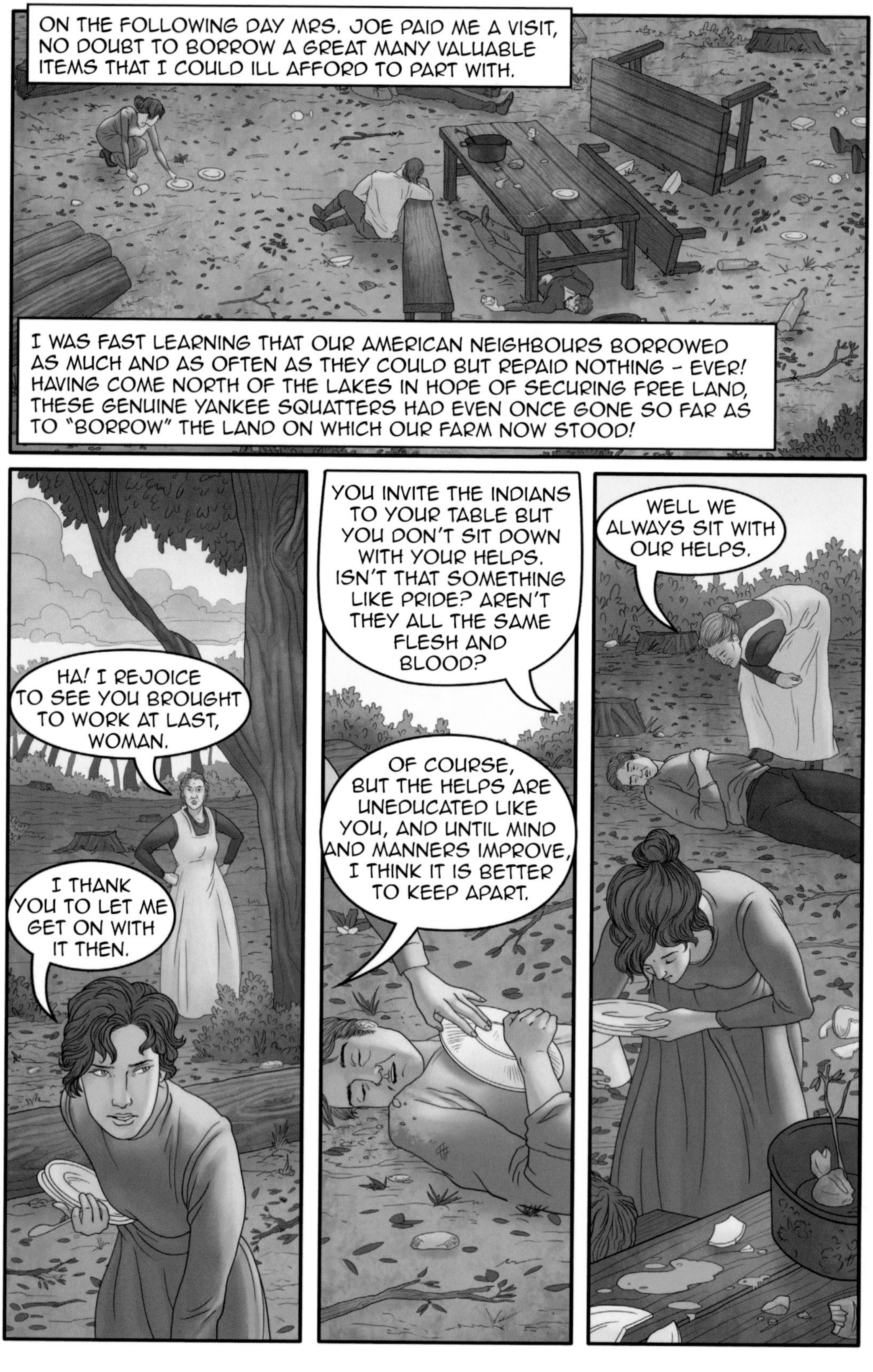
ON THE FOLLOWING DAY MRS. JOE PAID ME A VISIT, NO DOUBT TO BORROW A GREAT MANY VALUABLE ITEMS THAT I COULD ILL AFFORD TO PART WITH.
I WAS FAST LEARNING THAT OUR AMERICAN NEIGHBOURS BORROWED AS MUCH AND AS OFTEN AS THEY COULD BUT REPAID NOTHING - EVER! HAVING COME NORTH OF THE LAKES IN HOPE OF SECURING FREE LAND, THESE GENUINE YANKEE SQUATTERS HAD EVEN ONCE GONE SO FAR AS TO "BORROW" THE LAND ON WHICH OUR FARM NOW STOOD!
HA! I REJOICE TO SEE YOU BROUGHT TO WORK AT LAST, WOMAN.
I THANK YOU TO LET ME GET ON WITH IT THEN.
YOU INVITE THE INDIANS TO YOUR TABLE BUT YOU DON'T SIT DOWN WITH YOUR HELPS. ISN'T THAT SOMETHING LIKE PRIDE? AREN'T THEY ALL THE SAME FLESH AND BLOOD?
OF COURSE, BUT THE HELPS ARE UNEDUCATED LIKE YOU, AND UNTIL MIND AND MANNERS IMPROVE, I THINK IT IS BETTER TO KEEP APART.
WELL WE ALWAYS SIT WITH OUR HELPS.

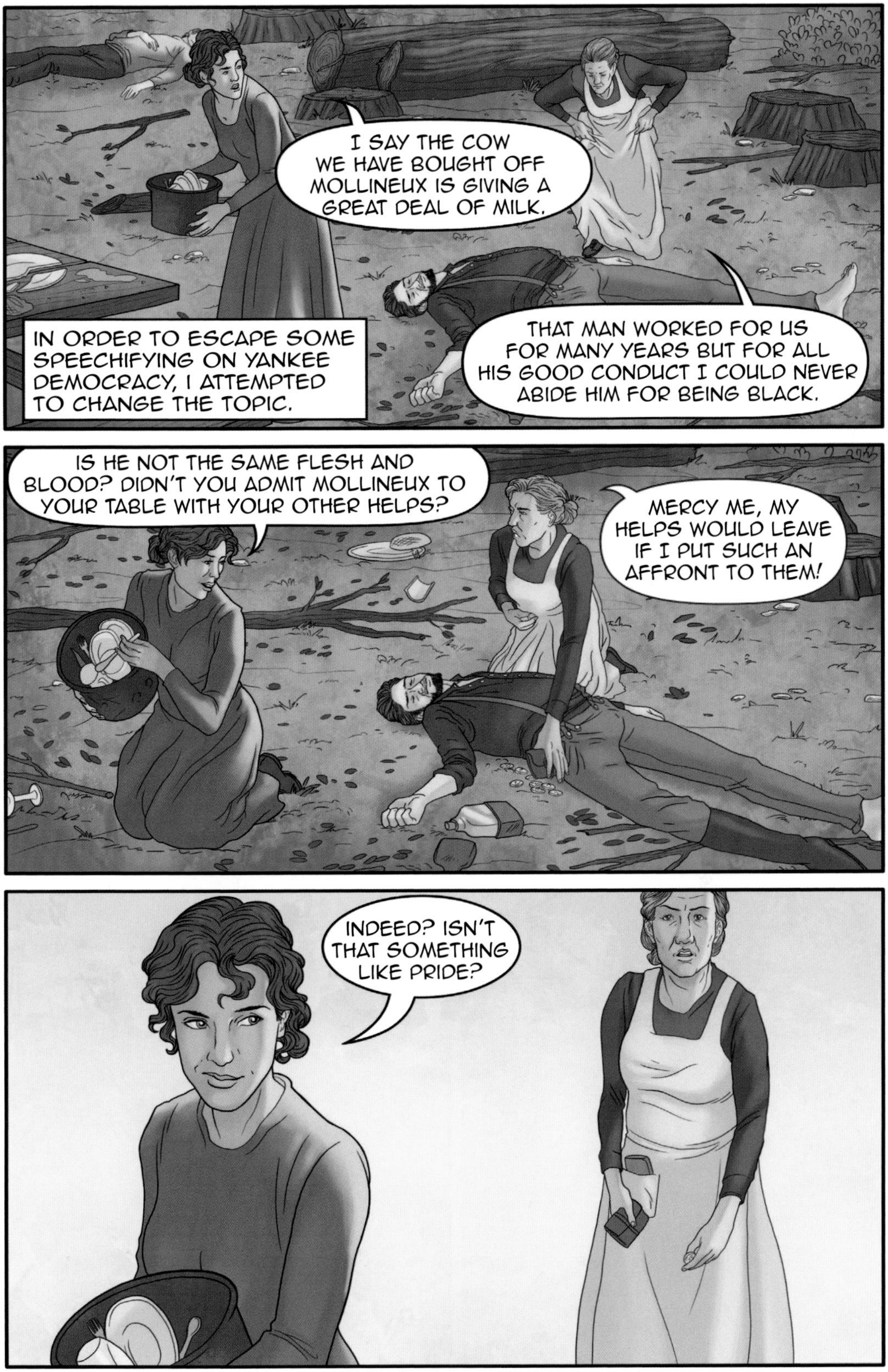
I SAY THE COW WE HAVE BOUGHT OFF MOLLINEUX IS GIVING A GREAT DEAL OF MILK.
IN ORDER TO ESCAPE SOME SPEECHIFYING ON YANKEE DEMOCRACY, I ATTEMPTED TO CHANGE THE TOPIC.
THAT MAN WORKED FOR US FOR MANY YEARS BUT FOR ALL HIS GOOD CONDUCT I COULD NEVER ABIDE HIM FOR BEING BLACK.
IS HE NOT THE SAME FLESH AND BLOOD? DIDN'T YOU ADMIT MOLLINEUX TO YOUR TABLE WITH YOUR OTHER HELPS?
MERCY ME, MY HELPS WOULD LEAVE IF I PUT SUCH AN AFFRONT TO THEM!
INDEED? ISN'T THAT SOMETHING LIKE PRIDE?

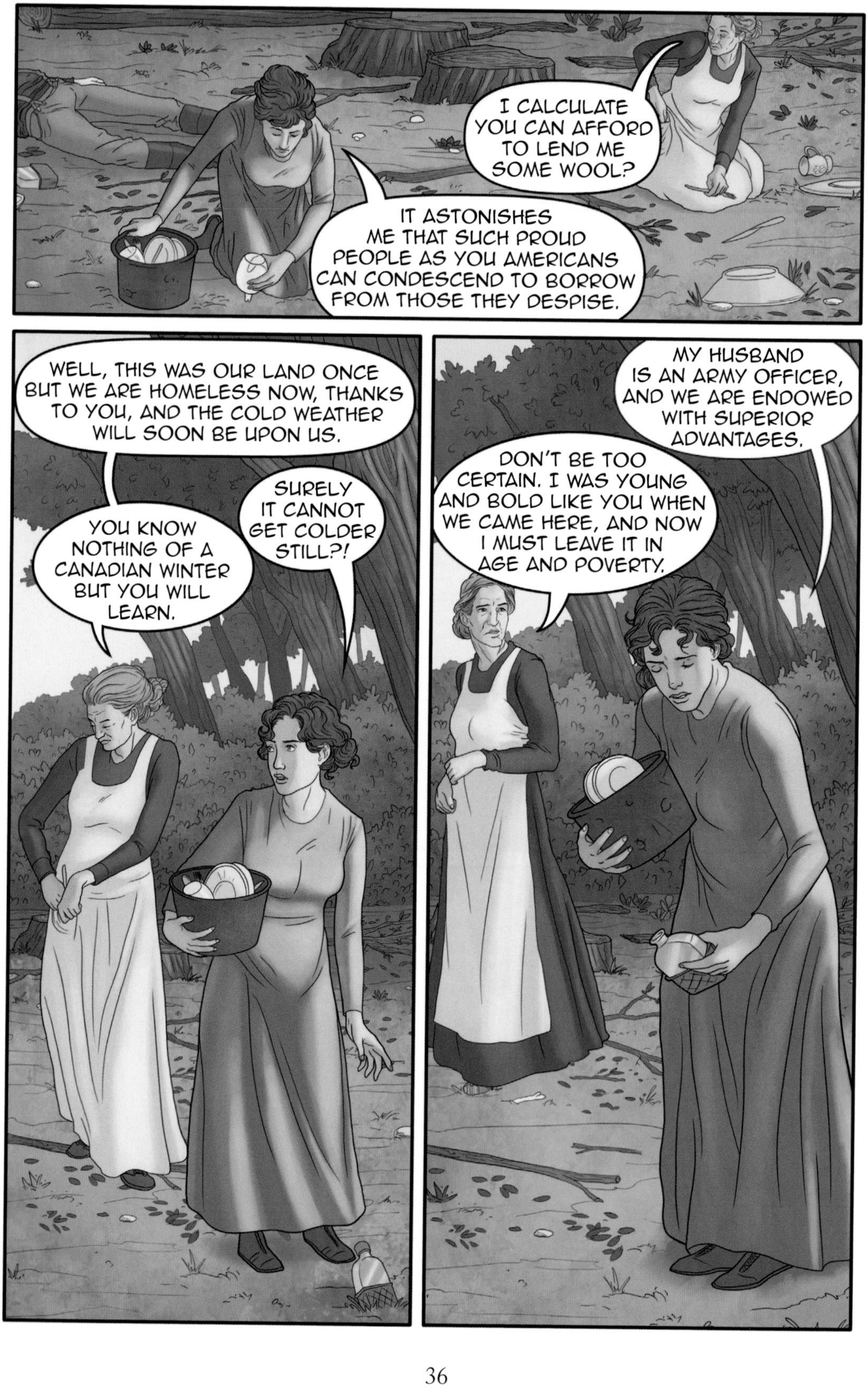
I CALCULATE YOU CAN AFFORD TO LEND ME SOME WOOL?
IT ASTONISHES ME THAT SUCH PROUD PEOPLE AS YOU AMERICANS CAN CONDESCEND TO BORROW FROM THOSE THEY DESPISE.
WELL, THIS WAS OUR LAND ONCE BUT WE ARE HOMELESS NOW, THANKS TO YOU, AND THE COLD WEATHER WILL SOON BE UPON US.
SURELY IT CANNOT GET COLDER STILL?!
YOU KNOW NOTHING OF A CANADIAN WINTER BUT YOU WILL LEARN.
MY HUSBAND IS AN ARMY OFFICER, AND WE ARE ENDOWED WITH SUPERIOR ADVANTAGES.
DON'T BE TOO CERTAIN. I WAS YOUNG AND BOLD LIKE YOU WHEN WE CAME HERE, AND NOW I MUST LEAVE IT IN AGE AND POVERTY.

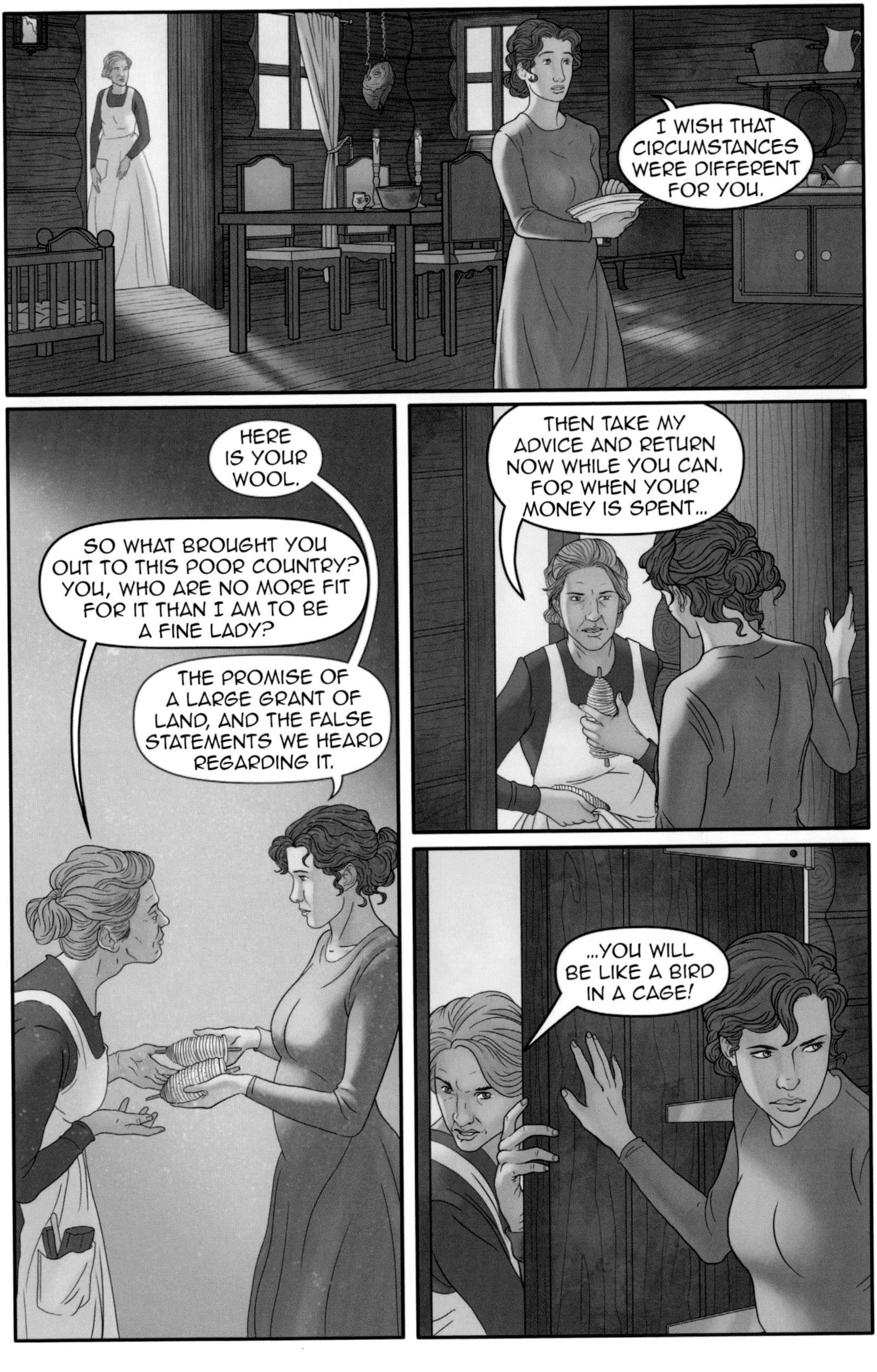
I WISH THAT CIRCUMSTANCES WERE DIFFERENT FOR YOU.
HERE IS YOUR WOOL.
SO WHAT BROUGHT YOU OUT TO THIS POOR COUNTRY? YOU, WHO ARE NO MORE FIT FOR IT THAN I AM TO BE A FINE LADY?
THE PROMISE OF A LARGE GRANT OF LAND, AND THE FALSE STATEMENTS WE HEARD REGARDING IT.
THEN TAKE MY ADVICE AND RETURN NOW WHILE YOU CAN. FOR WHEN YOUR MONEY IS SPENT...
...YOU WILL BE LIKE A BIRD IN A CAGE!

CHAPTER 5

SISTERS IN THE WILDERNESS

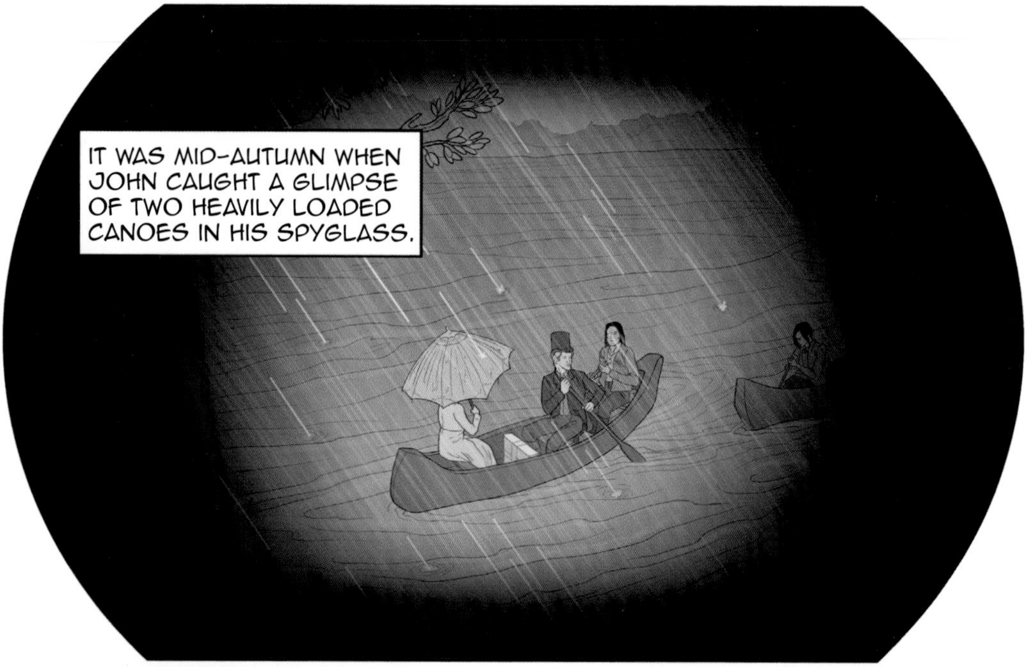
IT WAS MID-AUTUMN WHEN JOHN CAUGHT A GLIMPSE OF TWO HEAVILY LOADED CANOES IN HIS SPYGLASS.

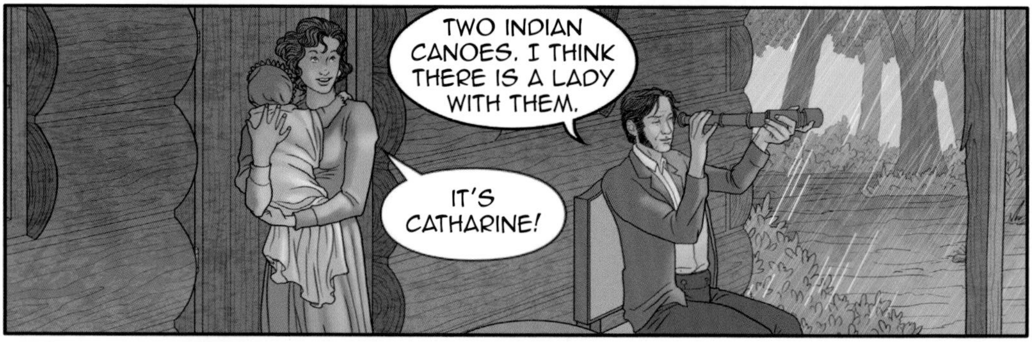
TWO INDIAN CANOES. I THINK THERE IS A LADY WITH THEM.
IT'S CATHARINE!

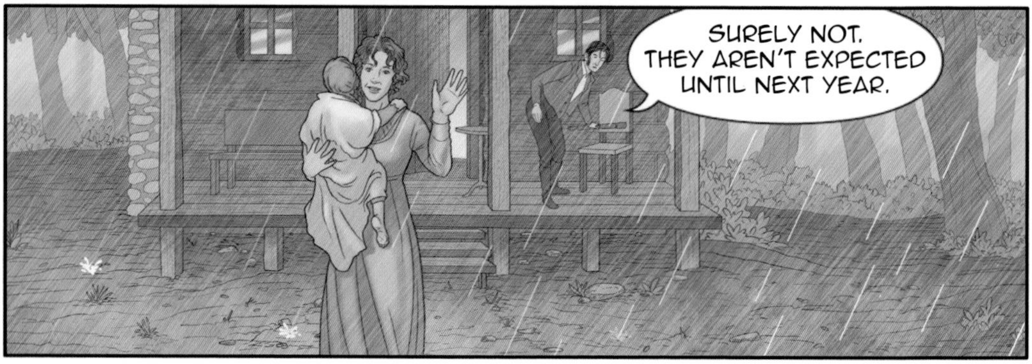
SURELY NOT. THEY AREN'T EXPECTED UNTIL NEXT YEAR.

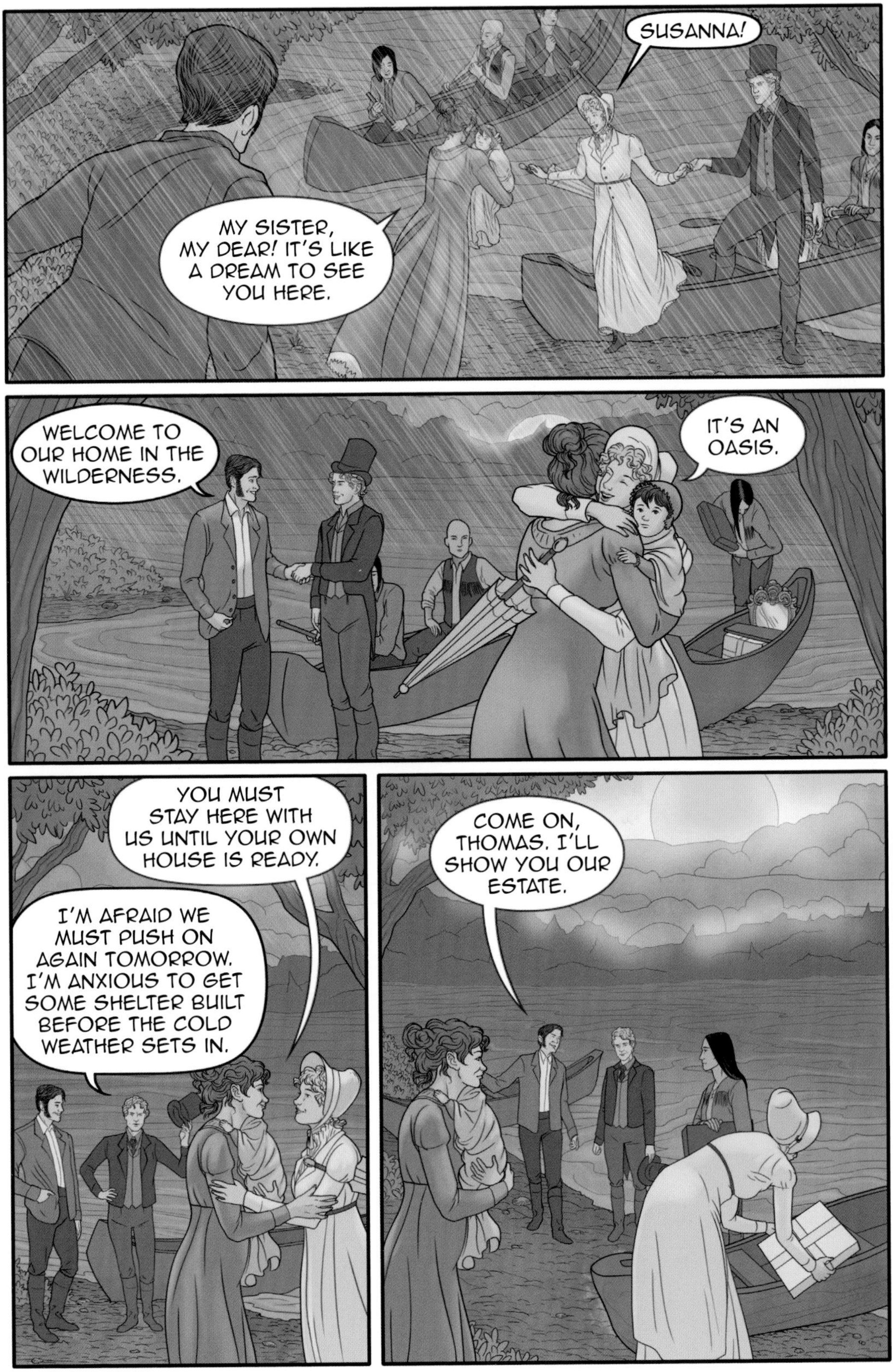
SUSANNA!
MY SISTER, MY DEAR! IT'S LIKE A DREAM TO SEE YOU HERE.
WELCOME TO OUR HOME IN THE WILDERNESS.
IT'S AN OASIS.
YOU MUST STAY HERE WITH US UNTIL YOUR OWN HOUSE IS READY.
I'M AFRAID WE MUST PUSH ON AGAIN TOMORROW. I'M ANXIOUS TO GET SOME SHELTER BUILT BEFORE THE COLD WEATHER SETS IN.
COME ON, THOMAS. I'LL SHOW YOU OUR ESTATE.

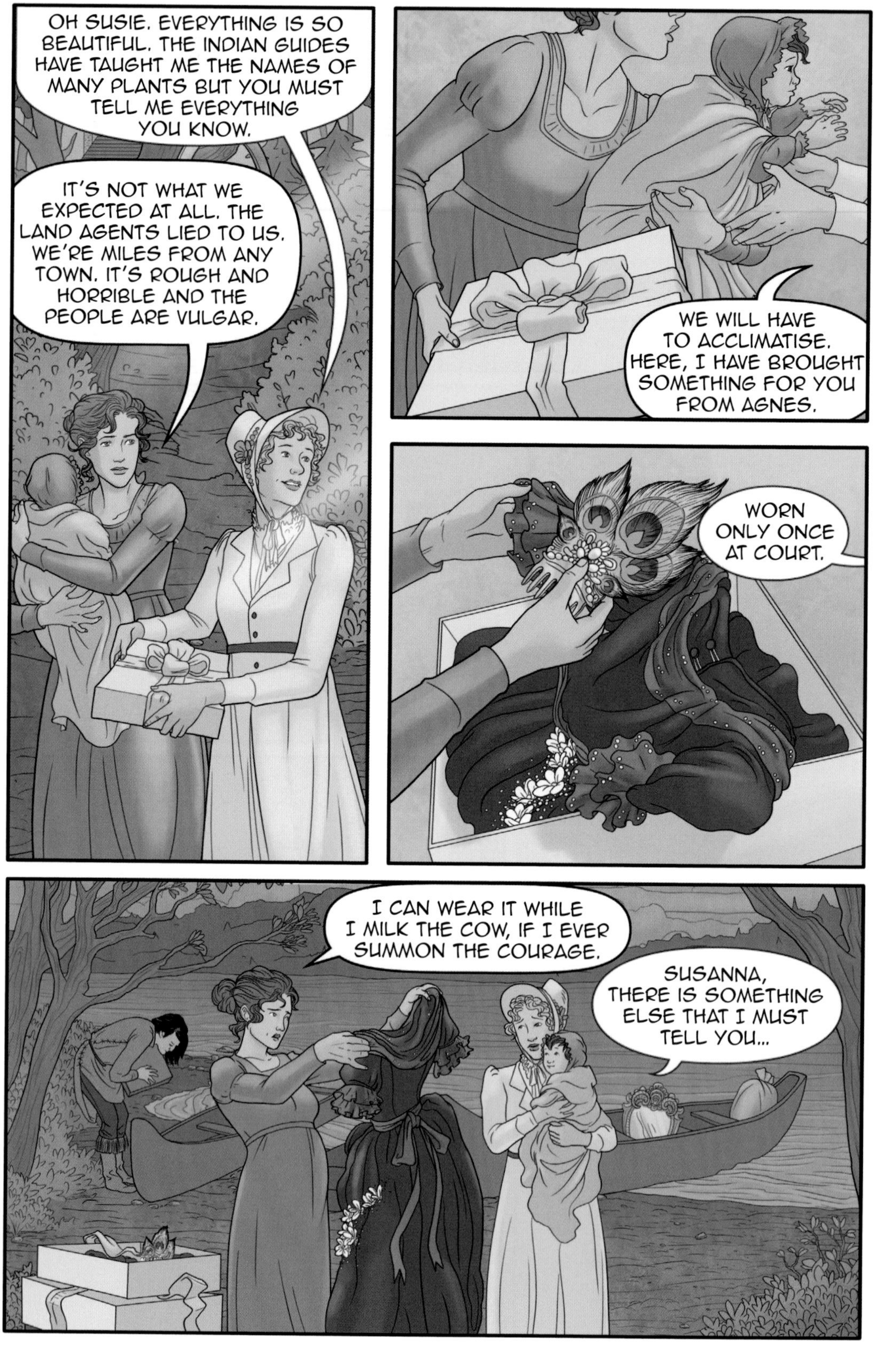
OH SUSIE. EVERYTHING IS SO BEAUTIFUL. THE INDIAN GUIDES HAVE TAUGHT ME THE NAMES OF MANY PLANTS BUT YOU MUST TELL ME EVERYTHING YOU KNOW.
IT'S NOT WHAT WE EXPECTED AT ALL. THE LAND AGENTS LIED TO US. WE'RE MILES FROM ANY TOWN. IT'S ROUGH AND HORRIBLE AND THE PEOPLE ARE VULGAR.
WE WILL HAVE TO ACCLIMATISE. HERE, I HAVE BROUGHT SOMETHING FOR YOU FROM AGNES.
WORN ONLY ONCE AT COURT.
I CAN WEAR IT WHILE I MILK THE COW, IF I EVER SUMMON THE COURAGE.
SUSANNA, THERE IS SOMETHING ELSE THAT I MUST TELL YOU...

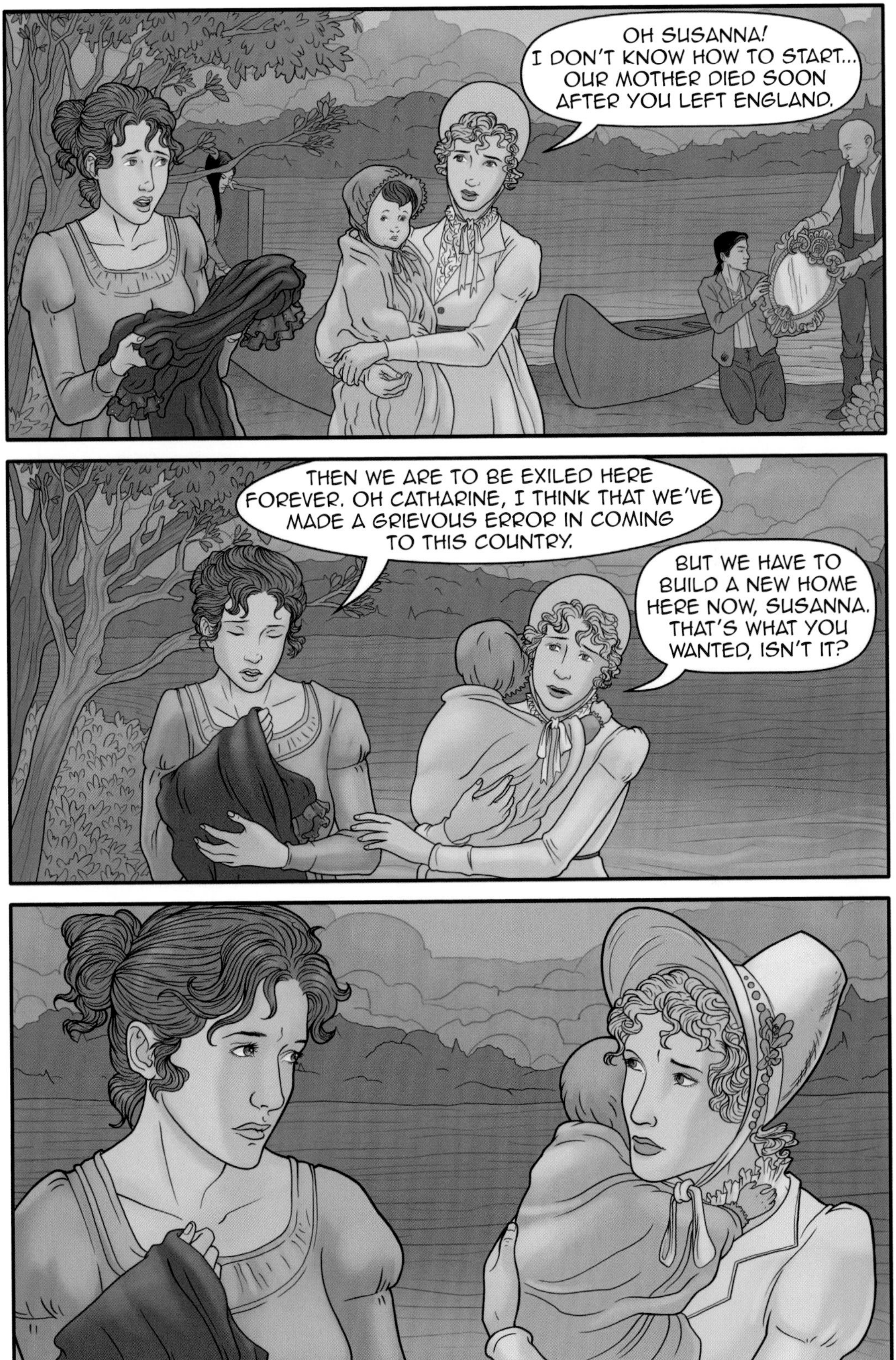
OH SUSANNA! I DON'T KNOW HOW TO START... OUR MOTHER DIED SOON AFTER YOU LEFT ENGLAND.
THEN WE ARE TO BE EXILED HERE FOREVER. OH CATHARINE, I THINK THAT WE'VE MADE A GRIEVOUS ERROR IN COMING TO THIS COUNTRY.
BUT WE HAVE TO BUILD A NEW HOME HERE NOW, SUSANNA. THAT'S WHAT YOU WANTED, ISN'T IT?

CHAPTER 6

THE SHIVAREE

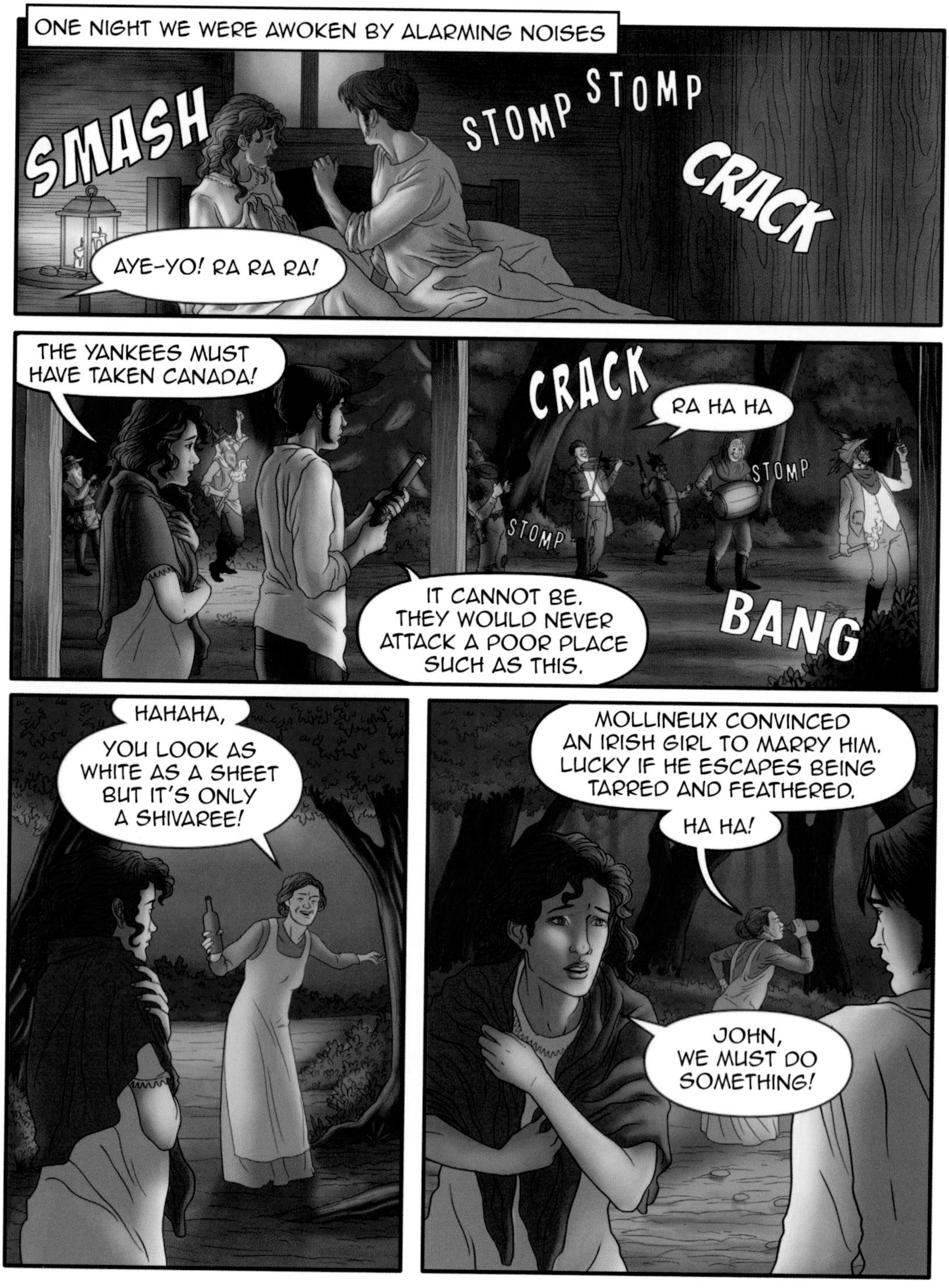
ONE NIGHT WE WERE AWOKEN BY ALARMING NOISES
SMASH
STOMP STOMP
CRACK
AYE-YO! RA RA RA!
THE YANKEES MUST HAVE TAKEN CANADA!
CRACK
RA HA HA
STOMP
STOMP
IT CANNOT BE. THEY WOULD NEVER ATTACK A POOR PLACE SUCH AS THIS.
BANG
HAHAHA,
YOU LOOK AS WHITE AS A SHEET BUT IT'S ONLY A SHIVAREE!
MOLLINEUX CONVINCED AN IRISH GIRL TO MARRY HIM. LUCKY IF HE ESCAPES BEING TARRED AND FEATHERED.
HA HA!
JOHN, WE MUST DO SOMETHING!

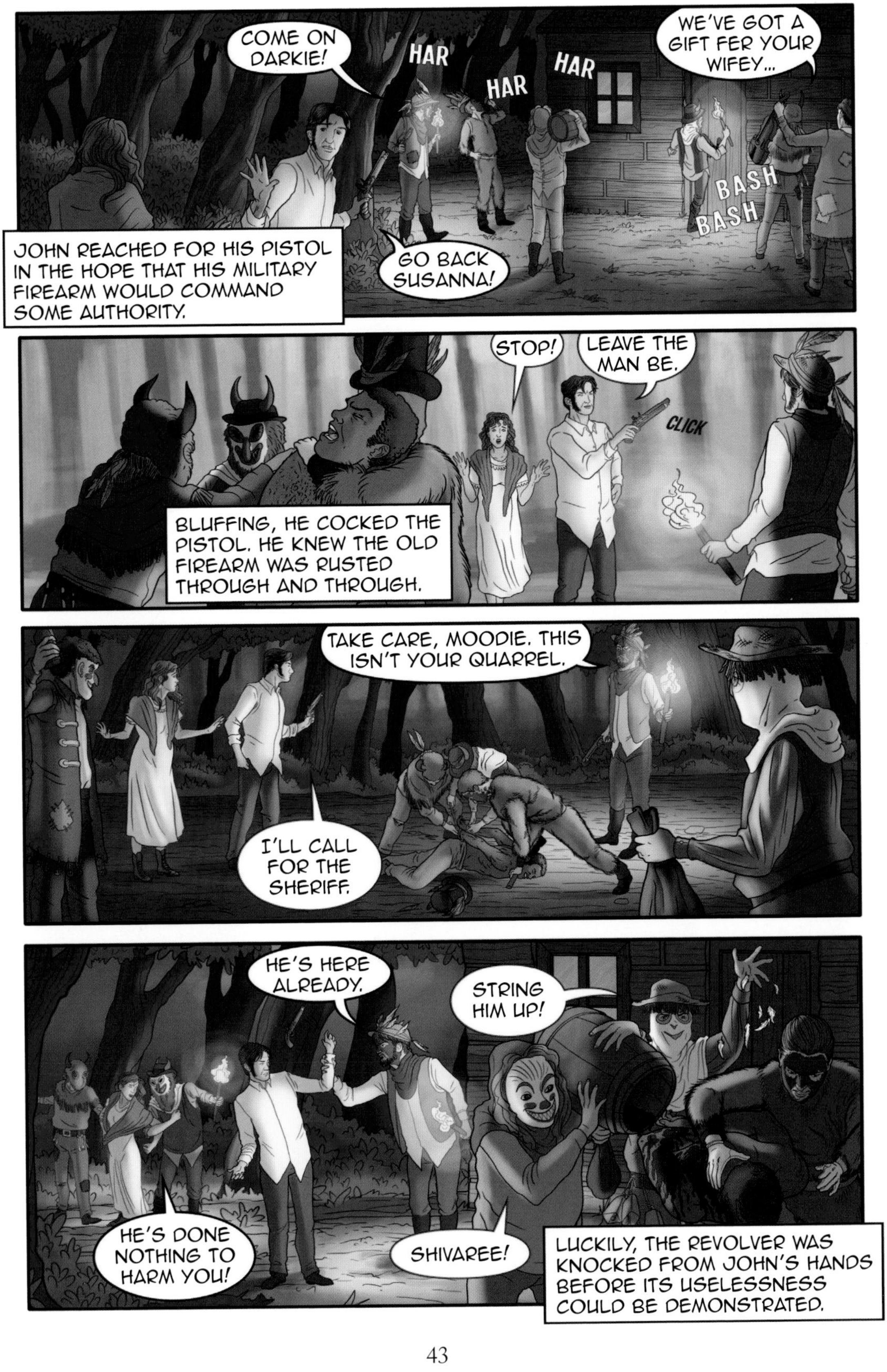

COME ON DARKIE!
HAR
HAR
HAR
WE'VE GOT A GIFT FER YOUR WIFEY...
BASH
BASH
JOHN REACHED FOR HIS PISTOL IN THE HOPE THAT HIS MILITARY FIREARM WOULD COMMAND SOME AUTHORITY.
GO BACK SUSANNA!
STOP!
LEAVE THE MAN BE.
CLICK
BLUFFING, HE COCKED THE PISTOL. HE KNEW THE OLD FIREARM WAS RUSTED THROUGH AND THROUGH.
TAKE CARE, MOODIE. THIS ISN'T YOUR QUARREL.
I'LL CALL FOR THE SHERIFF.
HE'S HERE ALREADY.
STRING HIM UP!
HE'S DONE NOTHING TO HARM YOU!
SHIVAREE!
LUCKILY, THE REVOLVER WAS KNOCKED FROM JOHN'S HANDS BEFORE ITS USELESSNESS COULD BE DEMONSTRATED.

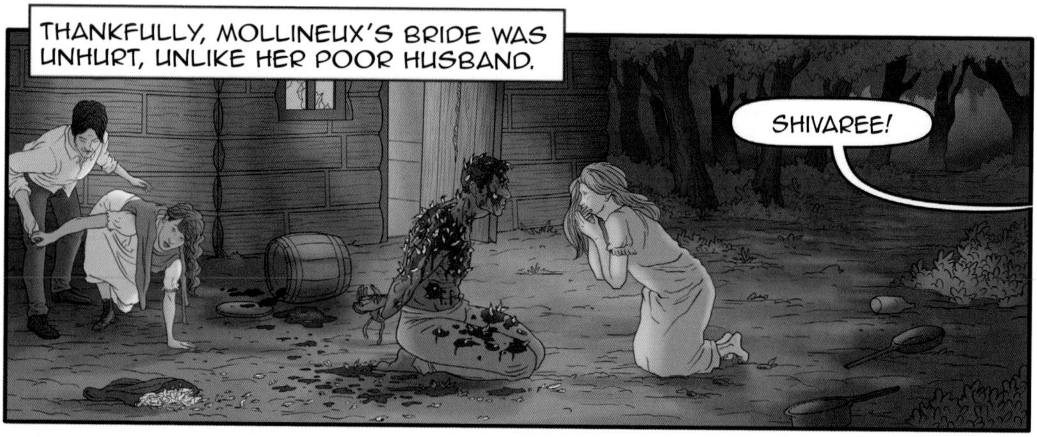
THANKFULLY, MOLLINEUX'S BRIDE WAS UNHURT, UNLIKE HER POOR HUSBAND.
SHIVAREE!

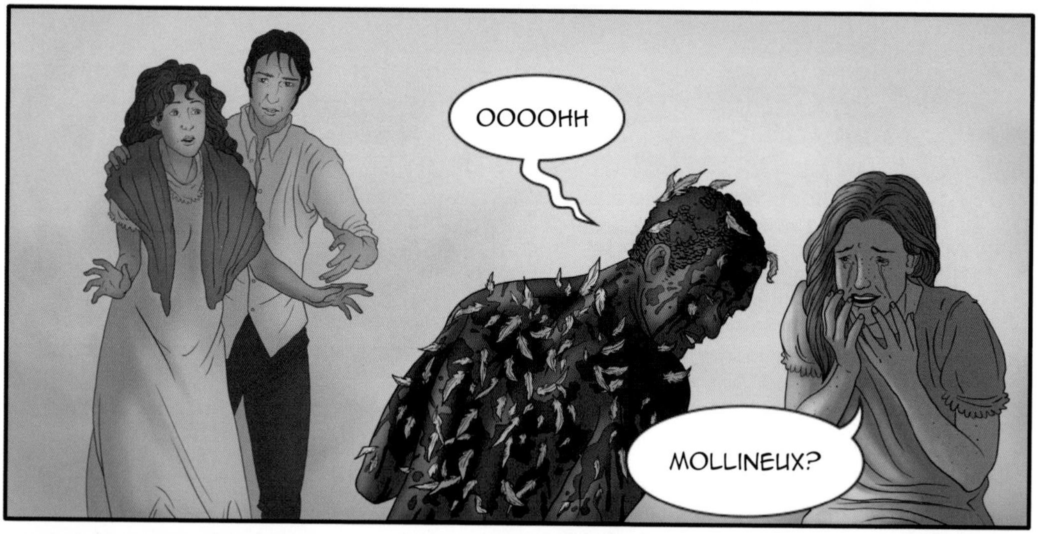
OOOOHH
MOLLINEUX?

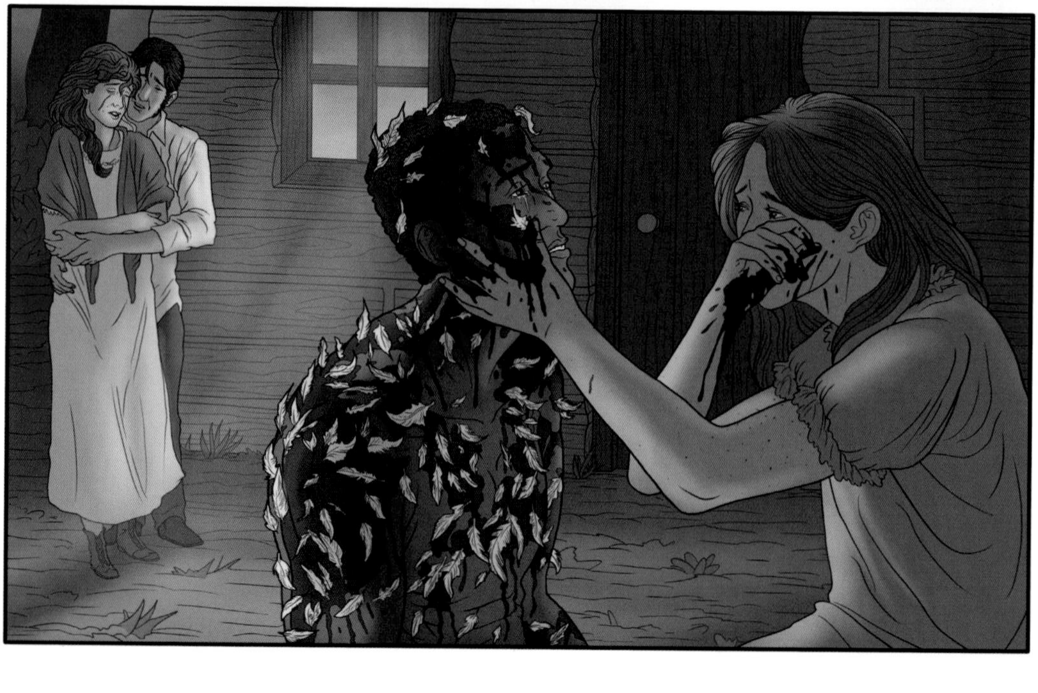

CHAPTER 7

JOHN MONAGHAN

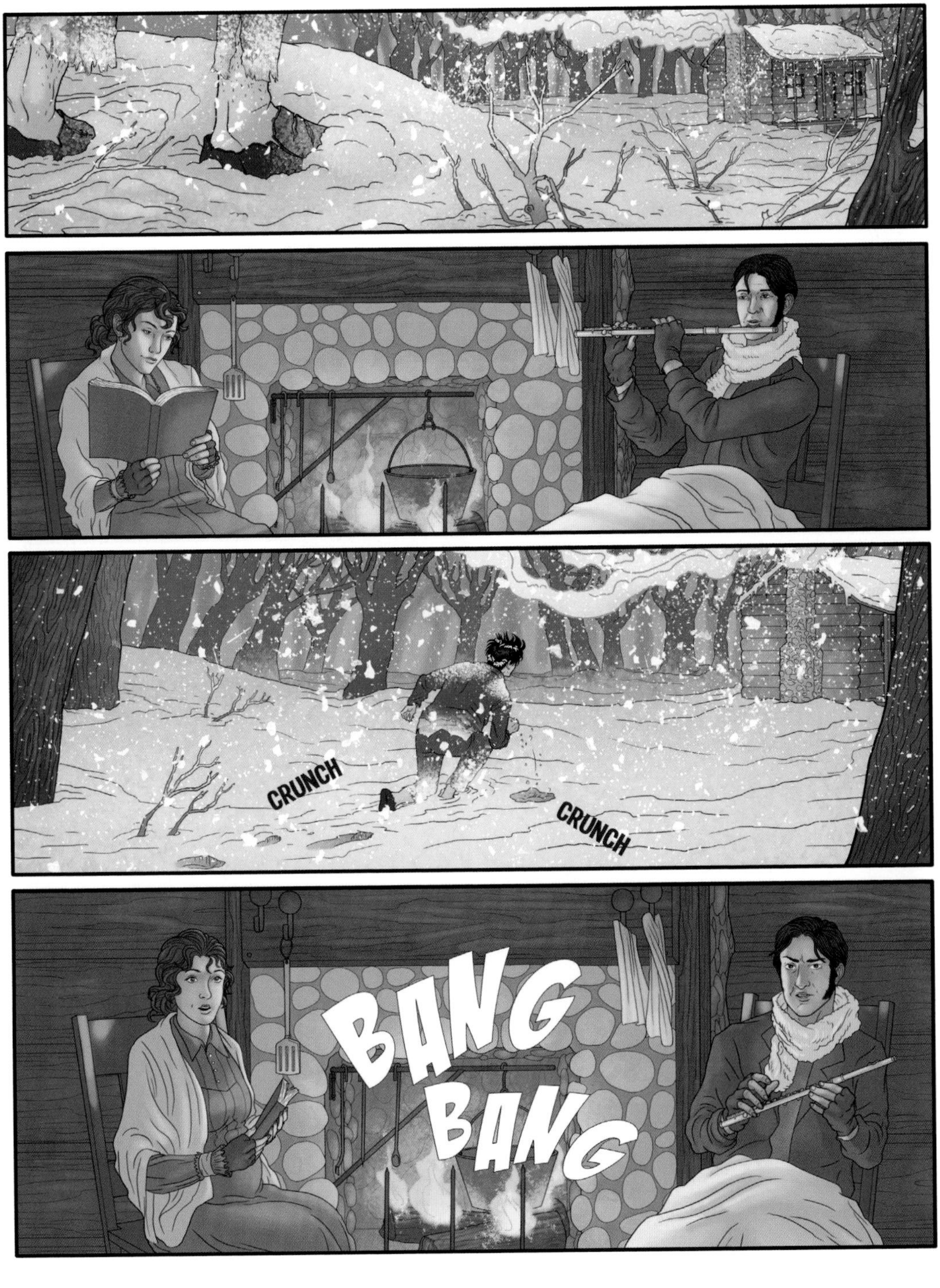
CRUNCH
CRUNCH
BANG
BANG
BANG

SIR, MY NAME IS JOHN MONAGHAN AND IF YOU WANT A LAD I WILL WORK FOR MY KEEP.

I RECOGNIZE HIM. HE WAS AT OUR LOGGING BEE.

I RAN AWAY FROM MY MASTER.

YOU'RE HURT!

ISOBEL, FETCH THE SALVE.

ISOBEL!

MY NEW SCOTTISH SERVANT REFUSED TO OFFER THE LEAST ASSISTANCE.

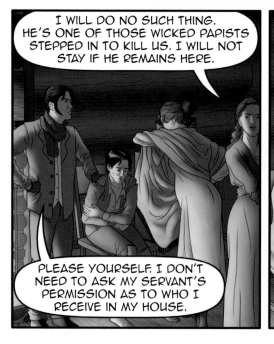

I WILL DO NO SUCH THING. HE'S ONE OF THOSE WICKED PAPISTS STEPPED IN TO KILL US. I WILL NOT STAY IF HE REMAINS HERE.

PLEASE YOURSELF. I DON'T NEED TO ASK MY SERVANT'S PERMISSION AS TO WHO I RECEIVE IN MY HOUSE.

ISOBEL'S IGNORANT FEAR OF ROMAN CATHOLICS WAS SADLY COMMONPLACE, AS ENMITIES BETWEEN PARTIES AND RELIGIONS RAN HIGH IN THOSE DAYS.

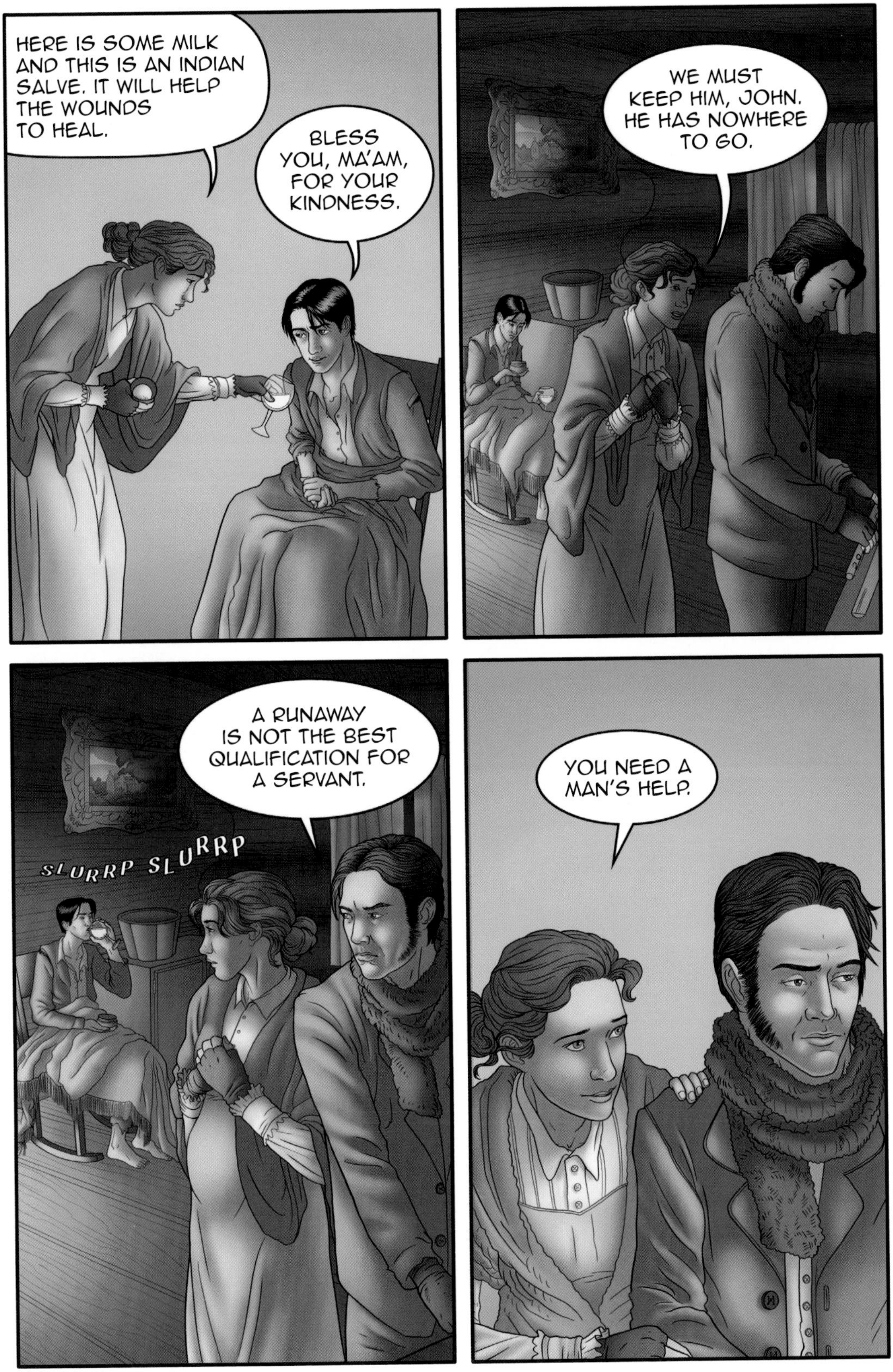
HERE IS SOME MILK AND THIS IS AN INDIAN SALVE. IT WILL HELP THE WOUNDS TO HEAL.
BLESS YOU, MA'AM, FOR YOUR KINDNESS.
WE MUST KEEP HIM, JOHN. HE HAS NOWHERE TO GO.
A RUNAWAY IS NOT THE BEST QUALIFICATION FOR A SERVANT.
SLURRP SLURRP
YOU NEED A MAN'S HELP.

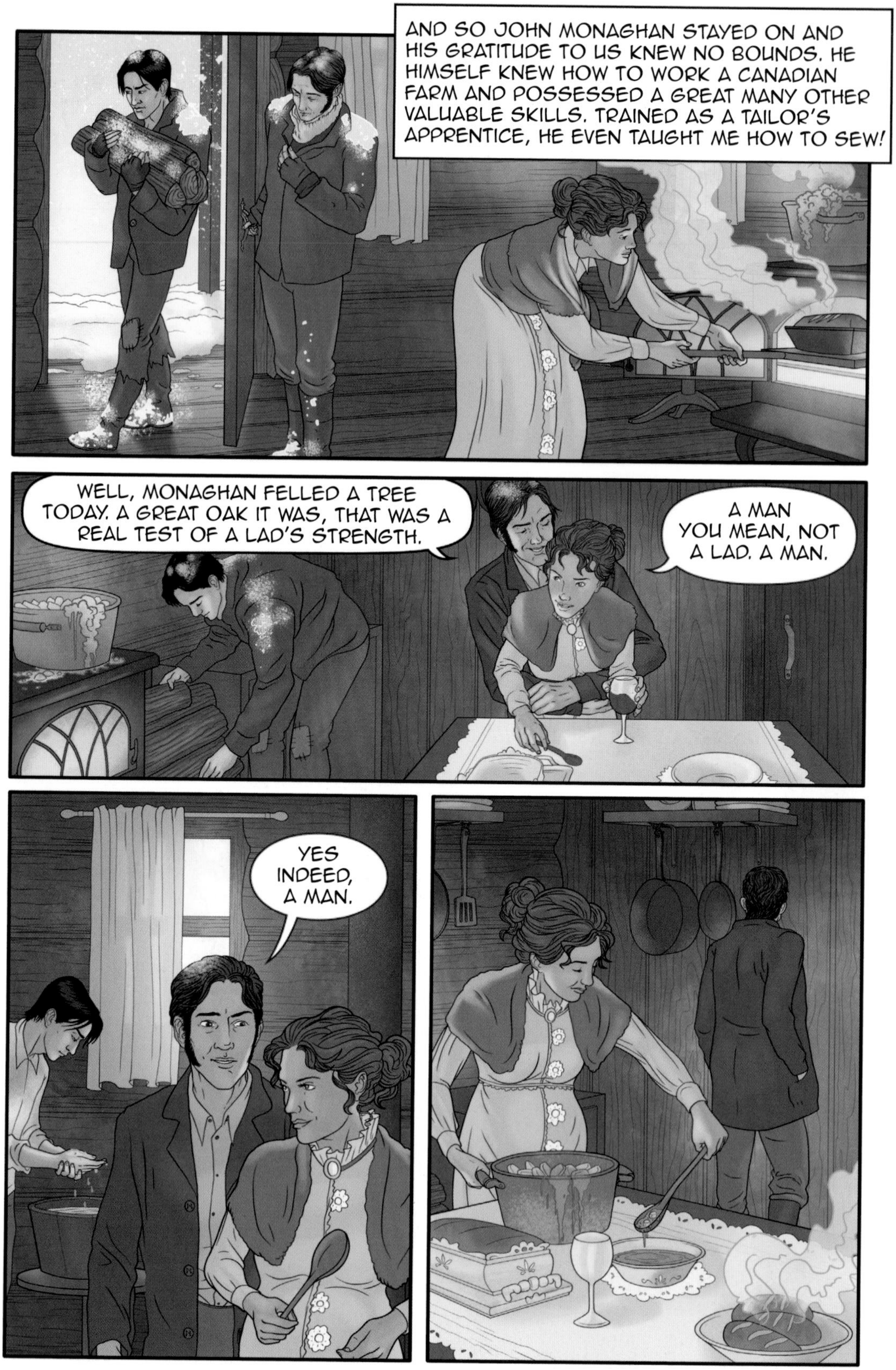
AND SO JOHN MONAGHAN STAYED ON AND HIS GRATITUDE TO US KNEW NO BOUNDS. HE HIMSELF KNEW HOW TO WORK A CANADIAN FARM AND POSSESSED A GREAT MANY OTHER VALUABLE SKILLS. TRAINED AS A TAILOR'S APPRENTICE, HE EVEN TAUGHT ME HOW TO SEW!
WELL, MONAGHAN FELLED A TREE TODAY. A GREAT OAK IT WAS, THAT WAS A REAL TEST OF A LAD'S STRENGTH.
A MAN YOU MEAN, NOT A LAD. A MAN.
YES INDEED, A MAN.

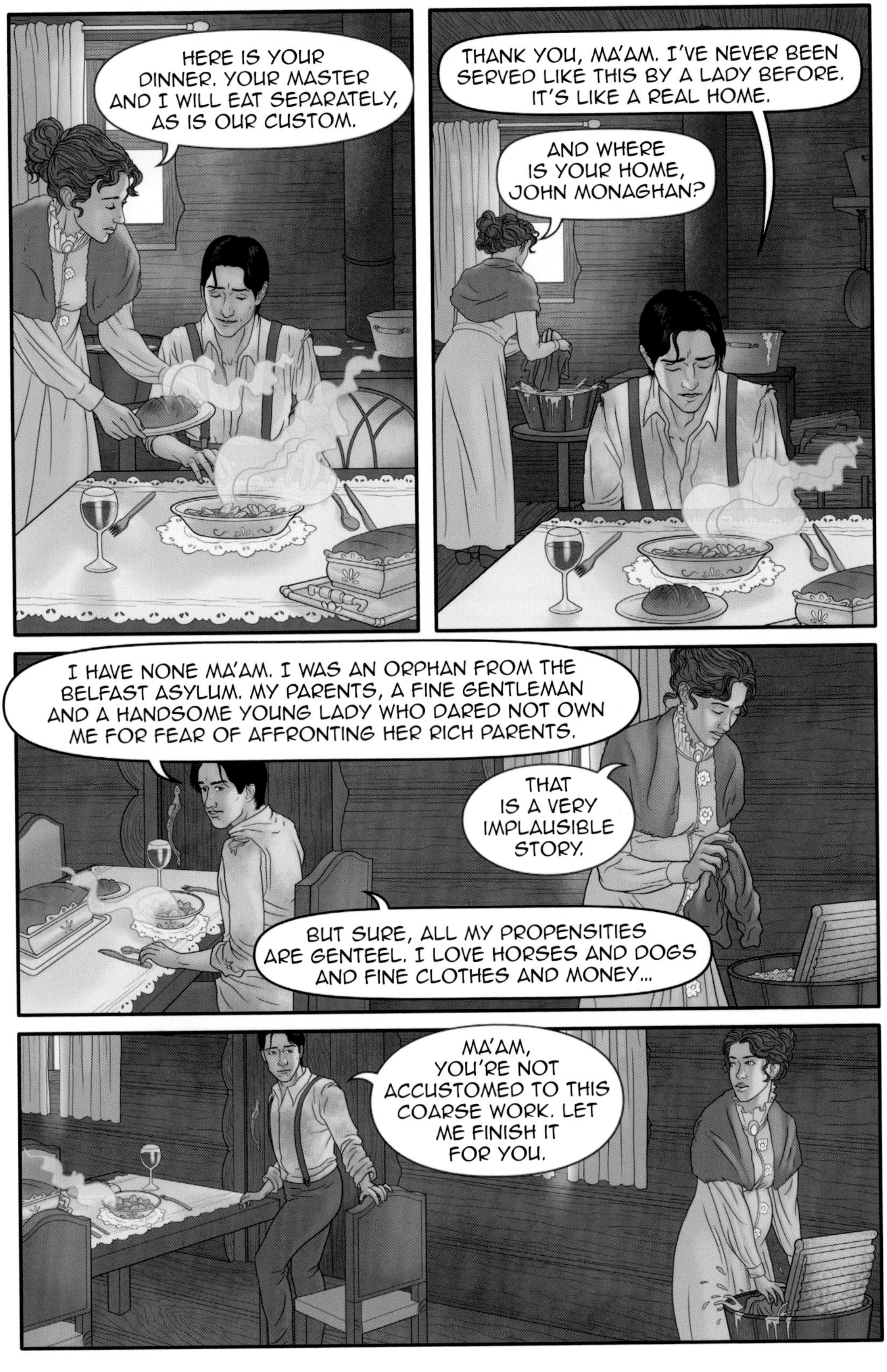
HERE IS YOUR DINNER. YOUR MASTER AND I WILL EAT SEPARATELY, AS IS OUR CUSTOM.
THANK YOU, MA'AM. I'VE NEVER BEEN SERVED LIKE THIS BY A LADY BEFORE. IT'S LIKE A REAL HOME.
AND WHERE IS YOUR HOME, JOHN MONAGHAN?
I HAVE NONE MA'AM. I WAS AN ORPHAN FROM THE BELFAST ASYLUM. MY PARENTS, A FINE GENTLEMAN AND A HANDSOME YOUNG LADY WHO DARED NOT OWN ME FOR FEAR OF AFFRONTING HER RICH PARENTS.
THAT IS A VERY IMPLAUSIBLE STORY.
BUT SURE, ALL MY PROPENSITIES ARE GENTEEL. I LOVE HORSES AND DOGS AND FINE CLOTHES AND MONEY...
MA'AM, YOU'RE NOT ACCUSTOMED TO THIS COARSE WORK. LET ME FINISH IT FOR YOU.

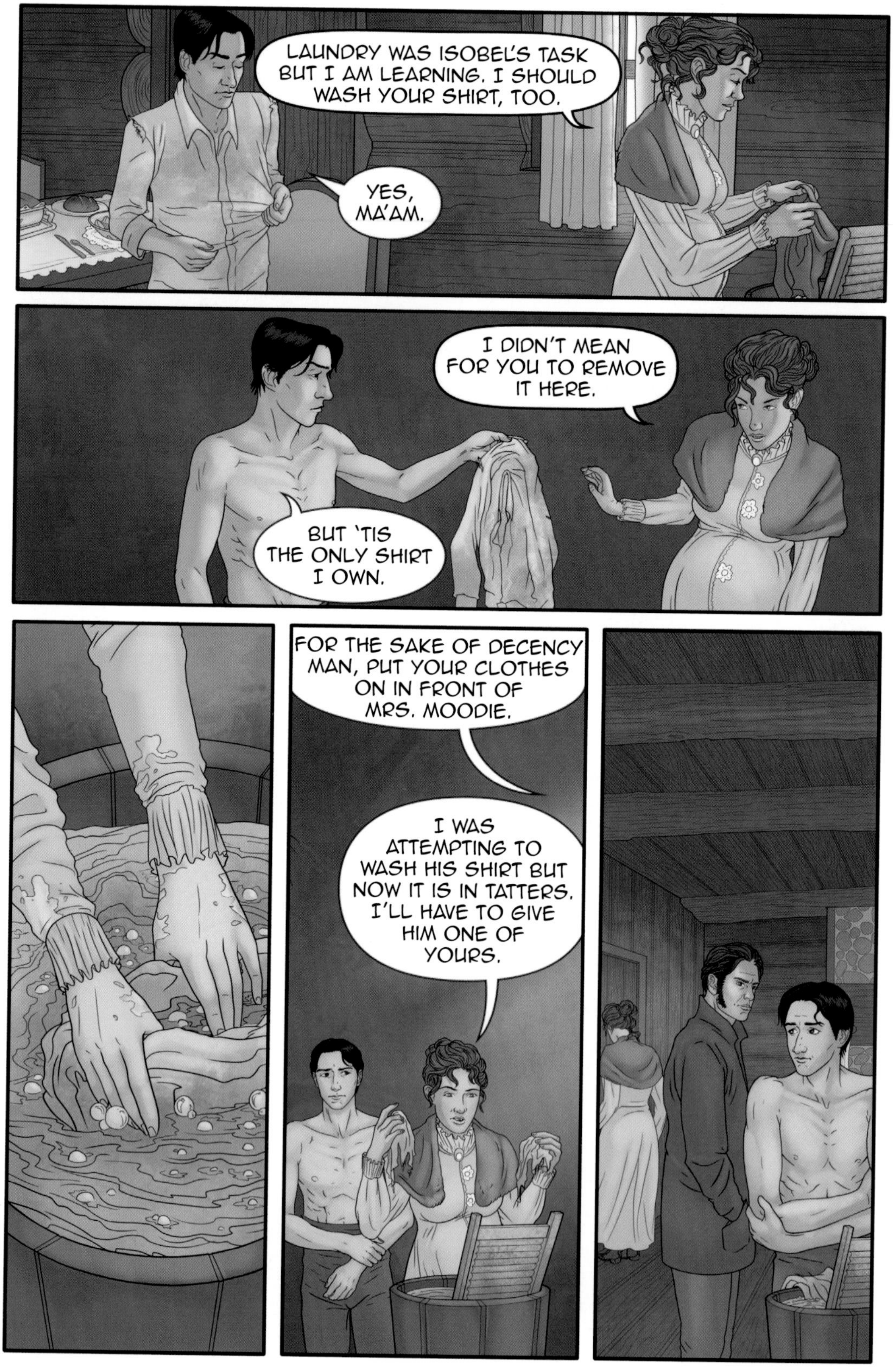
LAUNDRY WAS ISOBEL'S TASK BUT I AM LEARNING. I SHOULD WASH YOUR SHIRT, TOO.
YES, MA'AM.
I DIDN'T MEAN FOR YOU TO REMOVE IT HERE.
BUT 'TIS THE ONLY SHIRT I OWN.
FOR THE SAKE OF DECENCY MAN, PUT YOUR CLOTHES ON IN FRONT OF MRS. MOODIE.
I WAS ATTEMPTING TO WASH HIS SHIRT BUT NOW IT IS IN TATTERS. I'LL HAVE TO GIVE HIM ONE OF YOURS.

WHEN MY SECOND BABY ARRIVED MUCH SOONER THAN ANTICIPATED JOHN MONAGHAN WAS SENT WITH ALL HASTE TO FETCH THE MIDWIFE.

STEADY, SUSIE. THEY'RE HERE!

AAAAGGH

WHERE'S THE YANKEE WOMAN?

SHE IS SICK WITH FEVER. I SENT A LAD TO GO FOR MRS. TRAILL BUT–

AAAAAAA

I THINK WE'VE GOT TO HELP HER NOW.

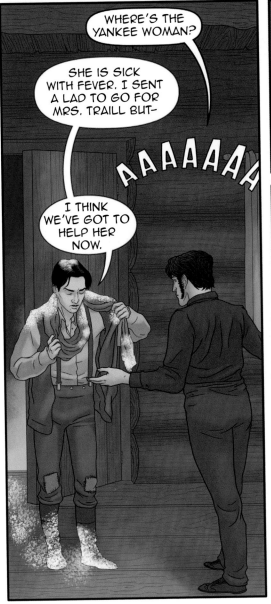

I SAW IT DONE ONCE. I CAN TELL YOU WHAT TO DO.

AAAAAAAAAA

TELL HER TO BREATHE.

BREATHE!

SUSIE, BREATHE!

PUT YOUR HANDS UNDERNEATH. DON'T PULL, JUST CATCH!

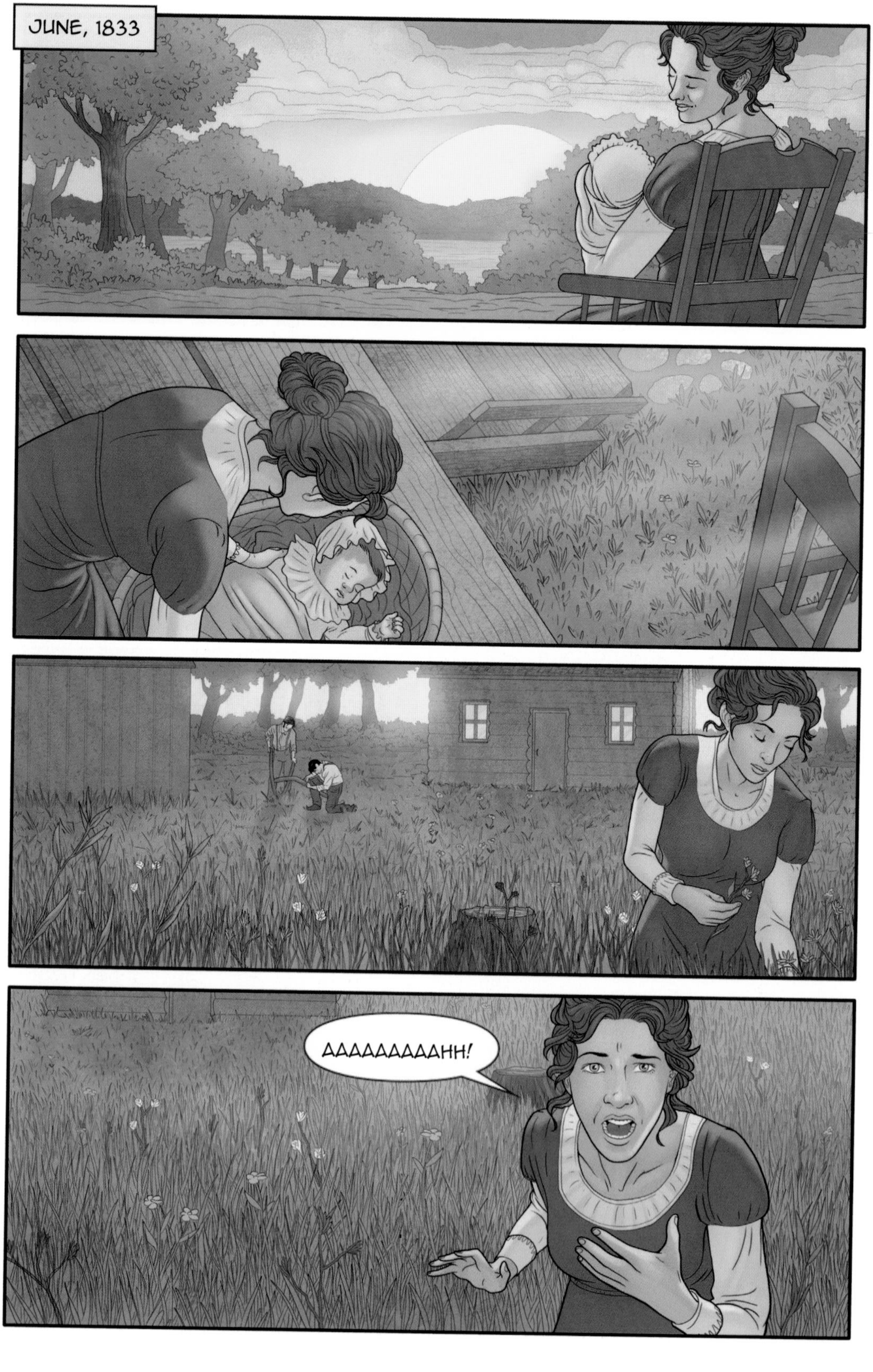
JUNE, 1833
AAAAAAAAAHH!

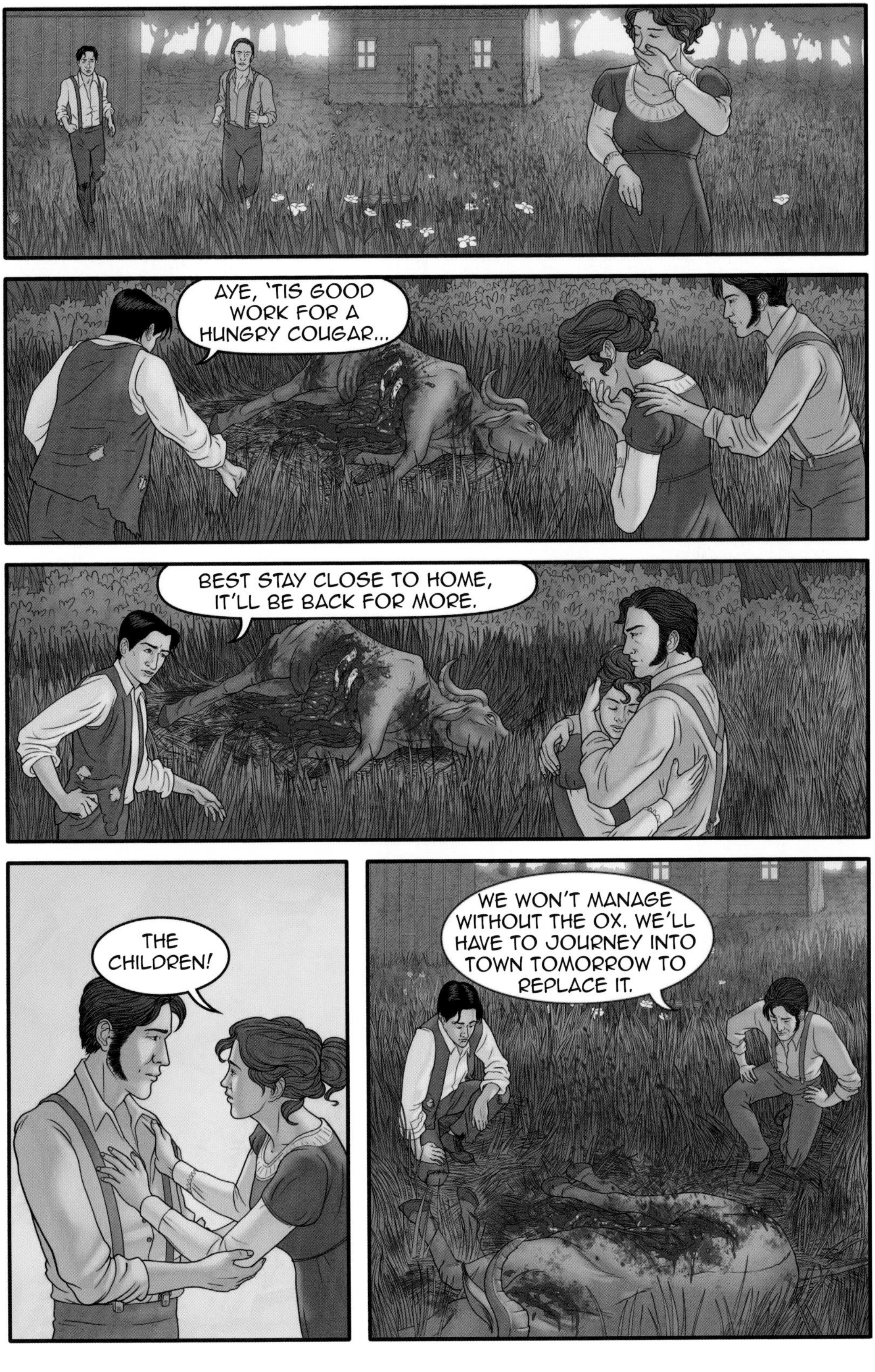
AYE, 'TIS GOOD WORK FOR A HUNGRY COUGAR...
BEST STAY CLOSE TO HOME, IT'LL BE BACK FOR MORE.
THE CHILDREN!
WE WON'T MANAGE WITHOUT THE OX. WE'LL HAVE TO JOURNEY INTO TOWN TOMORROW TO REPLACE IT.

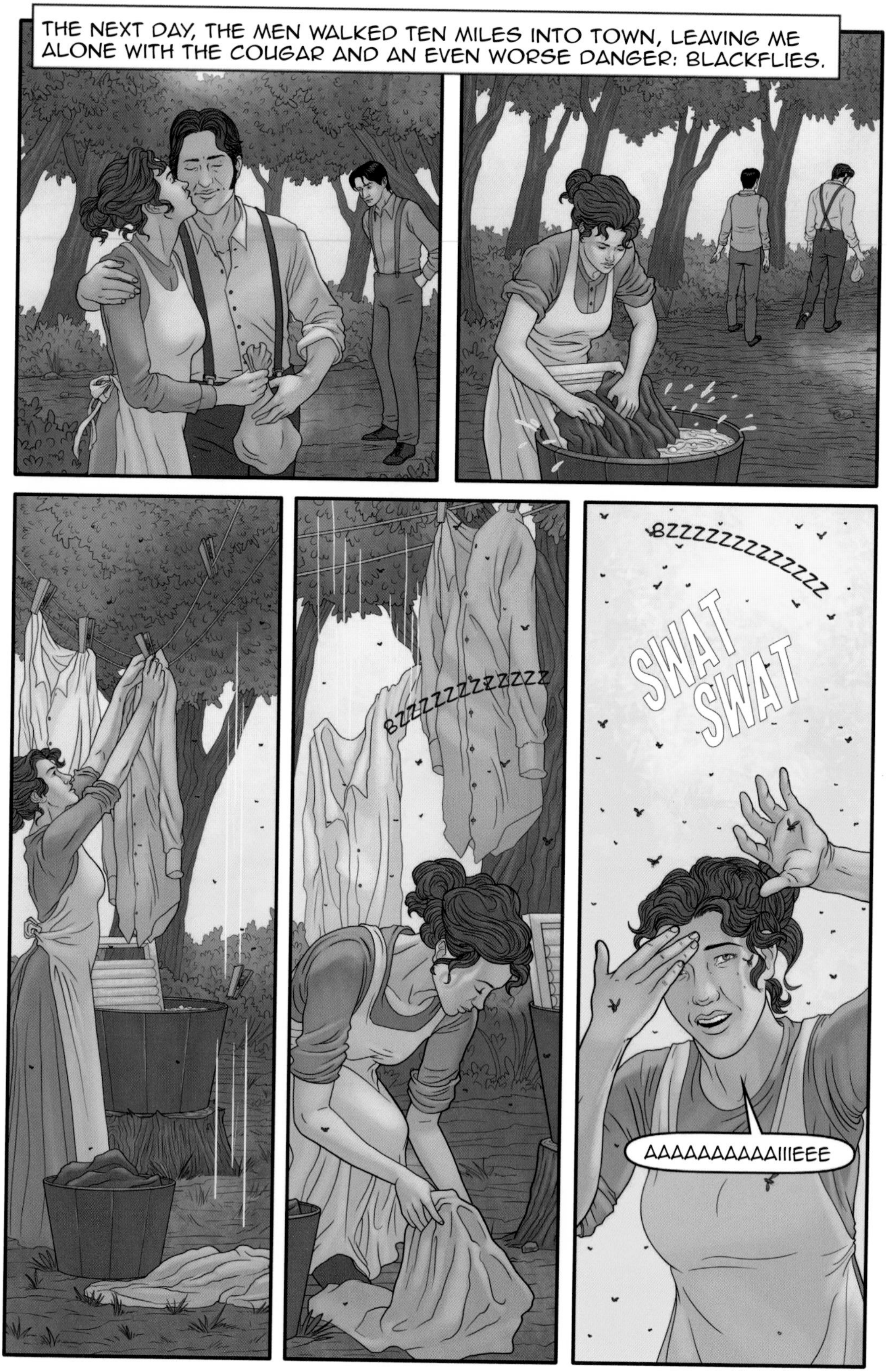
THE NEXT DAY, THE MEN WALKED TEN MILES INTO TOWN, LEAVING ME ALONE WITH THE COUGAR AND AN EVEN WORSE DANGER: BLACKFLIES.
BZZZZZZZZZZZZ
BZZZZZZZZZZZZZ
SWAT
SWAT
AAAAAAAAAAIIIEEE

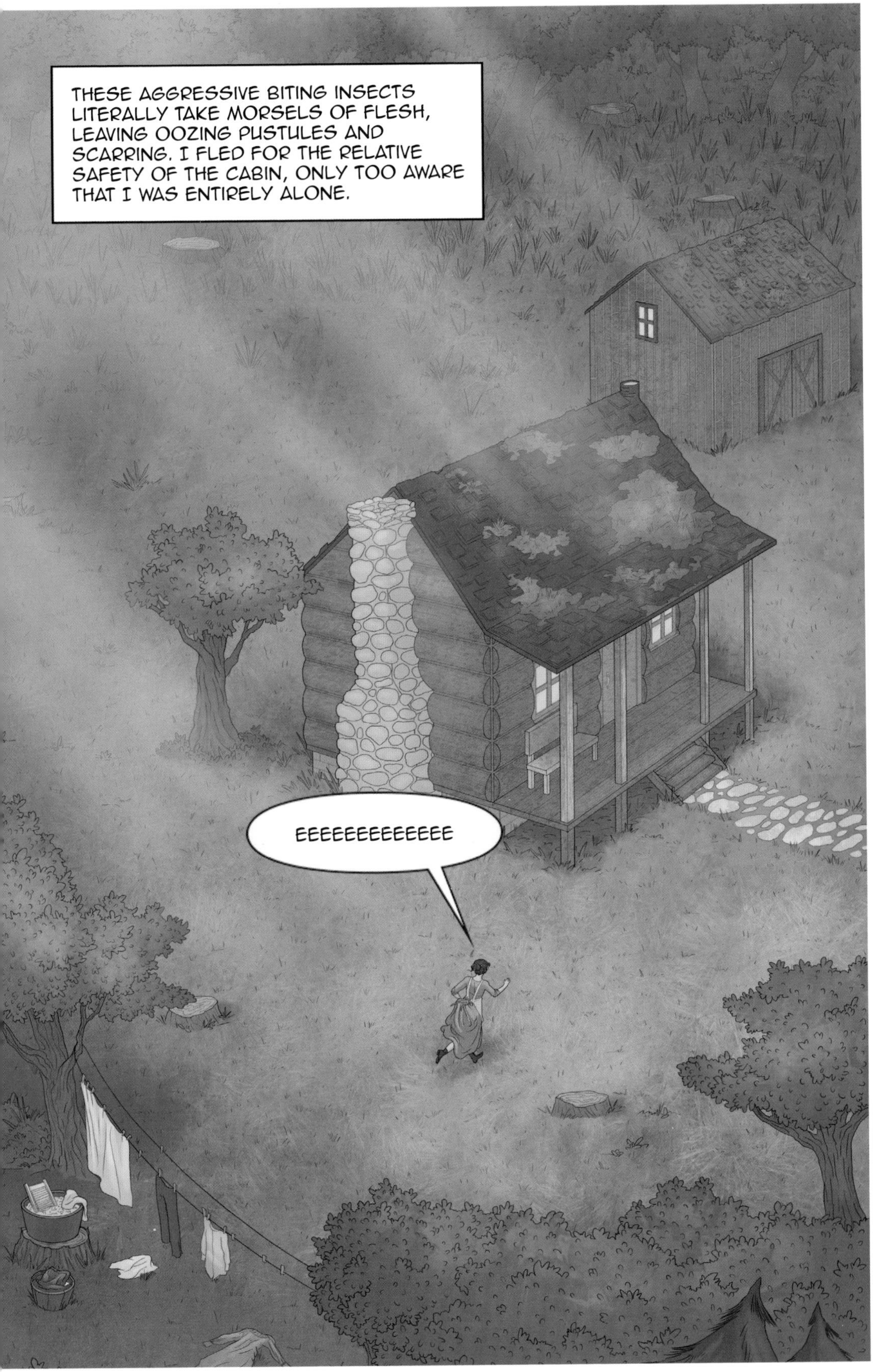
THESE AGGRESSIVE BITING INSECTS LITERALLY TAKE MORSELS OF FLESH, LEAVING OOZING PUSTULES AND SCARRING. I FLED FOR THE RELATIVE SAFETY OF THE CABIN, ONLY TOO AWARE THAT I WAS ENTIRELY ALONE.
EEEEEEEEEEEE

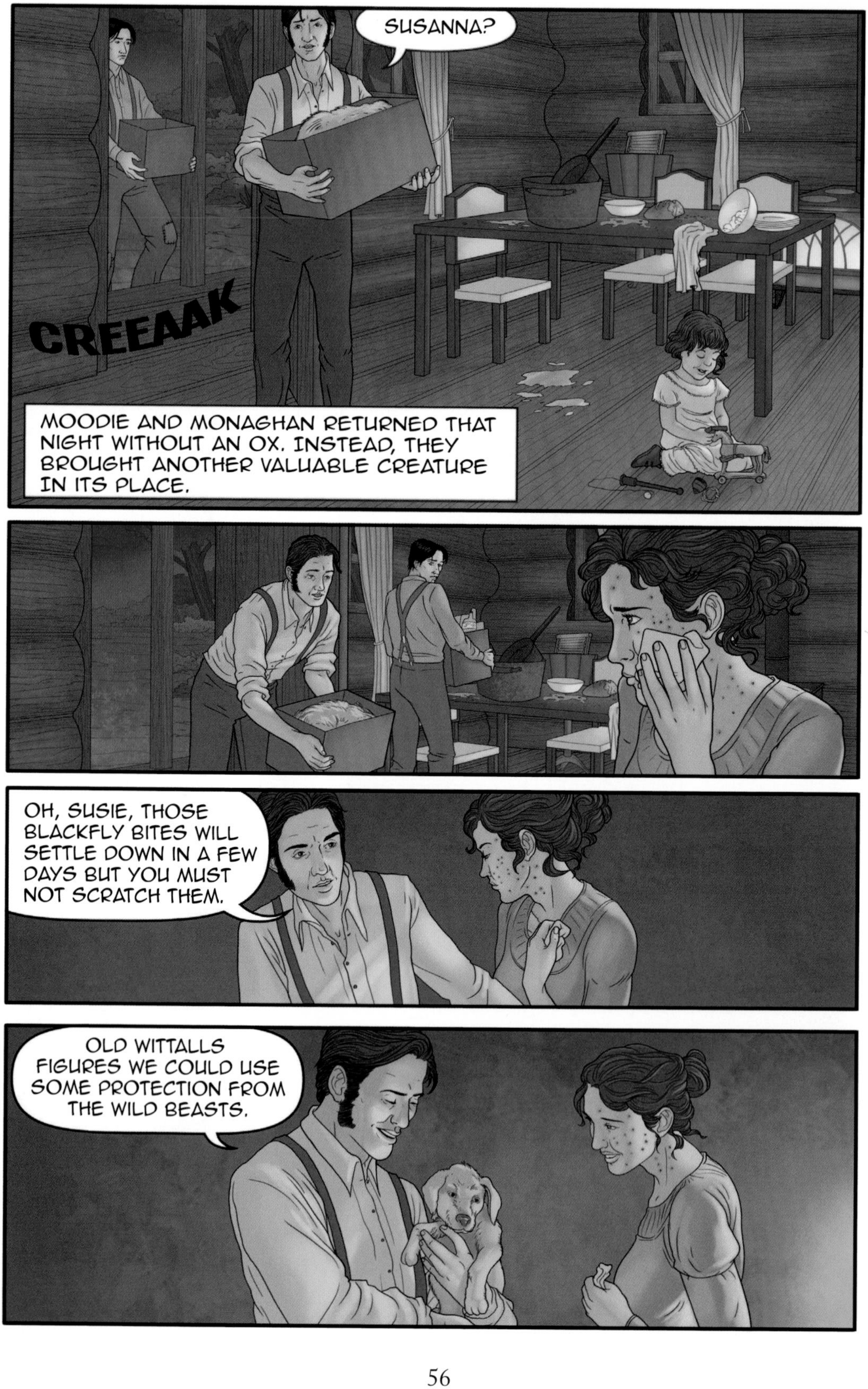
SUSANNA?
CREEAAK
MOODIE AND MONAGHAN RETURNED THAT NIGHT WITHOUT AN OX. INSTEAD, THEY BROUGHT ANOTHER VALUABLE CREATURE IN ITS PLACE.
OH, SUSIE, THOSE BLACKFLY BITES WILL SETTLE DOWN IN A FEW DAYS BUT YOU MUST NOT SCRATCH THEM.
OLD WITTALLS FIGURES WE COULD USE SOME PROTECTION FROM THE WILD BEASTS.

WERE YOU ABLE TO REPLACE THE OX?

WE'LL MANAGE WITH ONE FOR THE TIME BEING.

NO NEED TO FRET. WE'LL RECOVER THE LOSS COME HARVEST.

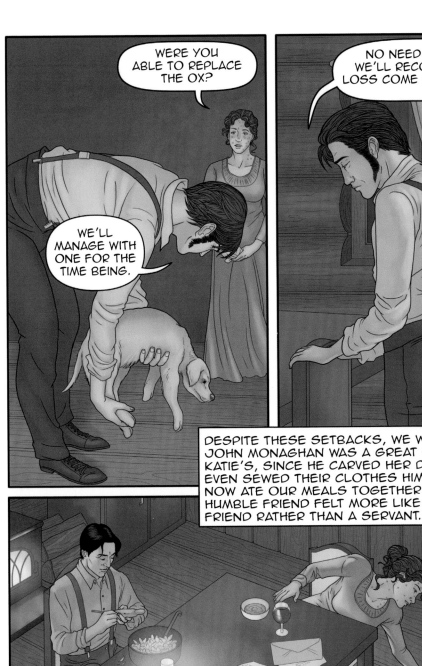

DESPITE THESE SETBACKS, WE WERE CONTENT. JOHN MONAGHAN WAS A GREAT FAVOURITE OF KATIE'S, SINCE HE CARVED HER DOLLS AND EVEN SEWED THEIR CLOTHES HIMSELF. WE ALL NOW ATE OUR MEALS TOGETHER, AND OUR HUMBLE FRIEND FELT MORE LIKE THAT – A FRIEND RATHER THAN A SERVANT.

CHAPTER 8
DISAPPOINTED HOPES

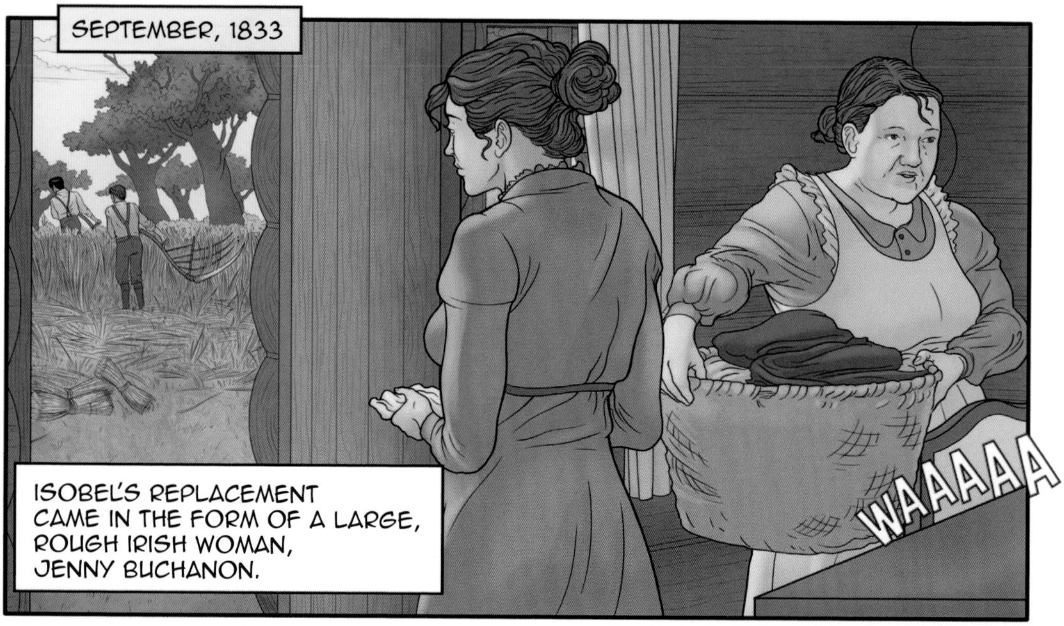
SEPTEMBER, 1833
ISOBEL'S REPLACEMENT CAME IN THE FORM OF A LARGE, ROUGH IRISH WOMAN, JENNY BUCHANON.
WAAAAA

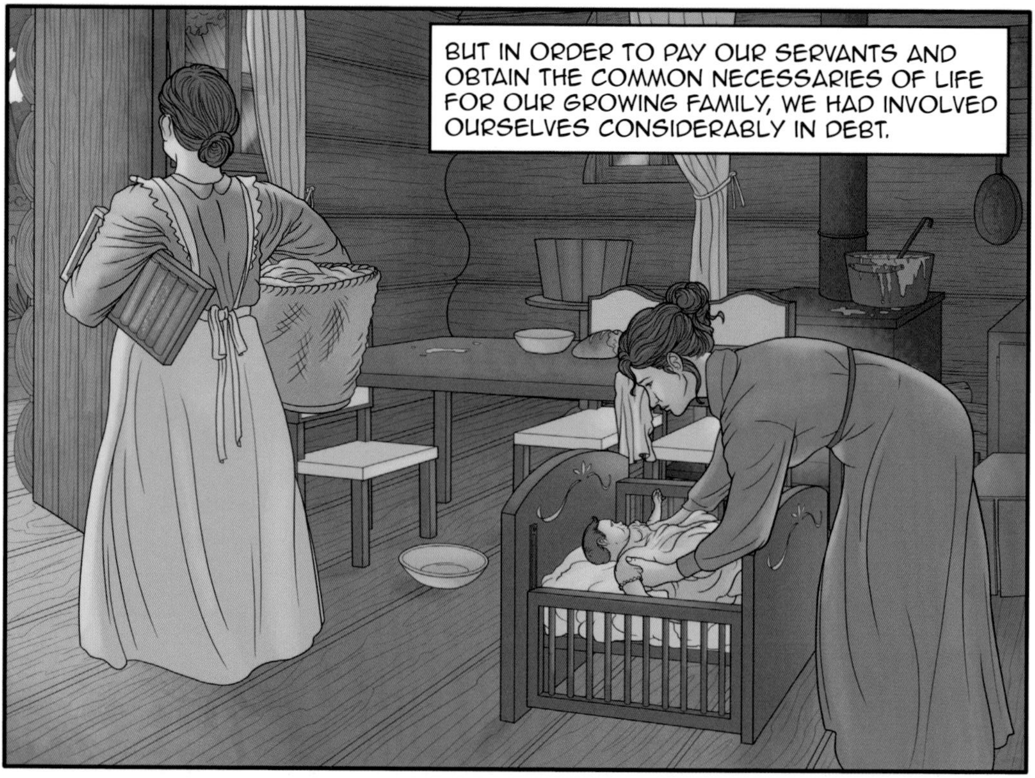
BUT IN ORDER TO PAY OUR SERVANTS AND OBTAIN THE COMMON NECESSARIES OF LIFE FOR OUR GROWING FAMILY, WE HAD INVOLVED OURSELVES CONSIDERABLY IN DEBT.

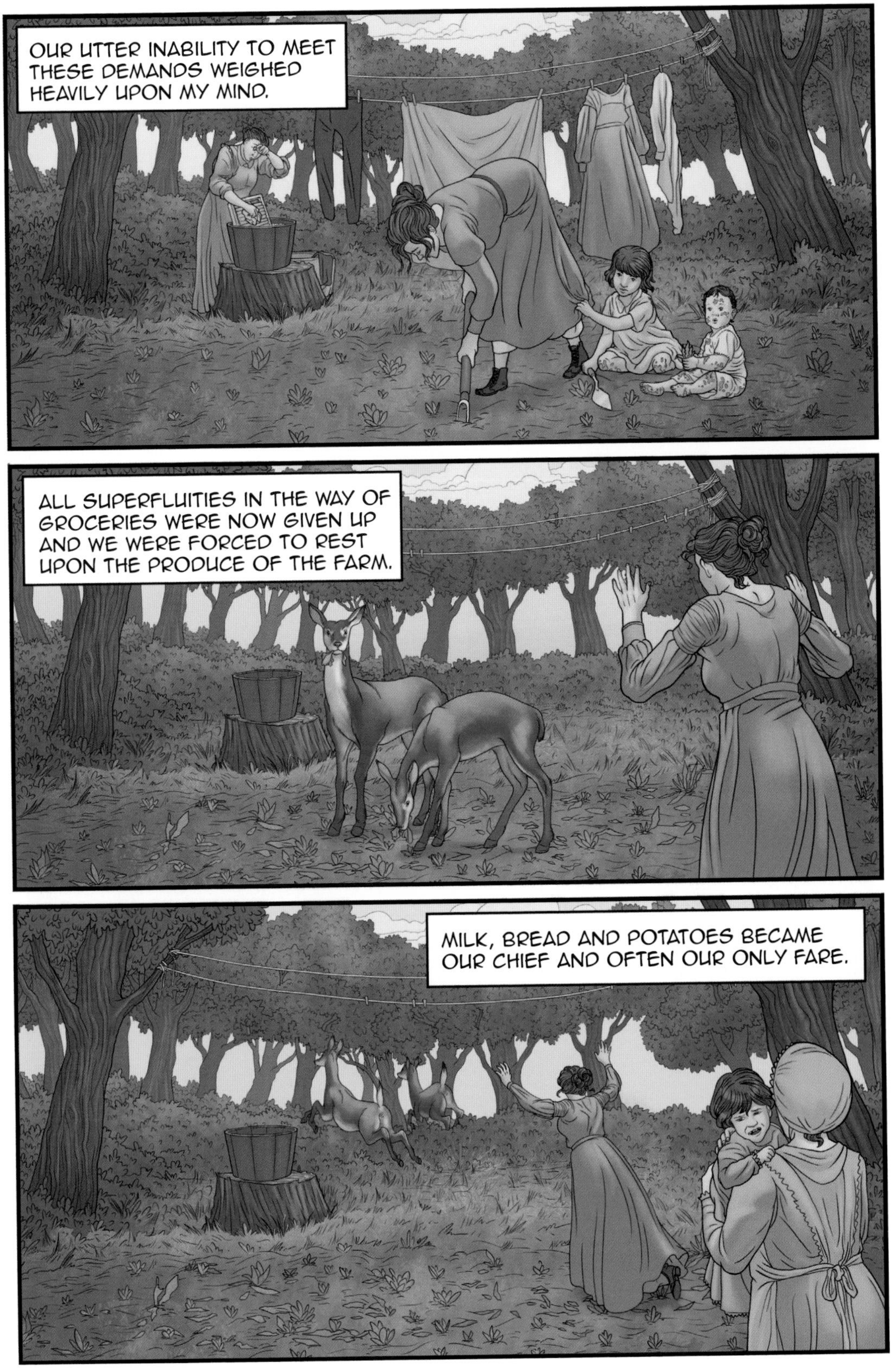
OUR UTTER INABILITY TO MEET THESE DEMANDS WEIGHED HEAVILY UPON MY MIND.
ALL SUPERFLUITIES IN THE WAY OF GROCERIES WERE NOW GIVEN UP AND WE WERE FORCED TO REST UPON THE PRODUCE OF THE FARM.
MILK, BREAD AND POTATOES BECAME OUR CHIEF AND OFTEN OUR ONLY FARE.

AND TOO OFTEN, THERE WAS NOT ENOUGH OF EVEN THESE SIMPLE FOODS.

POTATOE

WAAAAAAAAAAAAAAAAAAAAAAAA

EEEP!

KNOCK KNOCK

AAAAAAAAAAAAAA

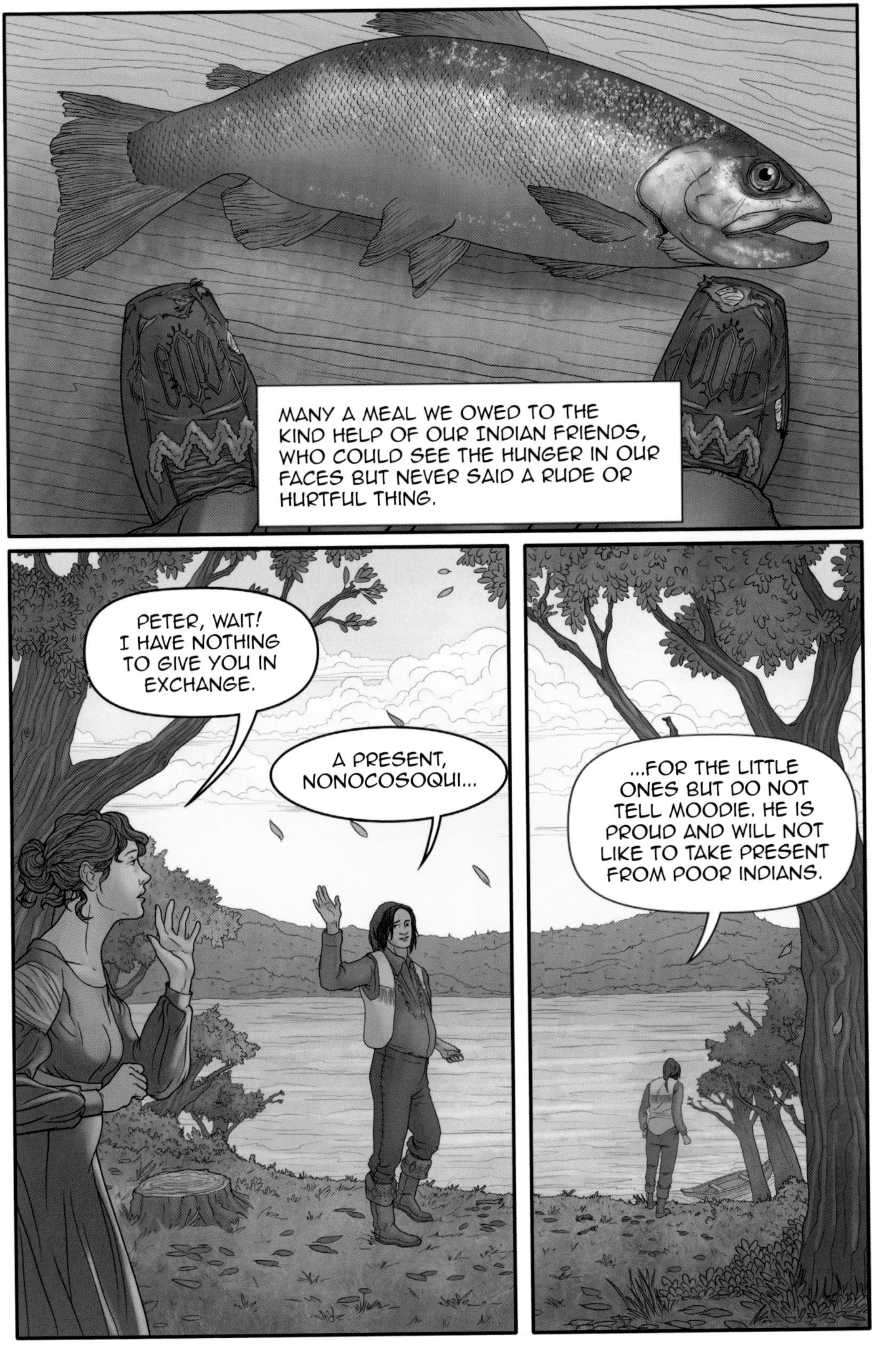
MANY A MEAL WE OWED TO THE KIND HELP OF OUR INDIAN FRIENDS, WHO COULD SEE THE HUNGER IN OUR FACES BUT NEVER SAID A RUDE OR HURTFUL THING.
PETER, WAIT! I HAVE NOTHING TO GIVE YOU IN EXCHANGE.
A PRESENT, NONOCOSOQUI...
...FOR THE LITTLE ONES BUT DO NOT TELL MOODIE. HE IS PROUD AND WILL NOT LIKE TO TAKE PRESENT FROM POOR INDIANS.

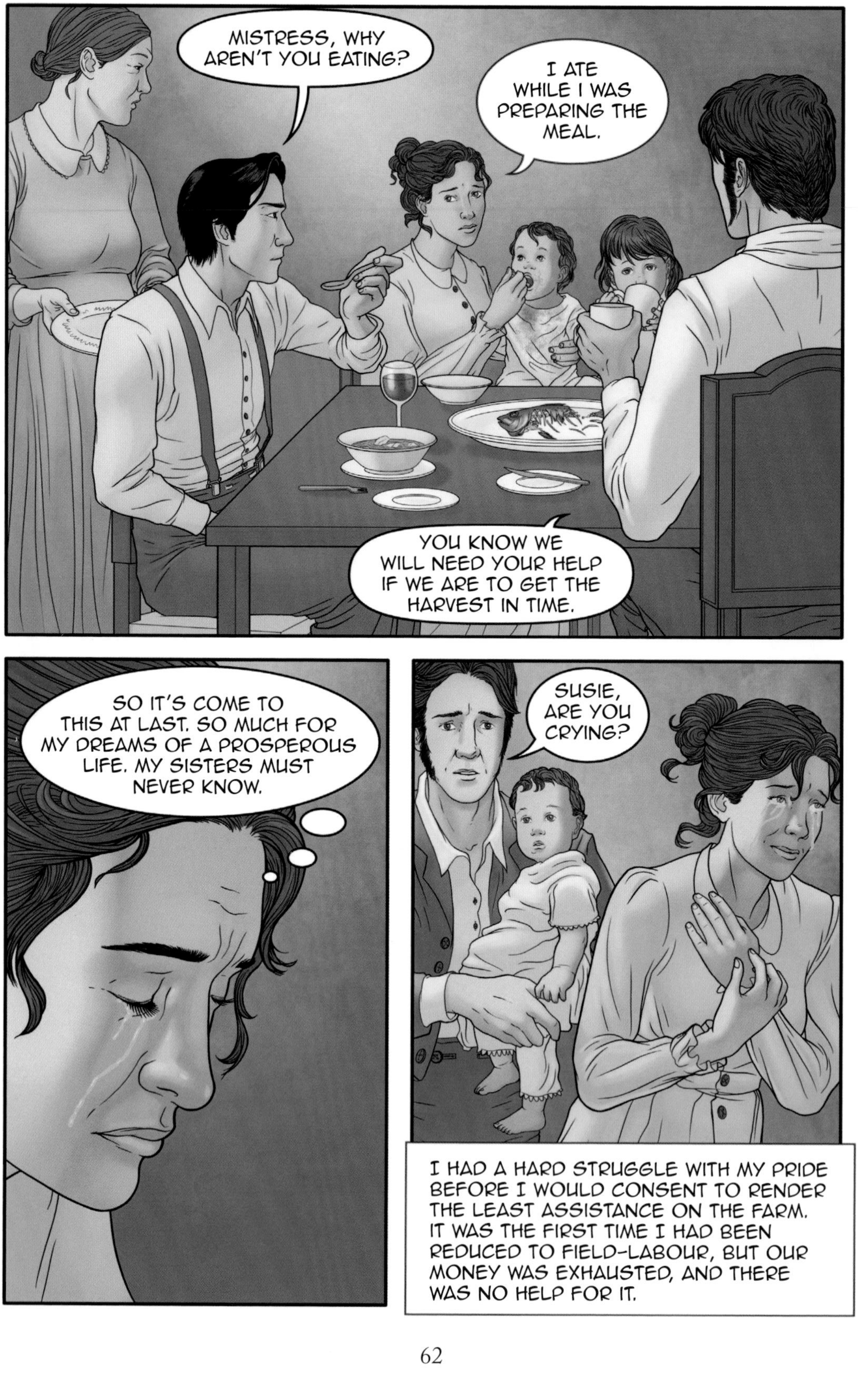
MISTRESS, WHY AREN'T YOU EATING?
I ATE WHILE I WAS PREPARING THE MEAL.
YOU KNOW WE WILL NEED YOUR HELP IF WE ARE TO GET THE HARVEST IN TIME.
SO IT'S COME TO THIS AT LAST. SO MUCH FOR MY DREAMS OF A PROSPEROUS LIFE. MY SISTERS MUST NEVER KNOW.
SUSIE, ARE YOU CRYING?
I HAD A HARD STRUGGLE WITH MY PRIDE BEFORE I WOULD CONSENT TO RENDER THE LEAST ASSISTANCE ON THE FARM. IT WAS THE FIRST TIME I HAD BEEN REDUCED TO FIELD-LABOUR, BUT OUR MONEY WAS EXHAUSTED, AND THERE WAS NO HELP FOR IT.

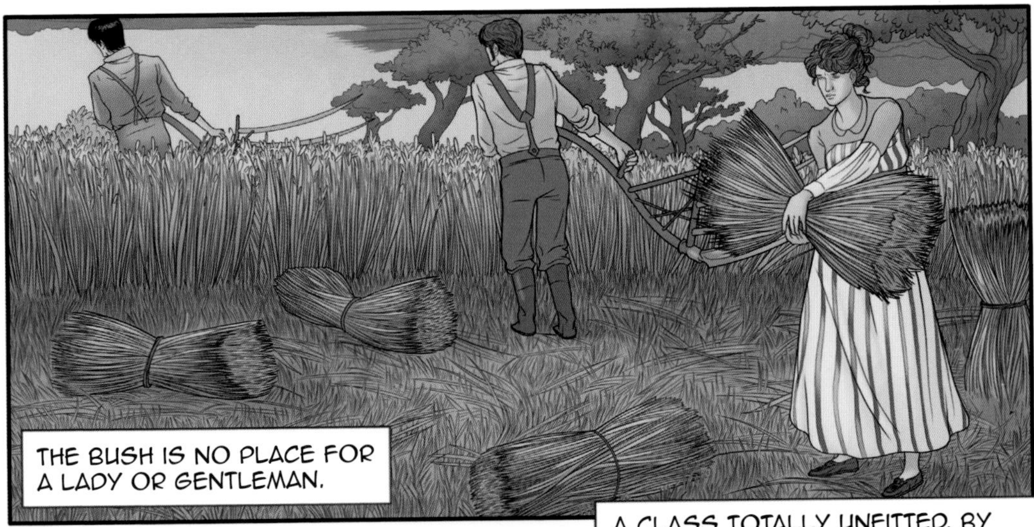
THE BUSH IS NO PLACE FOR A LADY OR GENTLEMAN.
A CLASS TOTALLY UNFITTED, BY PREVIOUS HABITS AND EDUCATION, TO BE HEWERS OF THE FOREST AND TILLERS OF THE SOIL.

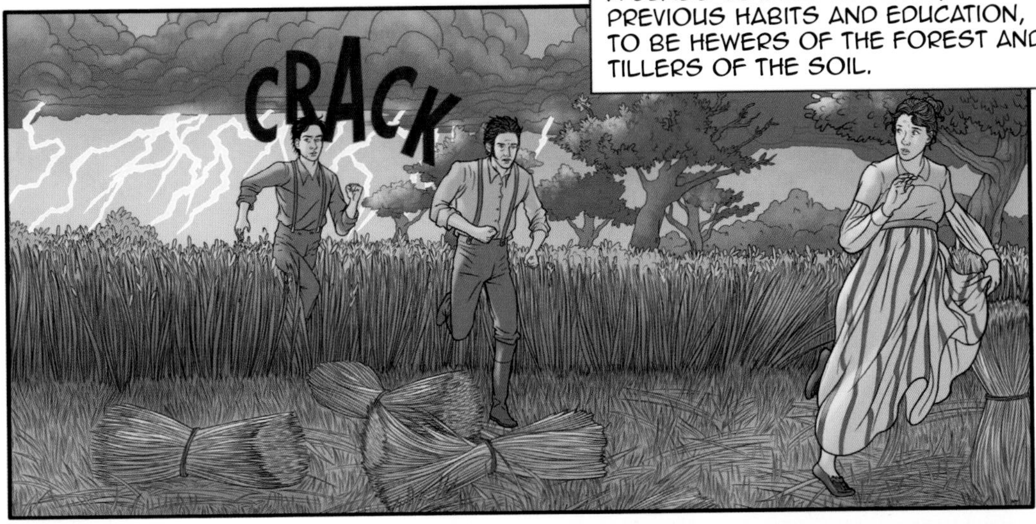
CRACK

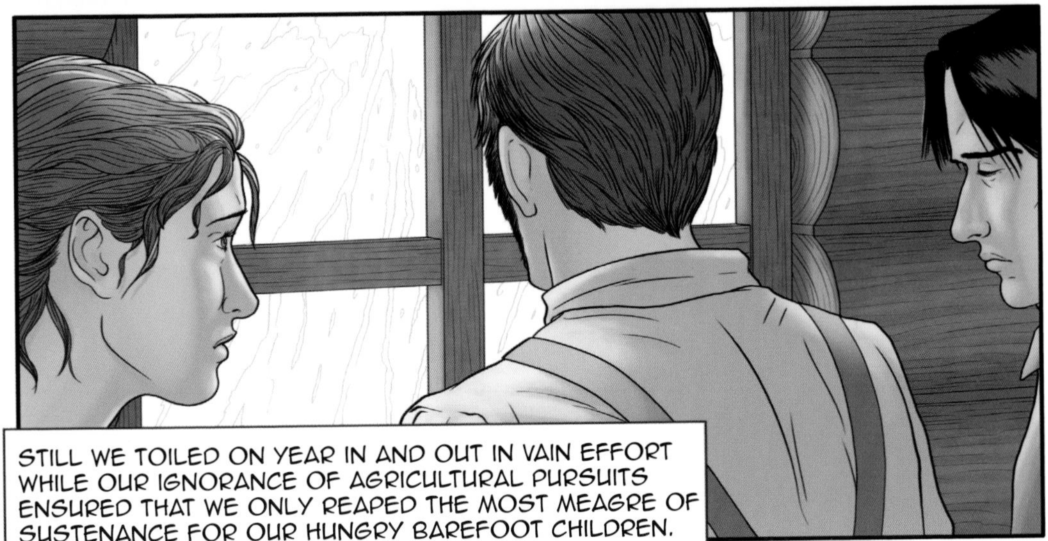
STILL WE TOILED ON YEAR IN AND OUT IN VAIN EFFORT WHILE OUR IGNORANCE OF AGRICULTURAL PURSUITS ENSURED THAT WE ONLY REAPED THE MOST MEAGRE OF SUSTENANCE FOR OUR HUNGRY BAREFOOT CHILDREN.

CHAPTER 9
THE BACKWOODS OF CANADA

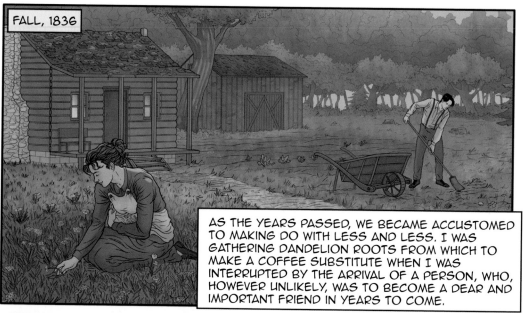

FALL, 1836

AS THE YEARS PASSED, WE BECAME ACCUSTOMED TO MAKING DO WITH LESS AND LESS. I WAS GATHERING DANDELION ROOTS FROM WHICH TO MAKE A COFFEE SUBSTITUTE WHEN I WAS INTERRUPTED BY THE ARRIVAL OF A PERSON, WHO, HOWEVER UNLIKELY, WAS TO BECOME A DEAR AND IMPORTANT FRIEND IN YEARS TO COME.

GOOD AFTERNOON.

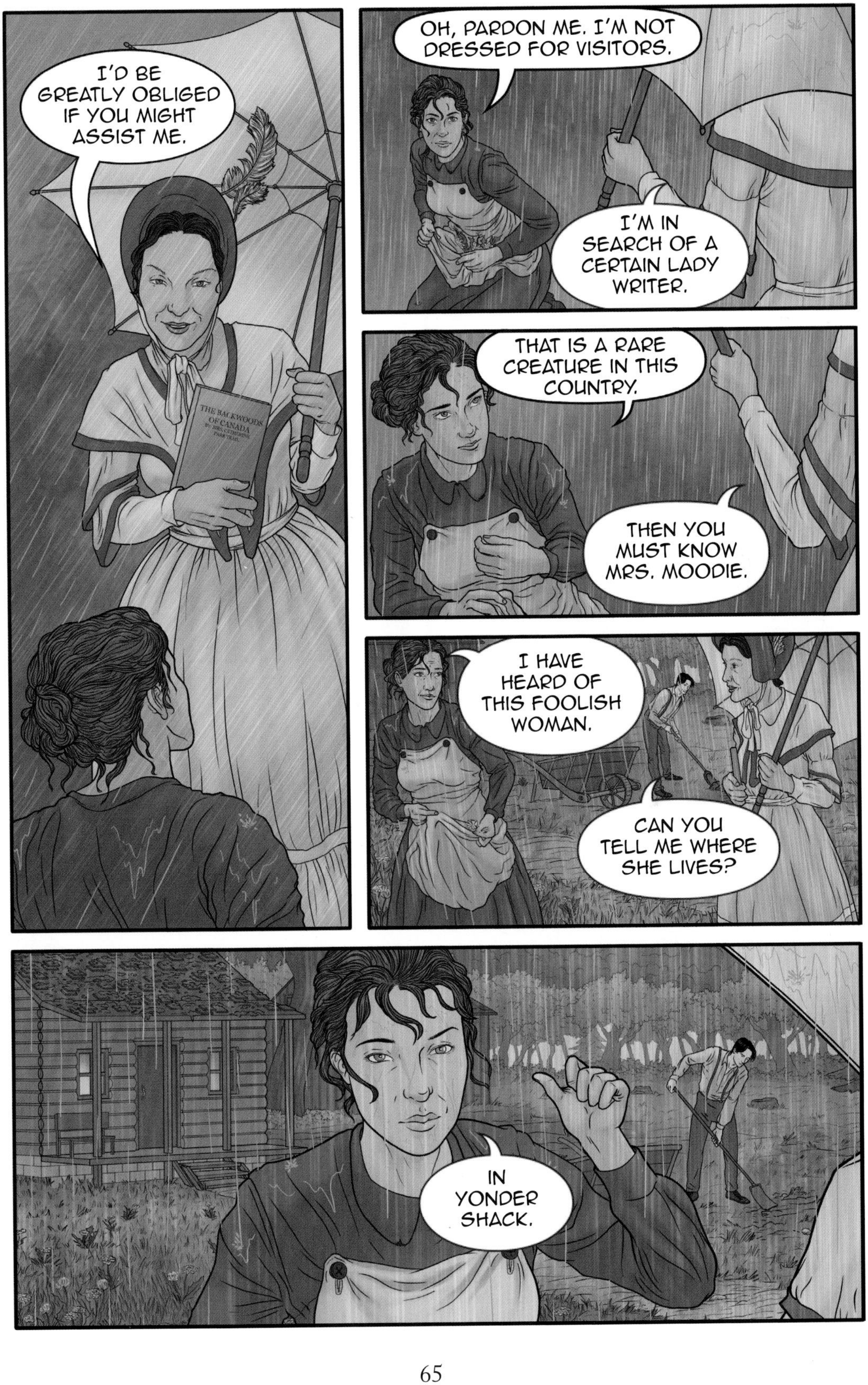
I'D BE GREATLY OBLIGED IF YOU MIGHT ASSIST ME.
OH, PARDON ME. I'M NOT DRESSED FOR VISITORS.
I'M IN SEARCH OF A CERTAIN LADY WRITER.
THAT IS A RARE CREATURE IN THIS COUNTRY.
THEN YOU MUST KNOW MRS. MOODIE.
I HAVE HEARD OF THIS FOOLISH WOMAN.
CAN YOU TELL ME WHERE SHE LIVES?
IN YONDER SHACK.

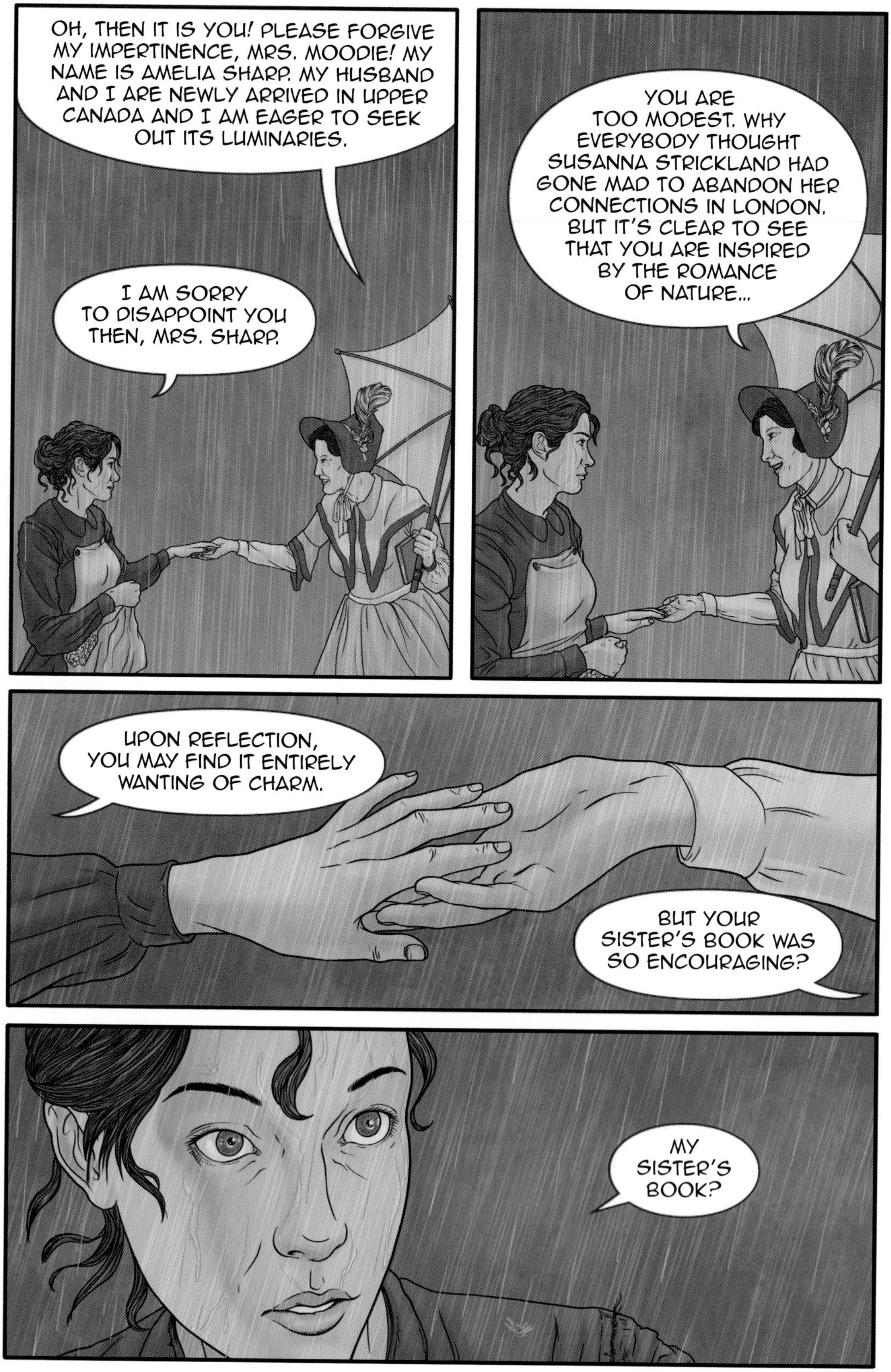
OH, THEN IT IS YOU! PLEASE FORGIVE MY IMPERTINENCE, MRS. MOODIE! MY NAME IS AMELIA SHARP. MY HUSBAND AND I ARE NEWLY ARRIVED IN UPPER CANADA AND I AM EAGER TO SEEK OUT ITS LUMINARIES.
I AM SORRY TO DISAPPOINT YOU THEN, MRS. SHARP.
YOU ARE TOO MODEST. WHY EVERYBODY THOUGHT SUSANNA STRICKLAND HAD GONE MAD TO ABANDON HER CONNECTIONS IN LONDON. BUT IT'S CLEAR TO SEE THAT YOU ARE INSPIRED BY THE ROMANCE OF NATURE...
UPON REFLECTION, YOU MAY FIND IT ENTIRELY WANTING OF CHARM.
BUT YOUR SISTER'S BOOK WAS SO ENCOURAGING?
MY SISTER'S BOOK?

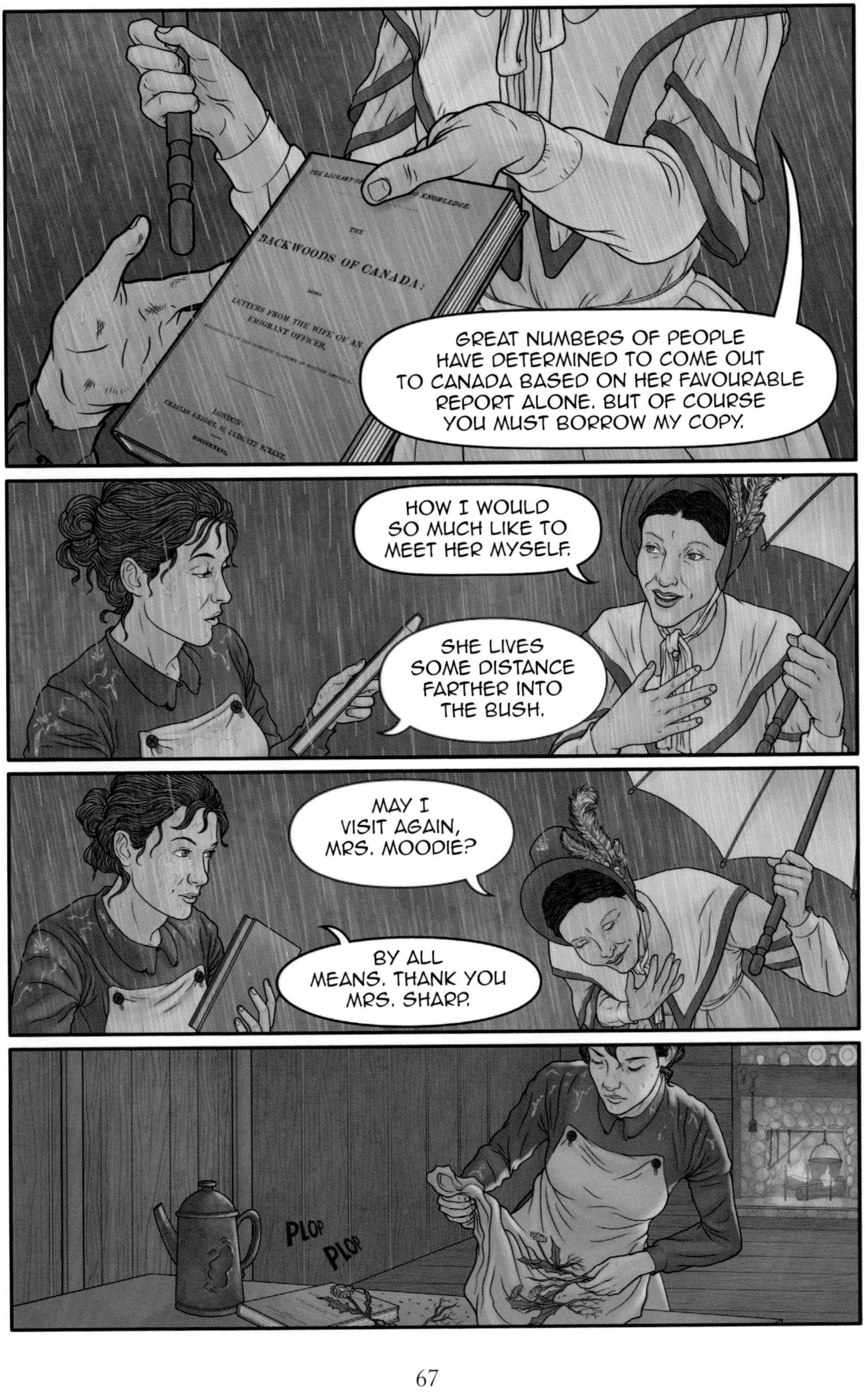
BACKWOODS OF CANADA:
LETTERS FROM THE WIFE OF AN EMIGRANT OFFICER,
GREAT NUMBERS OF PEOPLE HAVE DETERMINED TO COME OUT TO CANADA BASED ON HER FAVOURABLE REPORT ALONE. BUT OF COURSE YOU MUST BORROW MY COPY.
HOW I WOULD SO MUCH LIKE TO MEET HER MYSELF.
SHE LIVES SOME DISTANCE FARTHER INTO THE BUSH.
MAY I VISIT AGAIN, MRS. MOODIE?
BY ALL MEANS. THANK YOU MRS. SHARP.
PLOP
PLOP

–I CANNOT FORGIVE THIS BOOK!

SHE HASN'T WRITTEN A SINGLE WORD ABOUT THE HARDSHIPS, THE WILD ANIMALS, THE UNBEARABLE COLD...

FSSSSS

...GOING HUNGRY.

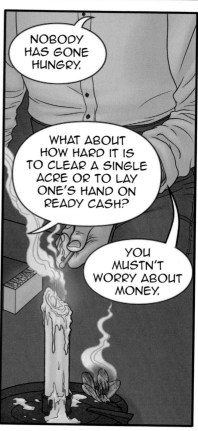

NOBODY HAS GONE HUNGRY.

WHAT ABOUT HOW HARD IT IS TO CLEAR A SINGLE ACRE OR TO LAY ONE'S HAND ON READY CASH?

YOU MUSTN'T WORRY ABOUT MONEY.

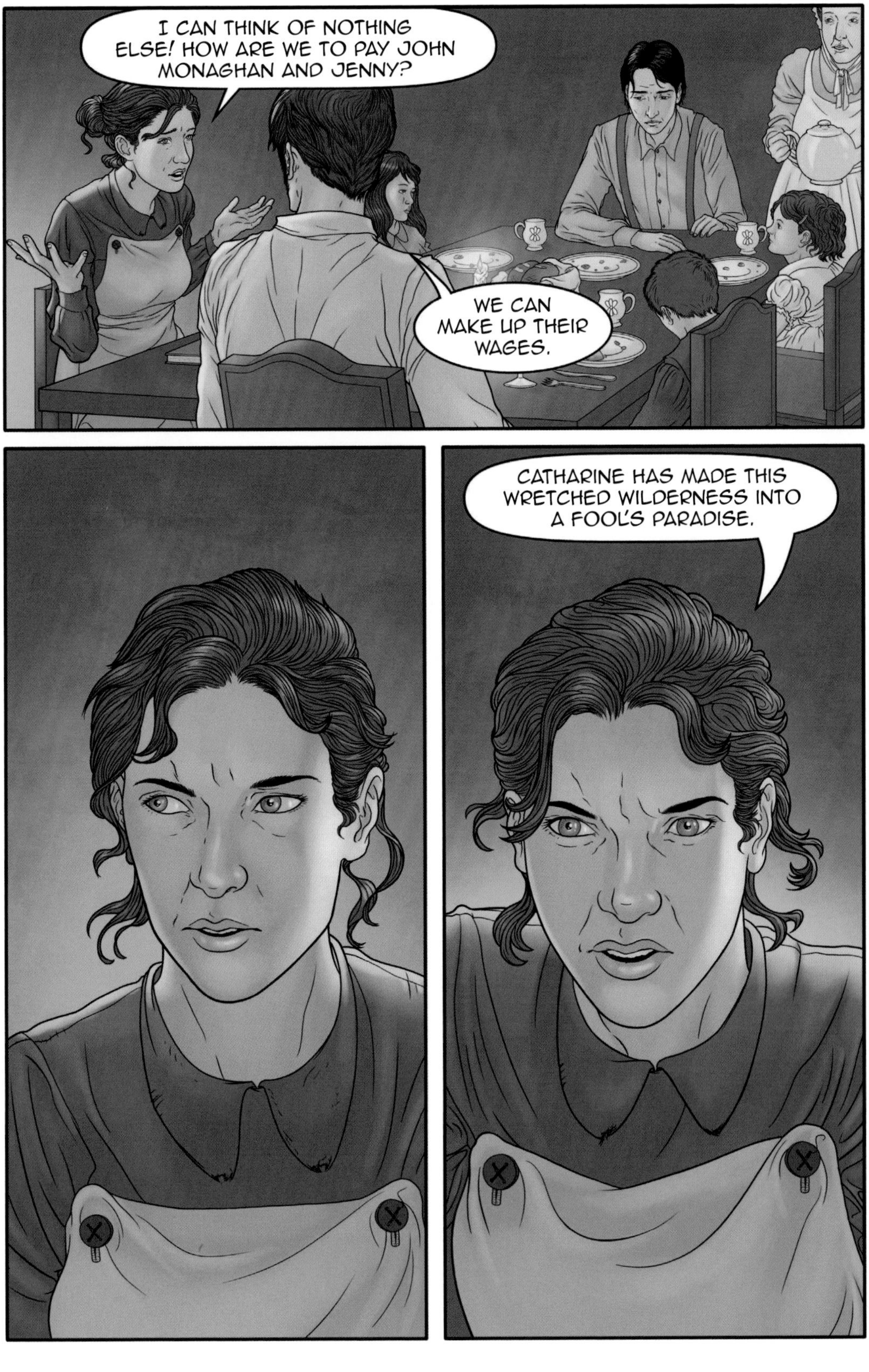
I CAN THINK OF NOTHING ELSE! HOW ARE WE TO PAY JOHN MONAGHAN AND JENNY?
WE CAN MAKE UP THEIR WAGES.
CATHARINE HAS MADE THIS WRETCHED WILDERNESS INTO A FOOL'S PARADISE.

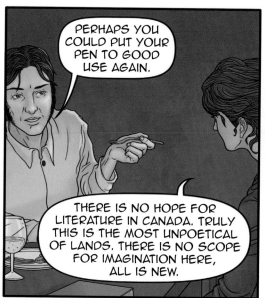
PERHAPS YOU COULD PUT YOUR PEN TO GOOD USE AGAIN.

THERE IS NO HOPE FOR LITERATURE IN CANADA. TRULY THIS IS THE MOST UNPOETICAL OF LANDS. THERE IS NO SCOPE FOR IMAGINATION HERE, ALL IS NEW.

PERHAPS YOU COULD WRITE ABOUT WHAT IS TRUE TO LIFE.

TO ADVERTISE OUR MISFORTUNES?

WHAT WOULD AGNES SAY? SHE IS A FAMOUS WRITER NOW, PRESENTED AT COURT.

SPLASH

WHAT WOULD HAPPEN IF IT BECAME KNOWN THAT HER SISTER LIVES IN A LOG HUT CONSORTING WITH VULGAR PEOPLE...WITH AMERICANS?

NO, I WILL MAINTAIN MY SILENCE.

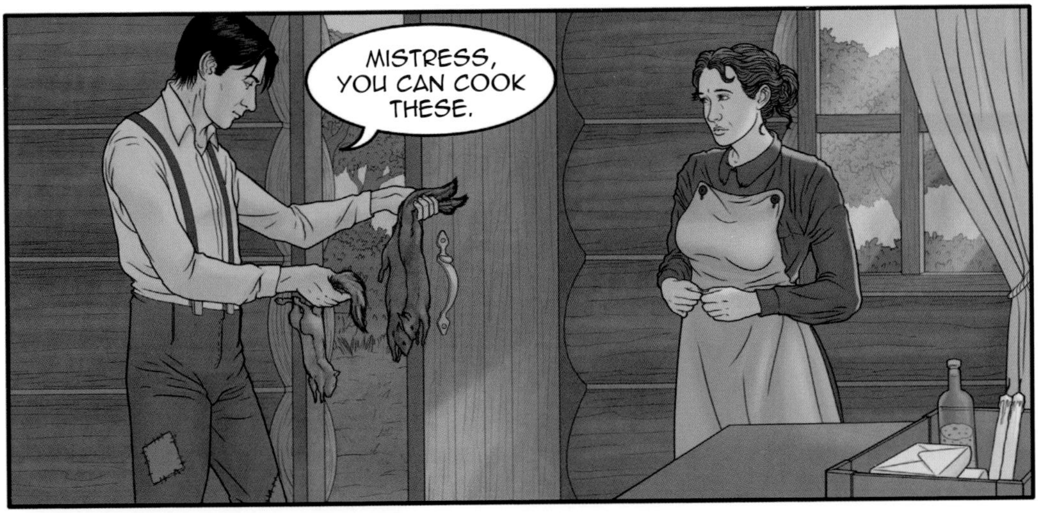
MISTRESS, YOU CAN COOK THESE.

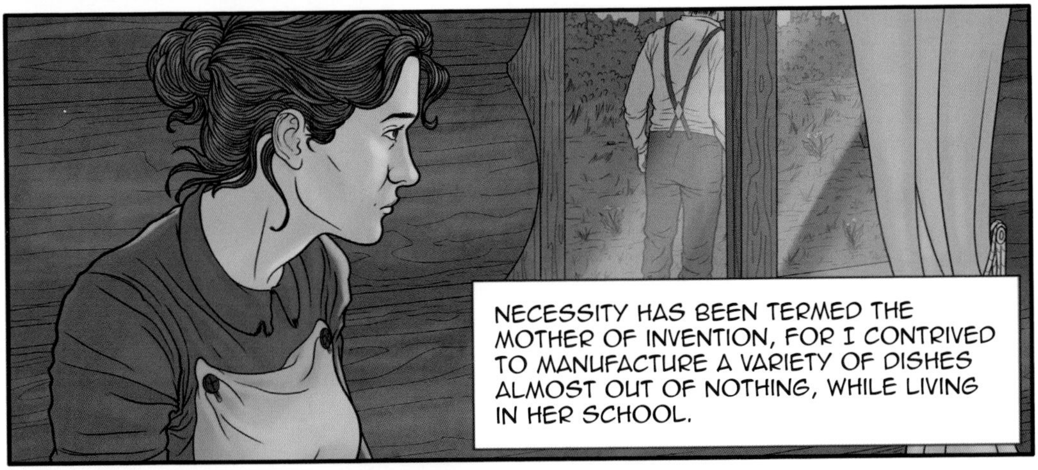
NECESSITY HAS BEEN TERMED THE MOTHER OF INVENTION, FOR I CONTRIVED TO MANUFACTURE A VARIETY OF DISHES ALMOST OUT OF NOTHING, WHILE LIVING IN HER SCHOOL.

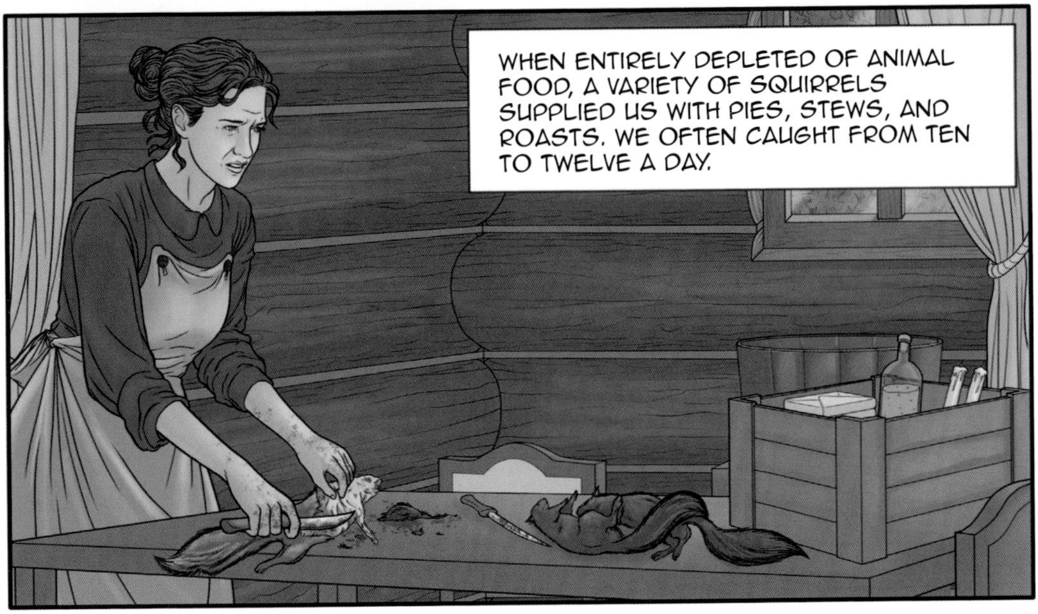
WHEN ENTIRELY DEPLETED OF ANIMAL FOOD, A VARIETY OF SQUIRRELS SUPPLIED US WITH PIES, STEWS, AND ROASTS. WE OFTEN CAUGHT FROM TEN TO TWELVE A DAY.

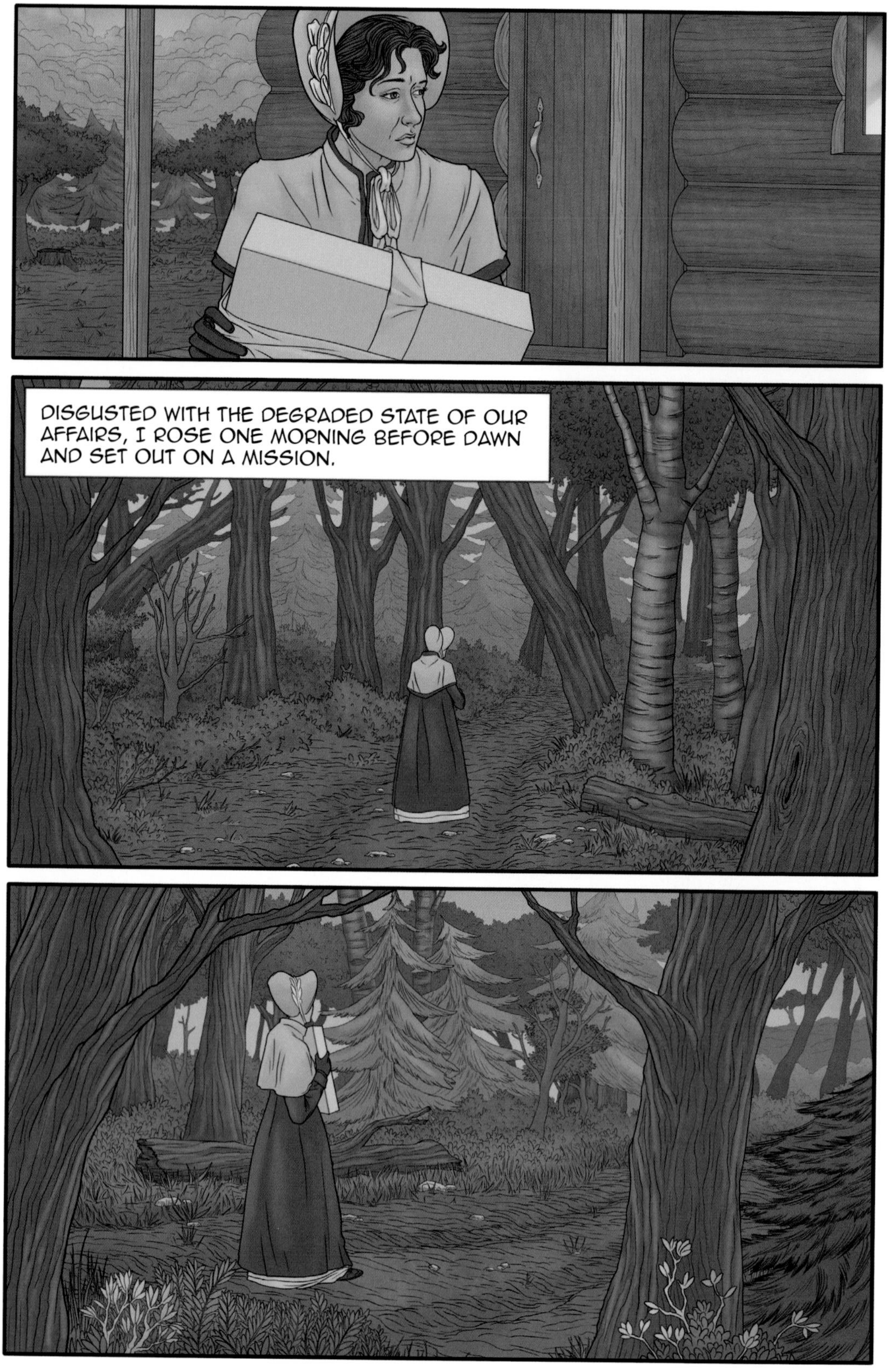
DISGUSTED WITH THE DEGRADED STATE OF OUR AFFAIRS, I ROSE ONE MORNING BEFORE DAWN AND SET OUT ON A MISSION.

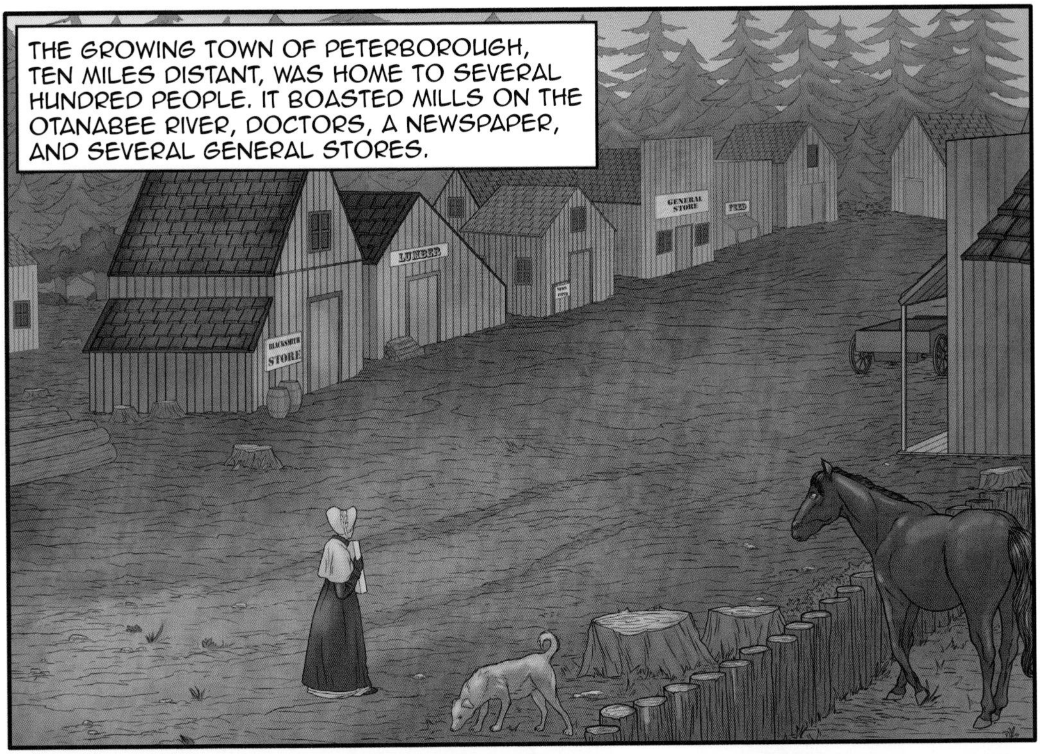
THE GROWING TOWN OF PETERBOROUGH, TEN MILES DISTANT, WAS HOME TO SEVERAL HUNDRED PEOPLE. IT BOASTED MILLS ON THE OTANABEE RIVER, DOCTORS, A NEWSPAPER, AND SEVERAL GENERAL STORES.
GENERAL STORE
LUMBER
BLACKSMITH STORE

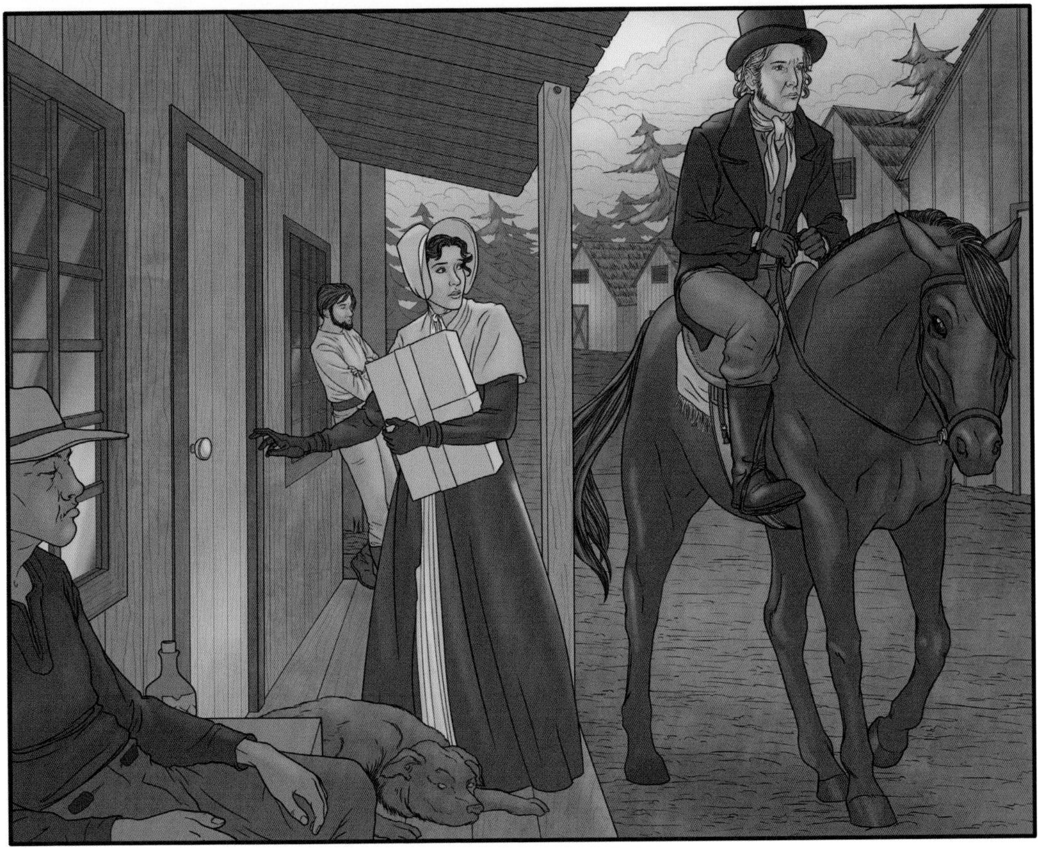

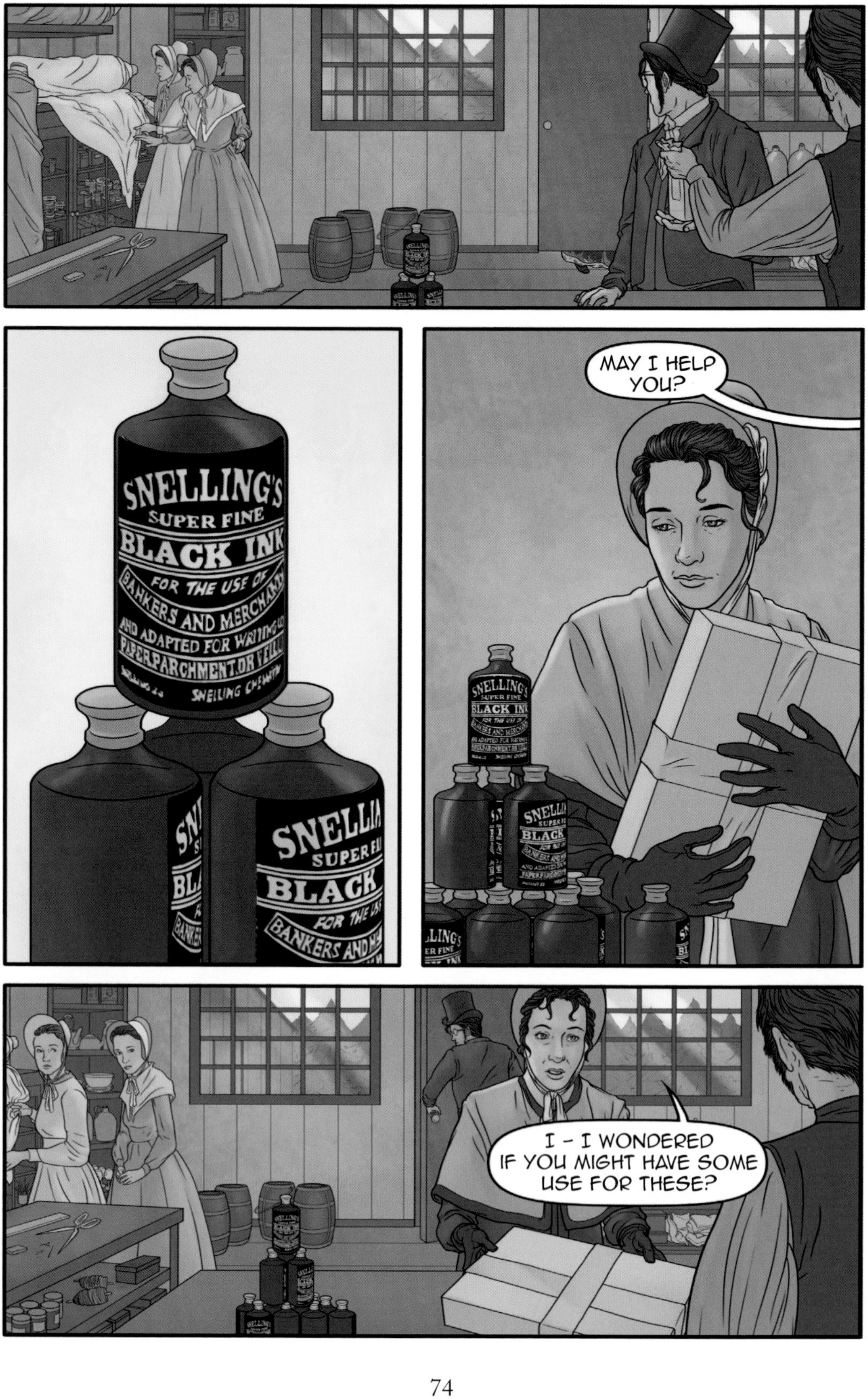
SNELLING'S
SUPER FINE
BLACK INK
FOR THE USE OF
MAY I HELP YOU?
I - I WONDERED IF YOU MIGHT HAVE SOME USE FOR THESE?

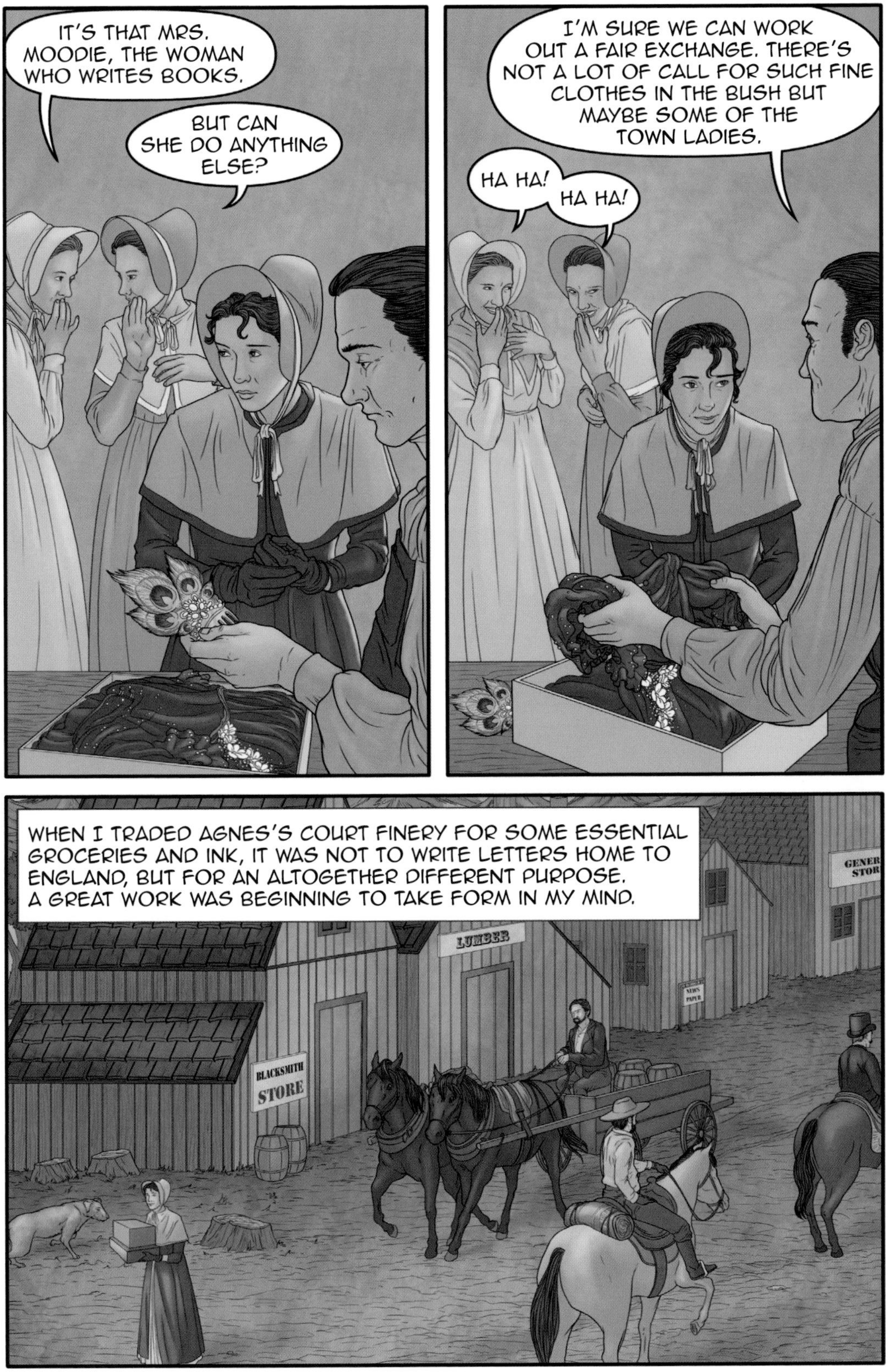
IT'S THAT MRS. MOODIE, THE WOMAN WHO WRITES BOOKS.
BUT CAN SHE DO ANYTHING ELSE?
I'M SURE WE CAN WORK OUT A FAIR EXCHANGE. THERE'S NOT A LOT OF CALL FOR SUCH FINE CLOTHES IN THE BUSH BUT MAYBE SOME OF THE TOWN LADIES.
HA HA!
HA HA!
WHEN I TRADED AGNES'S COURT FINERY FOR SOME ESSENTIAL GROCERIES AND INK, IT WAS NOT TO WRITE LETTERS HOME TO ENGLAND, BUT FOR AN ALTOGETHER DIFFERENT PURPOSE. A GREAT WORK WAS BEGINNING TO TAKE FORM IN MY MIND.
LUMBER
BLACKSMITH
STORE

CHAPTER 10

THE OUTBREAK

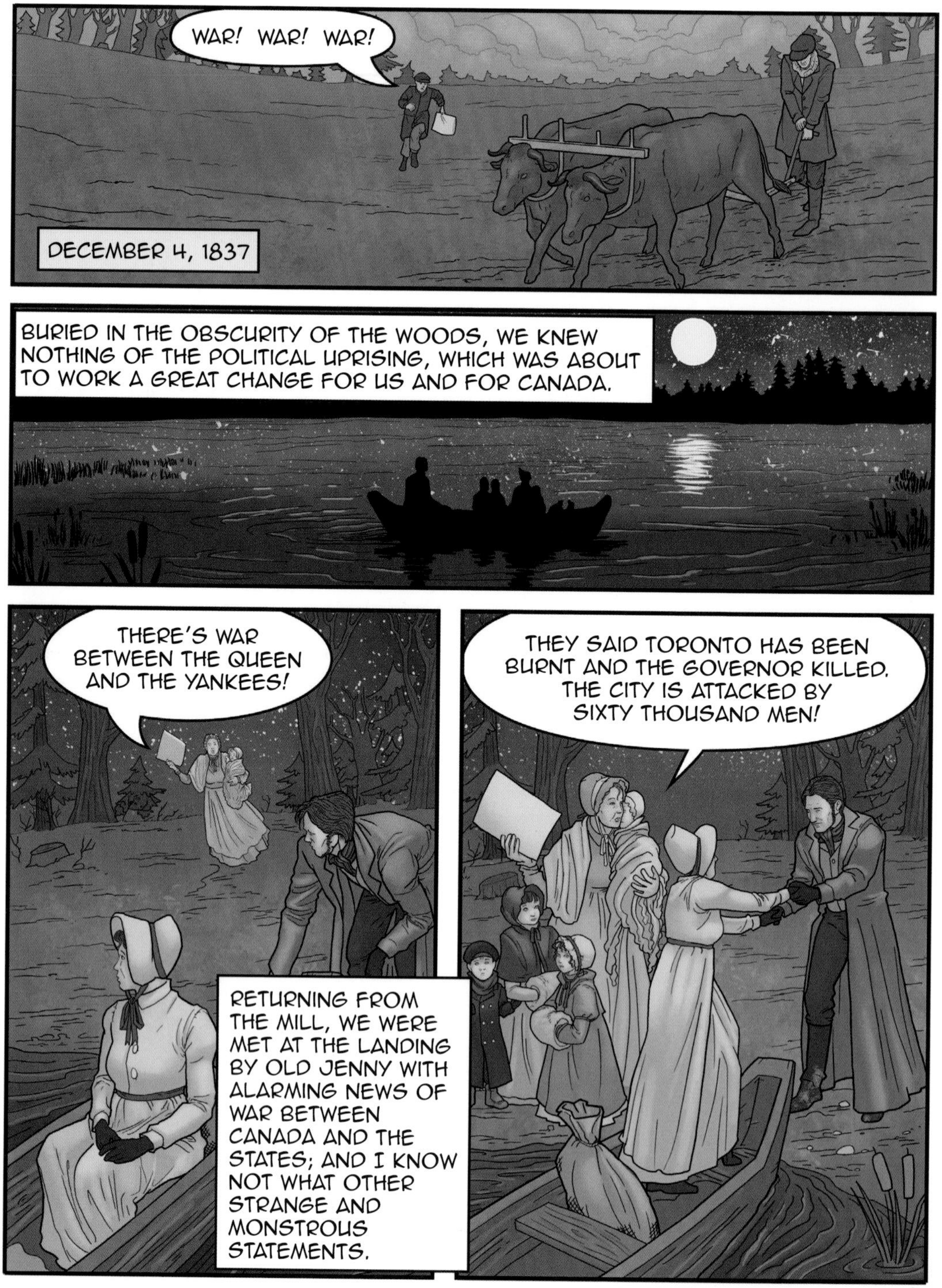

WAR! WAR! WAR!
DECEMBER 4, 1837
BURIED IN THE OBSCURITY OF THE WOODS, WE KNEW NOTHING OF THE POLITICAL UPRISING, WHICH WAS ABOUT TO WORK A GREAT CHANGE FOR US AND FOR CANADA.
THERE'S WAR BETWEEN THE QUEEN AND THE YANKEES!
RETURNING FROM THE MILL, WE WERE MET AT THE LANDING BY OLD JENNY WITH ALARMING NEWS OF WAR BETWEEN CANADA AND THE STATES; AND I KNOW NOT WHAT OTHER STRANGE AND MONSTROUS STATEMENTS.
THEY SAID TORONTO HAS BEEN BURNT AND THE GOVERNOR KILLED. THE CITY IS ATTACKED BY SIXTY THOUSAND MEN!

THERE WERE SOLDIERS HERE AND THEY LEFT THIS PAPER FOR THE MASTER AND IT'S ALL WRITTEN DOWN HERE.

THERE'S BEEN AN UPRISING. THE GOVERNOR IS MOBILIZING THE MILITIA, I'LL HAVE TO LEAVE IN THE MORNING.

JOHN, YOU CAN'T POSSIBLY GO!

I CAN'T IGNORE MY DUTY. I'M STILL AN OFFICER.

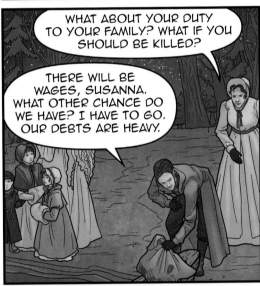

WHAT ABOUT YOUR DUTY TO YOUR FAMILY? WHAT IF YOU SHOULD BE KILLED?

THERE WILL BE WAGES, SUSANNA. WHAT OTHER CHANCE DO WE HAVE? I HAVE TO GO. OUR DEBTS ARE HEAVY.

LITTLE SLEEP VISITED OUR EYES THAT NIGHT. WE TALKED OVER THE STRANGE NEWS, AND THE POSSIBILITY THAT WE MIGHT NEVER SEE EACH OTHER AGAIN. OUR AFFAIRS WERE IN SUCH A DESPERATE CONDITION THAT MOODIE FELT ANY CHANGE MUST BE FOR THE BETTER; BUT THE POOR, ANXIOUS WIFE THOUGHT ONLY OF A PARTING, WHICH PUT A FINISHING STROKE TO ALL HER MISFORTUNES.

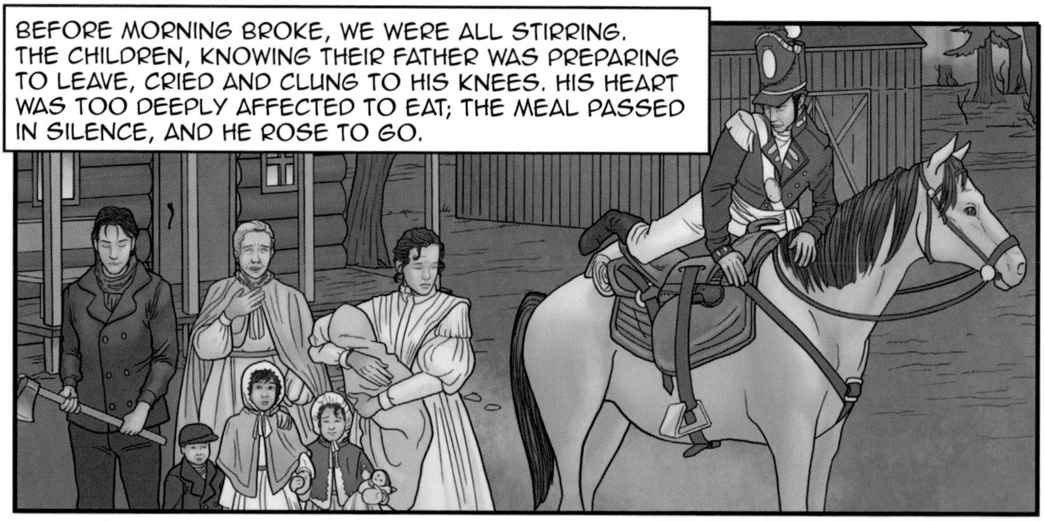
BEFORE MORNING BROKE, WE WERE ALL STIRRING. THE CHILDREN, KNOWING THEIR FATHER WAS PREPARING TO LEAVE, CRIED AND CLUNG TO HIS KNEES. HIS HEART WAS TOO DEEPLY AFFECTED TO EAT; THE MEAL PASSED IN SILENCE, AND HE ROSE TO GO.

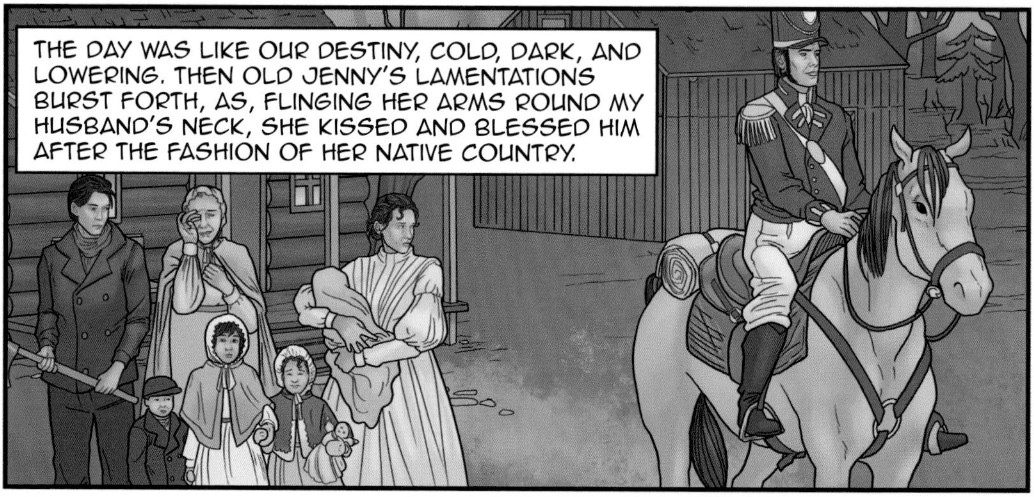
THE DAY WAS LIKE OUR DESTINY, COLD, DARK, AND LOWERING. THEN OLD JENNY'S LAMENTATIONS BURST FORTH, AS, FLINGING HER ARMS ROUND MY HUSBAND'S NECK, SHE KISSED AND BLESSED HIM AFTER THE FASHION OF HER NATIVE COUNTRY.

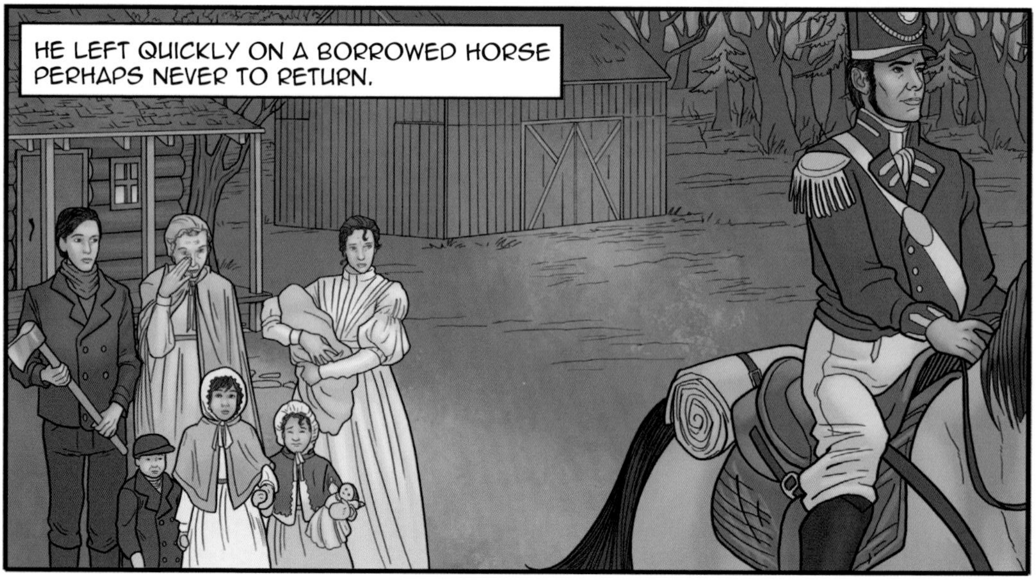
HE LEFT QUICKLY ON A BORROWED HORSE PERHAPS NEVER TO RETURN.

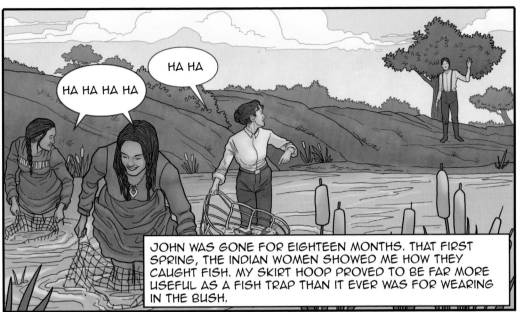

HA HA HA HA

HA HA

JOHN WAS GONE FOR EIGHTEEN MONTHS. THAT FIRST SPRING, THE INDIAN WOMEN SHOWED ME HOW THEY CAUGHT FISH. MY SKIRT HOOP PROVED TO BE FAR MORE USEFUL AS A FISH TRAP THAN IT EVER WAS FOR WEARING IN THE BUSH.

I ONCE HAD A LADY FRIEND IN LONDON WHO DRESSED AS A MAN.

SHE WORE TROUSERS?

YES. AND A WAISTCOAT AND A MAN'S HAT. SHE EXCITED A GREAT DEAL OF ATTENTION.

I CAN BELIEVE THAT.

OF COURSE SHE WAS QUITE RICH AND COULD DO AS SHE PLEASED. HOW WILHELMINA WOULD LAUGH IF SHE COULD SEE ME NOW.

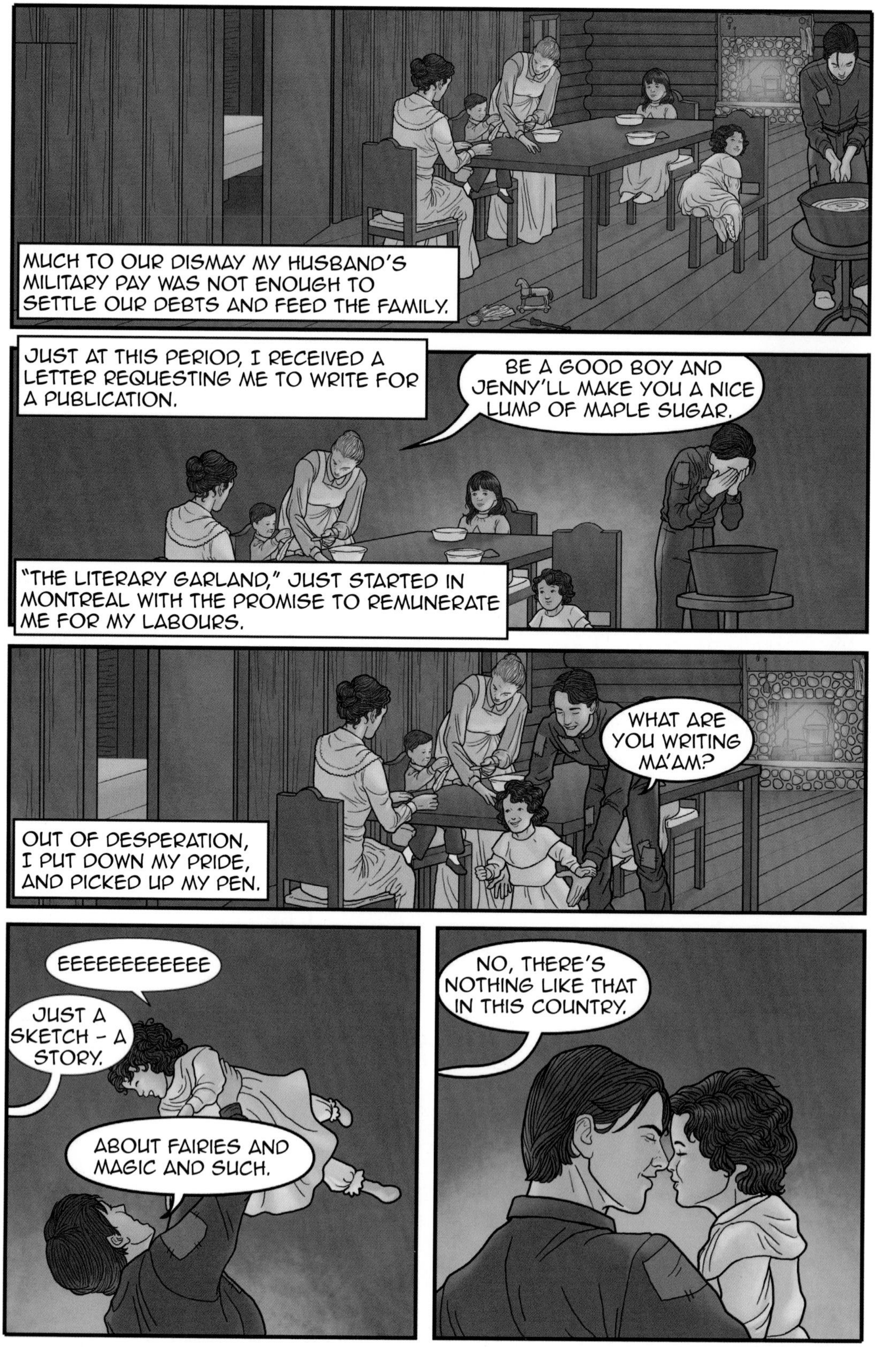
MUCH TO OUR DISMAY MY HUSBAND'S MILITARY PAY WAS NOT ENOUGH TO SETTLE OUR DEBTS AND FEED THE FAMILY.
JUST AT THIS PERIOD, I RECEIVED A LETTER REQUESTING ME TO WRITE FOR A PUBLICATION.
BE A GOOD BOY AND JENNY'LL MAKE YOU A NICE LUMP OF MAPLE SUGAR.
"THE LITERARY GARLAND," JUST STARTED IN MONTREAL WITH THE PROMISE TO REMUNERATE ME FOR MY LABOURS.
WHAT ARE YOU WRITING MA'AM?
OUT OF DESPERATION, I PUT DOWN MY PRIDE, AND PICKED UP MY PEN.
EEEEEEEEEEEE
JUST A SKETCH – A STORY.
ABOUT FAIRIES AND MAGIC AND SUCH.
NO, THERE'S NOTHING LIKE THAT IN THIS COUNTRY.

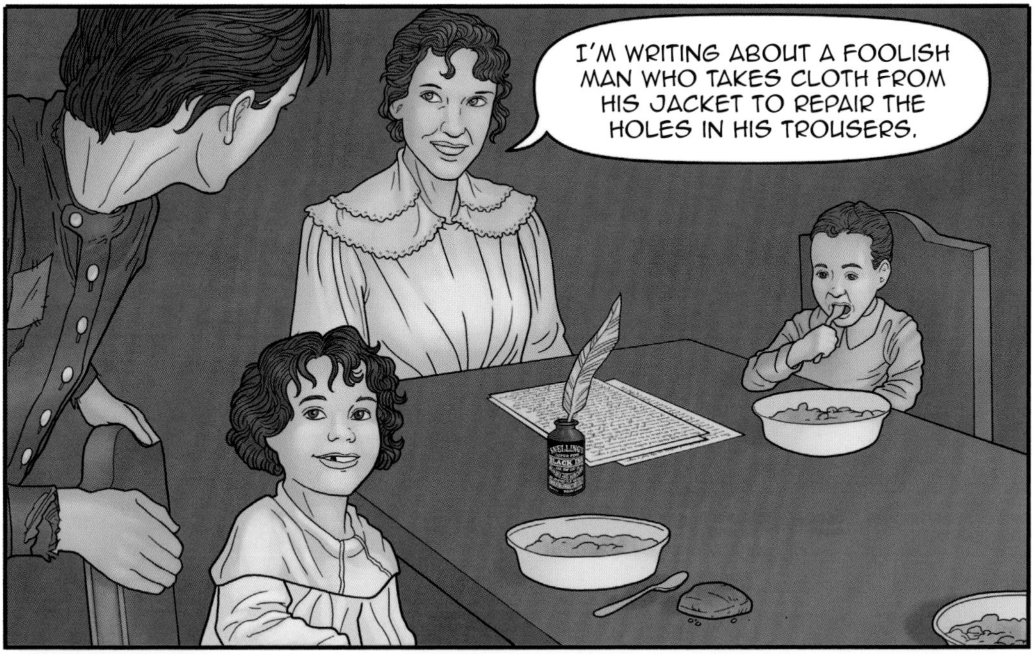
I'M WRITING ABOUT A FOOLISH MAN WHO TAKES CLOTH FROM HIS JACKET TO REPAIR THE HOLES IN HIS TROUSERS.

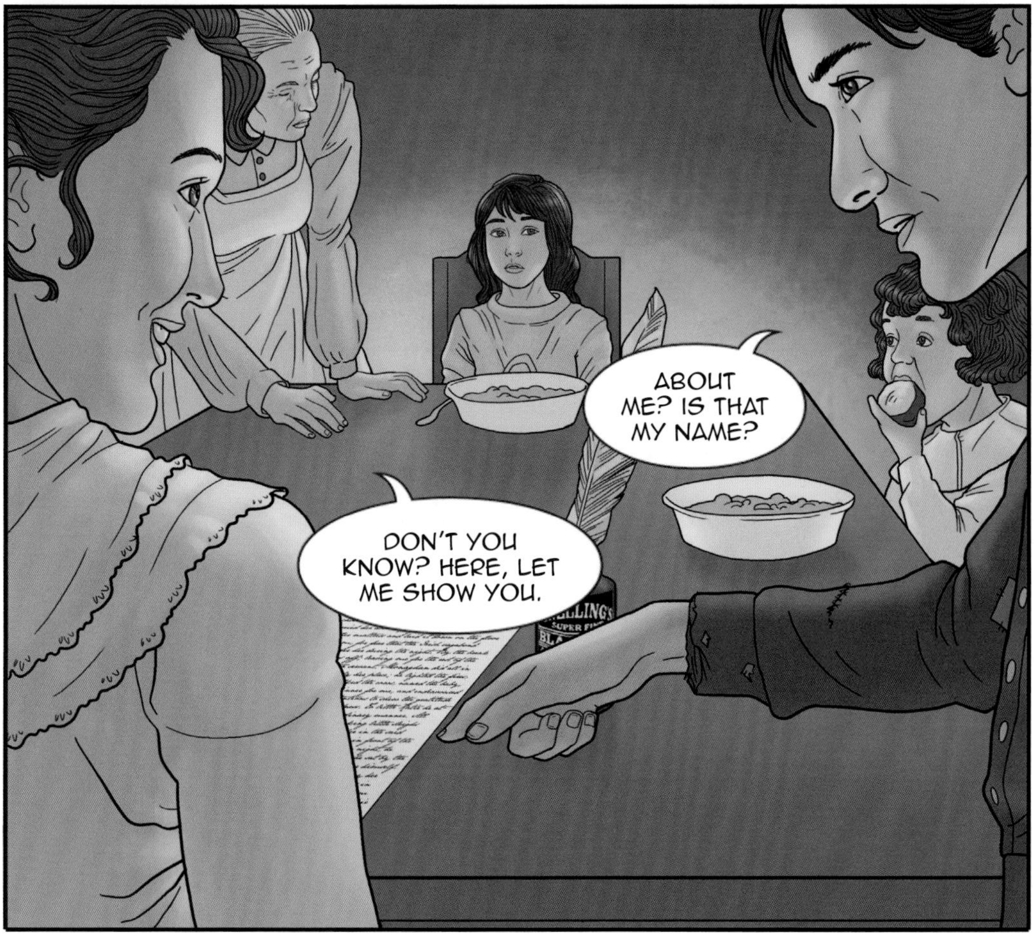
ABOUT ME? IS THAT MY NAME?
DON'T YOU KNOW? HERE, LET ME SHOW YOU.

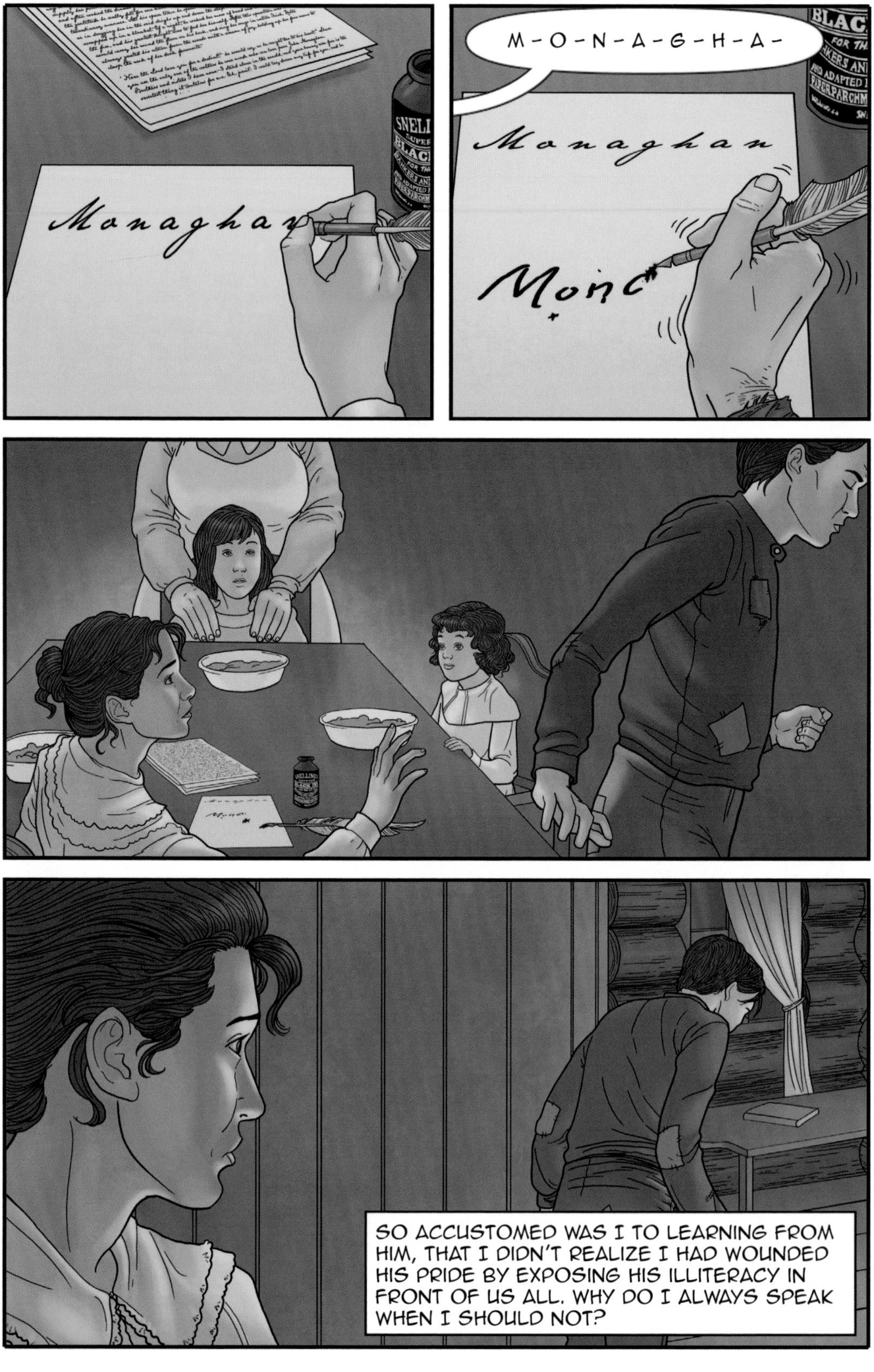
Monaghan
M-O-N-A-G-H-A-
Monaghan
Monc
SO ACCUSTOMED WAS I TO LEARNING FROM HIM, THAT I DIDN'T REALIZE I HAD WOUNDED HIS PRIDE BY EXPOSING HIS ILLITERACY IN FRONT OF US ALL. WHY DO I ALWAYS SPEAK WHEN I SHOULD NOT?

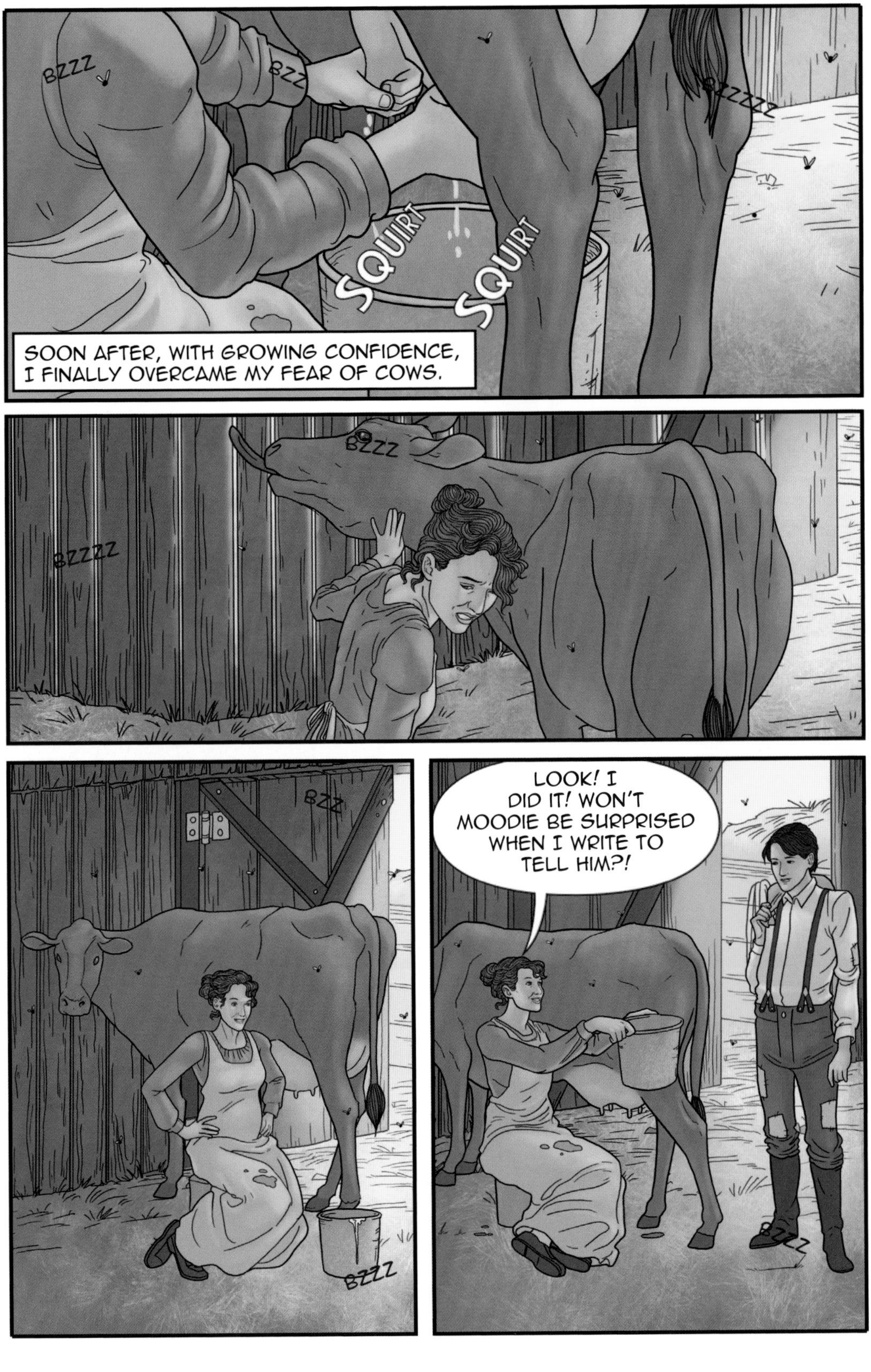
BZZZ
BZZ
BZZZZZ
SQUIRT
SQUIRT
SOON AFTER, WITH GROWING CONFIDENCE, I FINALLY OVERCAME MY FEAR OF COWS.
BZZZ
BZZZZ
BZZ
BZZZ
LOOK! I DID IT! WON'T MOODIE BE SURPRISED WHEN I WRITE TO TELL HIM?!
BZZZ

I – I'M GOING DOWN TO THE LUMBER CAMP BY THE FALLS. I'LL BE ABLE TO MAKE SOME MONEY THERE.

YOU CAN'T LEAVE AT SUCH A TIME WITH THE MASTER AWAY.

I'VE CHOPPED ENOUGH WOOD AND I CAN COME BACK EVERY WEEK AT LEAST. YOU NEEDN'T WORRY.

THAT'S NOT WHAT I MEANT.

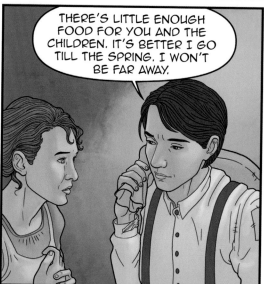

THERE'S LITTLE ENOUGH FOOD FOR YOU AND THE CHILDREN. IT'S BETTER I GO TILL THE SPRING. I WON'T BE FAR AWAY.

BUT WHAT IF THE REBELS COME?

THOSE SCOUNDRELS ARE NO MATCH FOR YOU...SUSANNA.

CHAPTER 11

ROUGHING IT

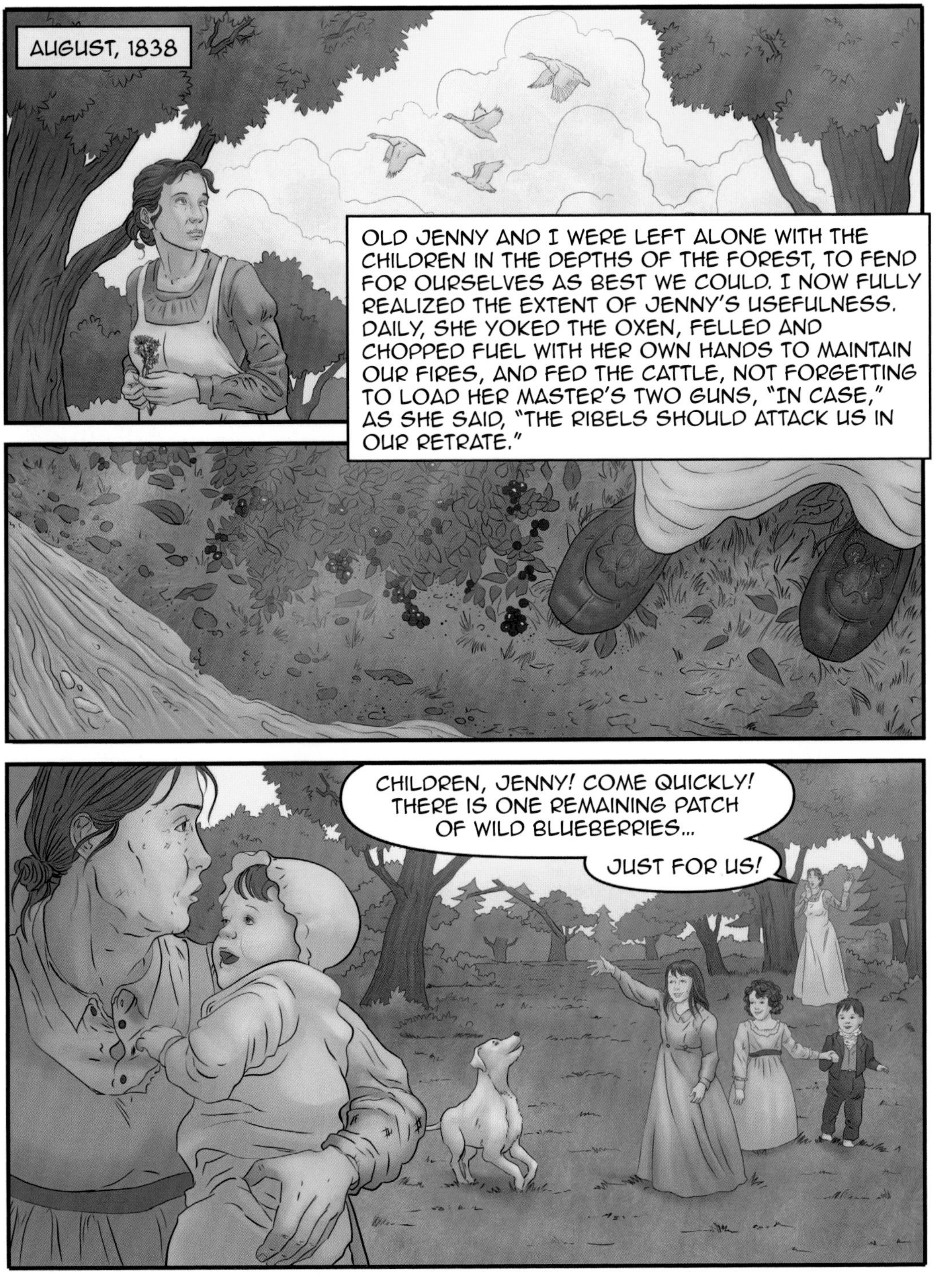
AUGUST, 1838
OLD JENNY AND I WERE LEFT ALONE WITH THE CHILDREN IN THE DEPTHS OF THE FOREST, TO FEND FOR OURSELVES AS BEST WE COULD. I NOW FULLY REALIZED THE EXTENT OF JENNY'S USEFULNESS. DAILY, SHE YOKED THE OXEN, FELLED AND CHOPPED FUEL WITH HER OWN HANDS TO MAINTAIN OUR FIRES, AND FED THE CATTLE, NOT FORGETTING TO LOAD HER MASTER'S TWO GUNS, "IN CASE," AS SHE SAID, "THE RIBELS SHOULD ATTACK US IN OUR RETRATE."
CHILDREN, JENNY! COME QUICKLY! THERE IS ONE REMAINING PATCH OF WILD BLUEBERRIES...
JUST FOR US!

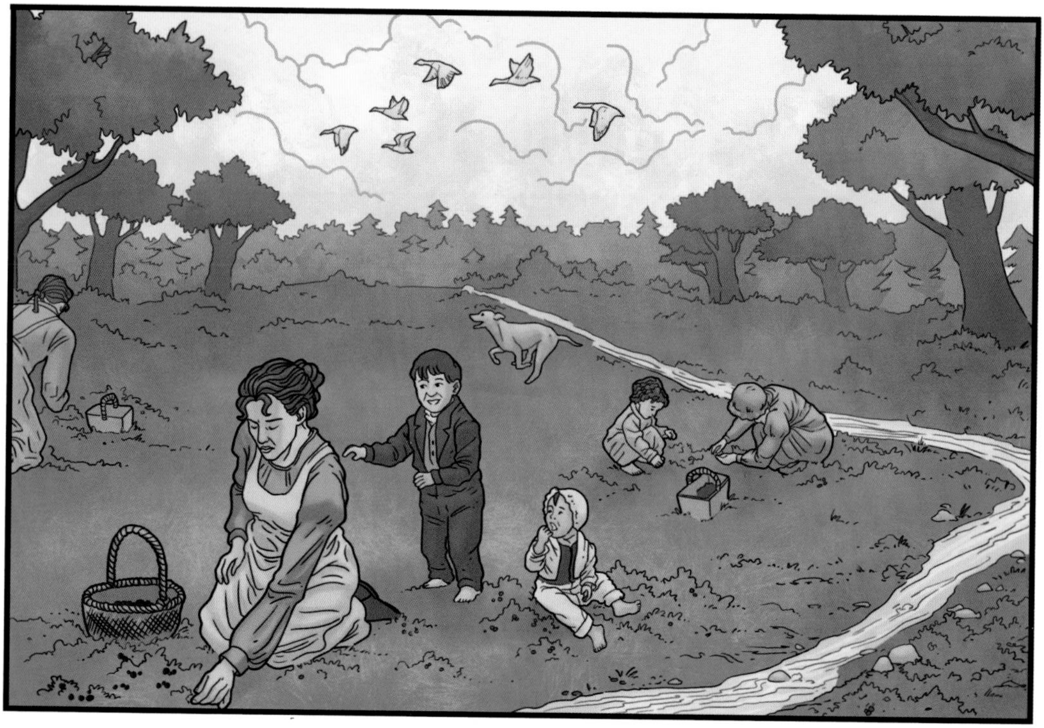

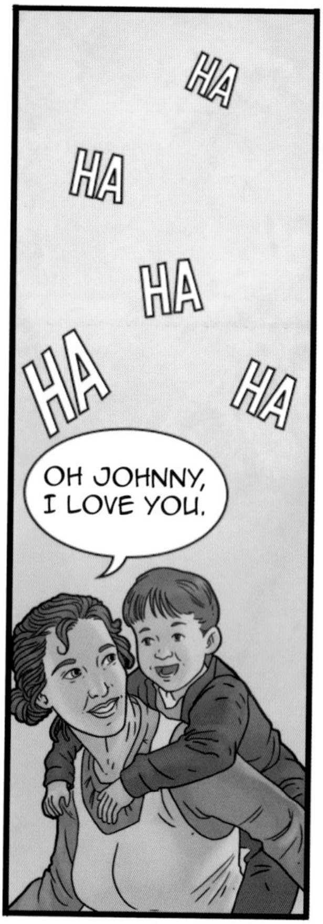

HA
HA
HA
HA
HA
OH JOHNNY, I LOVE YOU.

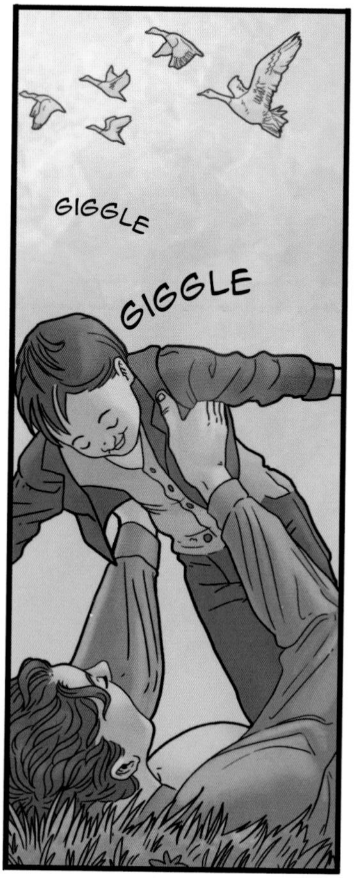

GIGGLE
GIGGLE

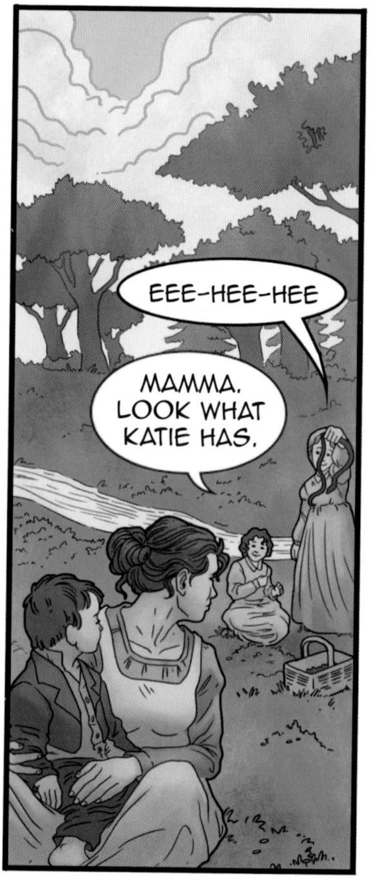

EEE-HEE-HEE
MAMMA. LOOK WHAT KATIE HAS.

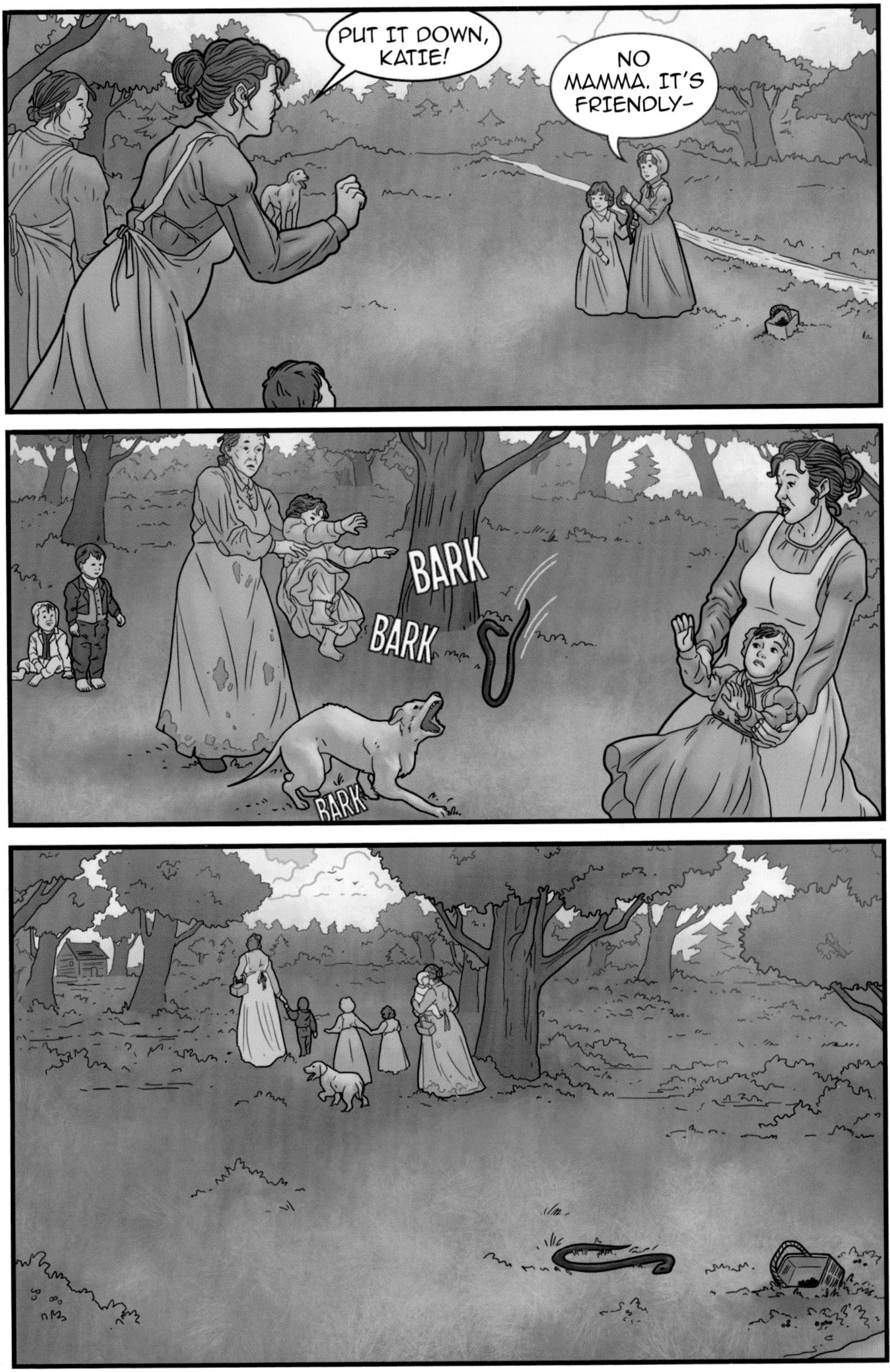
PUT IT DOWN, KATIE!
NO MAMMA. IT'S FRIENDLY-
BARK
BARK
BARK

ENERGIZED BY MY WRITING, I NO LONGER RETIRED TO BED WHEN THE LABOURS OF THE DAY WERE OVER. I SAT UP LATE, AND WROTE BY CANDLELIGHT. JENNY, THE FAITHFUL OLD CREATURE, REGARDED MY WRITINGS WITH A JAUNDICED EYE.

SCRITCH SCRITCH

JENNY, BE CAREFUL. NO, NONE FOR ME.

ALWAYS WITH THAT DIRTY WRITING.

DO YOU BELIEVE IN MAGIC, JENNY?

AYE.

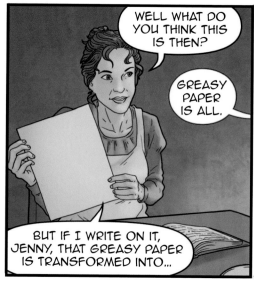

WELL WHAT DO YOU THINK THIS IS THEN?

GREASY PAPER IS ALL.

BUT IF I WRITE ON IT, JENNY, THAT GREASY PAPER IS TRANSFORMED INTO...

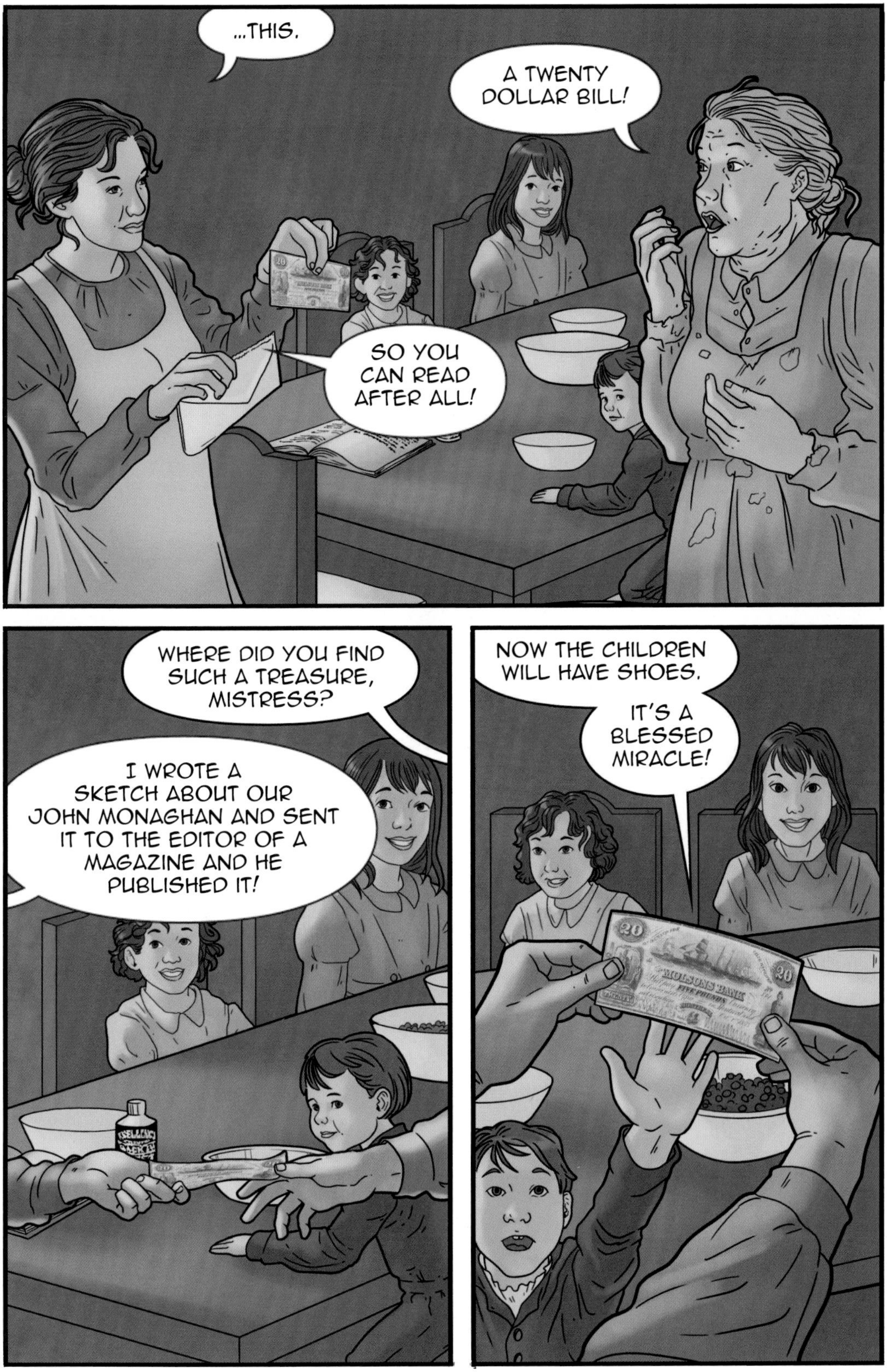
...THIS.
A TWENTY DOLLAR BILL!
SO YOU CAN READ AFTER ALL!
WHERE DID YOU FIND SUCH A TREASURE, MISTRESS?
I WROTE A SKETCH ABOUT OUR JOHN MONAGHAN AND SENT IT TO THE EDITOR OF A MAGAZINE AND HE PUBLISHED IT!
NOW THE CHILDREN WILL HAVE SHOES.
IT'S A BLESSED MIRACLE!
MOLSONS BANK

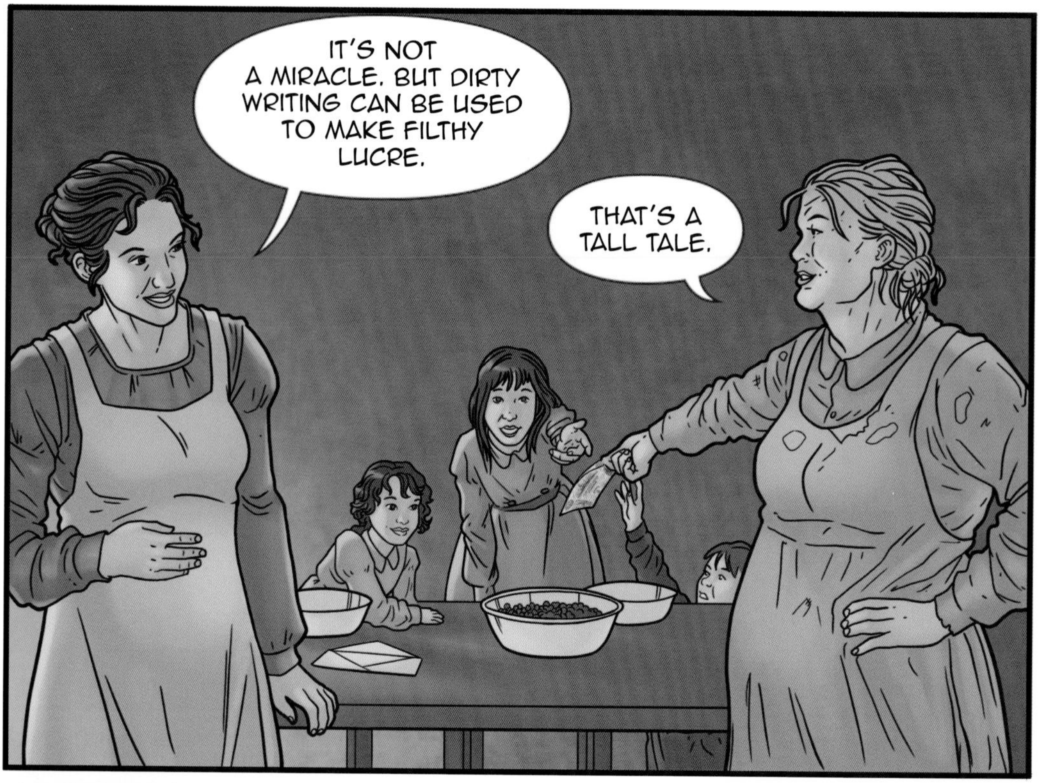
IT'S NOT A MIRACLE. BUT DIRTY WRITING CAN BE USED TO MAKE FILTHY LUCRE.
THAT'S A TALL TALE.

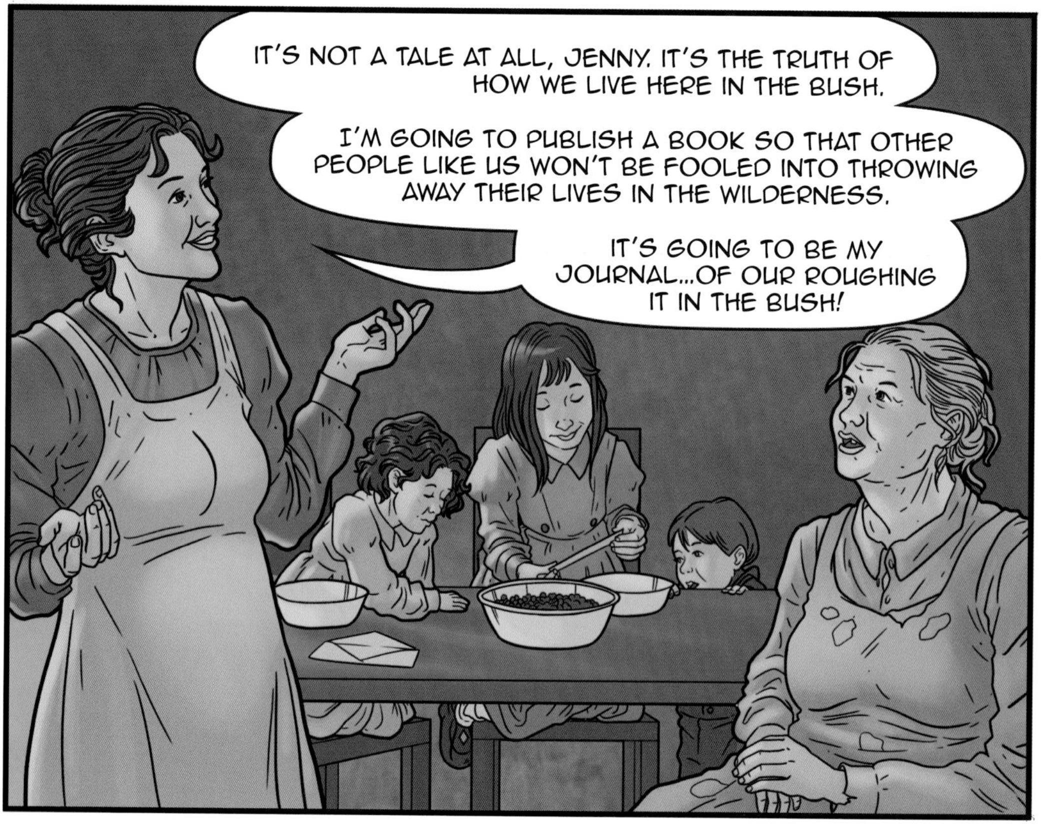
IT'S NOT A TALE AT ALL, JENNY. IT'S THE TRUTH OF HOW WE LIVE HERE IN THE BUSH.
I'M GOING TO PUBLISH A BOOK SO THAT OTHER PEOPLE LIKE US WON'T BE FOOLED INTO THROWING AWAY THEIR LIVES IN THE WILDERNESS.
IT'S GOING TO BE MY JOURNAL...OF OUR ROUGHING IT IN THE BUSH!

CHAPTER 12

TERRA INCOGNITA

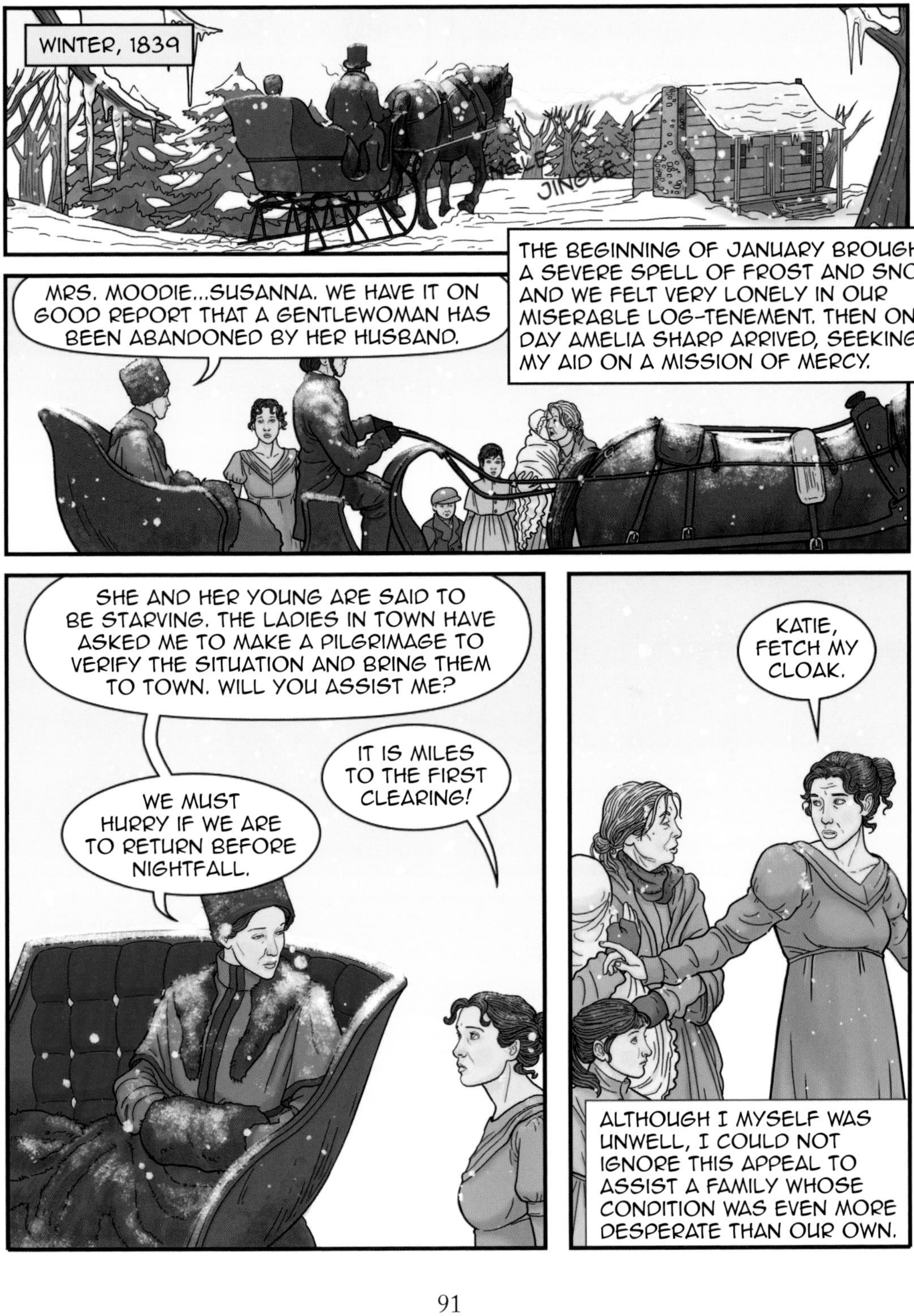

WINTER, 1839
JINGLE
JINGLE
THE BEGINNING OF JANUARY BROUGHT A SEVERE SPELL OF FROST AND SNOW AND WE FELT VERY LONELY IN OUR MISERABLE LOG-TENEMENT. THEN ONE DAY AMELIA SHARP ARRIVED, SEEKING MY AID ON A MISSION OF MERCY.
MRS. MOODIE...SUSANNA. WE HAVE IT ON GOOD REPORT THAT A GENTLEWOMAN HAS BEEN ABANDONED BY HER HUSBAND.
SHE AND HER YOUNG ARE SAID TO BE STARVING. THE LADIES IN TOWN HAVE ASKED ME TO MAKE A PILGRIMAGE TO VERIFY THE SITUATION AND BRING THEM TO TOWN. WILL YOU ASSIST ME?
IT IS MILES TO THE FIRST CLEARING!
WE MUST HURRY IF WE ARE TO RETURN BEFORE NIGHTFALL.
KATIE, FETCH MY CLOAK.
ALTHOUGH I MYSELF WAS UNWELL, I COULD NOT IGNORE THIS APPEAL TO ASSIST A FAMILY WHOSE CONDITION WAS EVEN MORE DESPERATE THAN OUR OWN.

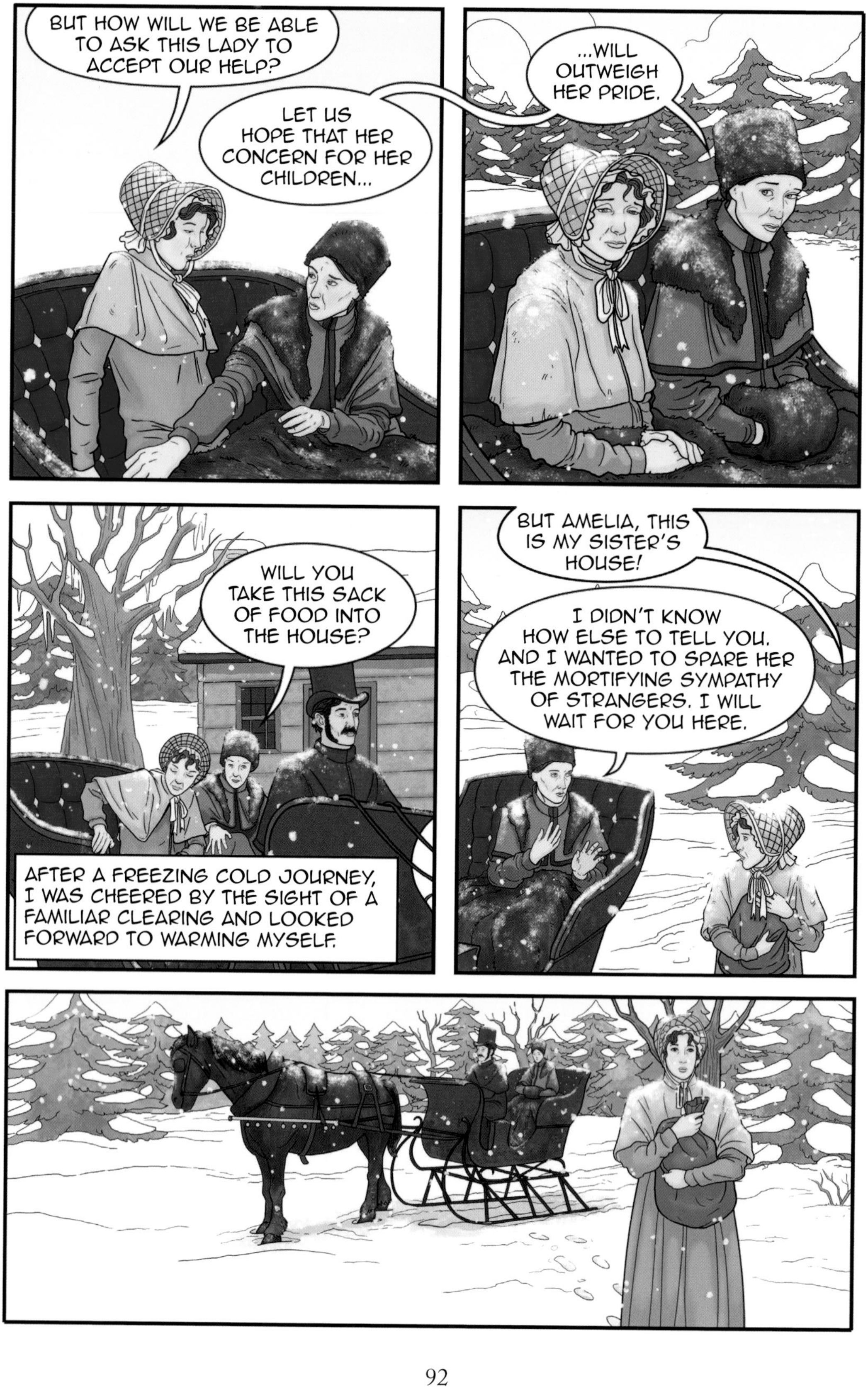
BUT HOW WILL WE BE ABLE TO ASK THIS LADY TO ACCEPT OUR HELP?
LET US HOPE THAT HER CONCERN FOR HER CHILDREN...
...WILL OUTWEIGH HER PRIDE.
WILL YOU TAKE THIS SACK OF FOOD INTO THE HOUSE?
AFTER A FREEZING COLD JOURNEY, I WAS CHEERED BY THE SIGHT OF A FAMILIAR CLEARING AND LOOKED FORWARD TO WARMING MYSELF.
BUT AMELIA, THIS IS MY SISTER'S HOUSE!
I DIDN'T KNOW HOW ELSE TO TELL YOU. AND I WANTED TO SPARE HER THE MORTIFYING SYMPATHY OF STRANGERS. I WILL WAIT FOR YOU HERE.

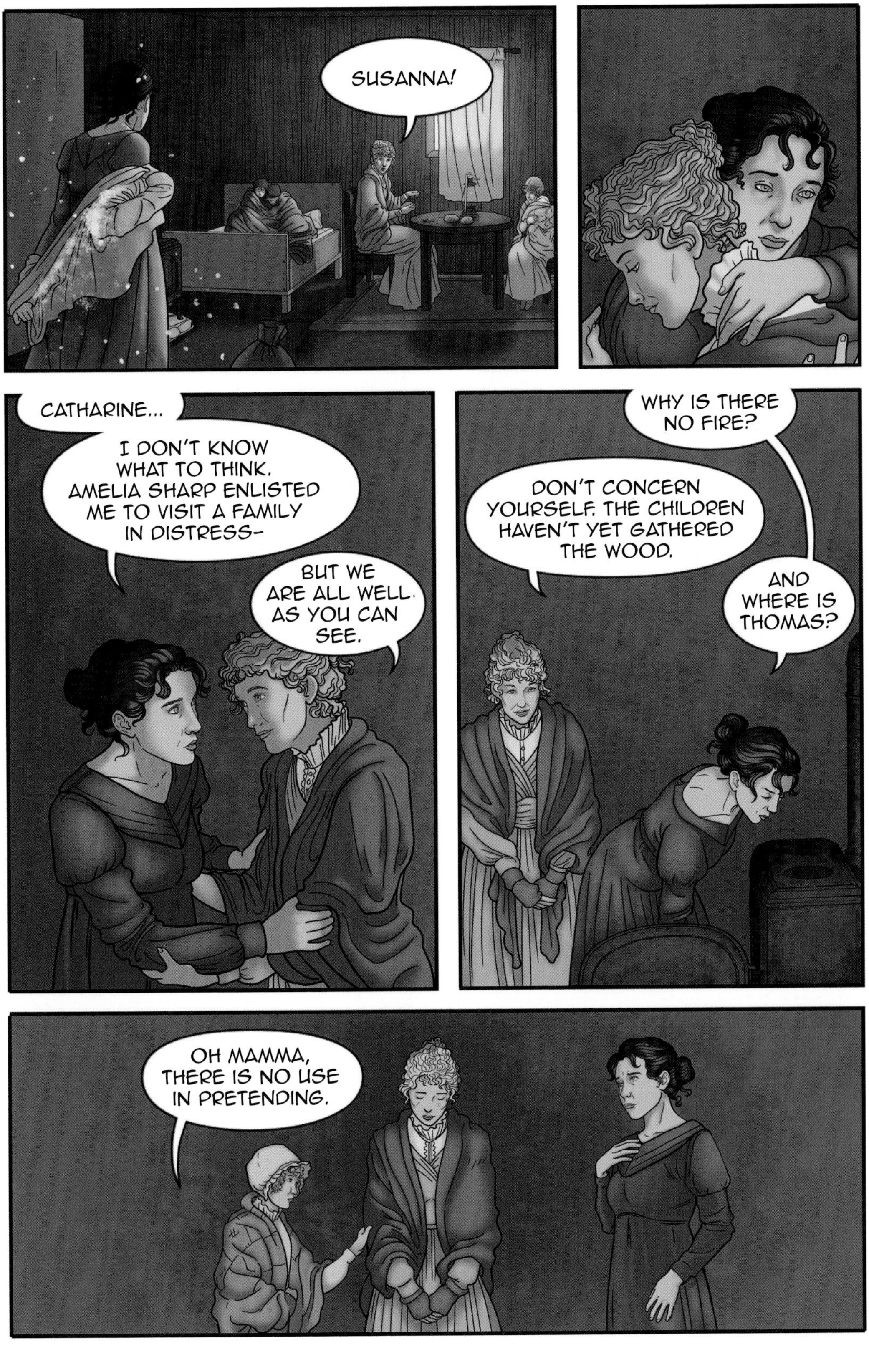
SUSANNA!
CATHARINE...
I DON'T KNOW WHAT TO THINK. AMELIA SHARP ENLISTED ME TO VISIT A FAMILY IN DISTRESS-
BUT WE ARE ALL WELL AS YOU CAN SEE.
WHY IS THERE NO FIRE?
DON'T CONCERN YOURSELF. THE CHILDREN HAVEN'T YET GATHERED THE WOOD.
AND WHERE IS THOMAS?
OH MAMMA, THERE IS NO USE IN PRETENDING.

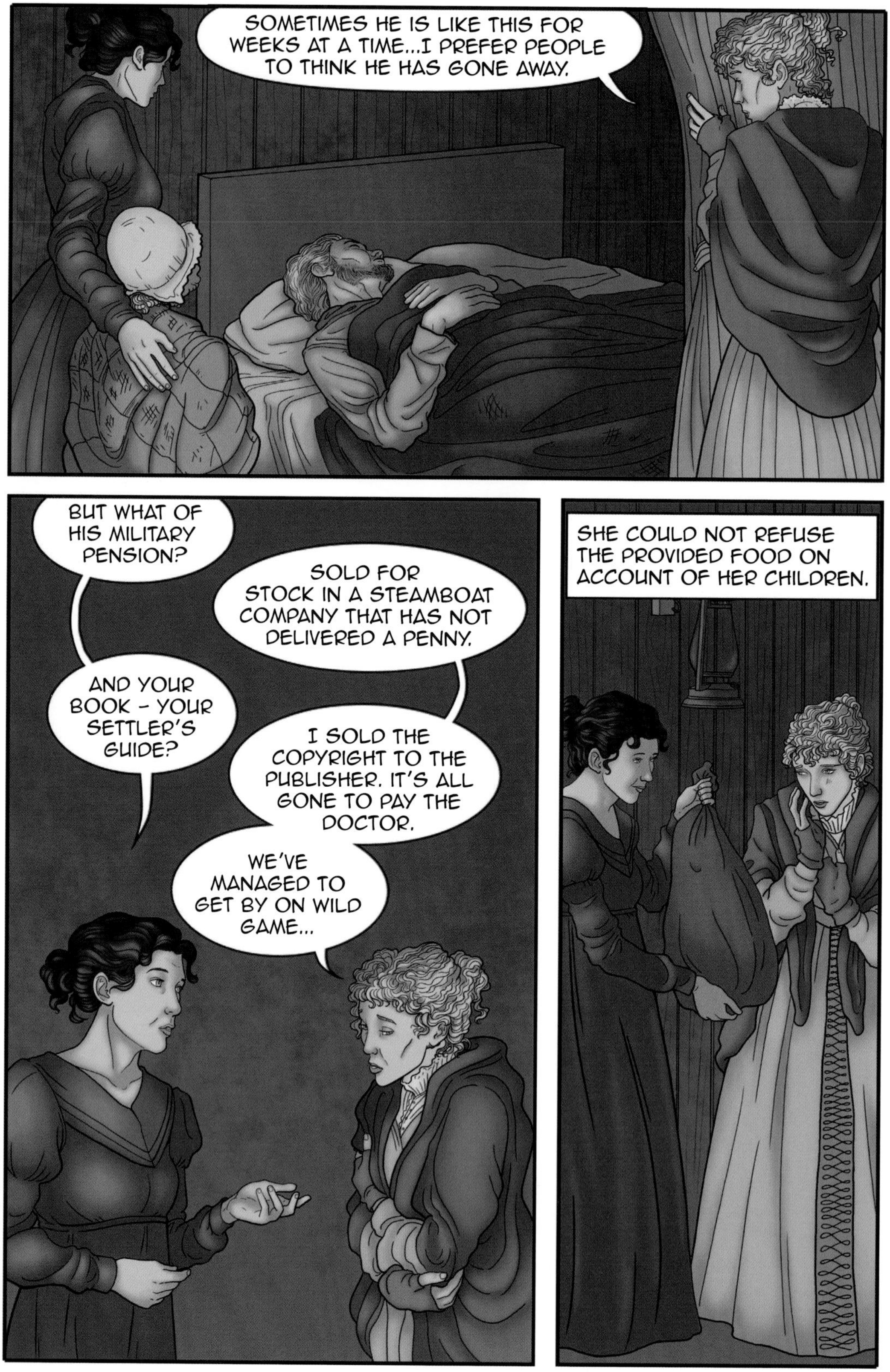
SOMETIMES HE IS LIKE THIS FOR WEEKS AT A TIME...I PREFER PEOPLE TO THINK HE HAS GONE AWAY.
BUT WHAT OF HIS MILITARY PENSION?
SOLD FOR STOCK IN A STEAMBOAT COMPANY THAT HAS NOT DELIVERED A PENNY.
AND YOUR BOOK - YOUR SETTLER'S GUIDE?
I SOLD THE COPYRIGHT TO THE PUBLISHER. IT'S ALL GONE TO PAY THE DOCTOR.
WE'VE MANAGED TO GET BY ON WILD GAME...
SHE COULD NOT REFUSE THE PROVIDED FOOD ON ACCOUNT OF HER CHILDREN.

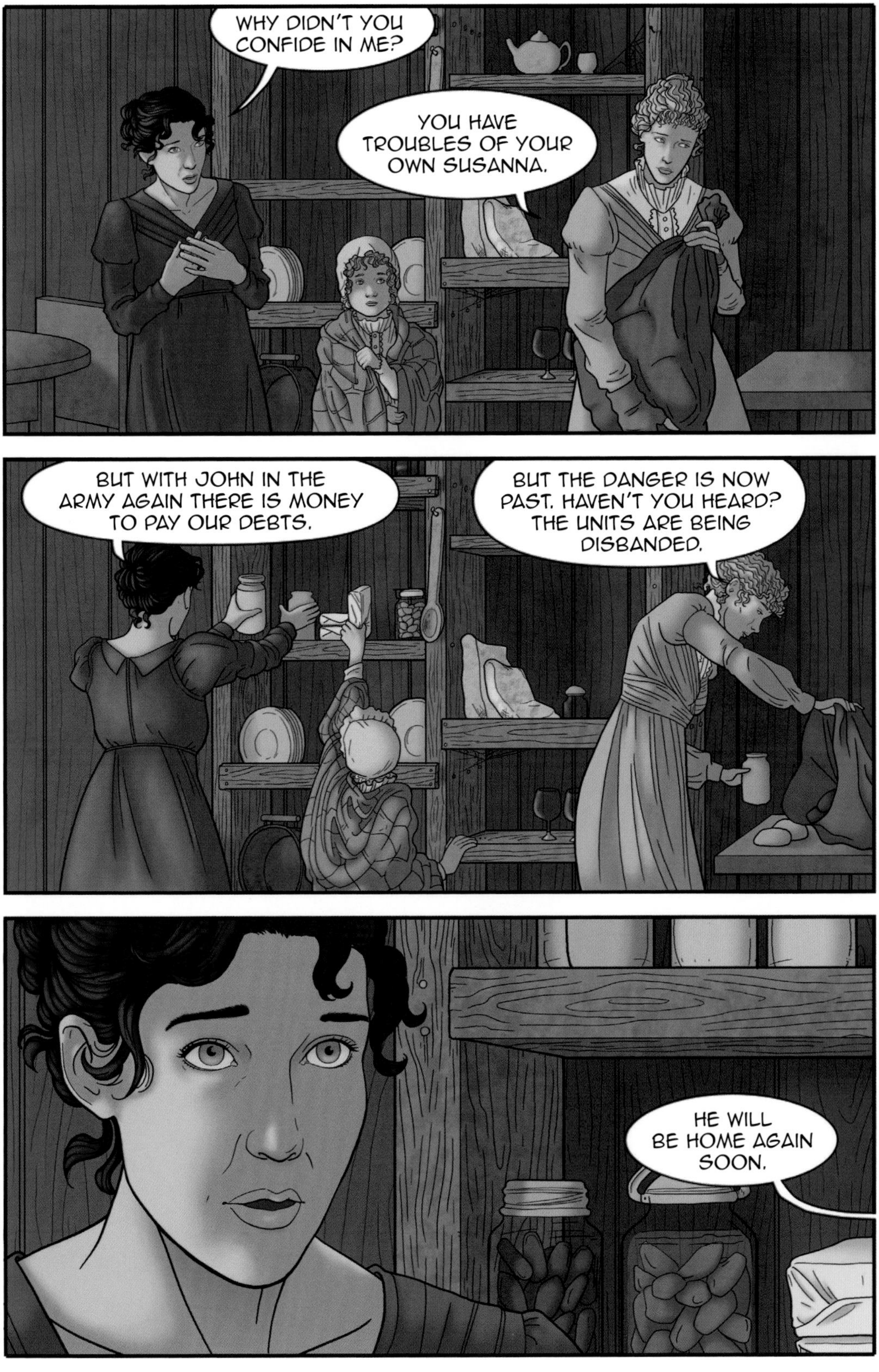
WHY DIDN'T YOU CONFIDE IN ME?
YOU HAVE TROUBLES OF YOUR OWN SUSANNA.
BUT WITH JOHN IN THE ARMY AGAIN THERE IS MONEY TO PAY OUR DEBTS.
BUT THE DANGER IS NOW PAST. HAVEN'T YOU HEARD? THE UNITS ARE BEING DISBANDED.
HE WILL BE HOME AGAIN SOON.

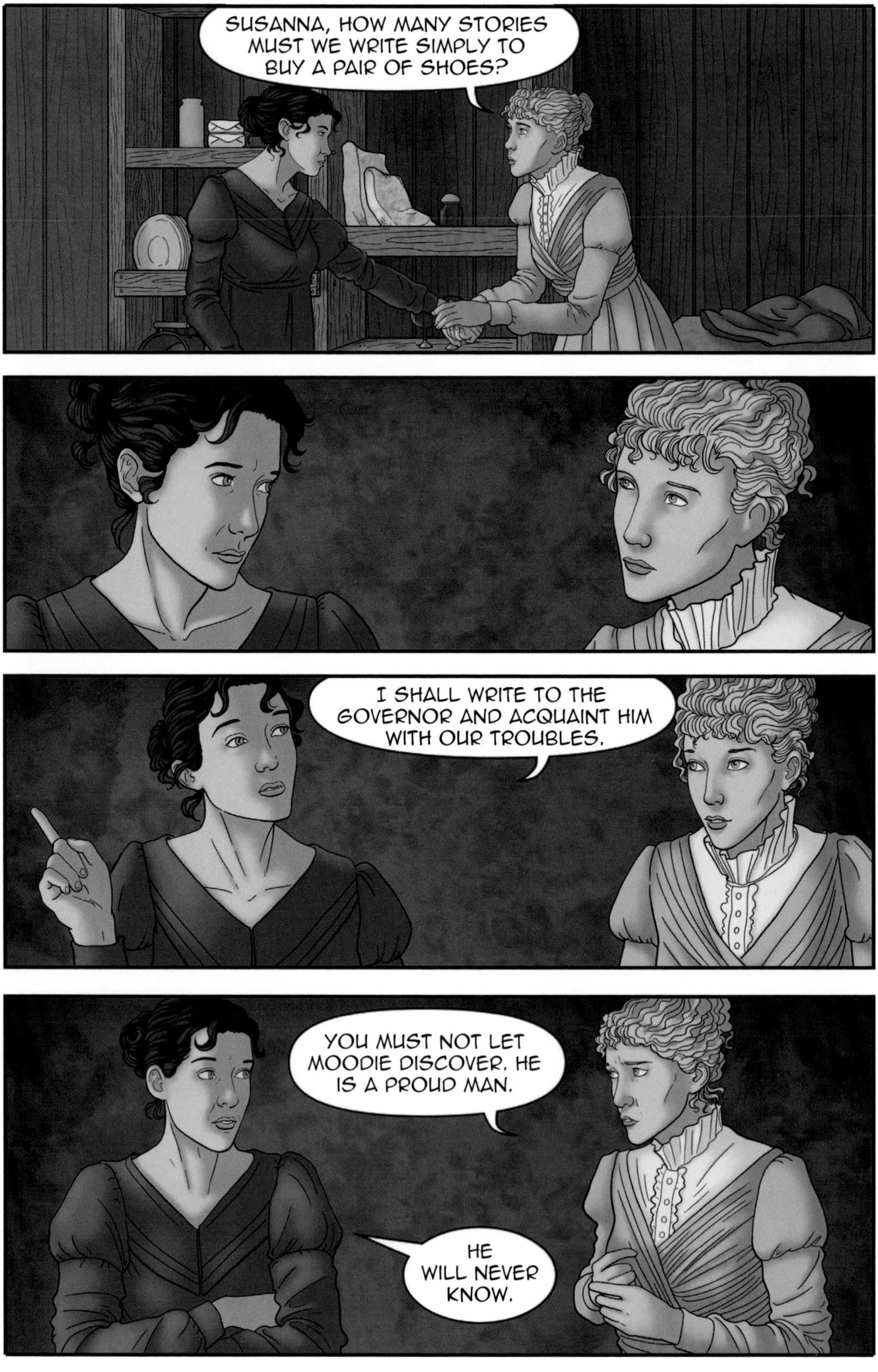
SUSANNA, HOW MANY STORIES MUST WE WRITE SIMPLY TO BUY A PAIR OF SHOES?
I SHALL WRITE TO THE GOVERNOR AND ACQUAINT HIM WITH OUR TROUBLES.
YOU MUST NOT LET MOODIE DISCOVER. HE IS A PROUD MAN.
HE WILL NEVER KNOW.

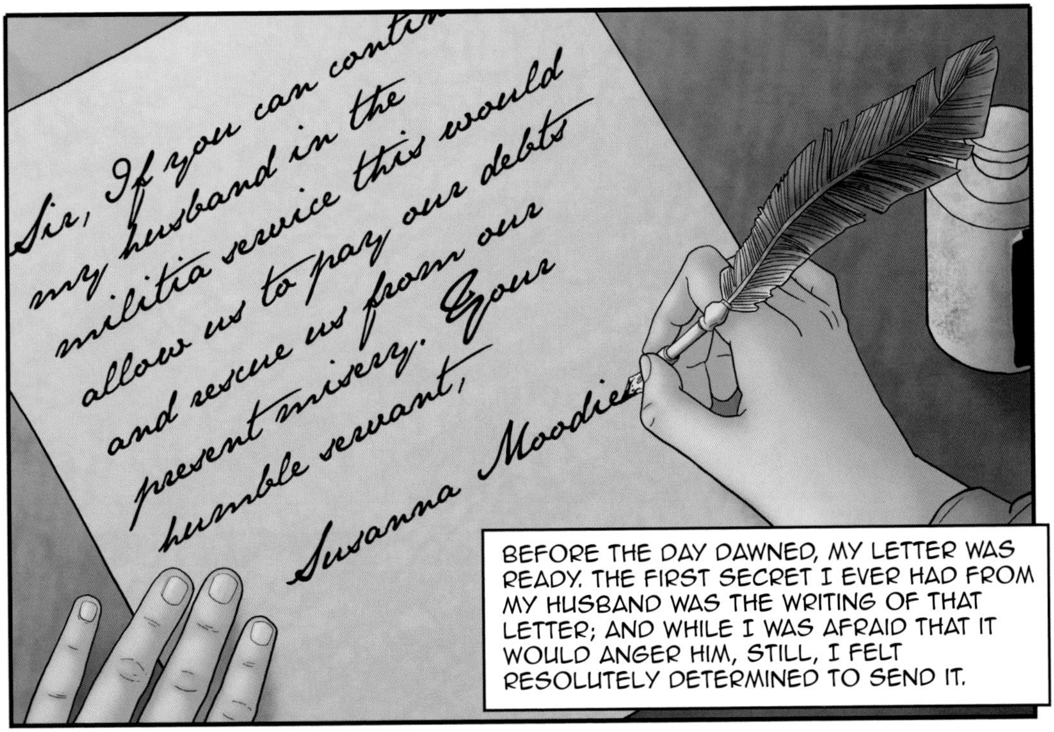
Sir, If you can contin
my husband in the
militia service this would
allow us to pay our debts
and rescue us from our
present misery. Your
humble servant,
Susanna Moodie
BEFORE THE DAY DAWNED, MY LETTER WAS READY. THE FIRST SECRET I EVER HAD FROM MY HUSBAND WAS THE WRITING OF THAT LETTER; AND WHILE I WAS AFRAID THAT IT WOULD ANGER HIM, STILL, I FELT RESOLUTELY DETERMINED TO SEND IT.

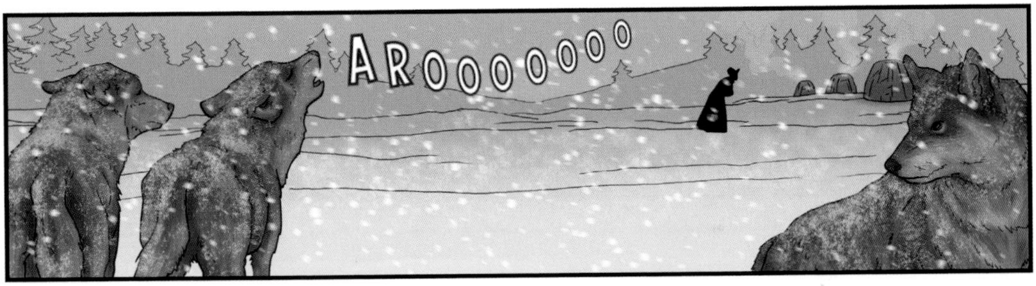
AROOOOOOO

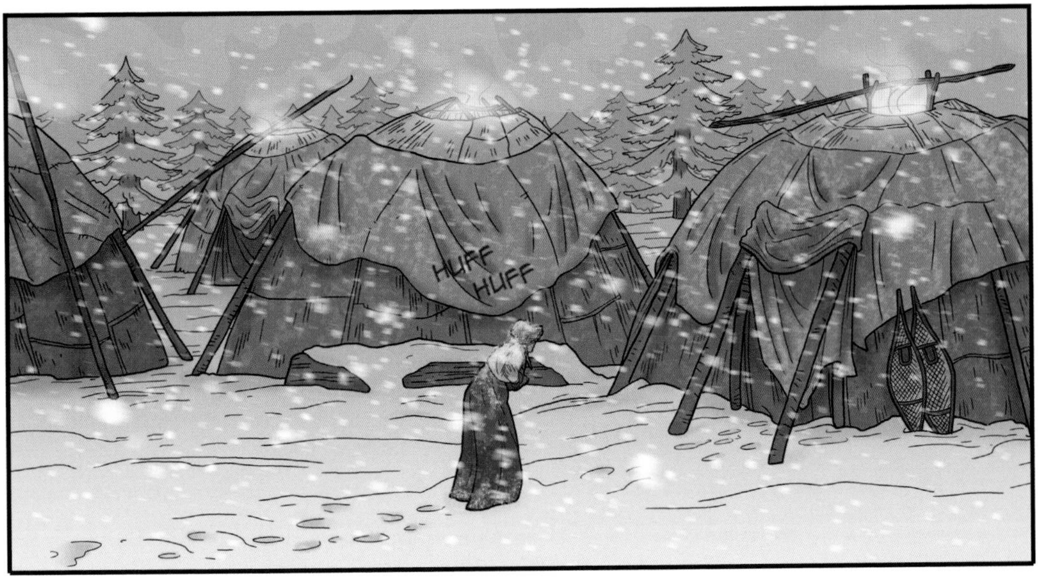
HUFF
HUFF

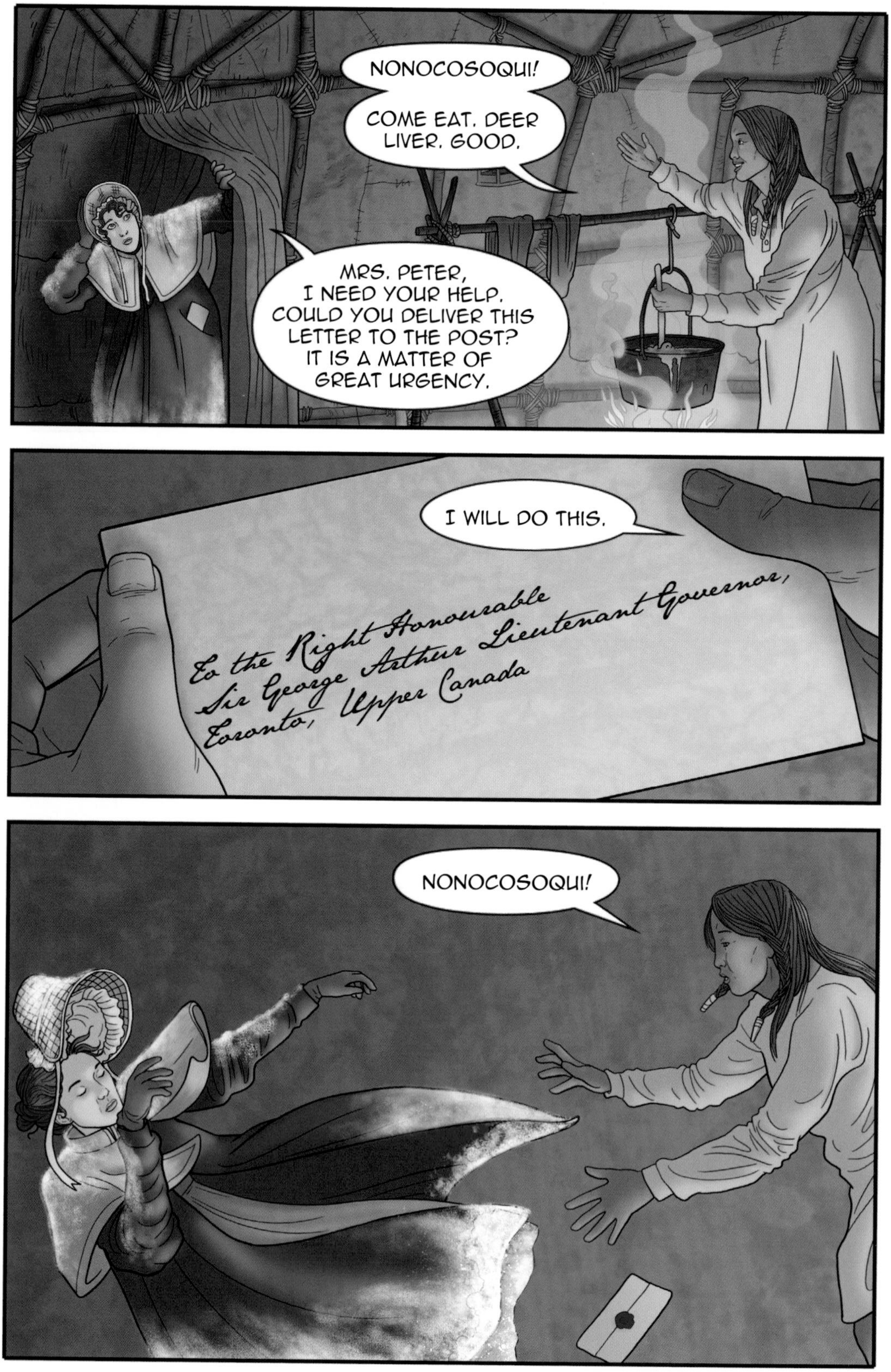
NONOCOSOQUI!
COME EAT. DEER LIVER. GOOD.
MRS. PETER, I NEED YOUR HELP. COULD YOU DELIVER THIS LETTER TO THE POST? IT IS A MATTER OF GREAT URGENCY.
I WILL DO THIS.
To the Right Honourable
Sir George Arthur Lieutenant Governor,
Toronto, Upper Canada
NONOCOSOQUI!

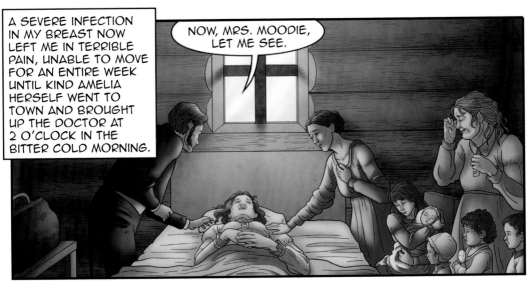

A SEVERE INFECTION IN MY BREAST NOW LEFT ME IN TERRIBLE PAIN, UNABLE TO MOVE FOR AN ENTIRE WEEK UNTIL KIND AMELIA HERSELF WENT TO TOWN AND BROUGHT UP THE DOCTOR AT 2 O'CLOCK IN THE BITTER COLD MORNING.

NOW, MRS. MOODIE, LET ME SEE.

GHASP!

HOW LONG HAS IT BEEN LIKE THIS?

SHE HASN'T MOVED IN A WEEK, LIKE A CRUSHED SNAKE.

SEND THE CHILDREN FROM THE ROOM.

COME ALONG, LET'S COLLECT SOME CEDAR CHIPS FOR THE FIRE.

IS THERE ANY WHISKEY?

NOT A DROP IN THE HOUSE.

THEN GIVE HER SOMETHING TO BITE ON.

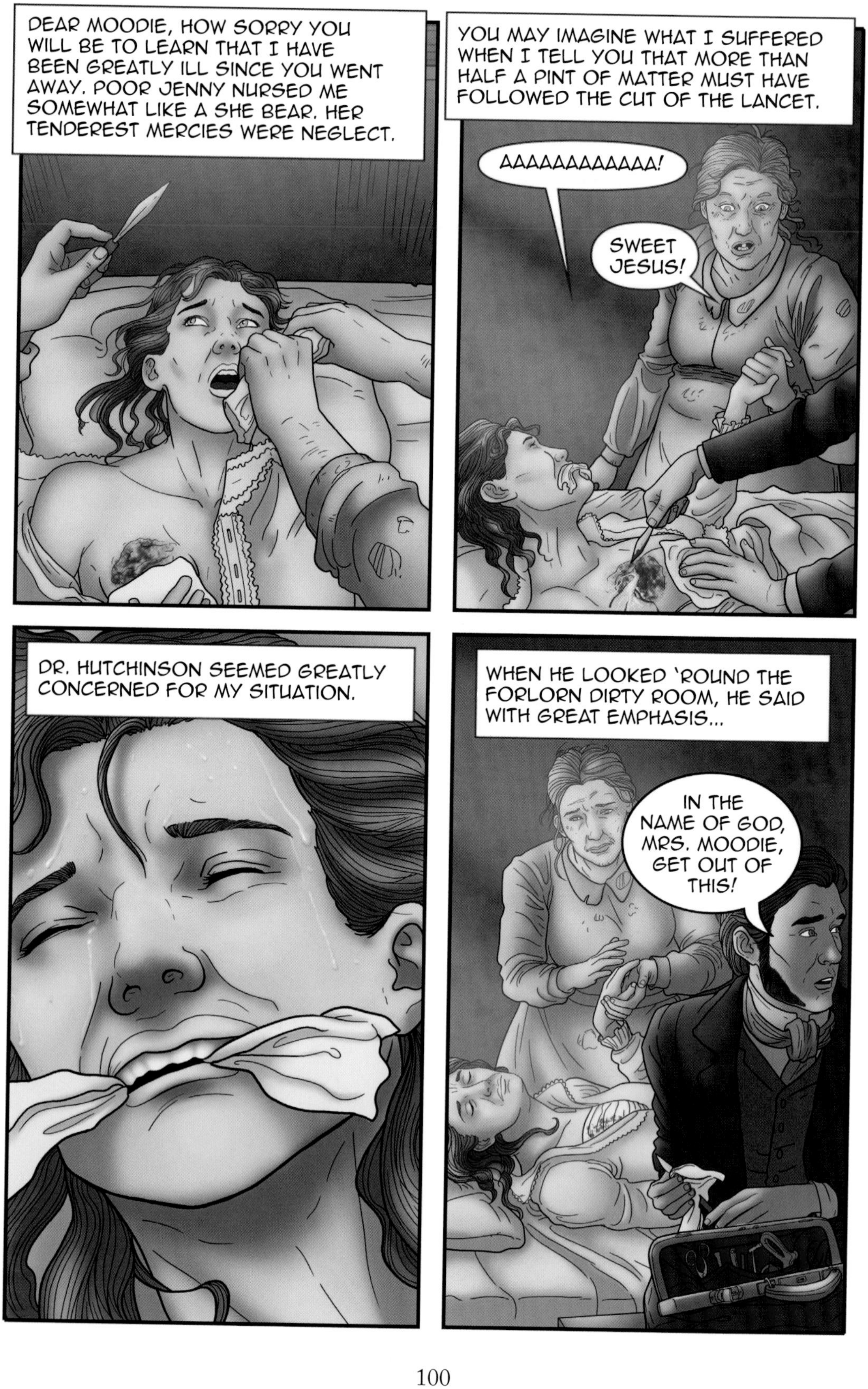
DEAR MOODIE, HOW SORRY YOU WILL BE TO LEARN THAT I HAVE BEEN GREATLY ILL SINCE YOU WENT AWAY. POOR JENNY NURSED ME SOMEWHAT LIKE A SHE BEAR. HER TENDEREST MERCIES WERE NEGLECT.
YOU MAY IMAGINE WHAT I SUFFERED WHEN I TELL YOU THAT MORE THAN HALF A PINT OF MATTER MUST HAVE FOLLOWED THE CUT OF THE LANCET.
AAAAAAAAAAAA!
SWEET JESUS!
DR. HUTCHINSON SEEMED GREATLY CONCERNED FOR MY SITUATION.
WHEN HE LOOKED 'ROUND THE FORLORN DIRTY ROOM, HE SAID WITH GREAT EMPHASIS...
IN THE NAME OF GOD, MRS. MOODIE, GET OUT OF THIS!

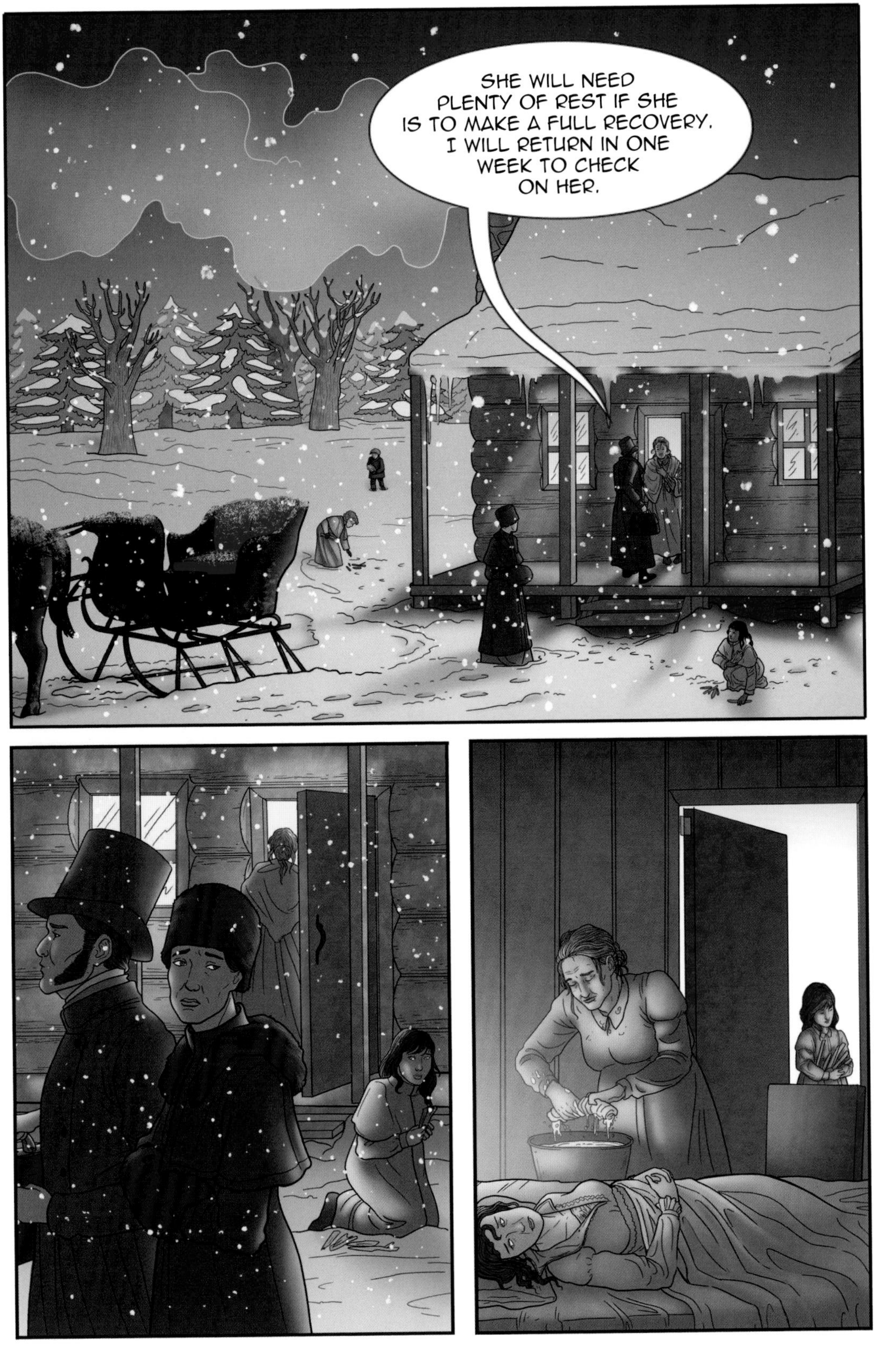
SHE WILL NEED PLENTY OF REST IF SHE IS TO MAKE A FULL RECOVERY. I WILL RETURN IN ONE WEEK TO CHECK ON HER.

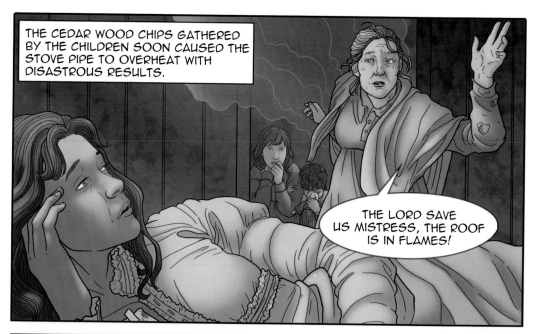

THE CEDAR WOOD CHIPS GATHERED BY THE CHILDREN SOON CAUSED THE STOVE PIPE TO OVERHEAT WITH DISASTROUS RESULTS.

THE LORD SAVE US MISTRESS, THE ROOF IS IN FLAMES!

IT IS ALL ABLAZE NOW! WHAT SHALL WE DO?

GO AND FETCH MONAGHAN AT THE LUMBER CAMP!

KATIE, WE MUST SAVE WHAT WE CAN. TAKE THE BEDDING OUTSIDE.

BRING THE POTATOES!

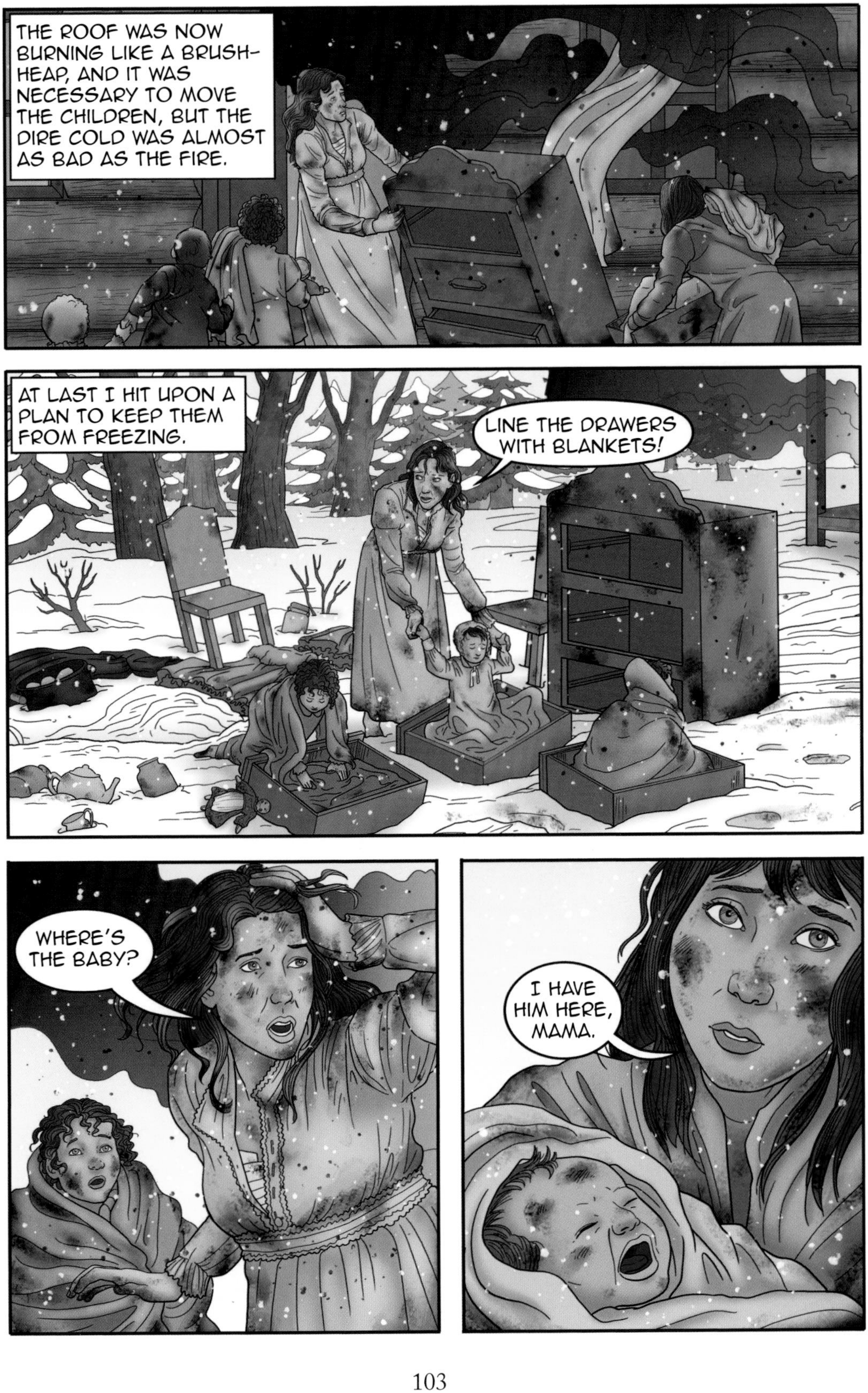
THE ROOF WAS NOW BURNING LIKE A BRUSH-HEAP, AND IT WAS NECESSARY TO MOVE THE CHILDREN, BUT THE DIRE COLD WAS ALMOST AS BAD AS THE FIRE.
AT LAST I HIT UPON A PLAN TO KEEP THEM FROM FREEZING.
LINE THE DRAWERS WITH BLANKETS!
WHERE'S THE BABY?
I HAVE HIM HERE, MAMA.

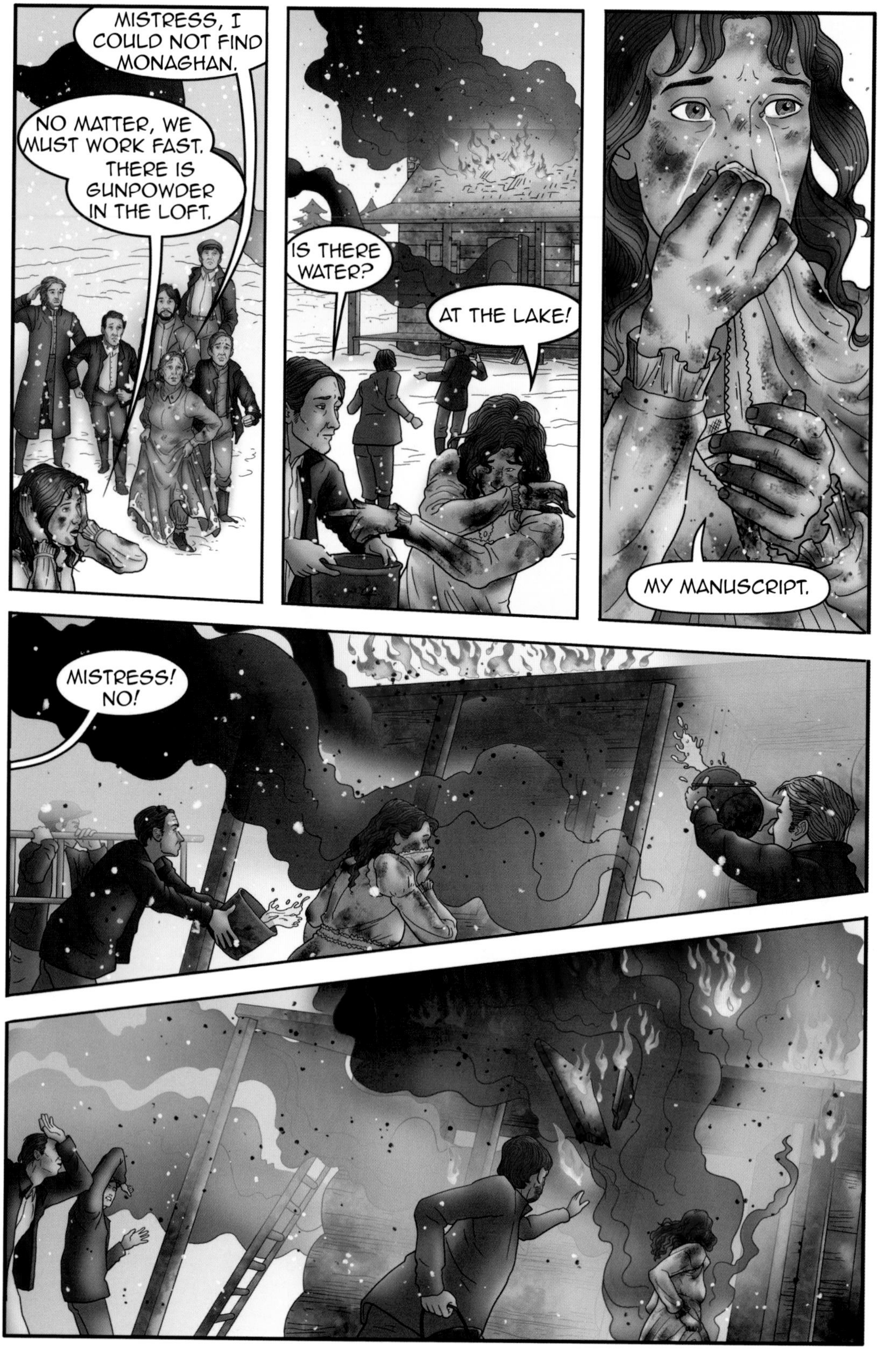
MISTRESS, I COULD NOT FIND MONAGHAN.
NO MATTER, WE MUST WORK FAST.
THERE IS GUNPOWDER IN THE LOFT.
IS THERE WATER?
AT THE LAKE!
MY MANUSCRIPT.
MISTRESS! NO!

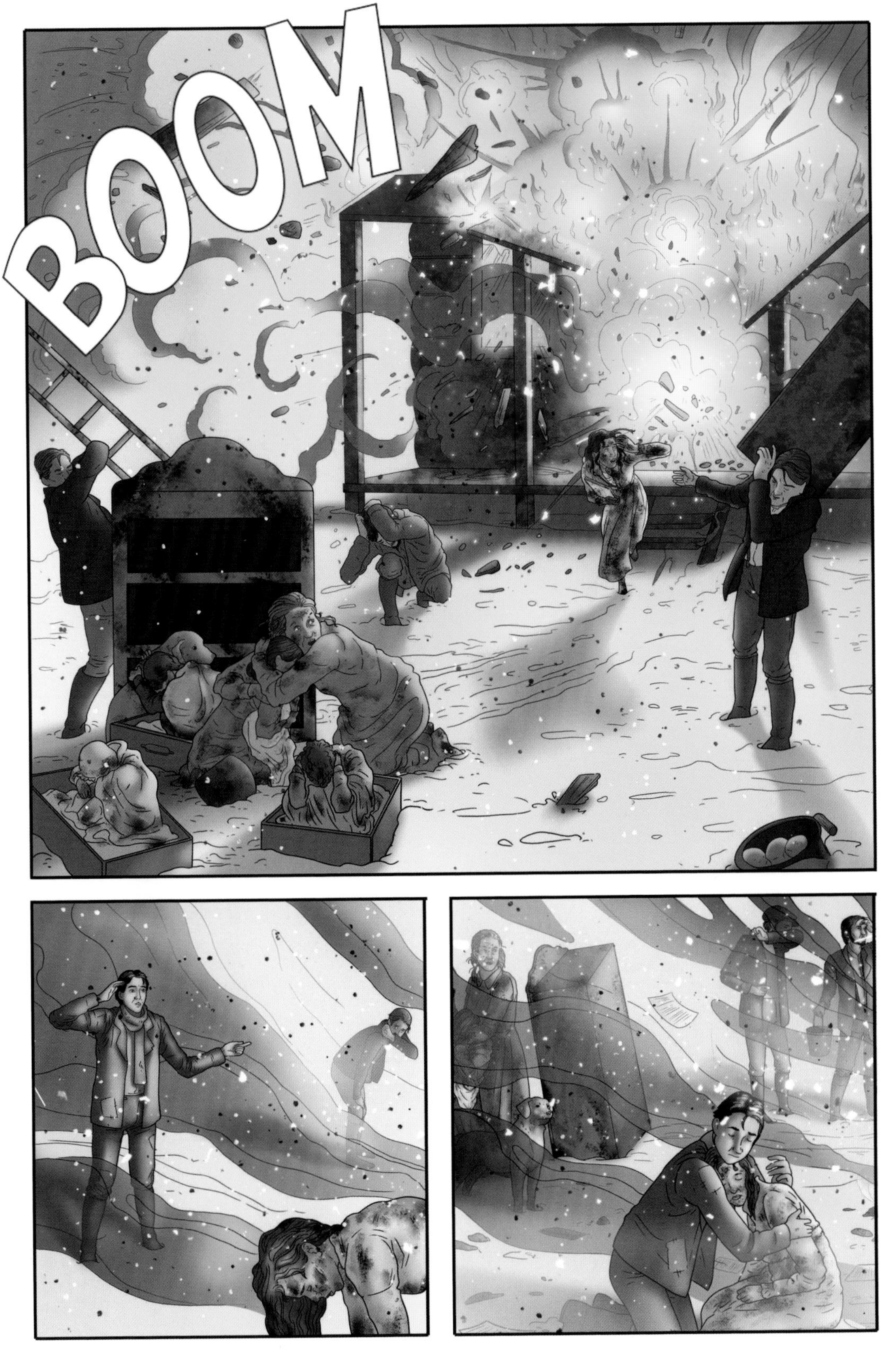
BOOM

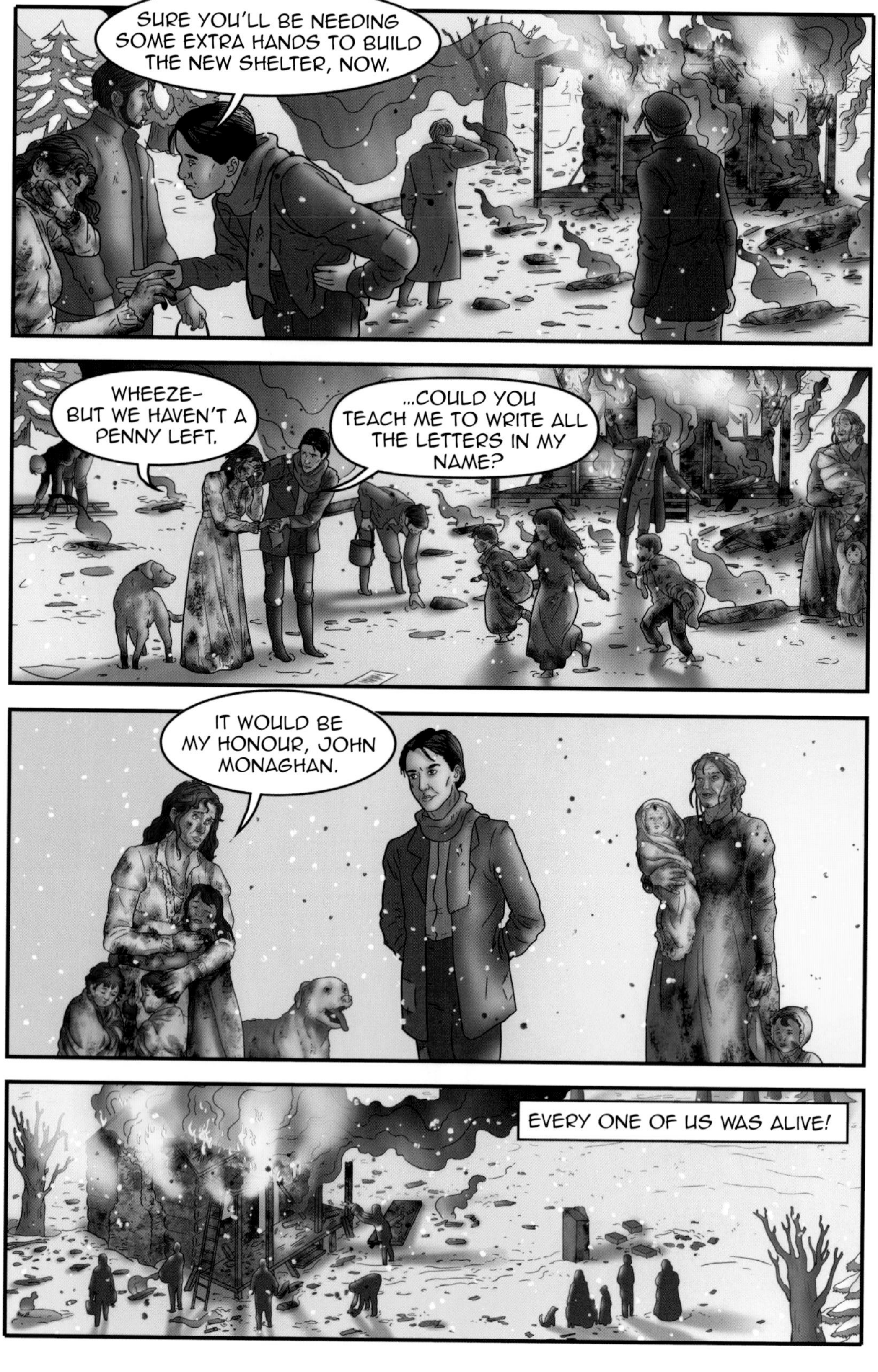
SURE YOU'LL BE NEEDING SOME EXTRA HANDS TO BUILD THE NEW SHELTER, NOW.
WHEEZE- BUT WE HAVEN'T A PENNY LEFT.
...COULD YOU TEACH ME TO WRITE ALL THE LETTERS IN MY NAME?
IT WOULD BE MY HONOUR, JOHN MONAGHAN.
EVERY ONE OF US WAS ALIVE!

CHAPTER 13

HOMECOMING

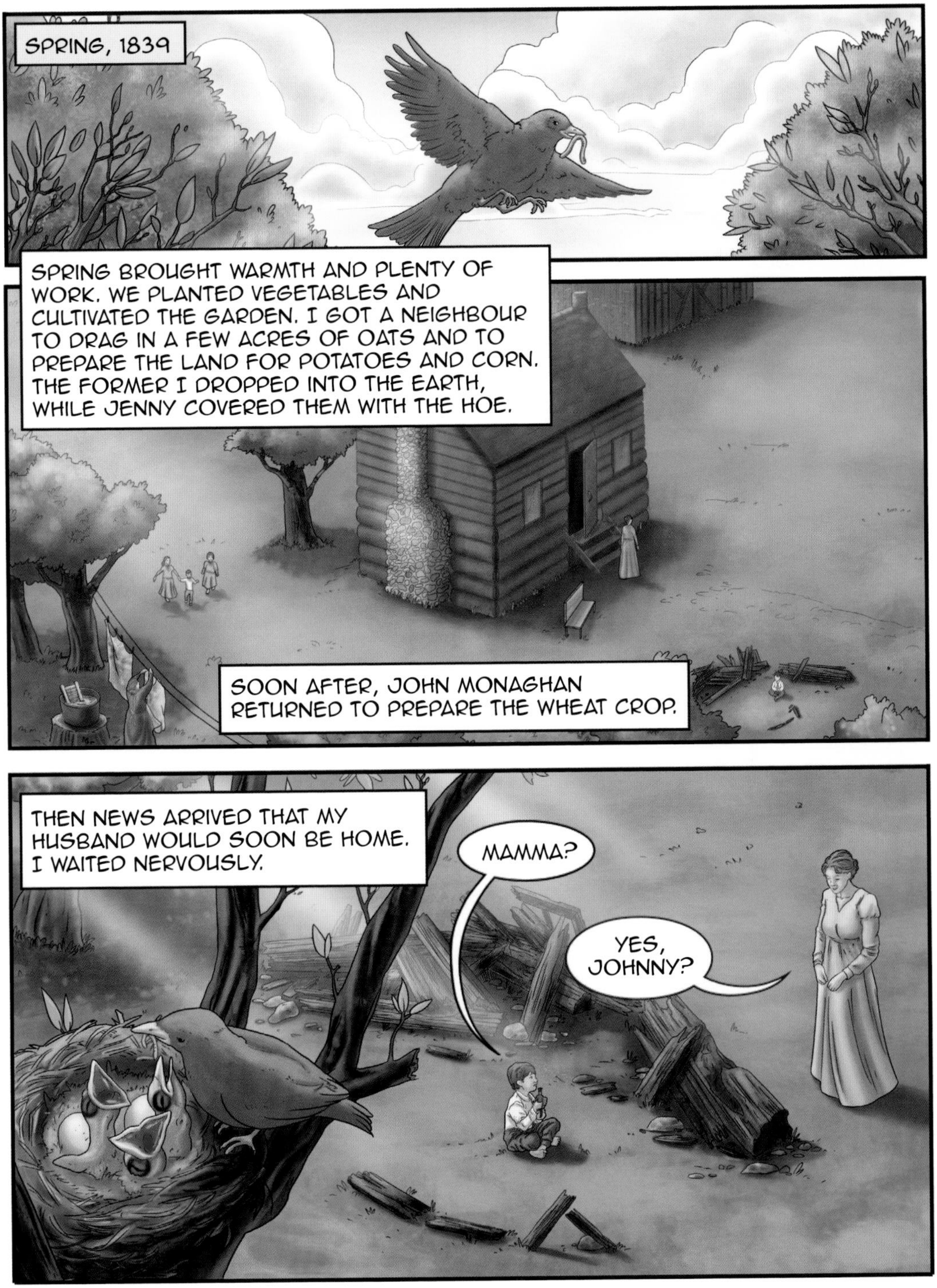
SPRING, 1839
SPRING BROUGHT WARMTH AND PLENTY OF WORK. WE PLANTED VEGETABLES AND CULTIVATED THE GARDEN. I GOT A NEIGHBOUR TO DRAG IN A FEW ACRES OF OATS AND TO PREPARE THE LAND FOR POTATOES AND CORN. THE FORMER I DROPPED INTO THE EARTH, WHILE JENNY COVERED THEM WITH THE HOE.
SOON AFTER, JOHN MONAGHAN RETURNED TO PREPARE THE WHEAT CROP.
THEN NEWS ARRIVED THAT MY HUSBAND WOULD SOON BE HOME. I WAITED NERVOUSLY.
MAMMA?
YES, JOHNNY?

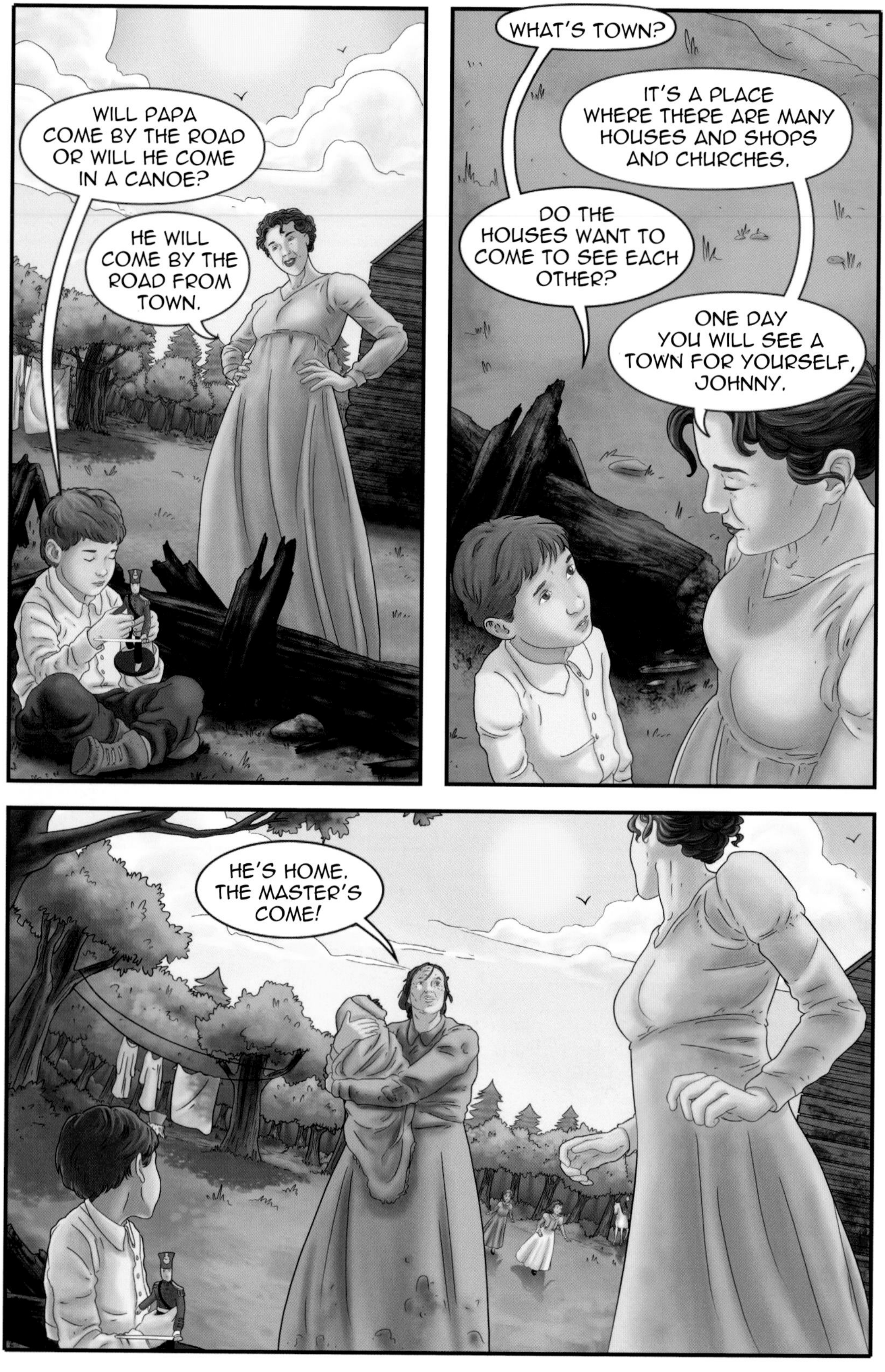
WILL PAPA COME BY THE ROAD OR WILL HE COME IN A CANOE?
HE WILL COME BY THE ROAD FROM TOWN.
WHAT'S TOWN?
IT'S A PLACE WHERE THERE ARE MANY HOUSES AND SHOPS AND CHURCHES.
DO THE HOUSES WANT TO COME TO SEE EACH OTHER?
ONE DAY YOU WILL SEE A TOWN FOR YOURSELF, JOHNNY.
HE'S HOME. THE MASTER'S COME!

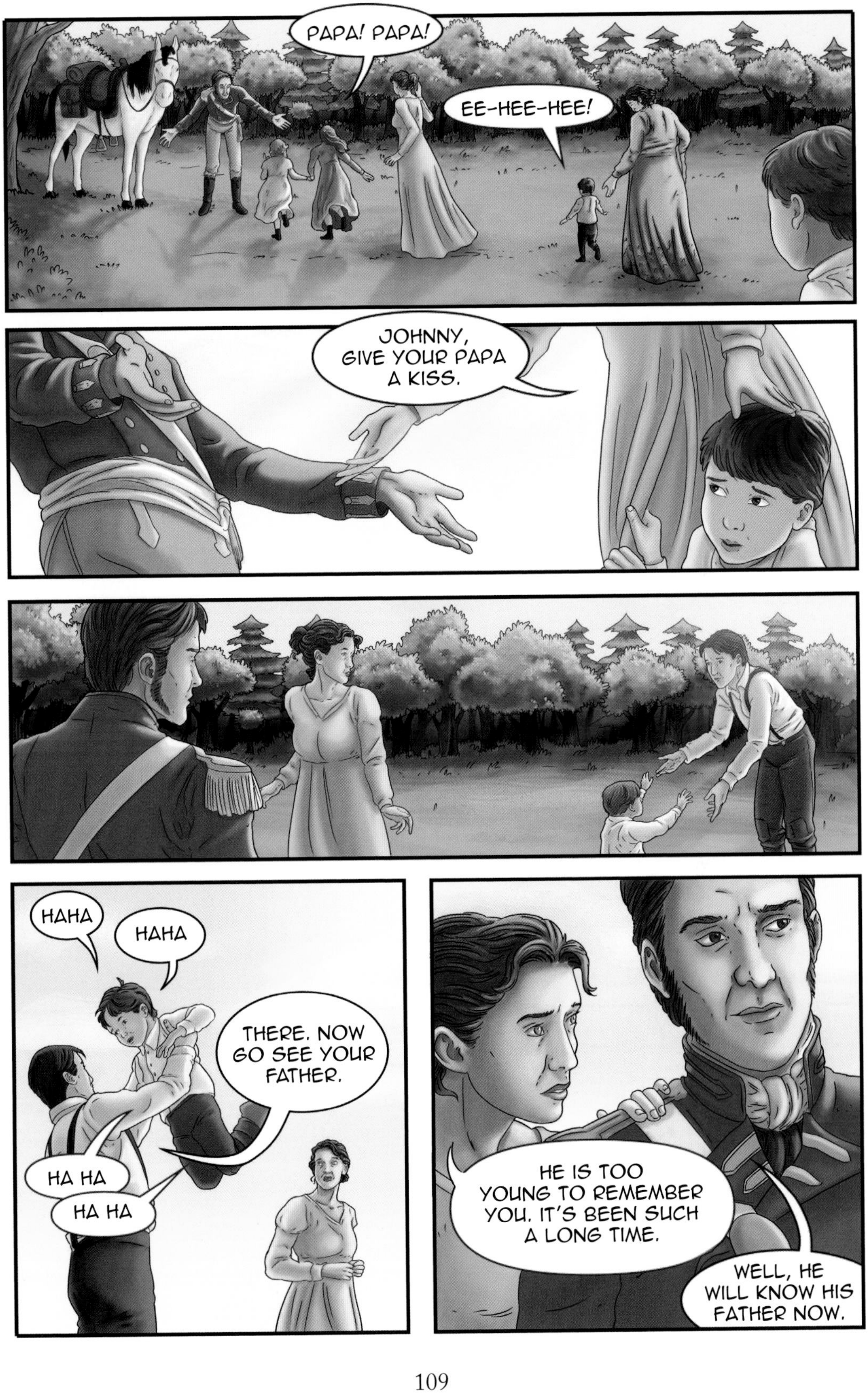

PAPA! PAPA!
EE-HEE-HEE!
JOHNNY, GIVE YOUR PAPA A KISS.
HAHA
HAHA
THERE. NOW GO SEE YOUR FATHER.
HA HA
HA HA
HE IS TOO YOUNG TO REMEMBER YOU. IT'S BEEN SUCH A LONG TIME.
WELL, HE WILL KNOW HIS FATHER NOW.

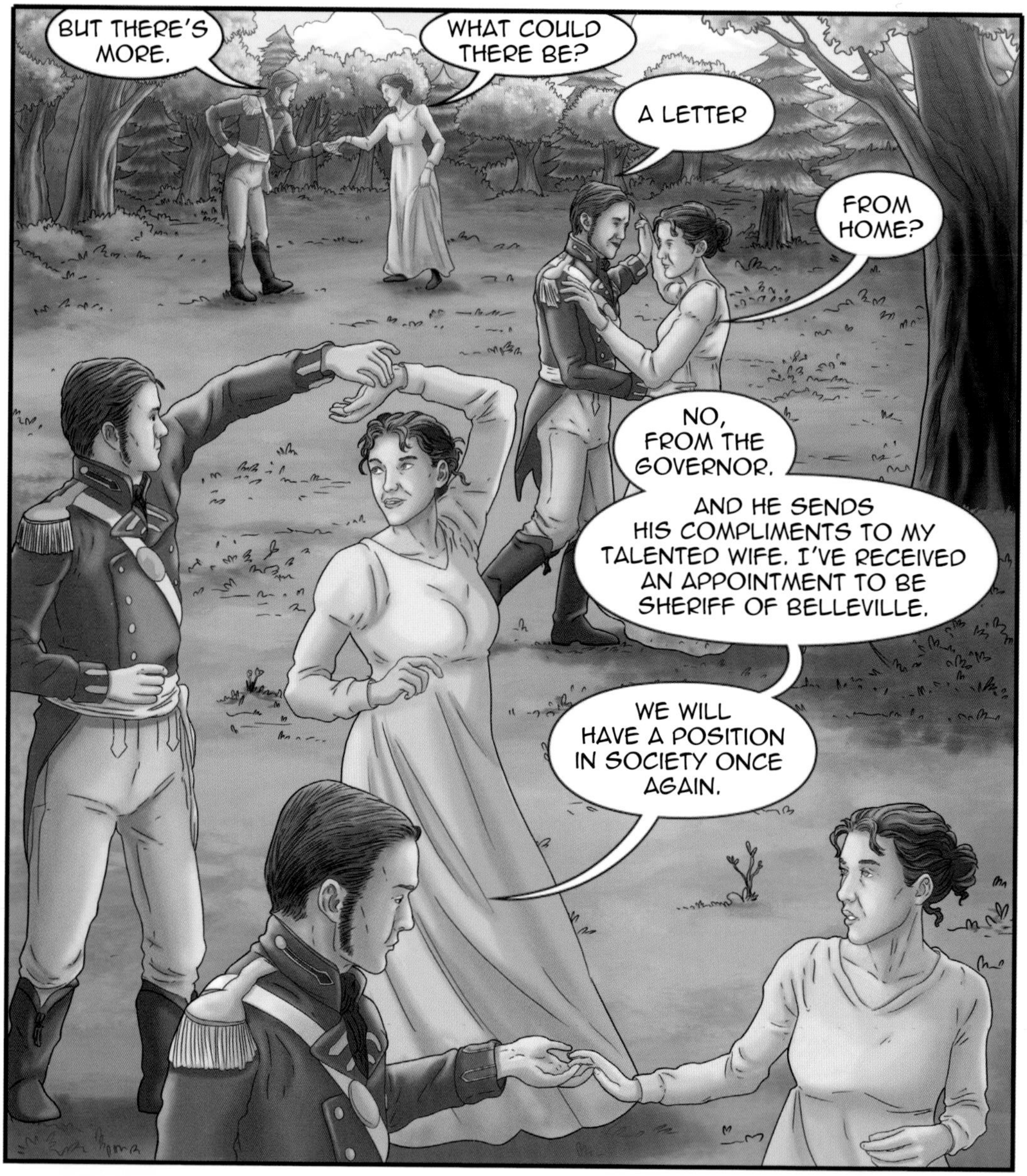
BUT THERE'S MORE.
WHAT COULD THERE BE?
A LETTER
FROM HOME?
NO, FROM THE GOVERNOR.
AND HE SENDS HIS COMPLIMENTS TO MY TALENTED WIFE. I'VE RECEIVED AN APPOINTMENT TO BE SHERIFF OF BELLEVILLE.
WE WILL HAVE A POSITION IN SOCIETY ONCE AGAIN.

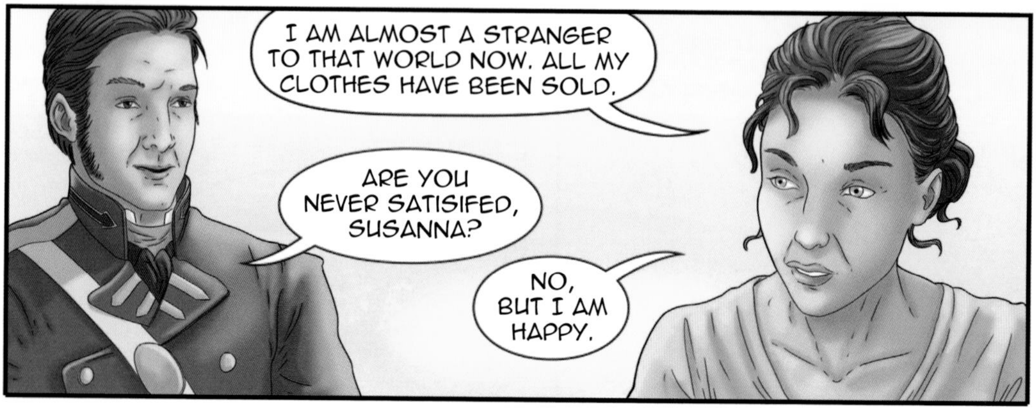
I AM ALMOST A STRANGER TO THAT WORLD NOW. ALL MY CLOTHES HAVE BEEN SOLD.
ARE YOU NEVER SATISIFED, SUSANNA?
NO, BUT I AM HAPPY.

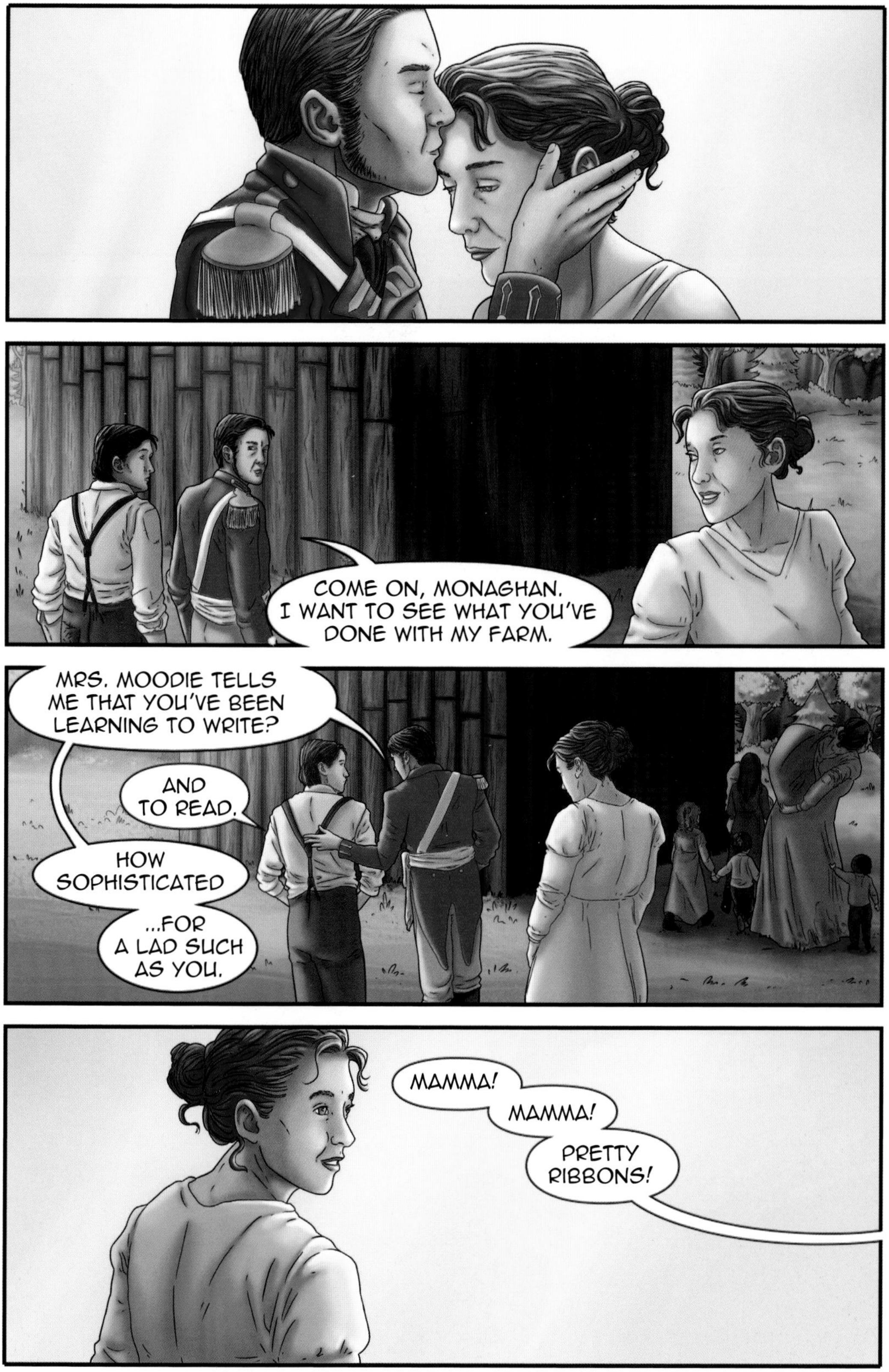
COME ON, MONAGHAN. I WANT TO SEE WHAT YOU'VE DONE WITH MY FARM.
MRS. MOODIE TELLS ME THAT YOU'VE BEEN LEARNING TO WRITE?
AND TO READ.
HOW SOPHISTICATED
...FOR A LAD SUCH AS YOU.
MAMMA!
MAMMA!
PRETTY RIBBONS!

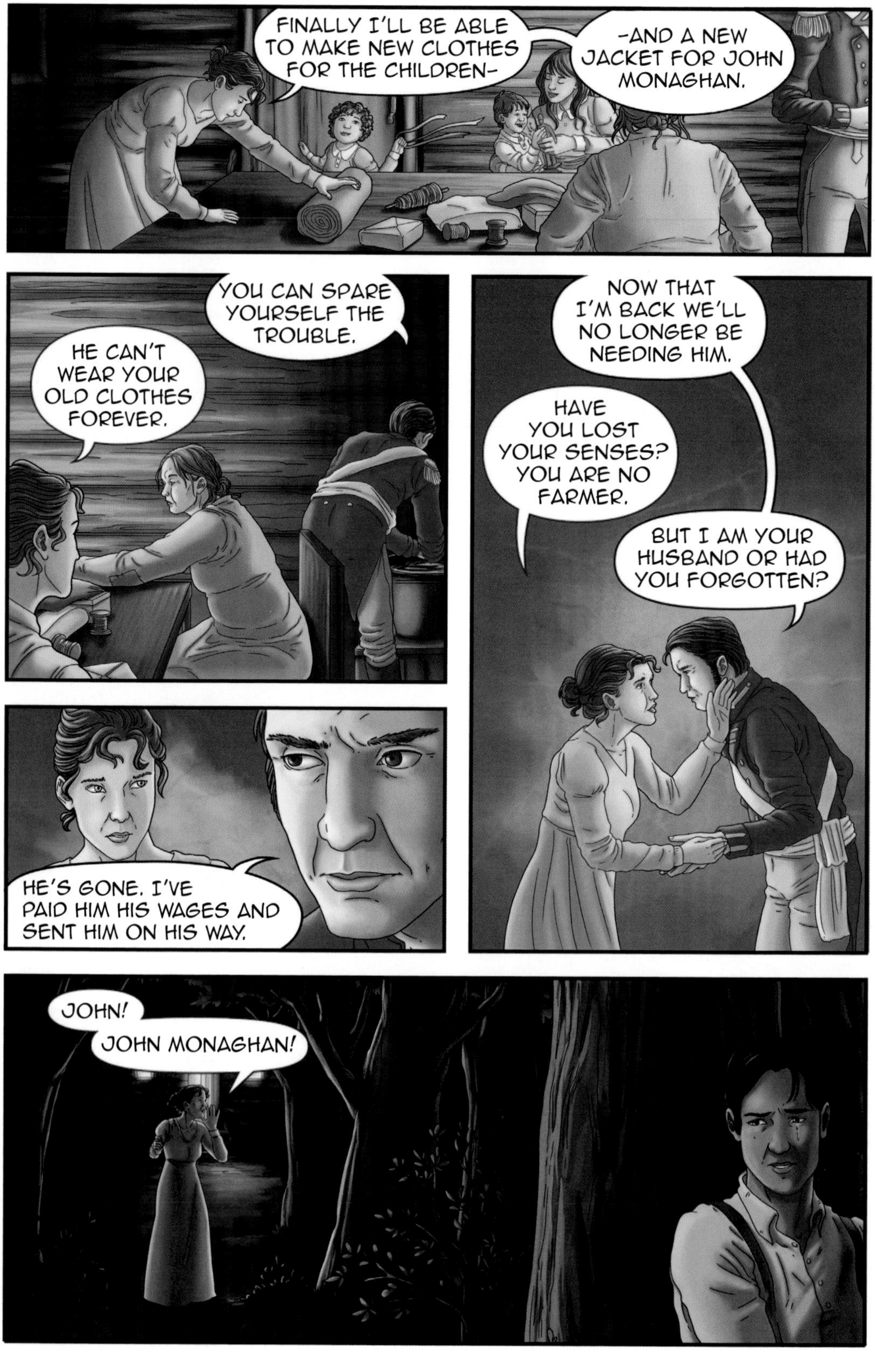
FINALLY I'LL BE ABLE TO MAKE NEW CLOTHES FOR THE CHILDREN-
-AND A NEW JACKET FOR JOHN MONAGHAN.
YOU CAN SPARE YOURSELF THE TROUBLE.
HE CAN'T WEAR YOUR OLD CLOTHES FOREVER.
HE'S GONE. I'VE PAID HIM HIS WAGES AND SENT HIM ON HIS WAY.
NOW THAT I'M BACK WE'LL NO LONGER BE NEEDING HIM.
HAVE YOU LOST YOUR SENSES? YOU ARE NO FARMER.
BUT I AM YOUR HUSBAND OR HAD YOU FORGOTTEN?
JOHN!
JOHN MONAGHAN!

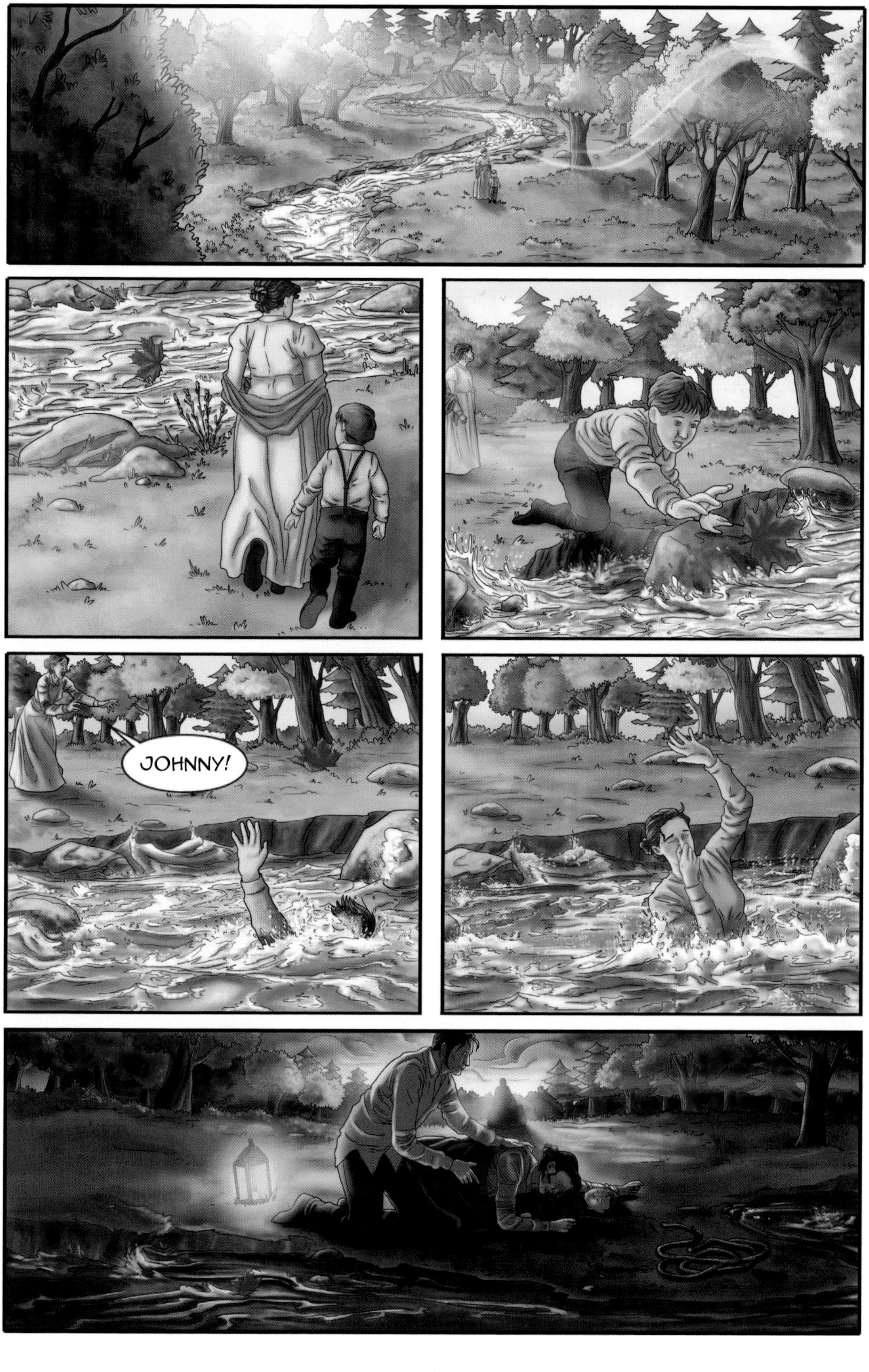
JOHNNY!

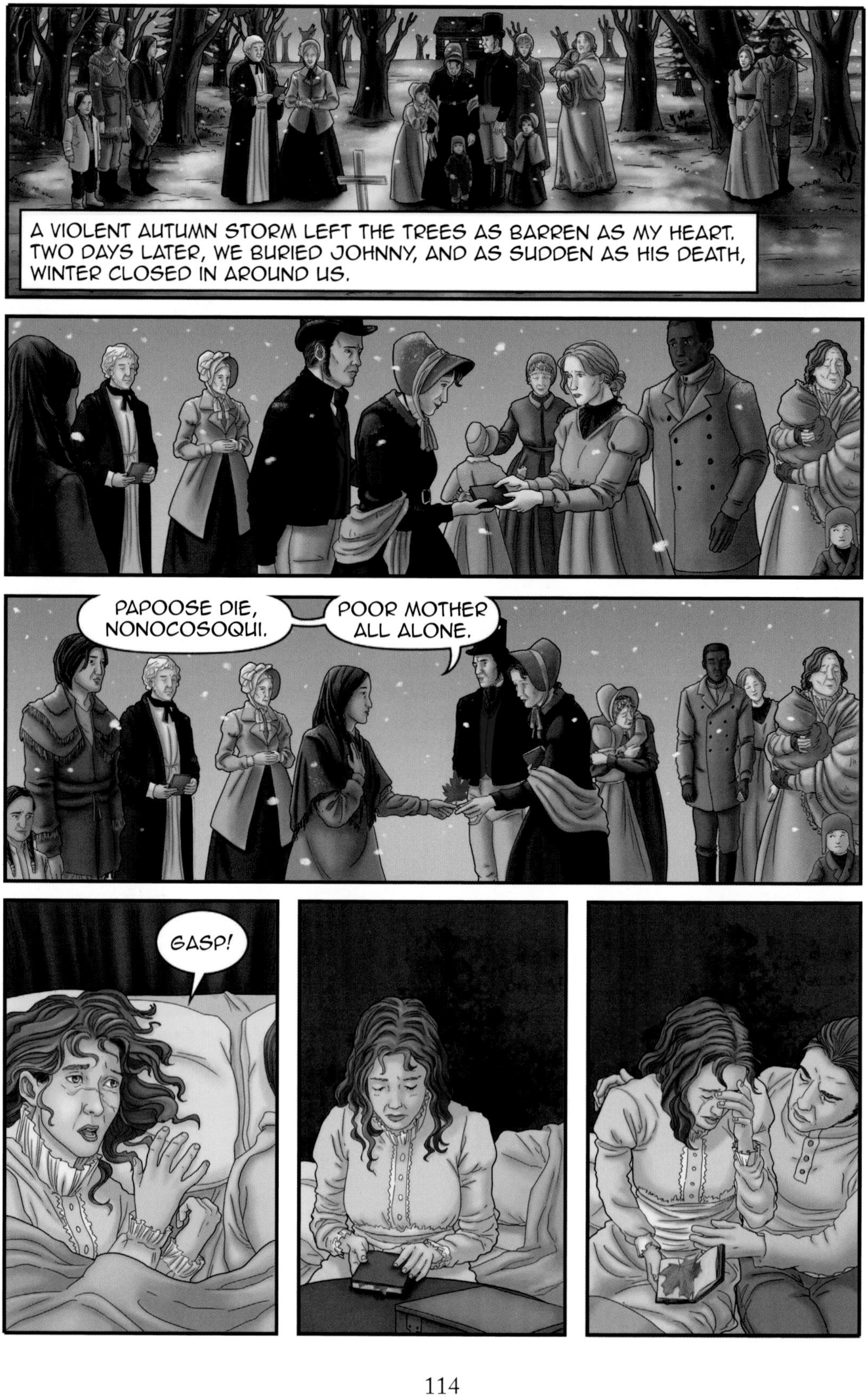
A VIOLENT AUTUMN STORM LEFT THE TREES AS BARREN AS MY HEART. TWO DAYS LATER, WE BURIED JOHNNY, AND AS SUDDEN AS HIS DEATH, WINTER CLOSED IN AROUND US.
PAPOOSE DIE, NONOCOSOQUI.
POOR MOTHER ALL ALONE.
GASP!

CHAPTER 14

DEPARTURE FROM THE BUSH

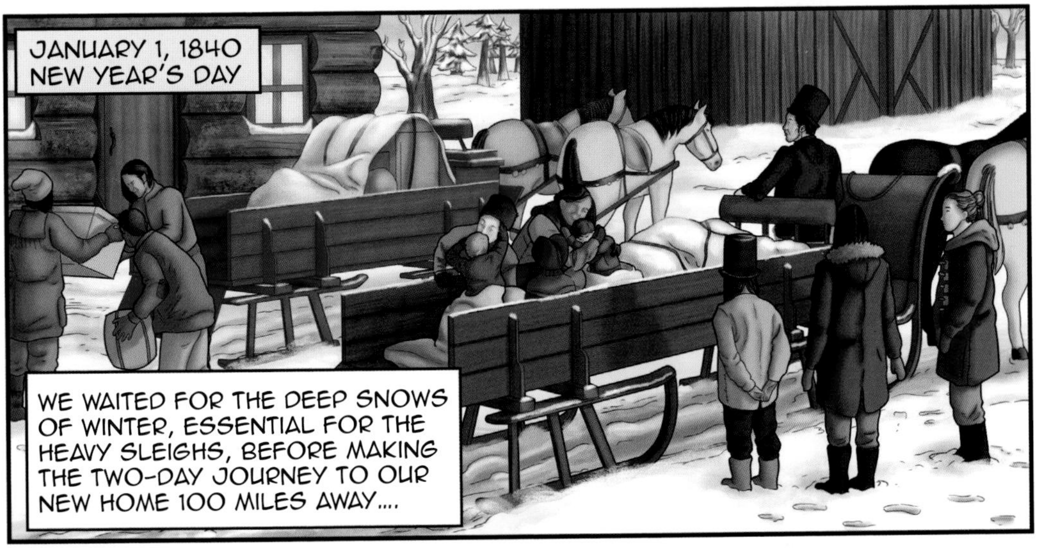
JANUARY 1, 1840
NEW YEAR'S DAY
WE WAITED FOR THE DEEP SNOWS OF WINTER, ESSENTIAL FOR THE HEAVY SLEIGHS, BEFORE MAKING THE TWO-DAY JOURNEY TO OUR NEW HOME 100 MILES AWAY....

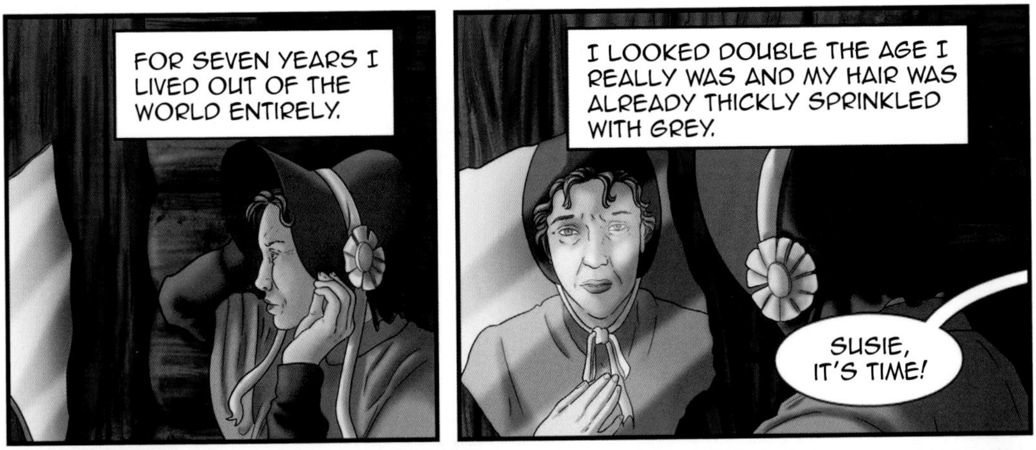
FOR SEVEN YEARS I LIVED OUT OF THE WORLD ENTIRELY.
I LOOKED DOUBLE THE AGE I REALLY WAS AND MY HAIR WAS ALREADY THICKLY SPRINKLED WITH GREY.
SUSIE, IT'S TIME!

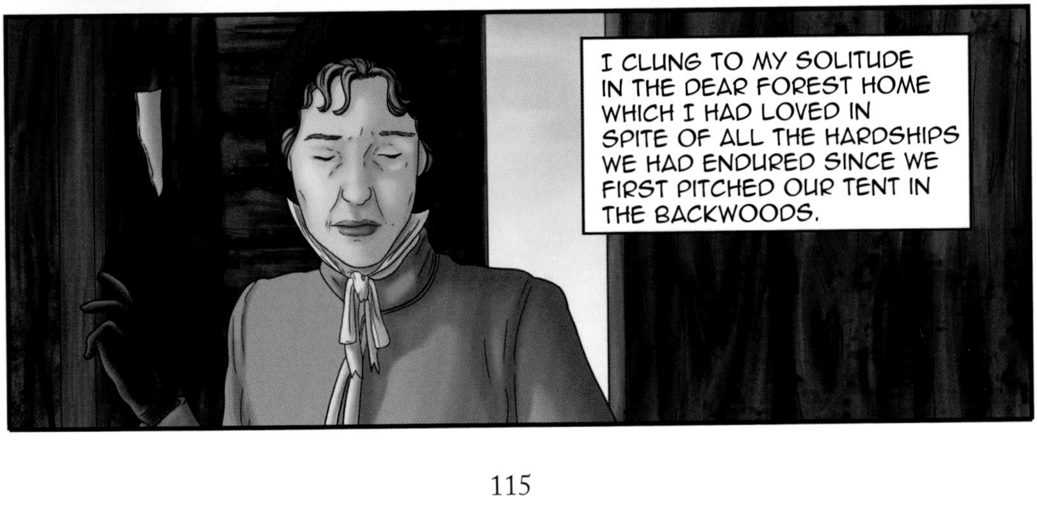
I CLUNG TO MY SOLITUDE IN THE DEAR FOREST HOME WHICH I HAD LOVED IN SPITE OF ALL THE HARDSHIPS WE HAD ENDURED SINCE WE FIRST PITCHED OUR TENT IN THE BACKWOODS.

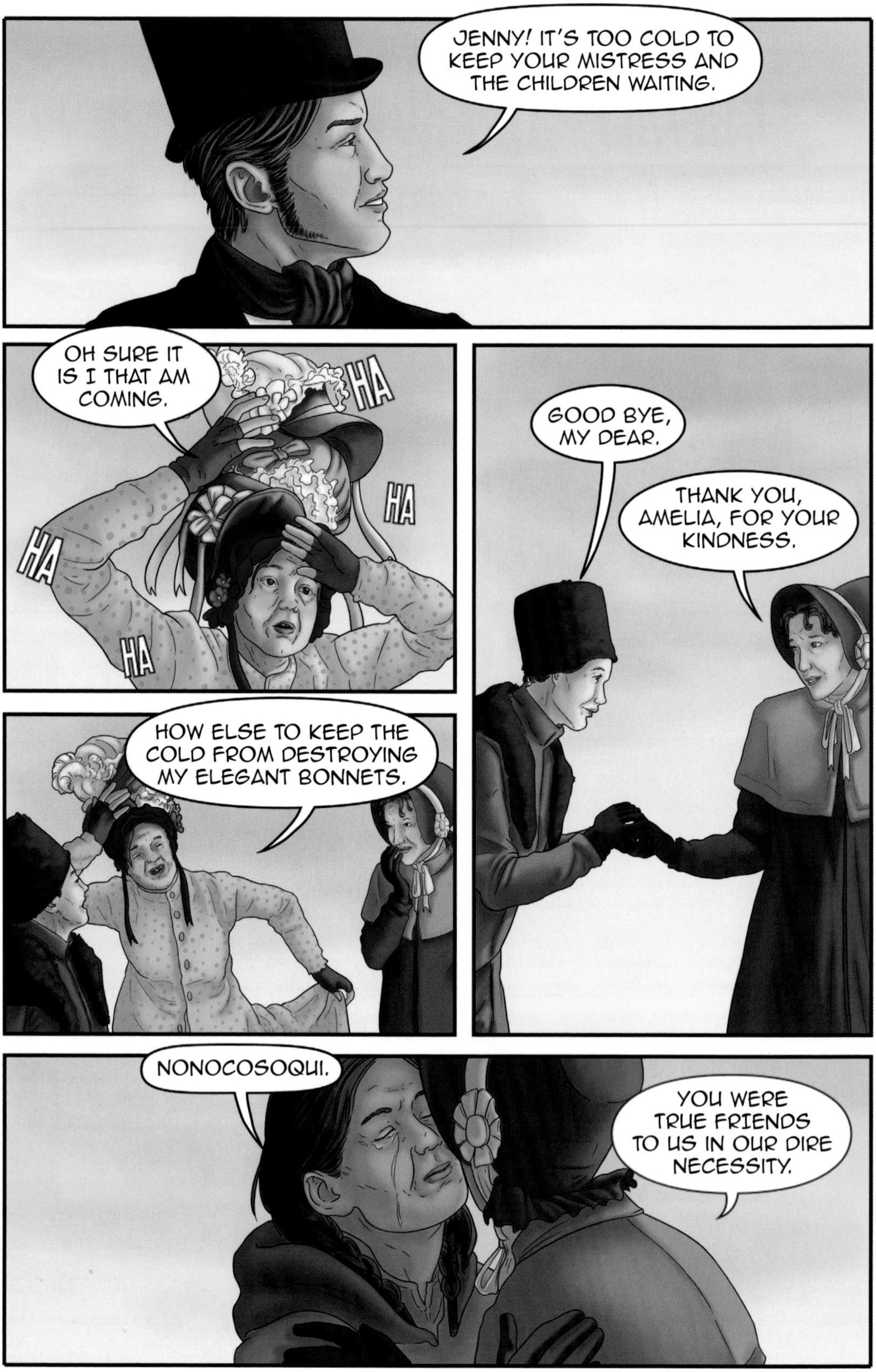
JENNY! IT'S TOO COLD TO KEEP YOUR MISTRESS AND THE CHILDREN WAITING.
OH SURE IT IS I THAT AM COMING.
HA
HA
HA
HA
HOW ELSE TO KEEP THE COLD FROM DESTROYING MY ELEGANT BONNETS.
GOOD BYE, MY DEAR.
THANK YOU, AMELIA, FOR YOUR KINDNESS.
NONOCOSOQUI.
YOU WERE TRUE FRIENDS TO US IN OUR DIRE NECESSITY.

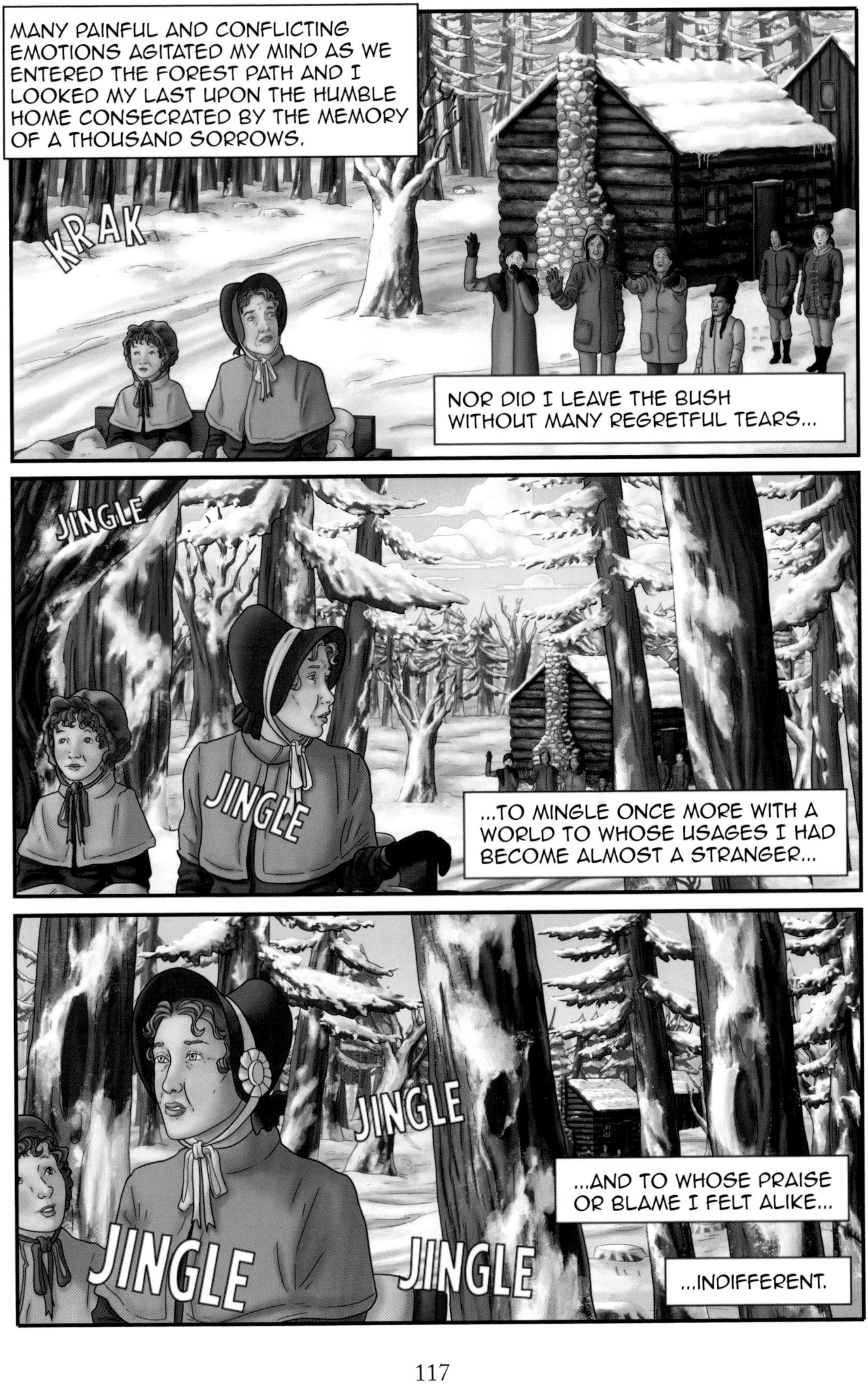
MANY PAINFUL AND CONFLICTING EMOTIONS AGITATED MY MIND AS WE ENTERED THE FOREST PATH AND I LOOKED MY LAST UPON THE HUMBLE HOME CONSECRATED BY THE MEMORY OF A THOUSAND SORROWS.
KRAK
NOR DID I LEAVE THE BUSH WITHOUT MANY REGRETFUL TEARS...
JINGLE
JINGLE
...TO MINGLE ONCE MORE WITH A WORLD TO WHOSE USAGES I HAD BECOME ALMOST A STRANGER...
JINGLE
...AND TO WHOSE PRAISE OR BLAME I FELT ALIKE...
JINGLE
JINGLE
...INDIFFERENT.

EPILOGUES

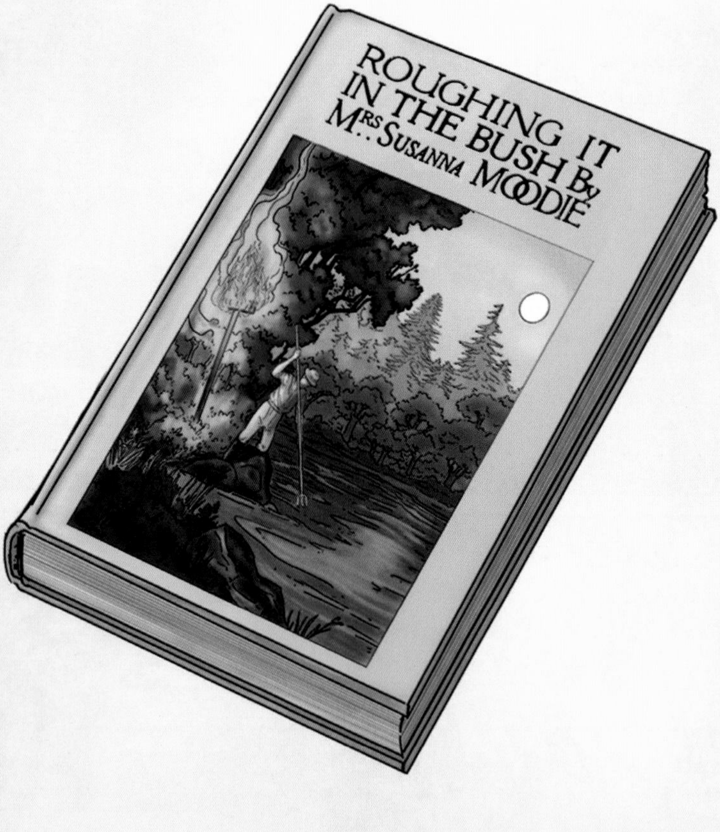

ROUGHING IT
IN THE BUSH By
MRS. SUSANNA MOODIE

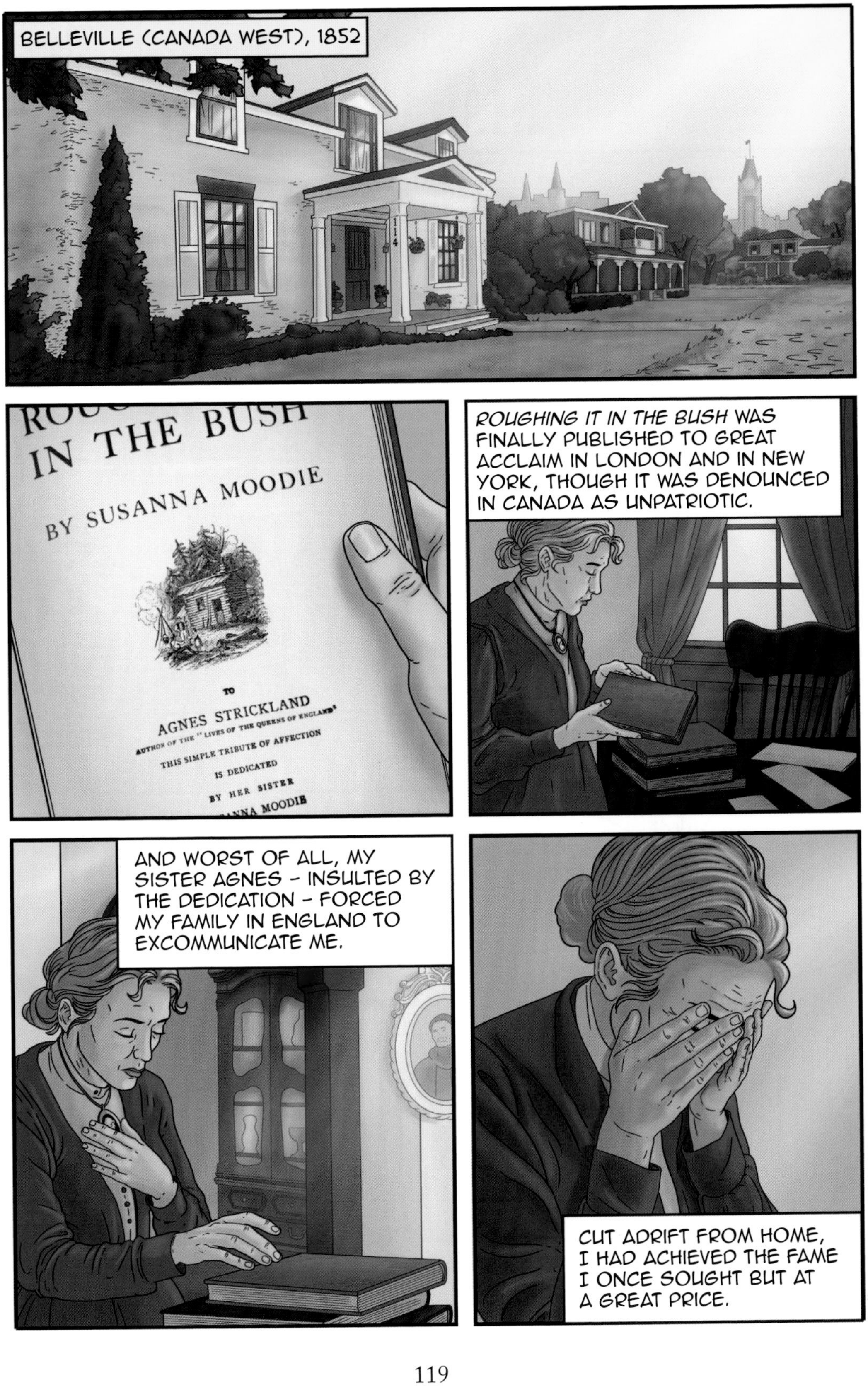
BELLEVILLE (CANADA WEST), 1852
114
IN THE BUSH
BY SUSANNA MOODIE
TO
AGNES STRICKLAND
AUTHOR OF THE "LIVES OF THE QUEENS OF ENGLAND"
THIS SIMPLE TRIBUTE OF AFFECTION
IS DEDICATED
BY HER SISTER
ANNA MOODIE
ROUGHING IT IN THE BUSH WAS FINALLY PUBLISHED TO GREAT ACCLAIM IN LONDON AND IN NEW YORK, THOUGH IT WAS DENOUNCED IN CANADA AS UNPATRIOTIC.
AND WORST OF ALL, MY SISTER AGNES - INSULTED BY THE DEDICATION - FORCED MY FAMILY IN ENGLAND TO EXCOMMUNICATE ME.
CUT ADRIFT FROM HOME, I HAD ACHIEVED THE FAME I ONCE SOUGHT BUT AT A GREAT PRICE.

CHAPTER 15

NIAGARA!

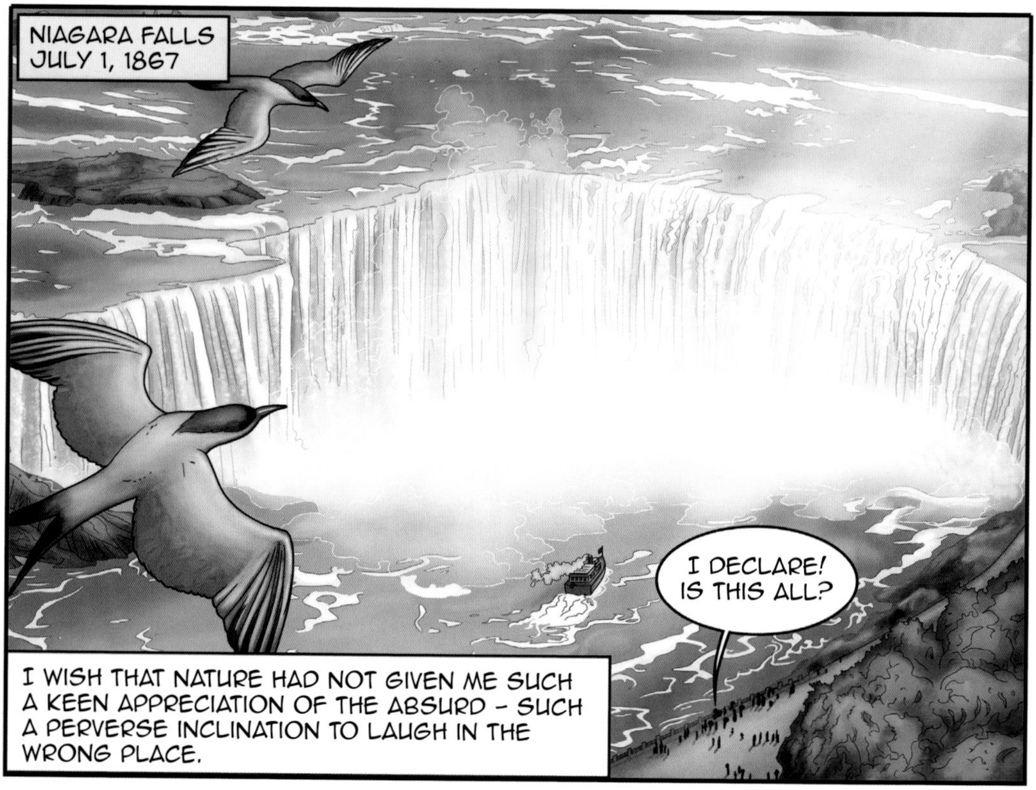
NIAGARA FALLS
JULY 1, 1867
I DECLARE! IS THIS ALL?
I WISH THAT NATURE HAD NOT GIVEN ME SUCH A KEEN APPRECIATION OF THE ABSURD - SUCH A PERVERSE INCLINATION TO LAUGH IN THE WRONG PLACE.

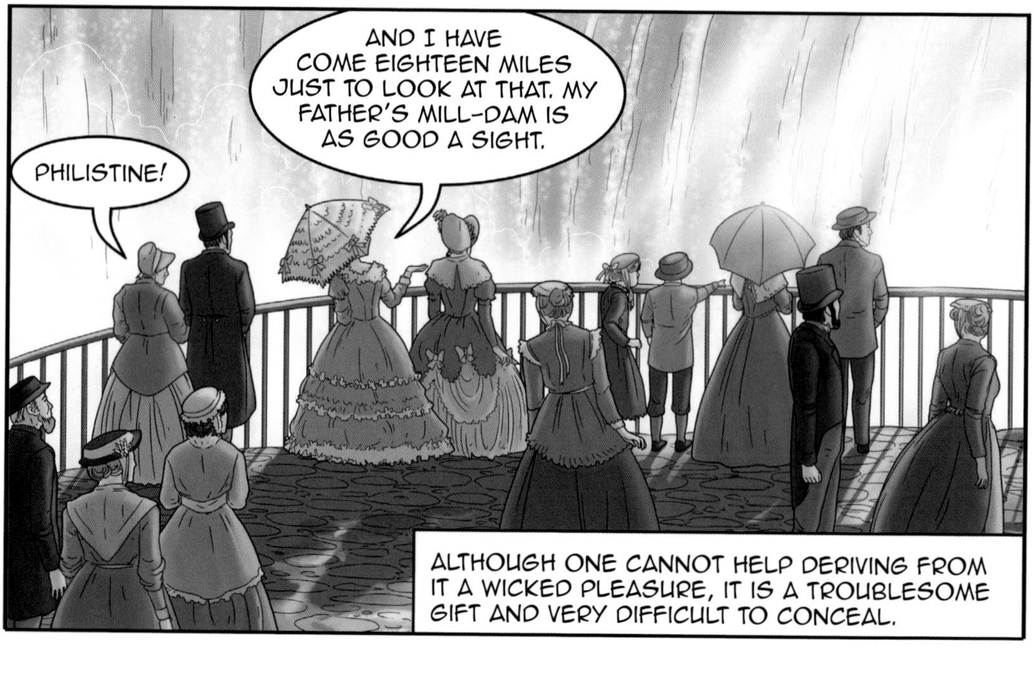
PHILISTINE!
AND I HAVE COME EIGHTEEN MILES JUST TO LOOK AT THAT. MY FATHER'S MILL-DAM IS AS GOOD A SIGHT.
ALTHOUGH ONE CANNOT HELP DERIVING FROM IT A WICKED PLEASURE, IT IS A TROUBLESOME GIFT AND VERY DIFFICULT TO CONCEAL.

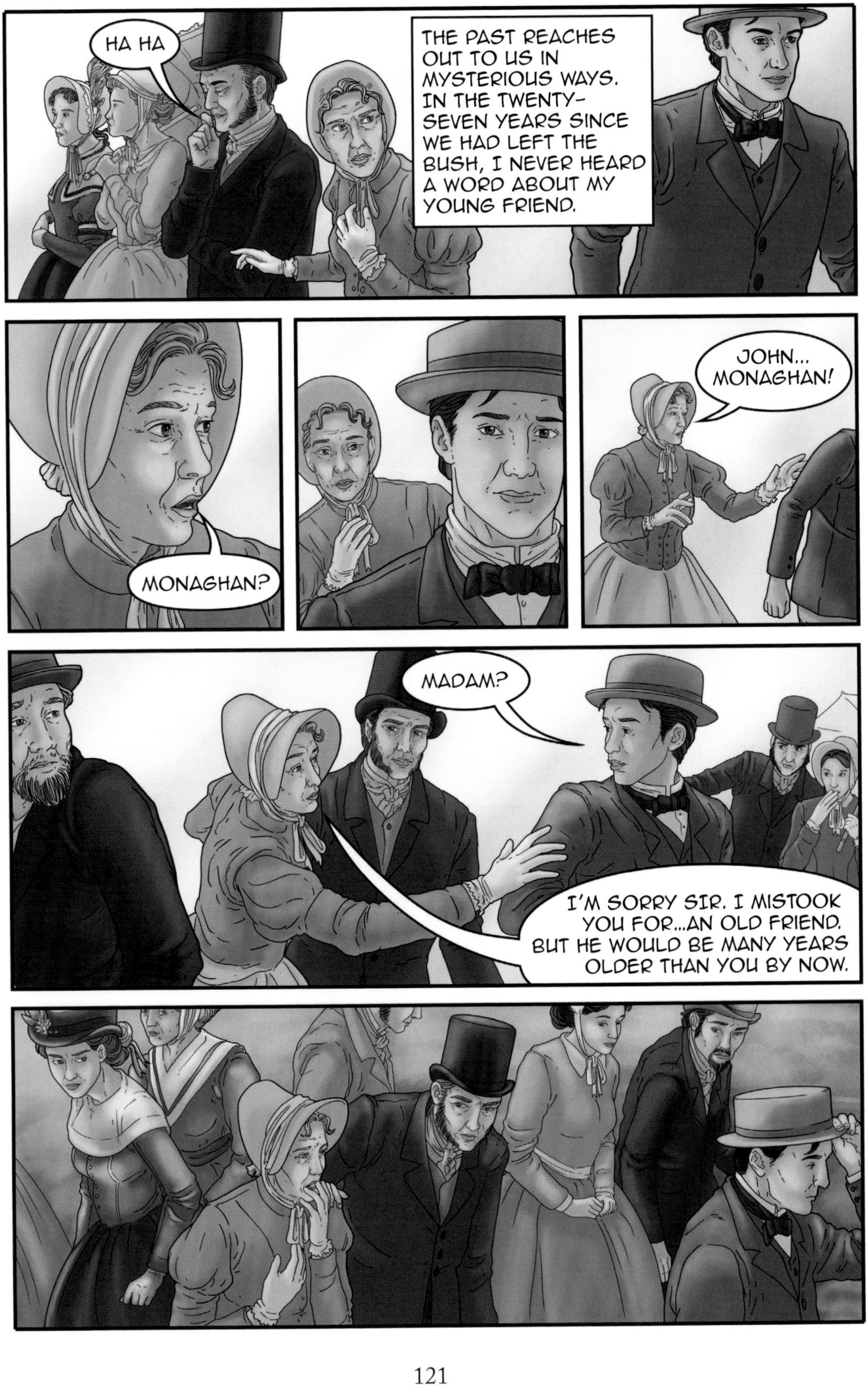
HA HA
THE PAST REACHES OUT TO US IN MYSTERIOUS WAYS. IN THE TWENTY-SEVEN YEARS SINCE WE HAD LEFT THE BUSH, I NEVER HEARD A WORD ABOUT MY YOUNG FRIEND.
MONAGHAN?
JOHN... MONAGHAN!
MADAM?
I'M SORRY SIR. I MISTOOK YOU FOR...AN OLD FRIEND. BUT HE WOULD BE MANY YEARS OLDER THAN YOU BY NOW.

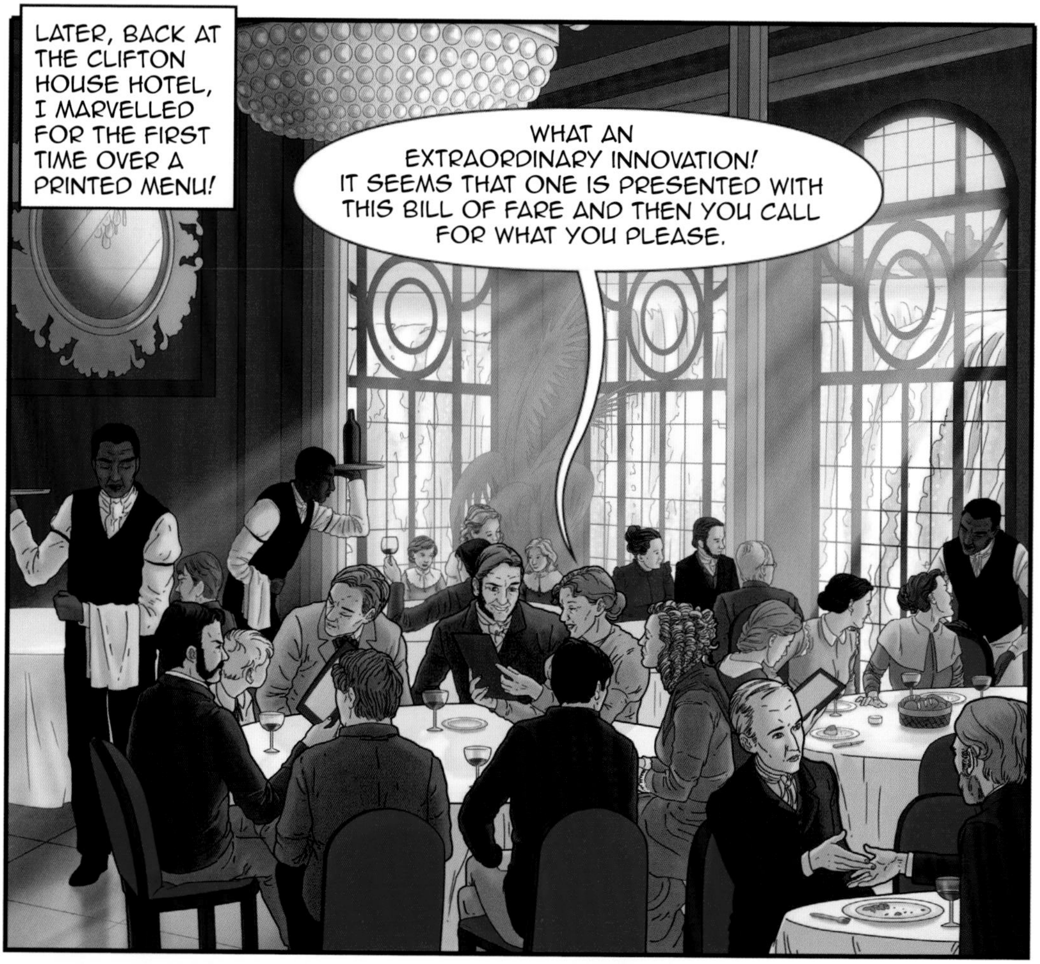
LATER, BACK AT THE CLIFTON HOUSE HOTEL, I MARVELLED FOR THE FIRST TIME OVER A PRINTED MENU!
WHAT AN EXTRAORDINARY INNOVATION! IT SEEMS THAT ONE IS PRESENTED WITH THIS BILL OF FARE AND THEN YOU CALL FOR WHAT YOU PLEASE.

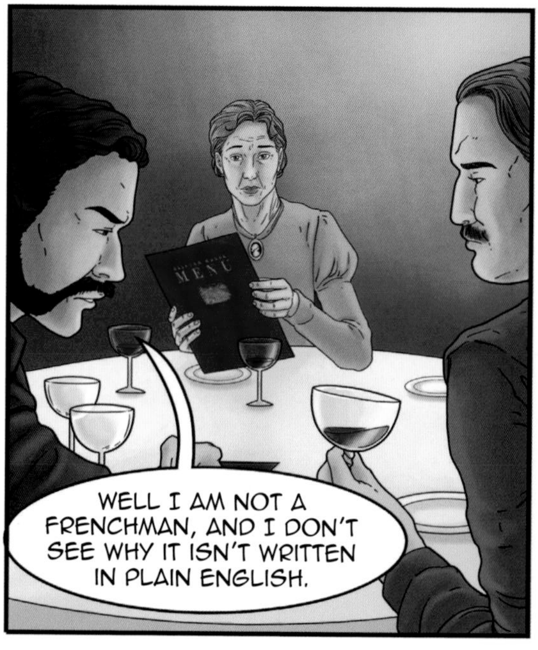
MENU
WELL I AM NOT A FRENCHMAN, AND I DON'T SEE WHY IT ISN'T WRITTEN IN PLAIN ENGLISH.

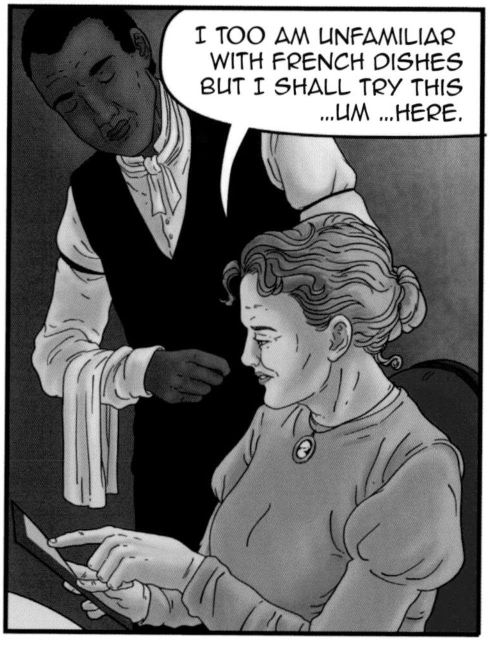
I TOO AM UNFAMILIAR WITH FRENCH DISHES BUT I SHALL TRY THIS ...UM ...HERE.

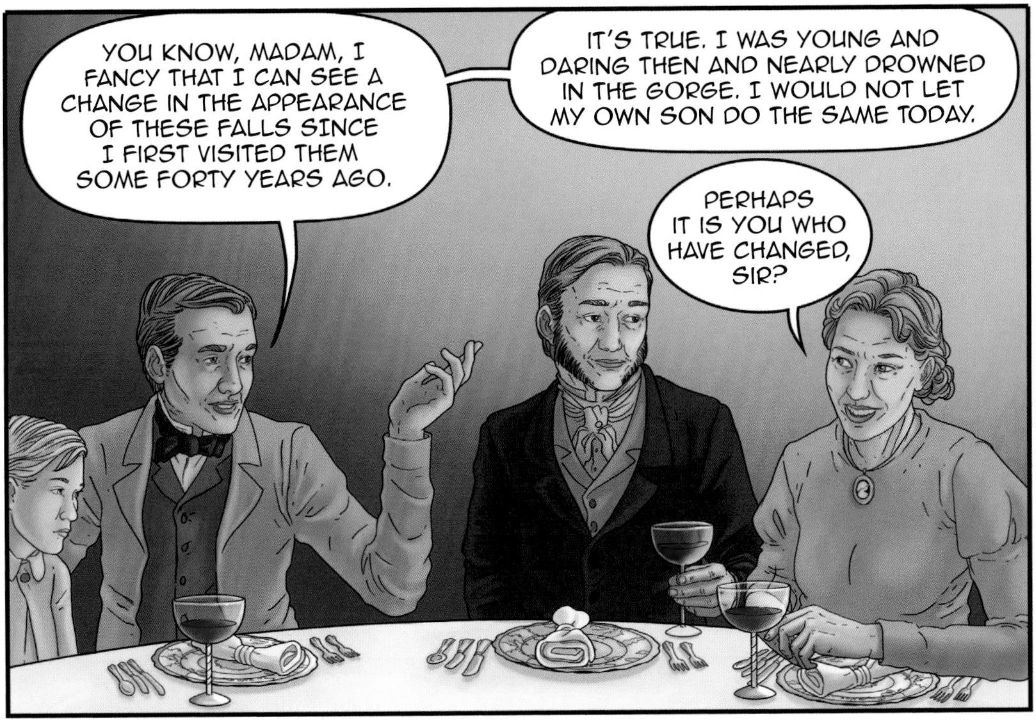
YOU KNOW, MADAM, I FANCY THAT I CAN SEE A CHANGE IN THE APPEARANCE OF THESE FALLS SINCE I FIRST VISITED THEM SOME FORTY YEARS AGO.
IT'S TRUE. I WAS YOUNG AND DARING THEN AND NEARLY DROWNED IN THE GORGE. I WOULD NOT LET MY OWN SON DO THE SAME TODAY.
PERHAPS IT IS YOU WHO HAVE CHANGED, SIR?

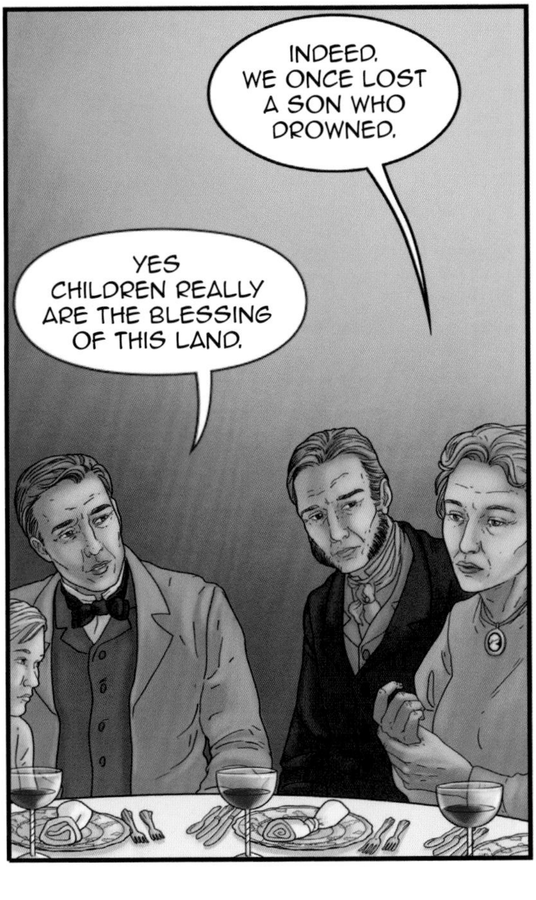
INDEED. WE ONCE LOST A SON WHO DROWNED.
YES CHILDREN REALLY ARE THE BLESSING OF THIS LAND.

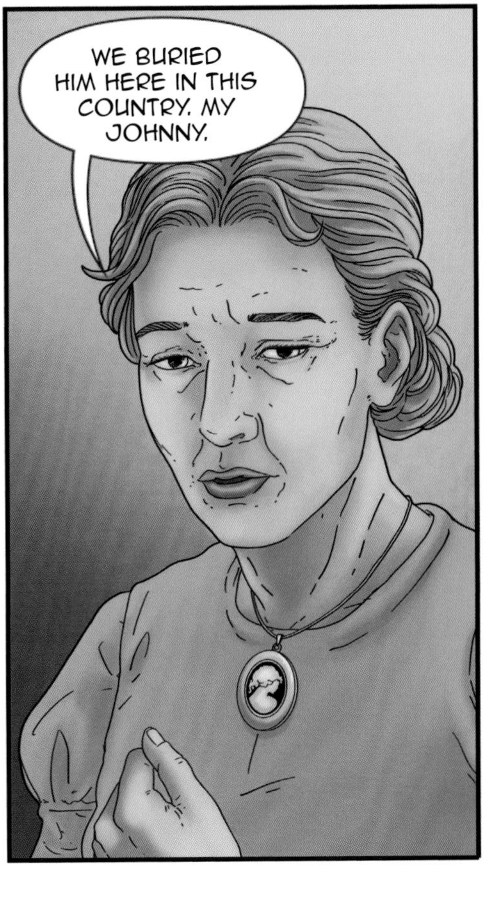
WE BURIED HIM HERE IN THIS COUNTRY. MY JOHNNY.

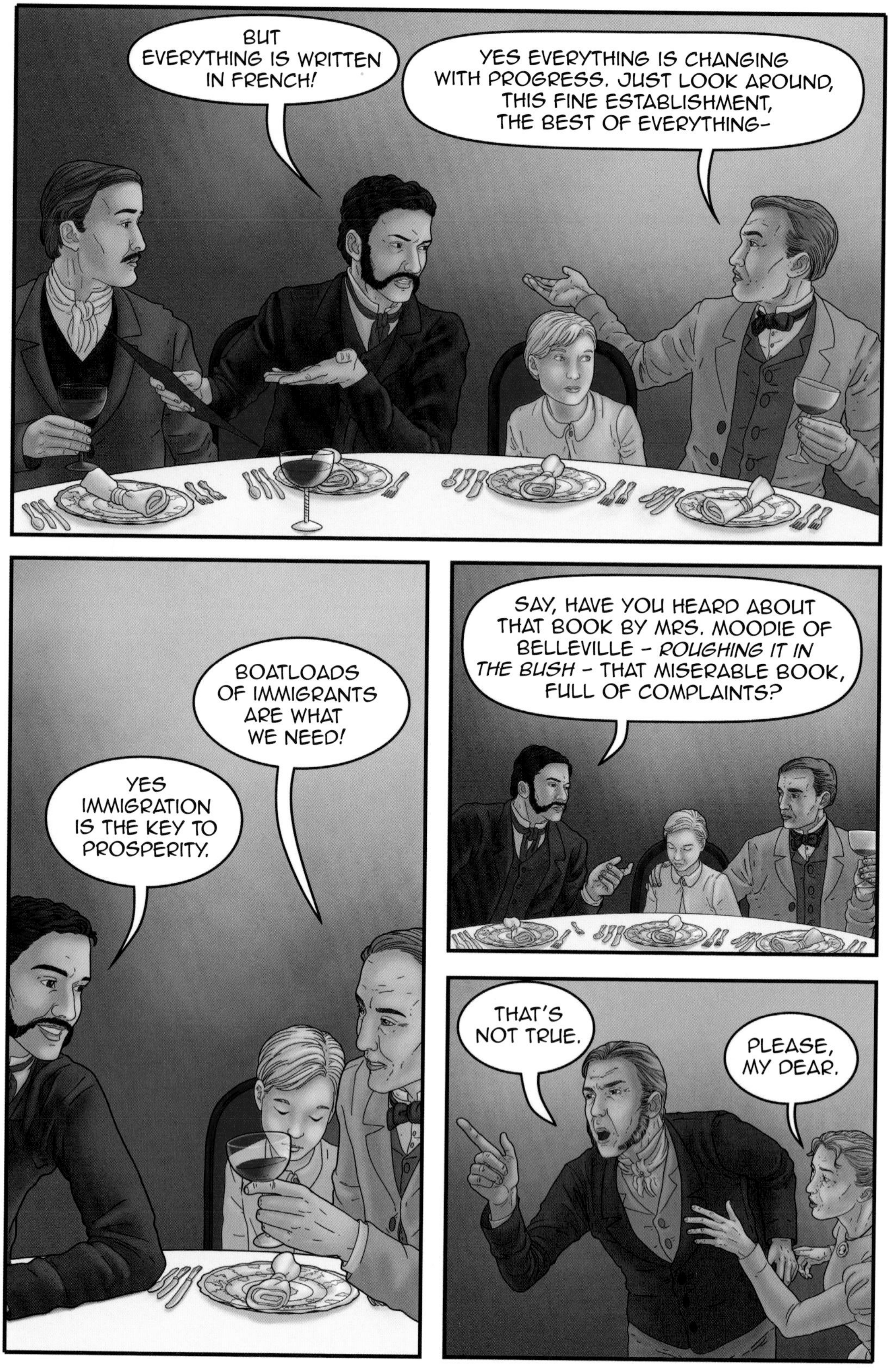
BUT EVERYTHING IS WRITTEN IN FRENCH!
YES EVERYTHING IS CHANGING WITH PROGRESS. JUST LOOK AROUND, THIS FINE ESTABLISHMENT, THE BEST OF EVERYTHING-
BOATLOADS OF IMMIGRANTS ARE WHAT WE NEED!
YES IMMIGRATION IS THE KEY TO PROSPERITY.
SAY, HAVE YOU HEARD ABOUT THAT BOOK BY MRS. MOODIE OF BELLEVILLE - *ROUGHING IT IN THE BUSH* - THAT MISERABLE BOOK, FULL OF COMPLAINTS?
THAT'S NOT TRUE.
PLEASE, MY DEAR.

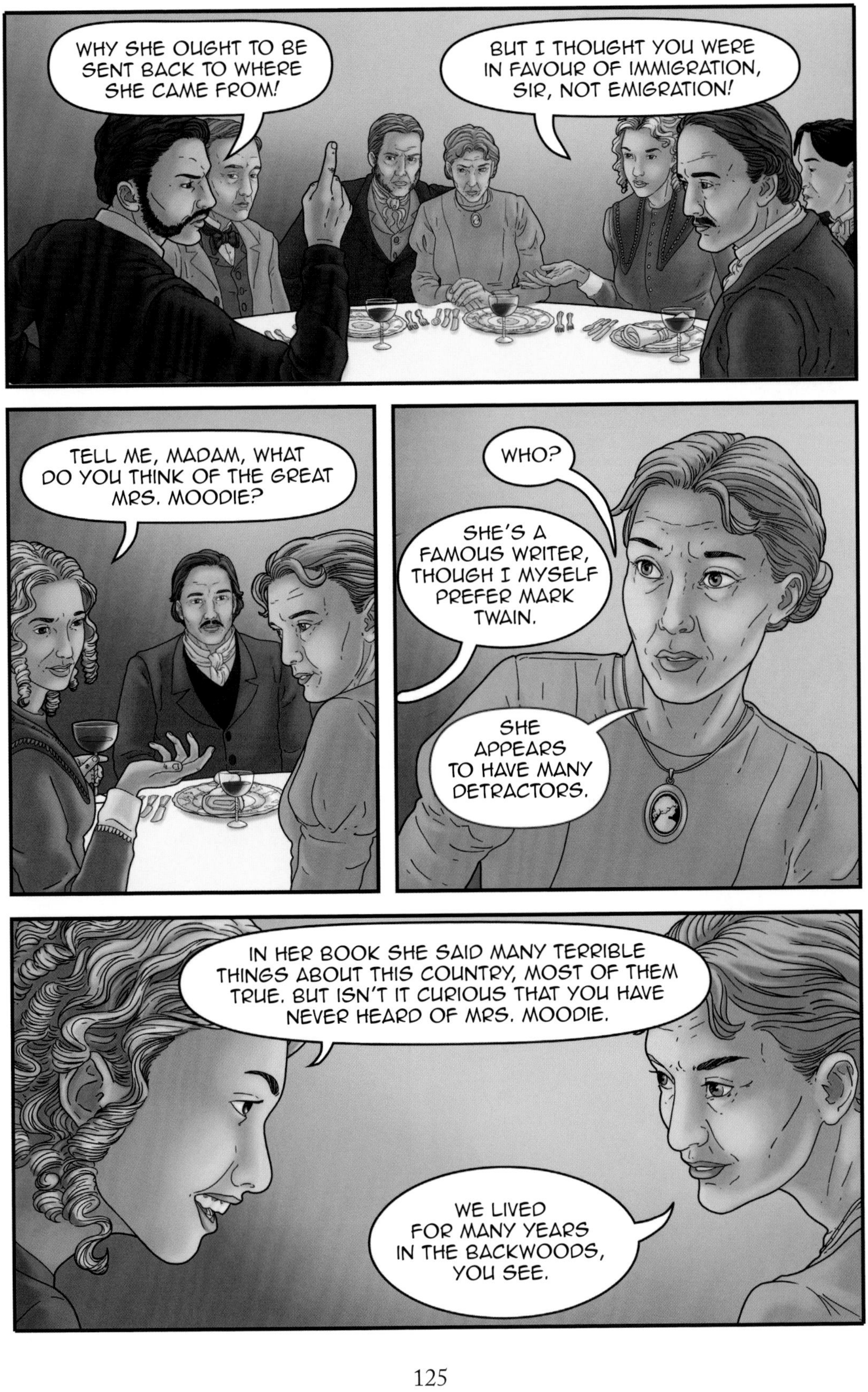
WHY SHE OUGHT TO BE SENT BACK TO WHERE SHE CAME FROM!
BUT I THOUGHT YOU WERE IN FAVOUR OF IMMIGRATION, SIR, NOT EMIGRATION!
TELL ME, MADAM, WHAT DO YOU THINK OF THE GREAT MRS. MOODIE?
WHO?
SHE'S A FAMOUS WRITER, THOUGH I MYSELF PREFER MARK TWAIN.
SHE APPEARS TO HAVE MANY DETRACTORS.
IN HER BOOK SHE SAID MANY TERRIBLE THINGS ABOUT THIS COUNTRY, MOST OF THEM TRUE. BUT ISN'T IT CURIOUS THAT YOU HAVE NEVER HEARD OF MRS. MOODIE.
WE LIVED FOR MANY YEARS IN THE BACKWOODS, YOU SEE.

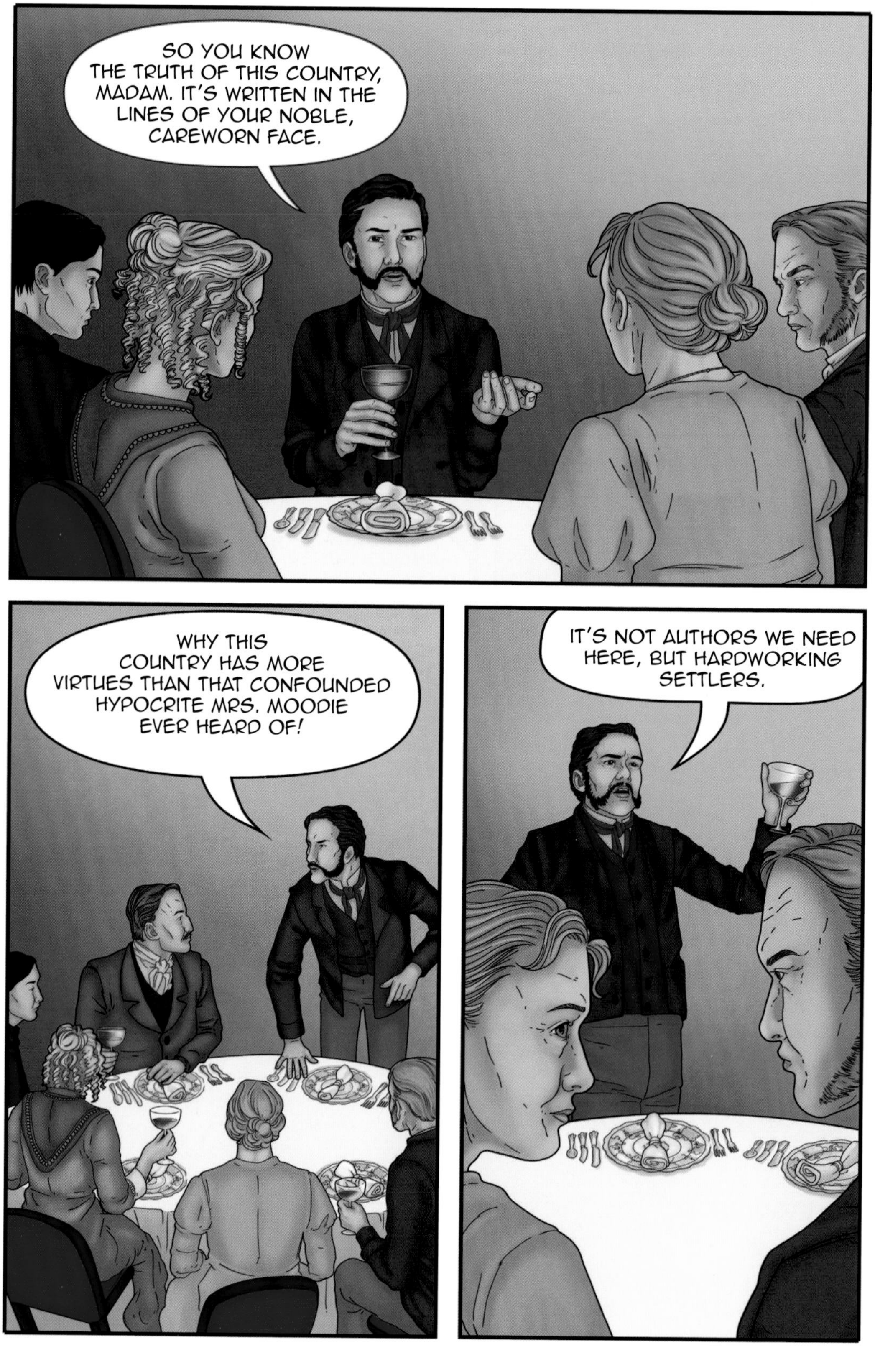
SO YOU KNOW THE TRUTH OF THIS COUNTRY, MADAM. IT'S WRITTEN IN THE LINES OF YOUR NOBLE, CAREWORN FACE.
WHY THIS COUNTRY HAS MORE VIRTUES THAN THAT CONFOUNDED HYPOCRITE MRS. MOODIE EVER HEARD OF!
IT'S NOT AUTHORS WE NEED HERE, BUT HARDWORKING SETTLERS.

AH, NOW HERE I MUST DISAGREE WITH YOU, SIR. LET US NOT FORGET THAT IT IS THE POET WHO FILLS OUR HEARTS WITH PURPOSE.
BUT THAT MOODIE WOMAN PAINTS A FALSE PORTRAIT!
ROUGHING IT IN THE BUSH IS A MOVING TESTAMENT OF PERSONAL FORTITUDE. I, FOR ONE, WOULD BE PROUD TO MEET THIS DISTINGUISHED WOMAN.
A DISTINGUISHED LADY!
LADIES AND GENTLEMEN, PERMIT ME TO PROPOSE A TOAST IN ABSENTIA TO A DISTINGUISHED LADY...
OUR OWN CELEBRATED CANADIAN AUTHOR...

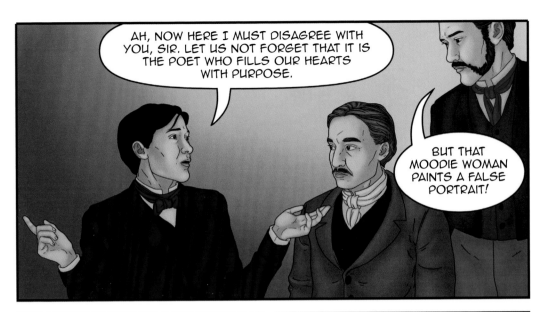

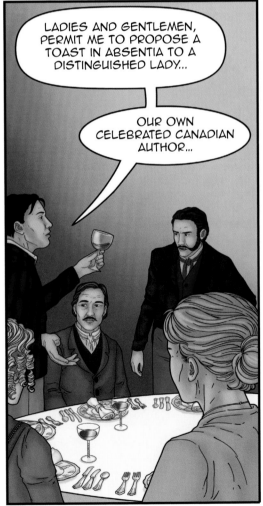

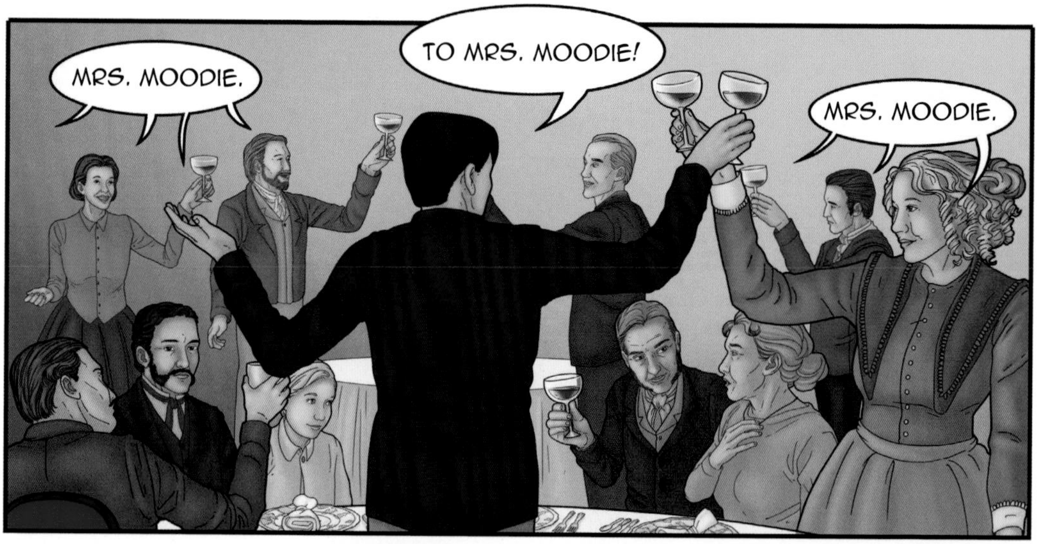
MRS. MOODIE.
TO MRS. MOODIE!
MRS. MOODIE.

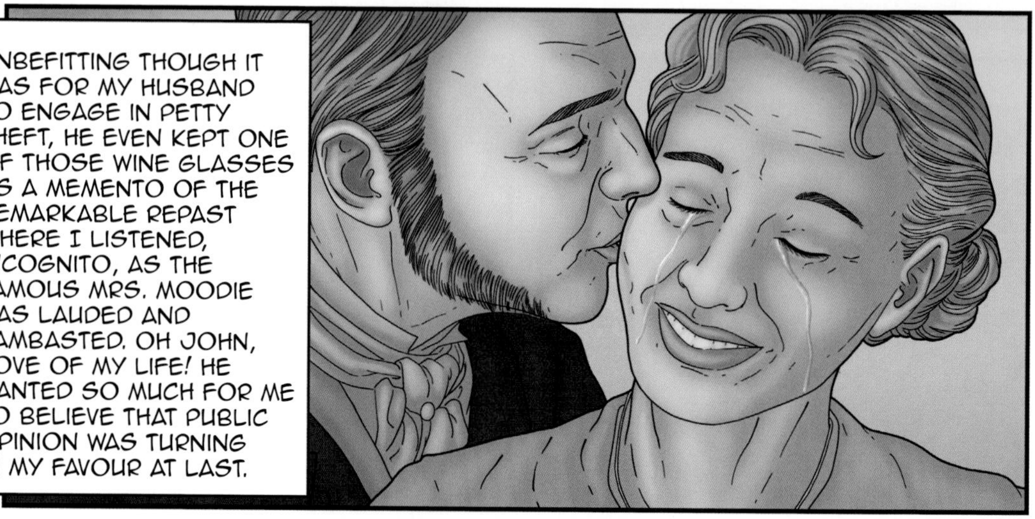
UNBEFITTING THOUGH IT WAS FOR MY HUSBAND TO ENGAGE IN PETTY THEFT, HE EVEN KEPT ONE OF THOSE WINE GLASSES AS A MEMENTO OF THE REMARKABLE REPAST WHERE I LISTENED, INCOGNITO, AS THE FAMOUS MRS. MOODIE WAS LAUDED AND LAMBASTED. OH JOHN, LOVE OF MY LIFE! HE WANTED SO MUCH FOR ME TO BELIEVE THAT PUBLIC OPINION WAS TURNING IN MY FAVOUR AT LAST.

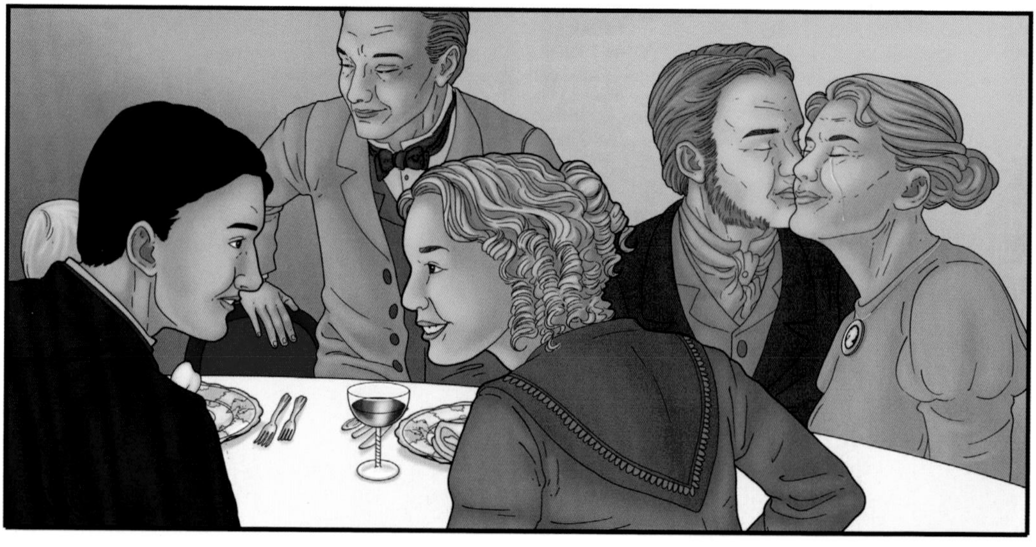

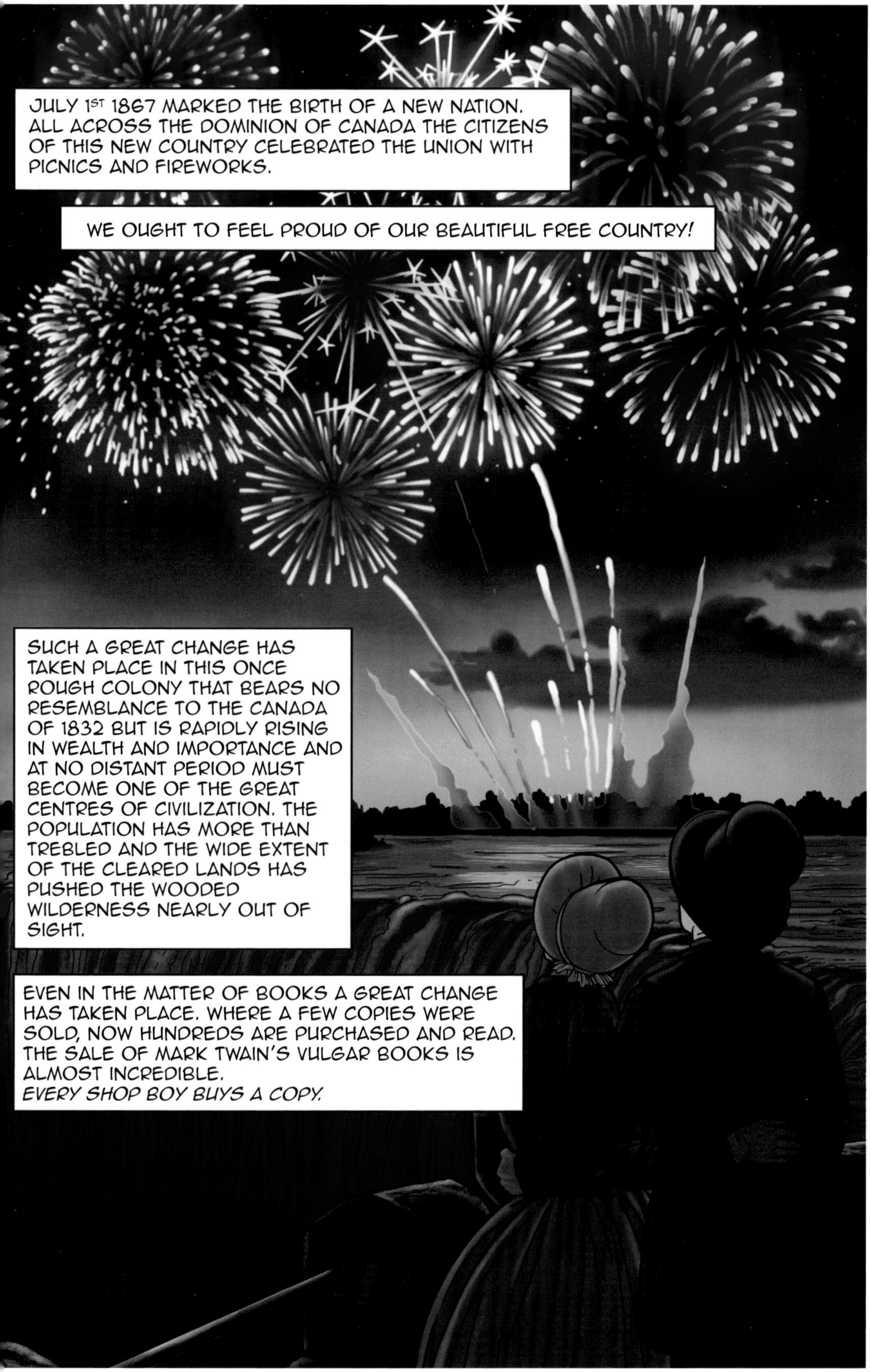
JULY 1ST 1867 MARKED THE BIRTH OF A NEW NATION. ALL ACROSS THE DOMINION OF CANADA THE CITIZENS OF THIS NEW COUNTRY CELEBRATED THE UNION WITH PICNICS AND FIREWORKS.
WE OUGHT TO FEEL PROUD OF OUR BEAUTIFUL FREE COUNTRY!
SUCH A GREAT CHANGE HAS TAKEN PLACE IN THIS ONCE ROUGH COLONY THAT BEARS NO RESEMBLANCE TO THE CANADA OF 1832 BUT IS RAPIDLY RISING IN WEALTH AND IMPORTANCE AND AT NO DISTANT PERIOD MUST BECOME ONE OF THE GREAT CENTRES OF CIVILIZATION. THE POPULATION HAS MORE THAN TREBLED AND THE WIDE EXTENT OF THE CLEARED LANDS HAS PUSHED THE WOODED WILDERNESS NEARLY OUT OF SIGHT.
EVEN IN THE MATTER OF BOOKS A GREAT CHANGE HAS TAKEN PLACE. WHERE A FEW COPIES WERE SOLD, NOW HUNDREDS ARE PURCHASED AND READ. THE SALE OF MARK TWAIN'S VULGAR BOOKS IS ALMOST INCREDIBLE.
EVERY SHOP BOY BUYS A COPY.

CHAPTER 16

THE BUSH GARDEN

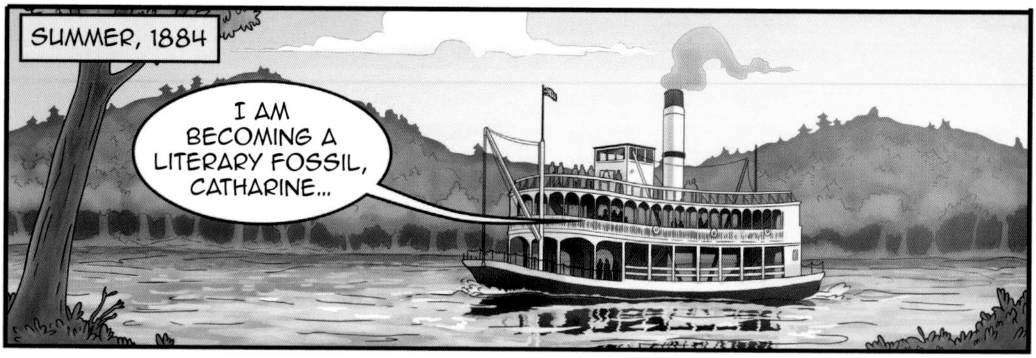
SUMMER, 1884
I AM BECOMING A LITERARY FOSSIL, CATHARINE...

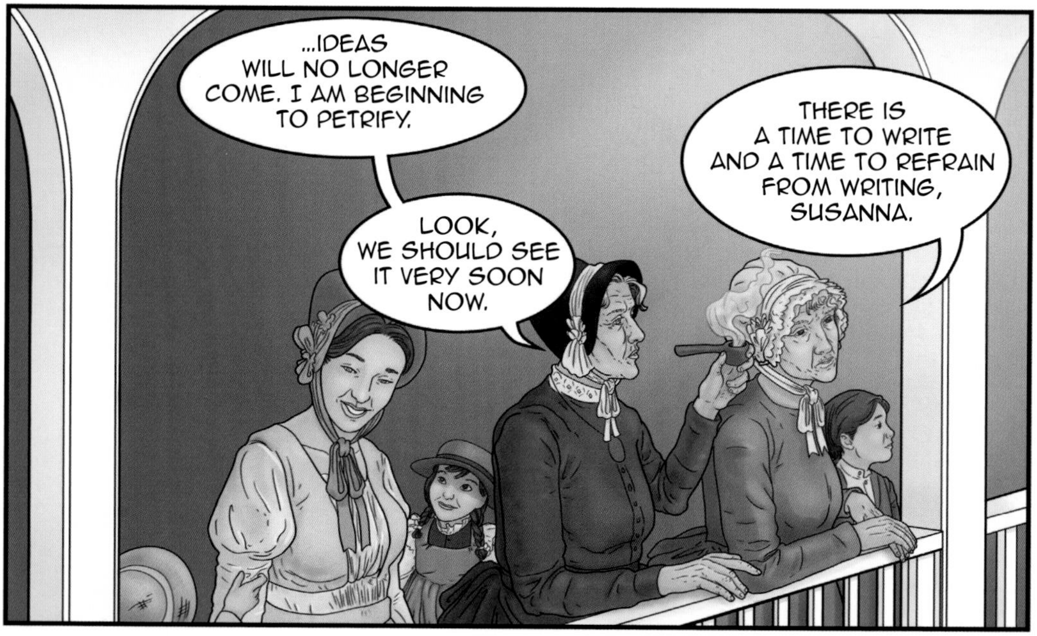
...IDEAS WILL NO LONGER COME. I AM BEGINNING TO PETRIFY.
THERE IS A TIME TO WRITE AND A TIME TO REFRAIN FROM WRITING, SUSANNA.
LOOK, WE SHOULD SEE IT VERY SOON NOW.

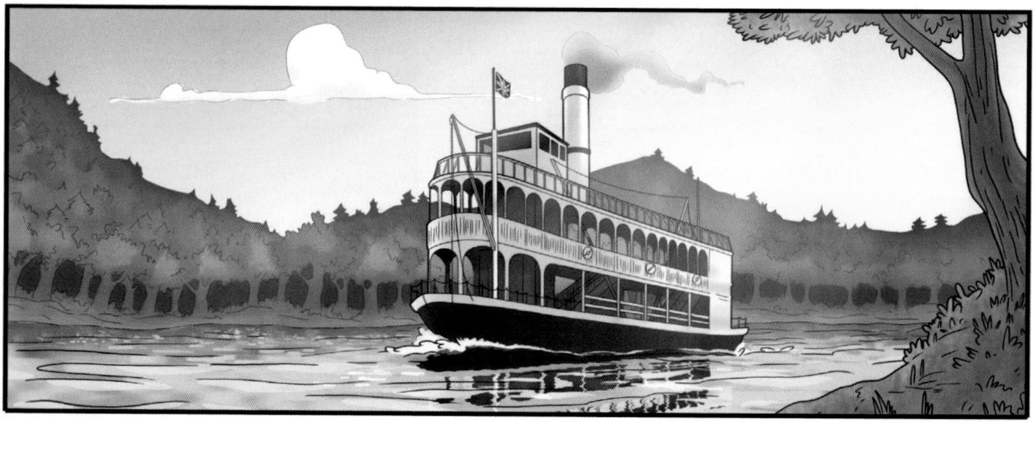

IS THIS WHERE YOU WERE BORN GRANDMA?

NO, I WAS BORN IN ENGLAND IN A BIG HOUSE WITH A WONDERFUL GARDEN.

WHERE ARE ALL THE FIELDS WE CLEARED?

THE TREES HAVE GROWN UP AGAIN.

HOW TIME CHANGES EVERYTHING.

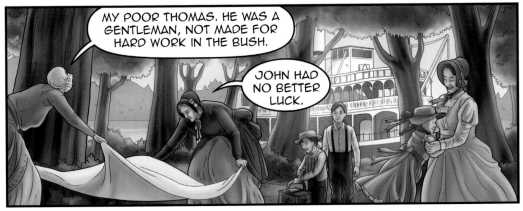

MY POOR THOMAS. HE WAS A GENTLEMAN, NOT MADE FOR HARD WORK IN THE BUSH.

JOHN HAD NO BETTER LUCK.

DID HE EVER LEARN THAT IT WAS YOU WHO SECURED HIS POSITION AS SHERIFF?

WHAT USE WOULD THAT HAVE SERVED?

131

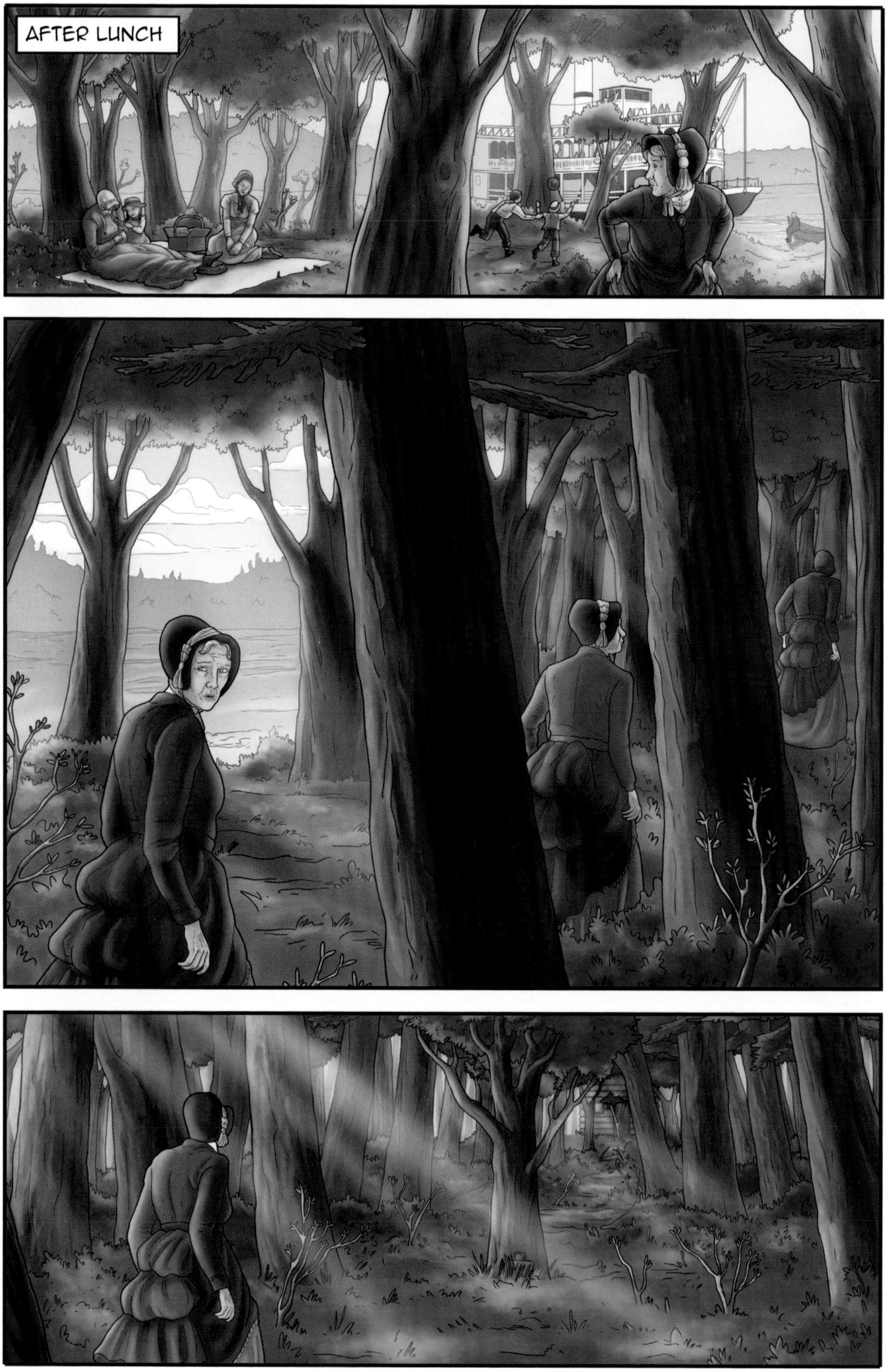
AFTER LUNCH

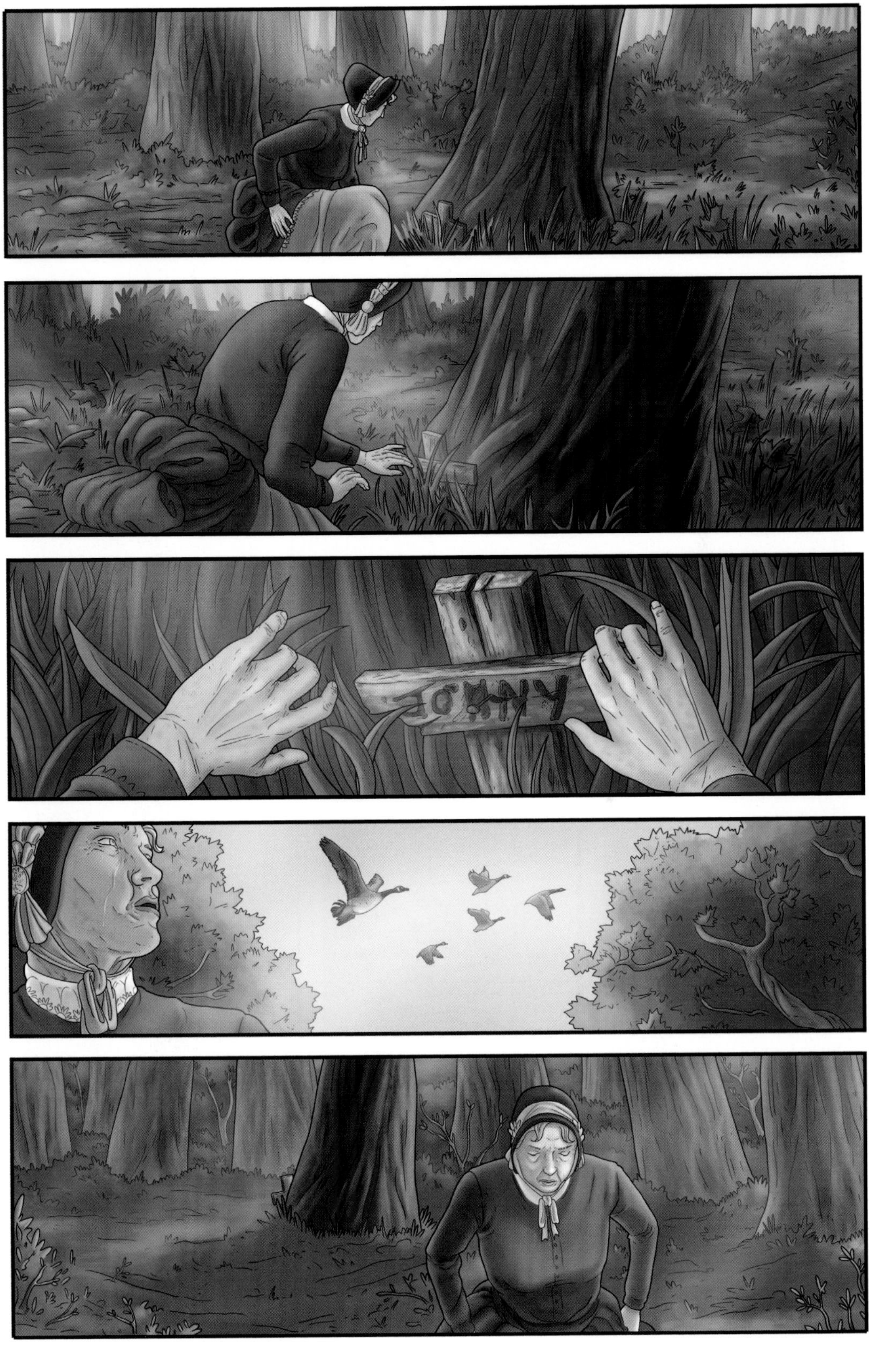
JOHNY

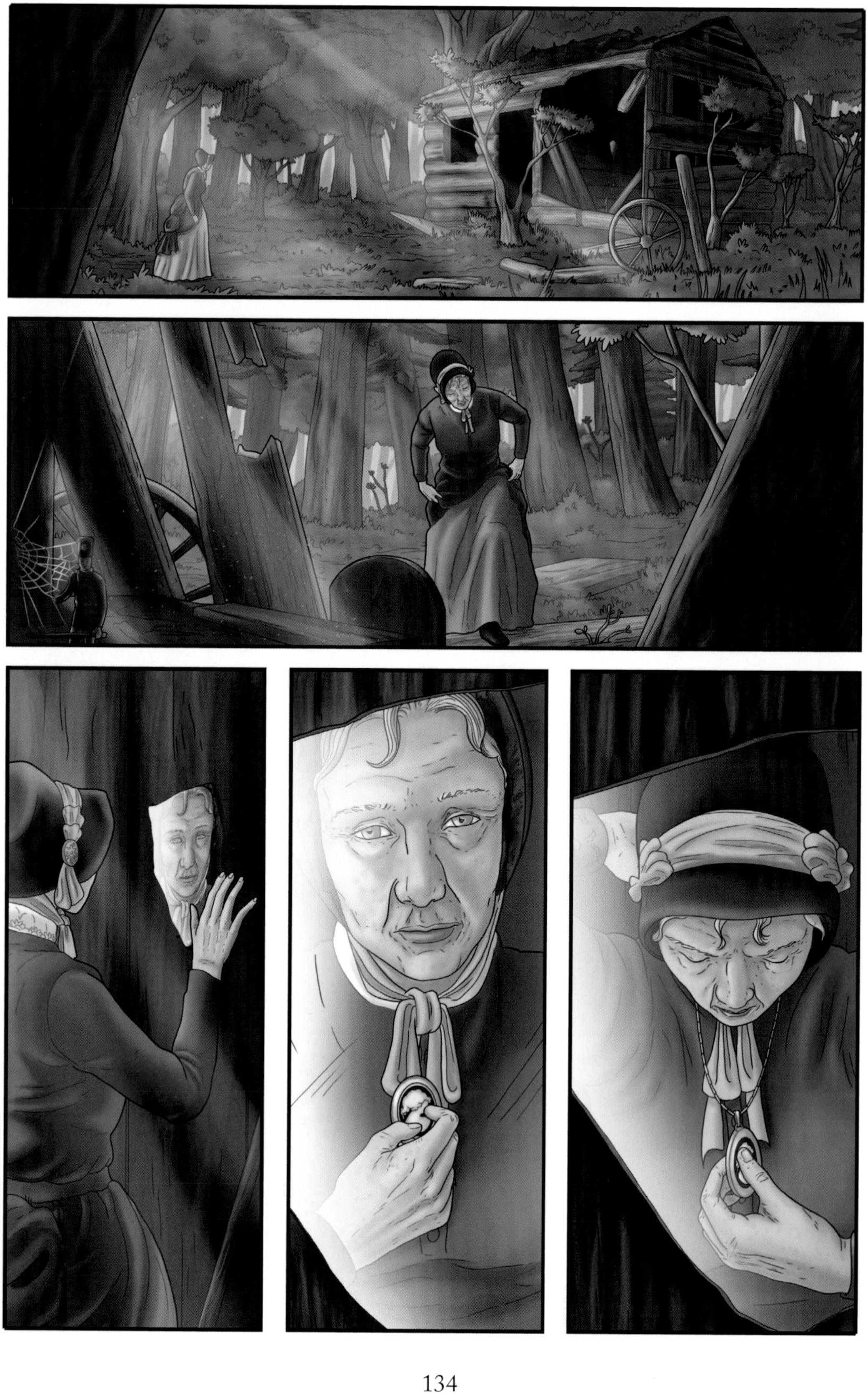

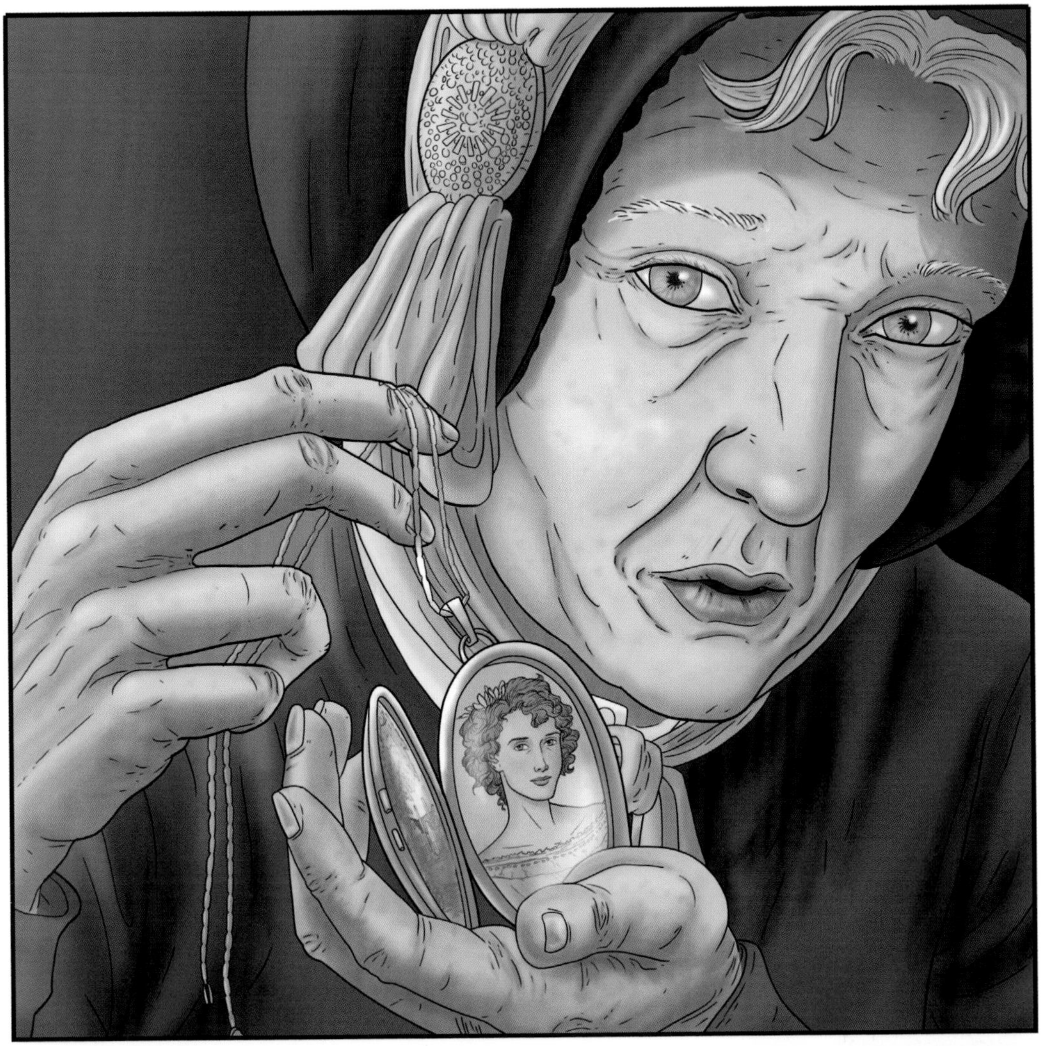

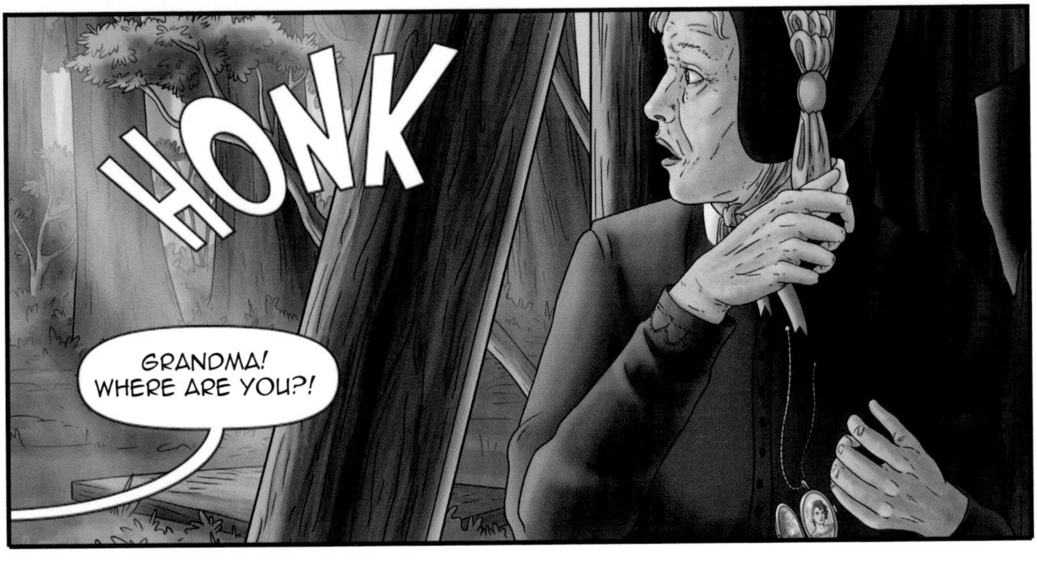
HONK
GRANDMA! WHERE ARE YOU?!

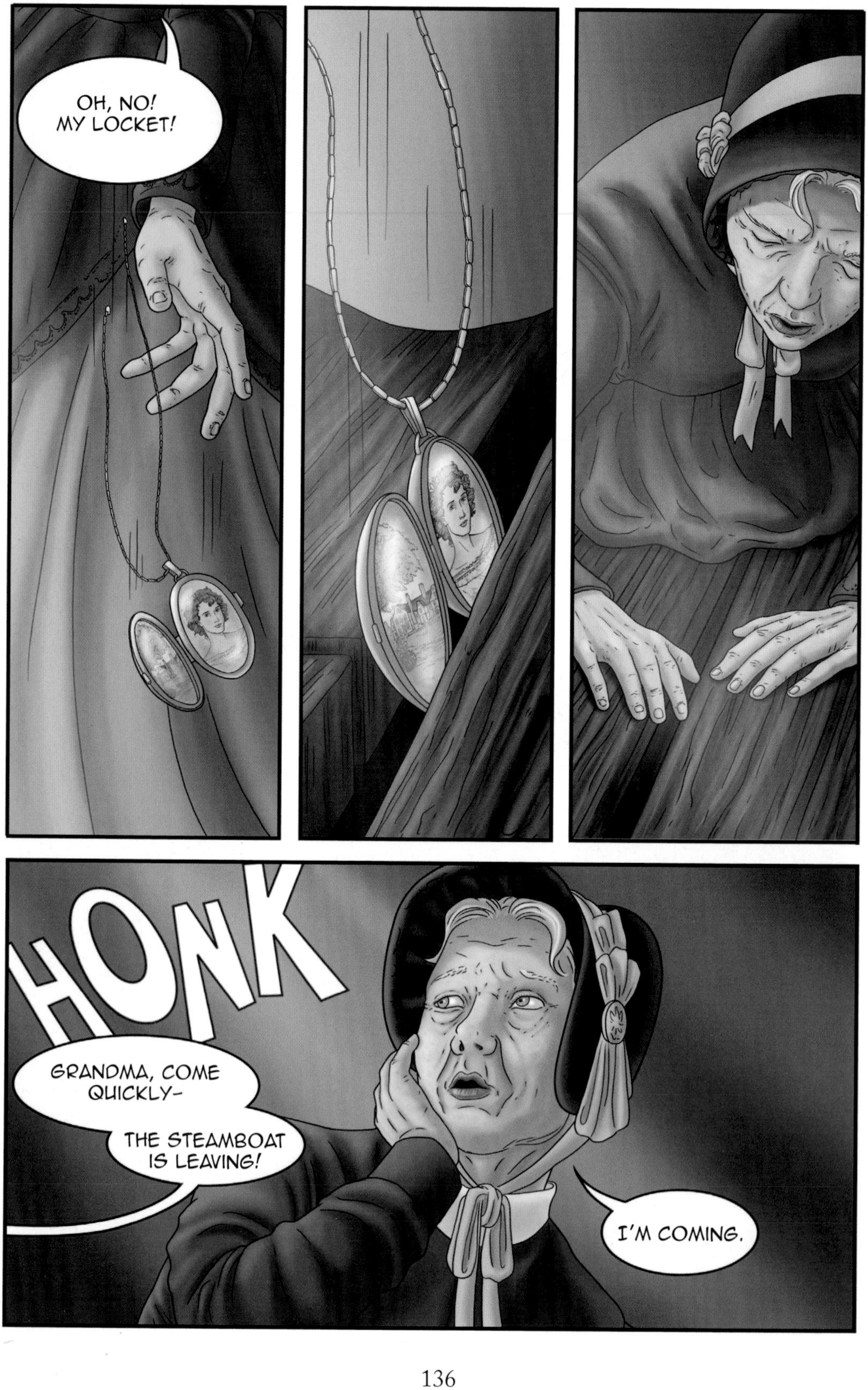
OH, NO! MY LOCKET!
HONK
GRANDMA, COME QUICKLY-
THE STEAMBOAT IS LEAVING!
I'M COMING.

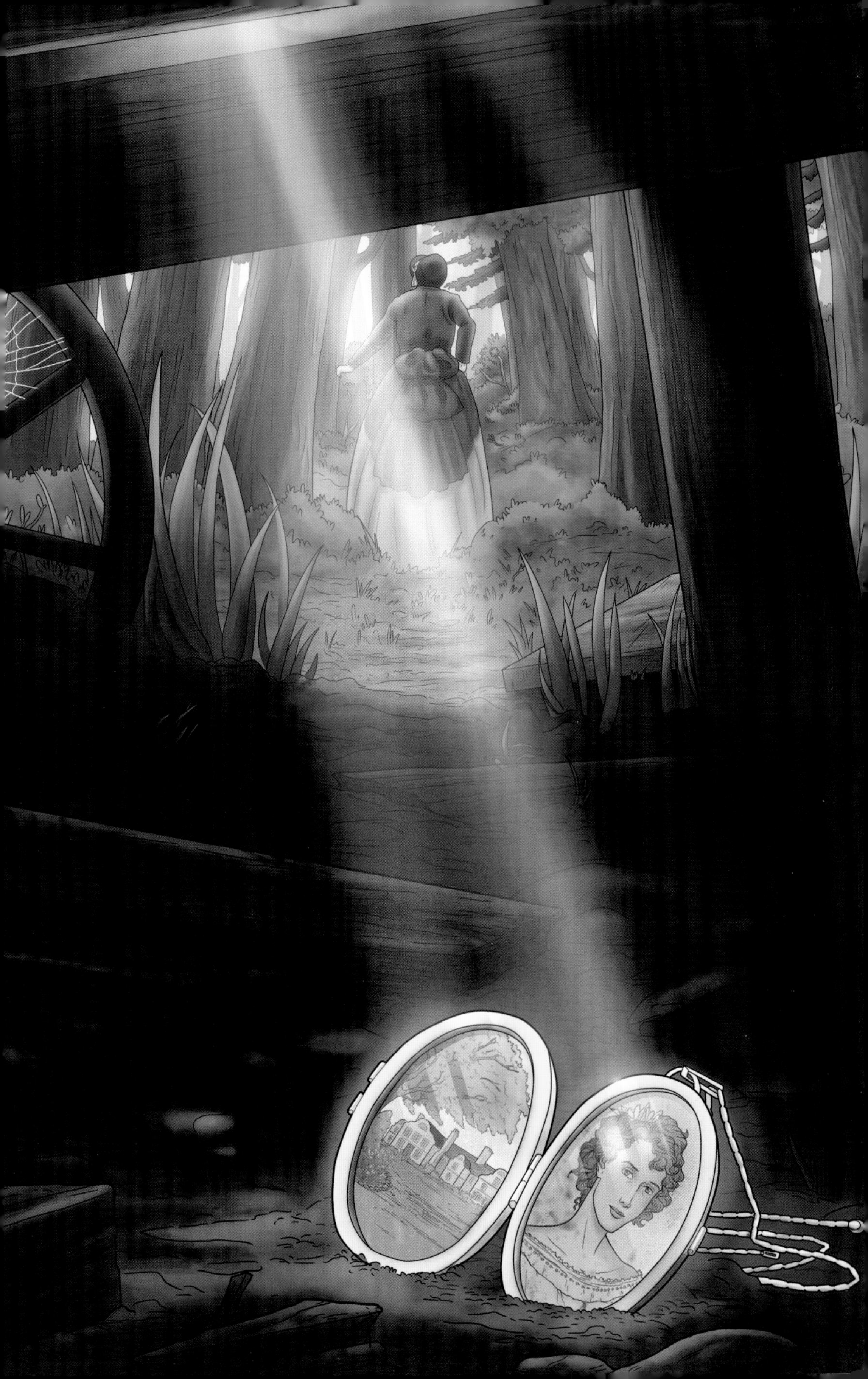

AUTHOR'S NOTE

Patrick Crowe and Carol Shields, Victoria, BC (2001)

Inspired by our shared vision of an epic story that we detected lurking between the pages of Susanna Moodie's cranky, meandering text, Carol Shields and I set out in 1998 to co-author the screenplay for a feature film. This graphic novel is the eventual result of our collaboration.

Carol and I first met in 1994 when I interviewed her for a documentary film. *The Enduring Enigma of Susanna Moodie* recounts Susanna's story through a series of spoken monologues intercut with scenes from an imagined epic from the silent movie era. However, the real focus of the film was not so much Susanna herself, as three present-day authors, namely Carol Shields, Margaret Atwood, and Timothy Findley. All three had consciously (or not) colluded on Moodie's cultural canonization by introducing her as a character in their writing.

Soon after the documentary launched, Carol was asked to write the screenplay for a "Susanna Moodie" feature film, and she accepted the challenge before realizing that she didn't really know how to write for film. Now, she wondered if I'd be willing to work with her as co-writer. I cautioned that my campy silent movie satire didn't exactly demonstrate proficiency with modern film drama, but Carol insisted so, of course, I agreed to work with her, and this would prove to be the most important mentorship from which I've ever benefitted.

After synthesizing the story structure, outline, and proposal, producer Keith Clarkson raised financing for the first draft. It was around this time that, Carol was diagnosed with breast cancer, which delayed, but did not deter our plans. Carol had a long history of collaboration with other writers, which seemed to me the result of her appealing self-assurance and respect for their ideas others. She was invariably indulgent of my worst ideas and never hesitated to provide her own (which were usually brilliant). Working separately in Toronto and Winnipeg, we took our outline and each began a scene, trading drafts back and forth via email for comments and revisions. The scenes that Carol began favoured dialogue over my own film school orientation toward visual storytelling, but most of her original character dialogue remains intact in the graphic novel.

One big challenge we faced was an overabundance of historic information, which kept suggesting a biographical approach. But the three-act feature film format did not correspond easily with the actual structure of Susanna's life nor the literary sketch format on which she relied.

With new insights emerging with the publication of Susanna's personal correspondence and even an archeological dig of the Moodies' log cabin, we were obliged to consciously make a work of fiction – albeit one highly influenced by personal and social history.

Carol felt strongly that our goal was a psychological, not historical truth, and that all our choices needed to reinforce the best dramatic arc for a feature film. Simply retelling Susanna's own story (itself highly edited, even redacted) would not realize the potential of film to inspire the viewer's imagination.

In order to simplify the narrative, we dispensed with the Moodies' first settlement near Cobourg, Ontario altogether. We had the Moodies arrive in the bush before the Traills and situated the families farther apart in order to enhance their sense of isolation. Timelines and the order of events were sometimes altered to fit the dramatic structure, and some of our characters were composites, but nonetheless we believed that the truth of Susanna's experience remained intact.

Carol and I had been originally connected through Michael Peterman of Trent University, who provided his guidance as historical consultant on the graphic novel. Michael is arguably the leading expert on the life and writing of Susanna Moodie and Catharine Parr Traill. While inspiring and advising, he researched and wrote a series of historic footnotes supporting the interactive book that also provide a comparative analysis between the historic Susanna and our own interpretation. Michael's many popular and scholarly works provide a more thorough depiction of Susanna's life than this graphic novel can attempt. Two of his works that we referenced repeatedly include: *Susanna Moodie: Letters of a Lifetime* (1993) and *Sisters in Two Worlds: A Visual Biography of Susanna Moodie and Catherine Parr Traill* (2007).

By January of 2001, Carol and I had delivered a first draft that clearly needed a lot of work. In August, I was able to spend two wonderful weeks with Carol and her husband, Don, at their home in Victoria where we plotted our second draft. But in November of that year, Carol's scan results showed that her cancer had spread. "It is time I got out of the Susanna business," she wrote to me in an email, so we set the writing aside with my implicit promise to complete the project.

After Carol's death in 2003, I missed my collaborator very badly and hadn't the heart to pursue the project. Over the next decade the growing popularity of graphic novels, especially the success of historic titles such as Chester Brown's *Louis Riel*, aligned with the vision for an entirely new interactive book format and reignited my enthusiasm for our venture, not as a film but as a very cinematic graphic novel.

Don Shields supported the idea, granting necessary rights, while daughter Anne Giardini acted as creative consultant for the Carol Shields Literary Trust. New to graphic novels, I aligned myself with Alex Jansen of Pop Sandbox, who introduced me to artist/author Willow Dawson and later, the brilliant young illustrator Selena Goulding.

One of the key players behind the project for many years has been our literary agent Michael Levine, who, along with the Publishing Team at Second Story Press, provided critical expertise. The entire project was made possible by key financial support from the Canada Media Fund through its innovative Experimental Stream.

Lastly, it is Margaret Atwood who first ignited contemporary curiosity in Susanna with her poem cycle *The Journals of Susanna Moodie* (1970) and who has now graciously provided the graphic novel with the best and most appropriate introduction imaginable.

My thanks to everyone who contributed.

–PATRICK CROWE
TORONTO, JANUARY 2016

BIOGRAPHIES

WILLOW DAWSON
STORY EDITOR, GRAPHIC NOVEL ADAPTATION

British Columbia native Willow Dawson is an illustrator and graphic novelist who now lives in Toronto. Her numerous award-winning books and graphic novels include: *Ghost Limb; Hyena in Petticoats: The Story of Suffragette Nellie McClung; Lila and Ecco's Do-It-Yourself Comics Club,* and *The Wolf-Birds.* In addition to teaching Creating Comics and Graphic Novels at the University of Toronto School of Continuing Studies, Willow also lectures and leads workshops in Ontario schools and libraries.

SELENA GOULDING
ILLUSTRATOR

Selena Goulding grew up on Vancouver Island and is a graduate of Toronto's Max the Mutt College of Animation, Art and Design. Selena's style is mature, technically sophisticated, and emotionally expressive in a way rarely seen in comic art. She is known for her work in young adult indie comics such as *Cobble Hill* and for her contribution to the *Secret Loves of Geek Girls* anthology. *Susanna Moodie: Roughing It in the Bush* is the first graphic novel illustrated in its entirety by Selena, taking eighteen months to complete.

ACKNOWLEDGEMENTS

The complete credits for this book can be found on www.susannamoodie.com

For their assistance and support we thank:

Margaret Atwood
Keith Clarkson
Doris Zibauer
Susan Jamieson
Michael Peterman
Elizabeth Hopkins
Carl Baldstadt
Charles Pachter
Timothy Findley
Elizabeth Thompson
Faye Hammill
Martin Zibauer
Blair Turner
Isolde O Neill
Hugh Brewster
Judy & Marc Glassman
Alex Jansen
Alex Mayhew
Emma and Lyra Westecott
Jack & Julia Barker
Julia, Adam and Piers Cubitt
Hazel Ecclestone
Evelyn Koski
Suzanne Mitchell & Fiona Gracie
Sara Diamond & Kellie Marlowe
Dan & Maria Farmer
Karen Farmer & Scott Broad
and Esprit Farmer Broad
Cheryl & Roger Parsons
Eugene Haluschak
Pat & Bernice Crowe
Arlette Baker, Don Shields and
the entire Shields Family

The Interactive Graphic Novel version of this book is produced with the support of:

ONTARIO ARTS COUNCIL
CONSEIL DES ARTS DE L'ONTARIO
an Ontario government agency
un organisme du gouvernement de l'Ontario

Ontario
Ontario Media Development Corporation
Ontario Interactive Digital Media Tax Credit

Canada Media Fund

Carol Shields Literary Trust

xenophile media

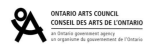

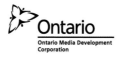

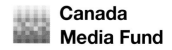

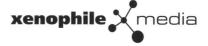